ONE MURDER MORE

ONE MURDER MORE

KRIS CALVIN

INKSHARES

SAN FRANCISCO

Written by Kris Calvin

Edited by Harrison Demchick
Design by MacFadden & Thorpe

This is a work of fiction. Names, characters, places, and incidents are either products of the author's imagination or are used fictitiously. Any resemblance to actual events or locales or persons, living or dead, is entirely coincidental.

Published by Inkshares, Inc. in San Francisco, California
Printed in the United States of America
First Edition

1 2 3 4 5 6 7 8 9 10

Library of Congress Control Number: 2015933322

ISBN 978-1-941758-08-3
(Hardcover)

CHAPTER 1

Maren Kane could barely make out the yellow dividing line a few feet in front of her through the thick, grey valley fog. Her shoulders tensed as she gripped the steering wheel, unsure which direction the narrow country highway would take next. The speed limit sign at 50 in reflective paint seemed a cruel joke.

Maren was in her fourth year as chief lobbyist at Ecobabe Inc., a start-up specializing in modern, environmentally friendly toys and games without screens—child-size entertainment that didn't need to be plugged in. She was late to a breakfast fundraiser with a local legislator in Clarksburg, fourteen miles south of her home in Sacramento.

A headache was building behind her eyes. Heavy mist wrapped the windshield like layers of gauze, rendering the wipers useless. Then she saw two glowing red spots ahead of her in the gloom—brake lights. Relieved at having someone else to rely upon to navigate, Maren released one hand from the wheel and cranked up the heat. It was forty-eight degrees outside and her old VW Beetle lacked insulation. She had just begun to relax when the red lights that had briefly been her guide rose vertically in the air and vanished. No screeching, no crashing sounds—just floating lights in space, then nothing. Maren braked, straining to see where the lead car might have gone.

Able to make out a yellow mile marker on the far side of the road—clear evidence of solid ground—she headed toward it, her Beetle coming to rest crookedly on the opposite shoulder. Heart pumping, she pulled on her coat, pushed the door open, and stepped out onto the blank landscape. Her long skirt already felt damp, her dark thick hair heavy against her neck. But her boots provided steady purchase on the slippery concrete.

Crossing, she could see the sudden turn the driver had missed, continuing instead straight off the unguarded edge of the road. The white sedan lay upside down in a deep drainage ditch full from recent rains. Only the tires and bottom half were visible above the waterline, like an albino turtle stuck on its back.

Her chest constricted as she imagined what the driver must be feeling trapped inside—assuming he or she could feel anything. She stretched her neck side to side, quickly, as though preparing for a race. Maren was on her school swim team as a kid and could still beat the clock at the pool.

Removing her boots and jacket, she sat down on the edge of the ditch and lowered herself feet first into the freezing, dirty water. It smelled agricultural and industrial at the same time, of horses, cows, and solvent. She couldn't quite touch bottom. Stroking head-up until even with the car, she inhaled deeply and went under.

Maren could see three figures: the driver in front and two small children in back. All suspended, inverted—feet up, heads down—held in by their seat belts as water slowly filled the vehicle through gaps in the metal, the windows tightly closed. A toddler, her fine brown hair in pink-ribboned pigtails, kicked and struggled against the restraints, crying frantically. A boy next to her, no more than five or six, was surprisingly stoic, reaching out his hand to pat his baby sister's arm.

The elderly woman behind the wheel appeared unconscious, eyes closed and mouth slack. Her arms hung loosely in midair, the tips of her fingers submerged an inch deep in water pooling on the car's ceiling, which now served as its floor.

Maren tried both front and back door handles—locked. The boy's eyes widened, his mouth opened at the mermaid-like apparition, Maren's face close to the glass, her dark curly hair flowing with the current.

Gasping for air, Maren came up to consider her strategy in time to see a man striding across the road, out of the fog. Tall, with short dark hair and black-framed glasses, he wore a white dress shirt, red tie, and charcoal-grey suit pants—a lawyer or accountant who had also stopped to help. Then she noticed the large handgun he was holding by his side.

Breaking into a jog, the man pulled off his glasses and dropped them to the pavement, then jumped into the overflowing drainage ditch, splashing gritty water in her face.

Is he planning to kill the car?

Maren submerged to find he had the gun flush against the front side window, angled up toward the floor. He pulled the trigger, the sound muffled, then repeated the process on the back window, aiming carefully above the young passengers' feet. The toddler's cries escalated to shrieks, audible even underwater.

On the plus side, he had opened an escape route by blasting out the glass. But the benefits were sure to be short-lived as water rushed into the car, threatening to envelop the occupants, helpless in their seats.

Maren surfaced, filled her lungs with air again, and dove down hard, swimming into the hull of the vehicle. She ignored the needle-like jabs on her right arm as she scraped across broken glass atop the door, and focused on working the booster seat clasp open for the older child as water rose rapidly around them. On the other side, the man was wielding a large bowie knife to cut the webbed straps on the girl's car seat.

Maren mimed to the boy to take a deep breath. He complied as she pulled him to her, kicking against the current. As she and the boy broke the surface he coughed violently. Once out of the ditch, Maren retrieved her coat from below the fog and wrapped it around the shaking child. Although pale, he stopped coughing and seemed to be breathing regularly. The man, his dress shoes sloshing and water dripping from his hair and clothes, appeared with the toddler. A muscular chest and well-defined arms clearly visible through his soaked shirt caused Maren to revise her earlier assessment of his profession—this was no desk jockey. She wondered if he might be an off-duty police officer or firefighter.

The girl was bawling loudly. When she saw her brother she tried to wriggle out of the man's arms, her round face getting redder as she gathered steam.

Maren scooped up the man's glasses just before he stepped on them. He freed one hand to take them, then gestured with his chin toward the fog-shrouded image of a large blue Ranger ahead by the side of the road, engine rumbling, lights on, and heater blasting.

"Please, get in the truck," he said. "We have to get the kids into town and medical care." His voice was calm despite the writhing girl in his charge.

He doesn't sound like a weapons dealer, Maren thought. *Although traveling with a handgun and bowie knife does raise questions.*

Then she remembered the woman.

"What about the driver?" she mouthed, not wanting the children to hear.

He shook his head.

She folded her lips tightly at the realization the woman hadn't made it.

The older child felt something between them. "I want Grandma," he said, looking up at Maren with clear, brown eyes and a deep frown, still shivering despite the jacket.

"We'll come back for her," Maren said, hating what that really meant, offering what she hoped would be true to soften it. "She would want us to get you somewhere warm."

As she spoke she became aware of a sensation of lightheadedness and weakness, the aftermath of the excess adrenaline she'd fired off in the rescue. Her arms threatened to give way under the weight of the boy.

The man was already at the truck, the toddler wailing now as the space between her and her brother had grown. Maren adjusted the boy more firmly against her hip, ignoring the resulting strain, and willed her legs to carry them across the road.

The large blue truck smelled like mint and something sweeter. As Maren opened the passenger door the little girl let out a sob of relief at the sight of her brother. Maren set him on the bench seat of the truck. His sister crawled onto his lap, her thumb in her mouth as she laid her head against his small chest.

Although the truck didn't look new, the interior was spotless—not a speck of dust in the nooks and crannies of the dashboard. The only thing out of place was a donut box askew on the floor. She lifted and opened it to give the girl a chocolate-covered donut. The child's crying slowed as she took a tentative bite, then another, alternately whimpering and chewing. The boy refused the treat. With his arms wrapped tightly around his sister, he focused his eyes on the water in the distance. Maren felt a chill as she wondered whether the intensity of the young boy's stare meant he was waiting for his grandma, or saying good-bye.

As Maren climbed in next to the two children, she noticed in the extended cab on the floor behind the driver's side a new-looking briefcase. It was emblazoned in gold with the initials "AJ" above an imprint of the official California state seal.

CHAPTER 2

"It's great to see you," Maren said, rising to give Noel a hug. He stood stiffly—not stepping away, but unresponsive. Maren knew Noel had difficulty with demonstrations of affection, but she occasionally needed to touch him. He was, after all, her baby brother. She smiled, for a moment able to leave behind thoughts of the submerged car.

Maren had secured one of the few remaining noon hour window seats at Café Trista. Two blocks from the capitol building, it was typical of casual eating spots in Sacramento—comfortable without being cozy, with tables far enough apart to avoid being easily overheard and ample lighting to see and be seen. In the familiar environment it seemed to Maren that days instead of only hours separated her from the morning's events.

In the emergency room a nurse had spirited away the children while Maren was ushered to a treatment room where another nurse cleaned her arm of glass from the car window. A tall, dour hospital representative appeared briefly to explain that the boy was able to provide a phone number for his parents, who were on their way. She also learned that her fellow Good Samaritan, "AJ," had stated he was unhurt and declined observation before leaving.

Once home, Maren had taken a hot shower. Then she made a cup of herbal tea. Settled on the sofa, she placed a call to Polly Grey, a state administrator originally from England who lived across the street and over the past five years had become Maren's closest friend. As Maren recounted the story to Polly she felt a lessening of her fatigue. Still, even her friend's reassuring words couldn't silence echoes of the fear Maren had felt when successful rescue of the children had seemed anything but certain. Nor had being safe at home eased Maren's memory of the driver's limp form, the elderly woman oblivious to the rushing water as it had engulfed her.

Maren forced her thoughts to the present.

"Why don't you order?" she asked Noel. "I'll hold our table."

Noel turned toward the counter abruptly, as though directed by remote control rather than a warm, sisterly suggestion. She watched his retreating figure. Tall and thin in an oversized, slouchy beige trench coat and 1930s-style fedora, he looked more like a wannabe FBI agent or a flasher than his true identity—a thirty-four-year-old scientist and epidemiology professor at the nearby University of California campus in Davis.

Maren and Noel shared piercing blue eyes, but the resemblance ended there. Noel's hair was sandy and Maren's deep auburn, nearly black. Maren, with high cheekbones, arched brows, and a beautiful smile, was generally viewed as on the right side of pretty. But while Noel had a nice face and strong chin, he missed being attractive due to an indefinable coldness that descended wherever he went. Not a dementor-level chill, but enough to make people start looking for the exit and a warmer setting not long after he arrived.

"You made the news," Noel said, returning with a heavy blue mug and joining her at the tiny table without removing his coat or hat. "Top of the hour, local and national."

Maren sighed, removed her tea bag, and set it on the saucer. When she'd learned that her partner in the roadside rescue wasn't Clark Kent sans Superman garb but instead Alec Joben, a former Marine and newly elected state senator, she knew the already dramatic incident would be irresistible to the press. That, and the use of a gun and knife in the rescue—*who doesn't love a gun and knife story with a happy ending?* Happy, since the death of the driver, Simone Booth, a longtime journalist turned freelance writer, appeared all but forgotten by everyone in the excitement and joy over rescue of the two children. Everyone except the little boy, who asked Maren in the emergency room when they were going back to get Grandma.

Maren had seen Alec Joben on TV that morning. With his shoulders back, the senator's military bearing was offset by a softness around his dark eyes. She liked that Joben didn't smile throughout the interview. He appeared to be genuinely affected by the tragic accident and disinterested in the attention he was getting for his role in the rescue.

Early reports were that it wasn't fog that had caused the older woman to miss the turn—her heart had failed. It cut too close to home for Maren, who was only eleven when she and Noel found their mother lying on the kitchen floor, her face contorted, documenting the terrible pain of a heart attack. Pieces of a broken green bowl and salad were everywhere, and dinner never did get made. In only two days the doctors pronounced the situation hopeless and pulled the plug in intensive care, and their mother was gone. Their father disappeared a few weeks later, leaving the children with their grandmother. Maren and Noel still didn't know where he was—if he was anywhere anymore.

Noel had never fully recovered. He'd learned too early that getting close to someone was a precursor to abandonment. Maren sometimes wondered what scars she carried that she didn't see. For the sixteen years since her mother's death and her father's abandonment Maren had worn her mother's simple gold wedding ring around a thin chain on her neck. Given to her mother by her father, it reminded Maren that she hadn't always been without them.

Maren glanced at her watch, confirming that she needed to leave for her scheduled lobbying appointment or she'd be late. After a last bite of blueberry scone she asked Noel whether he had time to walk with her to the capitol building—perhaps his stern expression and inability to make small talk would shield her from colleagues with questions about her newsworthy experience.

Noel didn't answer. She followed his gaze to his nearly full mug and wasn't surprised when he stood and returned to the counter to wait his turn politely behind several customers placing long orders even though all he needed was a disposable cup. In apparent compensation for the discomfort he knew he generated, her brother adhered to a strict code of manners to make his way through the world. If Noel had been born today, Maren suspected he would be tagged in childhood with one or more psychological or medical diagnoses—perhaps to a good end, perhaps not. She'd seen it go both ways.

While Noel navigated the coffee crowd, Maren watched out the window as the morning parade of legislators and lobbyists passed by. Most were in their Sacramento uniforms—dark suits, skirts, and sensible pumps for women, and red or blue ties for men. Maren dressed that way when she first started coming to Sacramento but learned over time that embracing her unique fashion sense yielded advantages. Legislators might not remember Maren Kane's name, but when they saw her red, western-style boots, they knew they could pick up on a conversation with her started months earlier.

Maren donned her coat and the siblings crossed L Street, passing through the rose garden behind the large, white-domed building that housed California legislators and their staff since the 1860s. Built in the same Roman style as the congressional building in Washington, D.C., though on a smaller scale, California's capitol building reflected the designers' decision to literally gild the lily, setting a gold cupola atop the white dome and capping that with a large copper ball, nearly three feet in diameter, plated in gold coins. Maren once reflected that while Hollywood might be California's uncontested modern seat of glamour, Sacramento had set the stage by dressing up its legislative quarters years earlier.

* * *

"You don't need to take those off."

The young man in front of Maren was kneeling and untying one shoe, his belt already unbuckled.

"It's not like the airport," Maren said. "The metal detector here is old school. With luck a gun might be enough to set it off."

Besides, she thought, in the capitol elected officials are most likely to kill one another, and they don't always get screened. She had an image of Alec Joben running, gun in hand.

Maren hadn't processed Joben's looks at the time of the rescue. In retrospect, she found he was undeniably "tall, dark, and handsome," almost to the point of cliché. Not a bad thing, but Maren was more intrigued by his demeanor and apparent compassion when he was interviewed about the accident. She found herself curious as to whether the new senator was married.

The young man stood awkwardly, restoring his belt to status quo while taking in Maren Kane's dark curly hair and western-style boots. "Are you one of the artists?" he asked.

Artists? Then she saw his name, scrawled on a sticker placed at a skewed angle on his chest. "Ed Howard, California Artists Association, Lobby Day in Sacramento."

"Maren!"

She was interrupted by Tamara Barnes, a young aide to the governor dressed in a chic cream-colored suit with a pleated skirt and fitted jacket, calling to her from the other side of security. Maren stepped out of line as a capitol guard approached her. "Ms. Kane, Ms. Barnes asked that you be given priority entrance."

By the time Maren produced her ID, twenty-six-year-old Tamara had started down the hall, her stylish grey pumps clicking efficiently on the tiled floor. She motioned to Maren to catch up.

Tamara Barnes had a classic Irish, shoulder-length red-orange hair that could never have come from a bottle, translucent skin peppered with barely-there freckles, and a lithe dancer's physique. It was rumored, bolstered by her new baby-blue BMW coupe, that she was a trust fund baby who didn't need a job but who chose public interest work for that rarest of reasons, a pure heart.

"I heard about this morning, the accident. Two children trapped—that must have been so frightening," Tamara said.

"It was Maren," said. "But once I was able to go home, dry off, and change, it felt better to be here."

Tamara nodded. A compulsion to work was a prerequisite to success in the capitol. They turned the corner and skirted three legislators in heated debate by the elevator. The two women stopped when they reached the heavy wooden double doors marking the outer entrance to the governor's suite of offices.

"Ecobabe have anything interesting this year?" Tamara asked.

Maren's Sacramento-based organization was known for sponsoring bills intended to protect children from environmental and safety hazards—time-consuming work, but consistent with the fledgling firm's desire to stand out in the highly competitive toy and game market. With a varied background that included economic and legal training, Maren juggled multiple responsibilities at the small start-up. But her primary role was as their registered lobbyist, enabling her to personally sell policymakers on Ecobabe's legislative ideas and, not incidentally, to save Ecobabe investors the hefty cost of external lobbying fees.

"Senate Bill 770, a ban on cell phone use while driving," Maren said.

"Didn't we do that already?" Tamara frowned, delicate lines creasing her forehead.

"Last year's law requires driver cell phones to be hands-free— with a headset or speakerphone. Our new proposal would prohibit all mobile phone use while operating a car in California, hands-free or not."

"That's not far afield for a toy company?" Tamara asked.

Market studies indicated that Ecobabe's promotion of the company's legislative activism on behalf of children's safety was instrumental in building the firm's small but loyal customer base. Far afield? Maybe. But definitely smart. At least when it succeeded. Ecobabe's recent highly-publicized campaign to prevent accidental childhood poisonings by requiring statewide curbside collection of hazardous household waste—like batteries, expired medicine and old lead-based paints— didn't get the votes it needed. So Maren was under extra pressure to produce a win.

"Safer, screen-free driving will save lives," Maren said. "And it reflects Ecobabe's ethos that simpler is better."

A reedy voice cut in. Caleb Waterston was out of breath, having hurried to intercept them. "Tamara, so good to see you. And Maren, I'd know those red boots anywhere, heh-heh-heh."

A successful contract lobbyist in his early fifties, Waterston was known for taking any client if the money was good. He also had a soft spot for Hollywood types. He had once bartered his lobbying services to a B-movie mogul who was seeking favorable zoning laws, in exchange for Waterston's name as an assistant producer when the credits rolled.

Maren regarded Caleb's ruddy, wizened face, the nearly colorless, deep-set grey eyes, and pencil-thin reddish mustache. His trendy suit and wild abstract-art tie were expensive but did little to complement his Ichabod-Crane-like physique. Waterston's ungainly head—the only big thing about him—seemed to perch precariously on his narrow neck. He reminded Maren of the "bobbleheads" they gave out at San Francisco's Candlestick Park when she went to baseball games there as a kid.

"I'm looking forward to our meeting, Tamara," he said. "Pointing the compass north, heh-heh-heh. I'll see you then."

Pointing the compass? The man makes no sense, Maren thought.

Waterston leaned in and kissed Tamara lightly on the cheek before leaving. Maren recoiled involuntarily despite the fact that Caleb hadn't touched her. But she noticed Tamara's expression was oddly flat. While some lobbyists were more touchy-feely than others, Maren didn't remember Waterston being one of them. In any case, such familiarity rarely extended to the governor's staff.

Tamara disappeared inside the suite without comment. She seemed to have forgotten Maren was there. But within a minute she'd returned—Maren was only a few steps down the hall.

"I'm sorry. That was rude of me," Tamara said.

"No, it's fine."

Tamara persisted. "I'd like to see your new bill on cell phones and driving—Senator Rickman's, is it?"

Tamara's parting offer to Maren was generous since lobbyists queued up to get the attention of the governor's staff. And Tamara was unaware that Maren's private history with Governor Raymond Fernandez meant Maren could ask him to look at the cell phone bill herself.

* * *

Senator Rorie Rickman's reception area was like a Minnie Mouse version of the real thing—two little chairs, a tiny desk, and a candy bowl. Maren was greeted by the senator's scheduler, Hannah Smart. Her dishwater blonde hair was in a ponytail. She wore no makeup and likely weighed in at under one hundred pounds.

Maybe she's all they have room for.

Still, Hannah seemed to know the drill, accepting Maren's Ecobabe business card and entering something on her computer in a professional manner. But whether it was Maren's vitals or the girl's Facebook status update, Maren couldn't tell.

As Maren was looking for a seat that would support a grown-up, Sean Verston, Senator Rickman's chief of staff, came out from a back office to greet her. Twenty-seven years old, over six feet tall with short, rusty-brown hair ending in bangs that flopped at odd angles over his forehead, there was something of an oversized, happy golden retriever in his demeanor.

"Nice tie," Maren said, a standing joke between them.

When Sean Verston graduated from Georgetown University he interned for a summer in Maren's office. When she decided to rent the attached studio at her new home he was her first tenant, staying until he completed his master's in public policy at Sacramento State. He moved closer to the capitol building when he entered the Young Fellows program, before being promoted by Rickman to be her right-hand man. Maren had recommended him for the position.

Maren felt maternal toward Sean, similar to the role she had with her brother Noel, but amplified by the fact that she experienced Sean as much younger than his chronological age. Partly, it was Sean's looks—he could have passed for twenty. But it was also that he didn't seem to have matured in the time she'd known him. A week rarely went by that he didn't check in with her with a question or a funny anecdote about a legislator's gaffe in the same manner and tone as when he was fresh out of college. For her part, Maren took seriously her role as Sean's mentor as he rose through the ranks of legislative staffers.

In all that time, Maren had never seen Sean take a fashion risk. He had many ties, but they were all some version of blue with red stripes. A few might be red with blue stripes, but really, that was it.

Sean's phone vibrated and they were called inside.

Rorie Rickman gestured for Maren to sit in one of the plush chairs across from her. Sean took the other.

"Good of you to wait," said the senator. "Are you okay? I saw the news."

A pediatrician and the only physician in the legislature, Rickman was in her sixties. Her southern California birthright showed. Tall, lean, with stylish, short blonde hair, she looked like a lifeguard who had aged well. A small gold cross on a chain around her neck, she was known to be a devout Catholic who carried do-gooder bills like the cell phone proposal and volunteered her medical services at the free clinic for homeless and foster children in West Sacramento. Rickman was rumored to be planning a run for governor when she finished her term as senator.

"It was...hard," Maren replied, searching for the right word. "But the doctors said the children will be fine." She didn't mention the journalist, not wanting to extend conversation about the morning's events. She sat up straight, all business, hoping Rickman would take the cue. "I'll have the press release ready for your office this afternoon. It highlights new evidence that driving using a hands-free cell phone is no safer than driving while holding the phone. It's the distraction that matters."

"Still, Health Committee won't be a walk in the park," Sean said. As he spoke he rested his phone on his thigh so he could eye incoming texts, using one hand to scroll down the screen.

"Sean's right," Maren said.

He looked up, grinning. "Could that be in doubt?"

Maren let out a breath, unaware she'd been holding it in. She realized Sean's was the first real smile directed at her that day. News of the accident and her perceived heroics had spread rapidly through the capitol—everyone seemed eager to convey concern, support, and sadness. But while it might have been immature of Sean to fail to take the early morning tragedy or her role in it to heart, she found the moment of normalcy to be exactly what she needed.

"We'll get the bill out of committee, we have the votes," Maren said. "But if there's a partisan fight, it will be tough to move it off the senate floor."

Rickman was reviewing a file on her desk while listening to the exchange—everyone in the capitol had to do two things at once most of the time. But at Maren's confirmation of potential problems, she pushed the folder aside. "Governor Raymond Fernandez ran on being able to forge bipartisan bonds. We'll need votes from both parties to get his signature." The senator's lips pursed tightly as she looked at Maren.

"Republican leadership will be tough to get on board," Maren acknowledged. "They'll likely view the bill as a government takeover of personal rights—not an unreasonable concern to raise. But evidence that driving while on the phone, hands-free or not, endangers others is compelling. Hilary Garrisey's death will make the case for us."

Ms. Garrisey, a high school prom queen from Huntington Beach, Orange County, died on her seventeenth birthday when her boyfriend, driving while joking with a buddy via a hands-free phone, misjudged a lane change and collided with another car—killing Hilary Garrisey instantly and putting a six-year-old child in the other vehicle in the hospital with two broken legs.

Sean looked at Maren to be sure she had finished. Then he turned his full attention to his boss. "That's true, we might pick up Republican votes there." Maren nodded. First stop would be the senator who represented the district where Hilary's tragic accident occurred, building from there.

The plan settled, Maren was gathering her things in preparation to stand and shake the senator's hand when she heard raised voices. Rickman's receptionist came in just ahead of Tamara Barnes, both looking flushed and upset.

"Senator, so sorry to disrupt the meeting, but Ms. Barnes..."

"That's all right, Hannah. Tamara, what is it?" Rickman looked, unsmiling, from one young woman to the other. The governor usually stayed out of the development of bills unless he had a serious objection, so an unscheduled visit from his staff was rarely good news for a legislator.

"She's here to see Sean," Hannah said.

Rickman's shoulders visibly relaxed.

"Hannah, thank you. Sean, you and Ms. Barnes may use my office, I have to get to a caucus meeting."

Maren reached for her bag to follow the senator out but stopped when she observed the expression on Tamara's face, eyes glassy, near tears as she shifted her weight from one foot to the other.

"I don't know what to do," Tamara said, focused only on Sean.

"It's okay," he said, placing an arm around her shoulder and guiding her toward the chair the senator had vacated. Tamara leaned against him, allowing herself to be helped into the seat. He knelt next to her, eye level, as one would do with a child.

"What is it?"

She didn't answer, tears now overflowing her bright green eyes.

Sean spoke softly. "Tamara. It's me. It's all right."

"I have to show you something," she said. "The governor...it's really too much to believe." The young woman was trembling, gripping the small, heart-shaped gold locket she was wearing as though it would hold her together. "We've done something awful," Tamara said. "I didn't know how awful."

CHAPTER 3

"I'd like the Veggie Korma."

Maren placed her order with the counter clerk at Saleha's and headed to one of the many vacant tables. Although bustling at lunchtime, few of the small, casual restaurants around the capitol building stayed open in the evening. They lacked the large and active bar considered essential by most lobbyists and legislators to unwind or to continue political deal-making. But Maren was looking only to relieve her hunger without running into more people who might ask about the morning news.

The delicious smell of curry and basil from the tiny kitchen convinced her she'd made the right choice.

Outside, the sun was down and the temperature was in the forties. Maren had her scarf off and one arm out of her coat and was considering what might be the cause of Tamara Barnes's distress—and how Ray Fernandez, who had only been governor for three months, could possibly be involved—when she saw Senator Joe Mathis seated at a table against the opposite wall, obscured by a tall, potted ficus plant.

Smaller in number than the student body of many high schools and with group dynamics nearly as adolescent, the 120 state-level California legislators, their staff, and lobbyists formed an exclusive Sacramento insider community. Members rarely ventured outside the capitol building or the few blocks around it during the workweek, leading to an "everyone in everybody's business" small-town atmosphere. This was made worse by the intensely confrontational nature of two-party politics—like the Hatfields and McCoys or the Capulets and Montagues, but in three-piece suits. Still, while Joe Mathis and Maren Kane had been adversaries on many bills, both knew it was nothing personal, just part of their respective jobs.

In his early seventies with a full head of greying hair, still trim and fit, the powerful leader of the Senate Republican Caucus raised his fork in greeting, his mouth full. Maren wondered why the senator was eating alone when his senate district was local and he lived nearby. Then she remembered having heard that his wife died recently after a long illness. Maren collected her coat and scarf and walked toward him.

"I've just started," Mathis said. "Join me?" Over thirty years her senior, he used a soft voice as he stood to pull out a molded plastic chair for her, then slid his dish over to make room on the small table.

It was an opportunity to educate Mathis on the merits of Eco-babe's cell phone bill, perhaps defuse Republican opposition. Maren knew lobbyists who would try to work the accidental meeting to their advantage. But weariness in the senator's eyes made her hold off. She smiled as she sat down.

Swallowing a bite of spicy chicken, Mathis coughed and reached for his water before asking, "Long day?" The waiter set Maren's colorful vegetable dish and a basket of freshly made flatbread in front of her. "I knew Simone Booth," Mathis said. "Funny old bird, but I remember when she was feted for her role in ferreting out the so-called soft-shell killers in New York—nominated for a Pulitzer, I think."

It was Maren's turn to cough and reach for water as she bit down hard on a small, hot chili. Before she recovered, Mathis continued—tired or not, he didn't need her to respond to carry on a conversation. Not an unusual trait in a powerful politician.

"A ring of hijackers would stop trucks at night filled with the day's fresh catch—lobster, fish, and soft-shell crabs—passing from Maryland into New York," Mathis said. "They'd sell the contents of the heist to restaurants with ties to organized crime—ones that weren't too picky about where they got their raw materials for the fancy dishes they served their clientele. A mobster in the mood for fresh seafood was not to be denied. It was the perfect crime since the evidence was eaten daily." Mathis smiled impishly at the thought. The pall that surrounded him lifted and he looked years younger.

"I know that story," Maren said. "Wasn't there a policeman who happened by one of the trucks as it was being robbed, tried to intervene, and was killed?"

"Yes. And Booth's dogged reporting brought so much pressure on the gang—she seemed close to uncovering their identities—that one of them broke, confessed, and the whole lot went down. Death penalty for the shooters. Quite dramatic."

But Maren had lost the thread. She paled as the thought of Simone's body returned to her.

Mathis cleared his throat and moved to easier topics—the unusually cold weather for March, the annoying construction on the north side of town. The rest of the meal passed pleasantly enough.

"Can I give you a lift?" Mathis asked as they bussed their dishes. He spoke casually, not looking at her. She suspected he was putting off the inevitability of being alone. Maren usually walked the fifteen blocks between the capitol and her home in Midtown—a way to fit exercise into her busy life. But she said yes to Joe Mathis. No harm in a warm ride home.

The senator wanted to retrieve a file from his office before picking up his car, so he and Maren walked to the capitol building first. As Mathis used his key card to access the private entrance for legislators and staff, they agreed they would meet by the governor's suite once Mathis had what he needed from his office upstairs. In the meantime, the multiple cups of tea and water Maren had drunk to offset her spicy entrée prompted her to visit the women's bathroom.

The halls of the statehouse were empty. In a place where conversation was prime currency the quiet was unsettling. Maren dismissed the prickly feeling as she passed the bronze statue of a grizzly bear donated by Governor Arnold Schwarzenegger when he was in office, the public restroom in sight. Her heavy satchel in one hand, she used her shoulder to push open the door. It was a large space meant to accommodate tourists, with places to sit and take a break from the crowded hallways. A lavender room-freshener-style scent did little to mask the odor of disinfectant. Bright fluorescent lights buzzed overhead.

Tamara Barnes lay on her back on a short sofa by the wall, just inside the entry. A full-length mirror reflected the girl's pale skin and soft features. Her eyes were lightly closed, her mouth relaxed, arms crossed over her stomach. Maren might have thought Tamara was resting if not for the blood covering the front of her cream-colored jacket and pooling on the cushions beneath her.

For a moment Maren wondered why people in movies were depicted as letting out a shrill scream when they saw a body. She was certain she couldn't make a sound if her life depended on it. Legs shaky, she crossed to the sofa and pressed her fingertips to the inside of the young woman's wrist. She couldn't locate a pulse. She leaned in, her cheek inches from Tamara's mouth, hoping to feel her breath.

Nothing.

Maren became acutely aware of her own heartbeat. It felt loud and uneven. She struggled to swallow. Two bodies in one day.

But she got hold of herself and retrieved her cell phone from her shoulder bag.

"9-1-1," the operator answered, his voice matter-of-fact.

"There's been…an accident," Maren said, her mouth dry, the words barely audible. She saw more blood—on the wall, on the floor. Deeper in tone than the girl's glossy hair, the splatter created a grotesque palette of reds in the white-tiled room.

Maren's vision blurred. She felt nauseous and cold.

"Ma'am? Are you there?" The dispatch operator tried again. "Ma'am, respond if you can."

His voice centered Maren, if barely. She mumbled, "I'm here," and then did as she was told, leaving the line open as she tucked the phone into her jacket pocket.

Pressing a palm flat against the wall to steady herself, Maren eased into a sitting position on the near end of the sofa. Concentrating on slowing her breathing, she gently lifted Tamara's hand and held it, offering comfort that could not be taken, and waited.

CHAPTER 4

There were a dozen chairs around the oval table shoehorned into a small conference room on the first floor of the capitol just down the hall from the governor's office. Maren felt as though the furniture had been placed first and the walls built tightly around it with no margin for error in design. She tried to slip sideways into a seat without scraping the chair against the wall behind her. That accomplished, she appraised the two men who had escorted her from the murder scene, where an army of professionals was now busy photographing, measuring, and bagging potential evidence.

Alibi Morning Sun, senior homicide detective at the Sacramento Police Department, stood in the doorway. In his fifties, medium height, broad with a slight paunch but mostly muscle, he had a nose that looked to have been broken at least once. His straight dark hair hung well below his shoulders. He was dressed in a brown blazer, deep green t-shirt, and tan chinos. Maren thought he would blend well into a mountainside. She recognized him from a photo that accompanied a profile earlier that year in the local paper reporting that rumor had it Alibi Morning Sun's mother chose his first name because the timing of his birth cleared his father from a murder rap.

Morning Sun's partner, Detective Carlos Sifuentes, sat to Maren's left at the head of the table. Early thirties, short and small-boned, he failed to fill out the high-backed chair. Dapper in a midnight-blue suit and gold tie, he had his jet-black hair slicked back from his forehead. His cologne, sandalwood and lime, was strong. He put Maren in mind of a jockey on his day off from the track away from the horse hair and mud, happy to dress up.

Detective Sifuentes powered up a small electronic computer tablet on the table in front of him. With a trace of a Spanish accent, he asked Maren to recount how it was that she happened to come upon the victim.

It hardly seemed mysterious to her—the women's restroom wasn't a destination that needed explaining for someone of the appropriate gender. But there was the matter of why she, a lobbyist and not on staff at the capitol, was there so late in the evening. And Maren was well aware that for most people, police officers included, lobbyists ranked somewhere below used-car salesmen and purveyors of snake oil in presumed trustworthiness.

She explained her impromptu dinner with Senator Joe Mathis and his need to return to the capitol building. Mathis made it from his upstairs office to the scene right after the paramedics. She had barely taken in Joe's presence then, and she didn't know where he was now.

"Did you know Ms. Barnes?" Sifuentes asked.

"I met her three years ago. When she first came to Sacramento as a member of the Young Fellows program."

"Do you remember specifically where and when you met?"

"No." She thought about what might be helpful to the officer. "The Young Fellows program is designed to bring the best and brightest college graduates into California public service. They get a modest stipend for living expenses and are placed in legislative and executive offices. My friend Polly Grey runs the program, so I'm in and out of their building. I'm familiar with many of the fellows."

Sifuentes typed as Maren spoke.

"Did you know Ms. Barnes well?"

Maren stretched her neck side to side, trying not to think about his use of the past tense.

"Not socially. Tamara was first placed as an intern in Governor Jack Caries' office and then became a staff member for him, a legislative aide. She stayed on in that position with Governor Fernandez when Caries left office. She and I worked together on a half dozen bills or more."

"When was the last time you saw the deceased alive?"

Deceased...Alive.

His words were jarring.

"Senator Rorie Rickman's office, around noon. Ms. Barnes— Tamara— came in without an appointment. She was extremely distressed." Maren looked down, smoothed her skirt. When she raised her head, her eyes were soft with tears.

"Ms. ..." Sifuentes consulted his notes to recall her name. "Ms. Kane, I know this is difficult. Can you remember exactly what Ms. Barnes said?"

"She said she had done something wrong. Awful, I think, was the word." She paused as she pictured the exchange. "No, it was *they*—that she and the governor—had done something wrong."

Carlos Sifuentes's eyebrows rose. He typed, deleted, typed again.

Alibi Morning Sun leaned against the doorjamb, arms crossed. His dark eyes focused on Sifuentes as though the young officer's questions mattered more than Maren's answers.

"She wanted to show Sean Verston something," she added. "Sean is Senator Rickman's chief of staff. He also started out in the Young Fellows program, I think the class before Tamara's."

Morning Sun turned his head toward Maren for the first time. His voice was deep and monotone. "She didn't say what it was?"

"No."

"Is there anyone you can think of who might have wanted to kill Tamara Barnes?"

In the shock of finding Tamara's body Maren had assumed the murderer was a deranged, archetypal slasher, not a person with discernible motives, and certainly not someone Maren knew. She tried now to connect the dots back to the real world, the world she and Tamara inhabited daily.

"Tamara Barnes was well-liked. She was nice, she..." Maren paused, picturing Tamara's warm, open expression that morning as she offered to review Ecobabe's cell phone legislation. Maren swallowed hard before continuing. "Still, everyone in the capitol has someone who wants them dead."

Sifuentes's writing hand hovered over the tablet.

Maren clarified. "It's common to have enemies here. It's part of the process of law making—there are allies and adversaries. There might have been a bill that Tamara recommended for veto that stopped a project or cost a company large sums of money. But for it to end in violence?"

She paused before continuing.

"I can't think of anyone…"

* * *

"Sean, pick up."

No answer on the landline in his apartment. Maren left another message on his cell.

She was certain the police would interview Scan. Maybe they already had. Then there was the governor—*Ray*—no point in trying to reach him after hours. It had been at least a dozen years since Maren had called him at home long before he made it to the statehouse, and even then it had been a bad idea. She decided to save that call for the next day.

After plugging in her phone to charge, Maren reheated leftovers from yesterday's pasta dish for a late-night snack and offered a little to Camper, a black pit bull/lab mix who had shown up starving on her doorstep three years ago. Despite reaching a hefty seventy pounds he was still making up for missed meals and would eat anything. Including an entire pizza if he could get to it before Maren noticed.

Maren changed into sweatpants and a faded blue T-shirt Noel had given her on her last birthday emblazoned with an image of the TARDIS, the time machine from the *Doctor Who* series of British sci-fi cult fame. She brought a comforter from her room and covered herself on the couch. Maren often feared nightmares and had trouble falling asleep, but tonight she felt justified indulging her belief that bad dreams would have a harder time finding her if she avoided her bed. Camper tried to play lapdog, but she pushed him firmly down to the vacant end of the large sofa.

* * *

Maren was swimming, holding the hand of the driver from the white sedan, Simone Booth. The old woman floated effortlessly at her side, smiling, her deep blue eyes—so similar to Maren's own—comforting and encouraging. Until a persistent drubbing sound started up and Maren could feel her grip on the woman's hand loosening, slipping away as the pounding got louder...

No. Please, no!

Maren opened her eyes to darkness, palms sweaty, her neck strained. She found she was on dry land, although the comforter was damp and twisted where she had tried to hold on. Fumbling for her cell phone on the end table, she checked the time. Two a.m. It seemed unlikely that anything good could come from a visitor this far past the witching hour. But Camper, usually a stalwart watchdog, was wagging his tail and barely suppressing a joyful bark. Maren pulled herself off the couch and asked who it was before opening the door, just in case Camper's judgment was off.

Sean Verston stood barely visible on the stoop in the dark—the front porch light was out. It looked as though he was wearing the same black suit he had on that morning in Rickman's office, although his clothes were distressingly homogeneous so it was impossible to tell. Once inside she saw that his eyes were red and circled in grey, his pallor sickly under a day's growth of beard.

Sean patted Camper absent-mindedly—when he had lived in the back studio he took the dog running with him. But tonight the young man's energy was palpably low, arms heavy at his sides.

"I'll make us tea," Maren said, almost at the stove since her kitchen and living room were open plan, only a counter in between. "You've heard…"

He nodded. She set a plate on the round pine table next to the fireplace—two fresh shortbread cookies from the local bakery—and sat down. Sean remained standing, his eyes shifting from the bookshelves to the floor.

"I need to use the bathroom." He knew where it was, down the hall and to the left.

When he returned, Sean paced the length of the small room several times before landing in front of an abstract painting over the mantel, greens and burnt orange open to interpretation—Maren thought it looked like trees.

"How did you find out?" she asked.

Sean seemed to notice the table, chairs and the cookies for the first time. He took one, crumbling the edges.

"Please, sit down," she urged. She had endured all the circling and shuffling she could at two in the morning.

He complied, hunched over in the chair, and continued to decimate the helpless shortbread.

"Did you see what Tamara wanted to show you?"

"No." He put what was left of the uneaten cookie onto the table next to the pile of crumbs he'd made. "Senator Rickman needed a briefing paper. There was a press event, I couldn't leave. Maybe if I had, maybe that's why…" He lowered his head, shaking it slowly side to side as though in internal argument.

"It's not your fault," Maren said softly. "But there might be something in what Tamara wanted to show you that would help the police. It seems as though they don't think this was random. Have you spoken with them?"

He looked up, his tired eyes for the first time alert, intent on hers. But he didn't respond.

"I told the police what happened with you and Tamara in Senator Rickman's office. Given that she works...that she worked with the governor." Maren had trouble shifting to the past tense, especially in front of Sean. He was slumped, limp, head down. She'd never seen him like this. "I'm the one who found her—or did you know that?"

Sean stood abruptly. "I can't go home tonight. My room-mates...I can't. Can I stay here?"

Six months ago when Maren found she could finally get by without collecting rent, she'd converted the studio into a com-bined home office and guest room with a foldout couch. She remembered telling Sean about it.

"Of course." Maren moved to get the spare key from a drawer in the kitchen. Although attached, there was no direct access between the house and the studio from the inside—the main door to the studio was on the left side of the property behind a gate securing privacy from neighbors.

"I'll help you get settled," she said, heading with him toward her front door.

"No, that's great." He smiled, reaching for the key, his color returning.

"There are towels, sheets, and blankets in a basket behind the couch." She touched him gently on the arm. "Let's talk tomorrow."

As she turned off the lights, Maren reflected on Sean's behavior. She didn't recall him ever having mentioned Tamara Barnes other than work-related. Certainly nothing personal between the two of them that might generate such a strong response. But she reasoned that the thoughtful young man would take the death of one of his own generation hard, particularly since Tamara had asked something of him that very day which he had failed to fulfill.

No question, she thought, *guilt regarding death is a determined partner.*

And this wasn't only death. It was murder.

CHAPTER 5

Sean's car wasn't out front when Maren left the next morning—
his classic 1982 gold Camaro would have been tough to miss.
Maren figured he went home to change before work, not that
anyone would notice. She hoped he was feeling better.

Ecobabe's offices were only a mile from her home—six blocks
up 22nd Avenue and two blocks over on K Street. A comfortable
walk. Tucked between a vegan restaurant and a folk art store
and across the street from a park where the homeless camped, it
was a classic urban workplace. Maren didn't get to spend much
time there since most of her work was done in the statehouse
with lawmakers and their staff, but this morning she needed
distance from the majestic white building where Tamara
Barnes's death had occurred, and where Maren was likely dou-
bly famous for finding bodies underwater and on dry ground.

The Ecobabe headquarters, where six full-time employees and two interns toiled loyally away, was less than two thousand square feet in size. Besides Maren, design and innovations director Dimitri Wong and sales and marketing VP Clay Zimbardo rounded out the senior staff. Each had a small office in the back. The main room was shared by office support, sales staff, and interns. When he wasn't traveling, Ecobabe CEO Martin Bogut worked from a home office. The actual design work of new toys and games was also done off-site.

Evie Allen, Maren's assistant, was overweight according to doctors' charts but undeniably gorgeous to everyone who met her. Loose ringlets of white-blonde hair ended just below her ears, and sparkling blue-grey irises under thick dark lashes resulted in what could only be described as bedroom eyes. Evie's brows went up when her boss came in, and she looked about to speak, but Maren waved her off and kept walking towards her small private office at the end of the hall.

Maren didn't want to be rude, but she couldn't start this new day with another round of "Yes, it was awful" and "Yes, I'm sure I want to be at work." She was acutely aware that despite the supportive words she'd conveyed to Senator Rickman, the cell phone bill's passage would take what was known in Sacramento as "a heavy lift." Plus, it's not like she was riding a wave of victories at Ecobabe—while plenty of factors had contributed to the death of the "Household Hazardous Waste" proposal (not the least of which might have been it's unappealing name) Maren had been in charge of the failed legislative strategy.

A desk facing the far wall of her office was saddled with an old computer. A framed picture, the only personal item on the desk, showed Noel sitting in the hot tub under the big oak tree in her backyard, the top of his thin chest and shoulders barely visible above the bubbles, his hat still on. Camper was in the background of the shot, both paws resting on the side of the spa as the big dog deftly stole a sandwich off Noel's plate.

The office walls were bracketed by bookcases filled with child health and injury prevention reports, a few novels, and an entire shelf devoted to outdated textbooks—evidence of Maren's winding educational path. First undergrad in economics, then training as a high school art teacher followed by a degree in forensic psychology with the intention of working with teens at a local halfway house. And finally, after she came to Ecobabe, a night school law degree so that she could better understand "legalese," the twisted verbiage of proposed laws and existing statutes.

A lifelong student by nature, Maren thought about going back to school some days, but the heavy volumes were a solid reminder of sleepless nights spent studying that made her think better of it.

There were no windows in the room, an unfortunate side effect of the landlord having divided the building's original floor plan into many smaller units. A print of a lush, tropical forest scene on one wall and a mirror over her desk facing it let Maren experience what it would be like to be able to see outside—at least if her office had been in Costa Rica.

When she opened the door today there was one addition. A large glass vase filled with rose-colored orchids filled the room with the unusual scent of toasted coconut. Maren was surprised to find that her first thought went to the handsome Senator Alec Joben, with whom she had shared underwater trauma and gunshots.

Not that he would have a reason...

But the card nestled among the greenery identified the sender as Liza Booth-Henry, Simone Booth's daughter and the mother of Zane and Zoey Booth-Henry. Liza and her husband John were inviting Maren to dinner Sunday to thank her in person. There was a phone number and e-mail address. Maren repositioned several of the flowers before sitting down in a tall desk chair of soft beige leather, the only extravagance in the small office.

Maren took in the beauty and rich fragrance of the bouquet, touched by the outpouring of gratitude from the family of the young children she had helped to save. But she was also shaken by the physical reminder of the loss suffered that day and wasn't sure she could face Zane's soulful eyes, which had seemed to blame Maren for not getting his grandma out alive. Plus, Sunday dinners were reserved for Noel. They made it a weekly family ritual, having been left to create their own. And then there was Tamara's death—Maren kept seeing the young woman's body, the blood on the floor, on Tamara's jacket, and on the sofa cushions. It didn't put Maren in the mood for small talk and socializing. She wondered if she would feel at all better when the police found the murderer.

Maren punched in the code on her office phone. The electronic voice informed her she had three messages. She hit speaker so she could go through her e-mail while she listened. Top of the queue was "Urgent: Investments!!" sent from senrabyllit@talk.com—an unknown address. *Undoubtedly a scam*, Maren thought, hitting delete without opening it. She felt for those who might be taken in—low-income elderly individuals who relied on their retirement to live and had everything to lose.

The first voice mail was from a coalition partner on the cell phone bill—the leader of a Girl Scout troop that lost two of its young members in a cell-phone-related crash. The second was a representative of the California District of the American Academy of Pediatrics. The academy had undertaken a public service campaign against texting while driving and teen cell phone use and was supporting Rickman's cell phone bill. Maren wrote a brief note to her assistant Evie asking her to contact both the Girl Scouts and the pediatric organization to confirm that their expert witnesses would be available to testify at the upcoming Senate Health Committee hearing. She had just finished typing when the third voice mail commenced and a confident male voice got her attention.

"Maren. My office. Eleven a.m. Let Delilah know if you need another time. Extension 4682 will get you the backline."

That call took him fifteen seconds, Maren thought. *Fifteen seconds to close a fifteen-year gap.*

Maren often saw Governor Raymond Fernandez in passing at meetings in the capitol and, of course, on the news. But hearing him on her voice mail took her back to being a volunteer on his first campaign for office, when she was besotted with love for him and certain he felt the same way.

Not an uncomplicated memory. Even setting aside the fact that he was married, it would have been nothing short of nuclear to add a relationship with a woman twenty years younger to Ray Fernandez's résumé, and a white woman at that, in a city heavy with Latino voters excited to have one of their own represent them in the legislature.

So Maren and Ray had looked and lusted and sparingly touched in private moments until the day Martha Santera

Lucinda Fernandez, Ray's childhood sweetheart and wife, saw them together, took stock, and demanded that Ray tell Maren to resign.

There had been rumors since of similar affronts to the Fernandez marriage, all with younger women. At first Maren hoped Ray's attraction to her had been unique, and that recent stories were the product of the idle gossip that follows every handsome man and woman in elected office. But as Maren got some distance from Ray, she decided what occurred between them so many years ago wasn't love—at least not for him.

Maren would have liked to thank Martha Fernandez for pulling the plug on the budding affair and putting Maren off married men for good. But she figured that expression of gratitude would not be well received by California's first lady.

CHAPTER 6

During his brief time in Africa, former governor Jack Caries
learned that a monsoon meant heavy wind coming from one
direction. It was defined by its single-mindedness. Despite what
most westerners thought, a monsoon might not bring rain.

*But five days of nonstop downpour rendering roads unusable and work
on construction impossible surely merits some special name*, Caries grum-
bled to himself. He paced back and forth the length of the
small sitting room in his suite at the Castle Hotel in Mombasa,
Kenya. While standard rooms in the hotel were furnished with
modest iron-frame double or twin beds, a desk with a TV, and
a single chair, Jack's suite was specially equipped for his longer
stay. It also took into account his status as a visiting dignitary,
an American politician.

The bedframe was a heavy black-red mahogany, the mattress
dressed in a tufted golden spread topped with six pillows cased

in royal purple with gold and green tassels. The sitting area featured a rattan couch and two matching chairs, all with colorful pillows. A well-stocked dark wood bar with two stools graced one wall.

It had been four months since Jack Caries stepped down as governor of California and saw Raymond Fernandez inaugurated as his successor. It shocked the public and angered Democratic leadership when Caries, a shoo-in for reelection with record-high approval ratings, chose not to run for a second term and to work instead with a nonprofit to establish schools in Africa.

Jack moved first to Nairobi, then on to Mombasa, the oldest city in East Africa. Located on an island connected to the Kenyan mainland by ferries and bridges, Mombasa was bursting with nearly a million inhabitants, many of whom lived in slums right outside the city. Nearly year-round hot and humid weather punctuated by an ungodly rainy season gave added armor to Mombasa's entrenched poverty, impossible to penetrate without a determination and resources that most men and women lacked. But not Jack Caries—when he set his mind to something, washed-out roads and the rotting stench of months of uncollected garbage weren't going to stop him. Despite the obstacles, Jack decided to build three primary schools in and around Mombasa, surprising his board and funders.

Unfortunately, the last of his planned Kenyan community schools currently sat unfinished in the torrential downpour. Caries poured himself a drink—straight rum, no ice—and contemplated going down to the hotel casino. But he figured *Been there, done that*. And HIV was rampant in Mombasa. Even condoms didn't make sex feel safe, taking the shine off hooking up with ready female company. Plus, Jack no longer found casual liaisons satisfying. He wanted the chance to put public office behind him, do meaningful work, and find Ms. Right.

He sipped his drink, shoulders slumped as though the deluge outside were directly pummeling him despite the solid walls of his suite. The alcohol did little to help—Caries' real drug of choice was music, or to be specific, jazz. When in office Jack worked with the California legislature to establish an annual jazz competition for middle school and high school students. He planned to continue to attend the auditions and to have lunch with the young winners each year.

But tonight's transmission from local Capital FM radio at 98.4 was mostly static. At odd moments the keystrokes of Adam Rambui, a Kenyan jazz pianist, broke through. Rambui had suffered severe burns in a childhood accident and said faith drove his beats. Although dramatic when the piece flowed intact, the intermittent chords were not enough to calm Jack. He physically ached to feel the Southern California sunshine and see the palm trees—the only water he wanted to hear was in the form of waves on the Pacific Ocean rhythmically striking the white sands of Malibu.

Jack had fallen in love with Los Angeles the first day he moved there from New York. His intention was to break into films with the help of a midlevel Hollywood producer, an old friend of his dad's. But with his JFK good looks and charm he ended up in politics instead—*another kind of acting,* Jack recalled.

A soft tapping sounded at the door to his suite.

Caries rose and opened it to find a petite hotel maid barely taller than her large wheeled cart stacked with towels and supplies. She looked young, not yet out of her teens. Her ebony skin blended into her black uniform; her white collar seemed somehow out of place.

"Turn-down service, mister?" she asked, then corrected herself. "Mister Governor. Turn-down service, sir?" Clearly, she had been coached to handle him as a VIP.

He nodded, and she withdrew a small silver tray with chocolates from a lower shelf of the cart. She moved quickly to set the tray on the table next to the bed, then efficiently folded back the blankets and plumped the pillows. She was halfway to the door to leave when she stopped.

"There is better music, Mister Governor," she said.

Jack had forgotten the mostly static playing in the background. "Yes," he laughed, "I imagine there is."

She raised an eyebrow and frowned. He felt reprimanded for having implied that a lack of music might be a laughing matter. Crossing quickly to the radio, the young woman turned the dial and a classical station at once filled the room with clear tones. She listened keenly for a moment, her head tilted to one side, and then seemed to remember where she was and left.

Despite the company of the Kenyan orchestra via the airwaves, his suite felt emptier to Jack now than before she had arrived.

More rain outside. It was endless. *Santa Fe might do*, Jack considered, *the Sangre de Cristo Mountains in the distance, clean, crisp air without an ounce of humidity*. But more than a stable climate, he wanted his money. Luxury in Mombasa wasn't close to luxury stateside. He dreamt of soft leather furniture, state-of-the-art electronics, and bricks and mortar built into a house that would be his forever. He and his sister would never want for anything. Something that early in their lives would have seemed impossible.

To Jack's mind, he should have been home by now. But his business manager kept putting him off. And Jack had to agree it was smart to be out of the public eye—abroad—when the final, multimillion-dollar deal went through. Still, he wanted details, to understand the persistent delays. But the Internet was unreliable on the Kenyan coast on the best of days, and in this brutal weather, forget it. Even international phone service was down. The last message on his investments was three days ago, a terse telegram that said only "Sale in process, hold tight."

CHAPTER 7

Not a fan of the gym, Maren designed her workout regimen
to consist of walking most everywhere, supplemented by time
at the pool and track when she could fit it in. So even though
yesterday the police had delivered her VW from the scene of
the accident to her home, she'd followed her usual routine and
left it parked in her driveway this morning. But she regretted
being on foot leaving her office, since being late for a meeting
with the governor might mean no meeting at all. The time
reserved would evaporate if a gap of minutes between appoint-
ments meant someone else could be wedged in.

As Maren racewalked from her office to the capitol building,
she tried Sean's cell. No answer. Then his work. Hannah Smart,
the receptionist at Senator Rickman's office, said Sean hadn't
come in or called.

"But isn't it just so awful what happened to Ms. Barnes?" Hannah said, her voice high and childlike. "I mean, we must have been among the last people to see her alive. I remember she was wearing that beautiful cream suit, I think it was a Marc Jacobs design, she was always so elegantly turned out. The rest of us didn't know how she could afford it."

Hannah clearly wanted to talk about anything having to do with Tamara, now the hottest topic in the capitol. Maren got off the phone as quickly as she could.

Moments later she entered the anteroom of the Horseshoe, the insiders' name for the U-shaped suite of offices on the first floor of the capitol building that housed California's governor and his entourage. Maren was out of breath, but on time. The waiting area, furnished in state-funded spartan style, featured four nondescript chairs and a drab blue sofa arranged tightly around a square coffee table. The receptionist, Delilah Wade—late twenties, blonde and buxom—was seated at a small desk in the corner. Maren introduced herself and offered a business card. Delilah reviewed it, then announced loudly to the empty chamber, "Governor Fernandez will see you now."

Delilah rose regally, revealing an Amazonian stature in proper proportion to her ample breasts. Her jade green, tightly fitted silk suit somehow defied wrinkles. She walked briskly the few steps to a narrow door opposite her desk. As she reached for the handle she nearly collided with a mousy-looking woman with large glasses weighed down by a colossal stack of folders coming through from the other side.

"Wallis, watch where you're going! The governor is expecting us."

The woman scuttled quickly past, trying to avoid further reprimand.

"Really, we have protocol here!" Delilah said, towering over her target, who was now hunched over and looked like she would fold into a ball and roll away if she could. Wallis managed instead to nod sheepishly, her eyes squeezed closed as though a glimpse of the angry goddess might prove fatal, converting flesh to stone.

Delilah turned to Maren, not bothering to lower her voice. "She's helping out in the first lady's office. Temporary," she added, in a tone one might use to describe a bug that crawled in under the window screen.

Delilah's attention diverted, Wallis exited into the main capitol hallway through the door Maren had come in. Maren wondered if Wallis was the woman's first name or last, and whether she would ever come back.

Recovering her excessive poise, Delilah tried the corner door again, this time successfully. She shepherded Maren through an oversized meeting room that housed a massive conference table and enough large, executive-style chairs to seat thirty. On the left were sliding glass doors leading to an astroturfed courtyard dotted with cheap, white plastic patio furniture. When Governor Arnold Schwarzenegger was in office, he enclosed the outdoor seating with fabric panels to create a private smoking tent at his own expense where he and fellow politicos could enjoy their cigars. The tent came down when Schwarzenegger left, and as Maren passed the area it looked abandoned and uninviting.

They passed through another door. The rapid tap of Delilah's shiny black heels and the clanging of her multiple bracelets echoed down the hallway. They finally arrived at a small, wood-paneled room with books floor to ceiling and several deep and comfortable high-backed armchairs. After indicating a warming pot of coffee in the corner Delilah left, executing a stylish turn that would do credit to a Versace runway show.

Maren took a breath and perused the shelves—Dickens's *Great Expectations*, Obama's *Dreams from My Father*, Ted Kennedy's auto-biography, and several Spanish-language novels that showed Raymond Fernandez's personal touch.

"You may borrow any you like. Although you've probably read them all."

Maren turned at the familiar voice. Medium height with deep black hair and a strong, patrician face, Ray Fernandez didn't so much enter a room as claim it. He still had his thick mustache, which bucked the clean-shaven look favored by most elected males.

Closing the space between them in seconds, Fernandez abruptly pulled Maren toward him as though to draw her into a passionate embrace, but instead barely grazed her cheek with an almost-kiss, then quickly released her.

Maren glared at him. Not the time, not the place, *and what the hell?*

Ray Fernandez caught the look, smiled, then seated himself in a leather armchair. Maren remained standing, not certain whether she wanted the relative height advantage or was pre-paring to flee.

"So…" Ray said, looking slowly from the crown of Maren's thick mane of hair down to her red boots and not missing any-thing in between.

This is your meeting, Maren thought, waiting him out.

"The girl, Tamara Barnes…" he began.

"Woman," Maren said without thinking.

"Yes, woman," he said, smiling even more broadly. Although not often corrected now that he was governor, it appeared to amuse him. "I understand from the police that you were there when Ms. Barnes made a comment about me." Again, he waited. An unnatural pause, but Maren wasn't ready to respond. She knew Ray. If he wanted something, he was good at waiting. It had almost worked on her years ago, his patience, those smiles. If his wife hadn't walked in on them...

But Maren had gotten better at waiting, too. Stretching her neck side to side, she seated herself in a red velvet chair.

He spoke first. "I gather she referred to something upsetting?" he asked.

"Yes, she said you and she had done something awful."

The governor's brow wrinkled deeply. "I can't imagine what that would be," he said, his eyes resting on Maren's neck. She felt he was watching her swallow. She tried not to, which made it impossible to avoid. He smiled again.

"Nothing?" she asked, her hand unconsciously rising to her throat to cover it.

He smiled again, "No, *mi amor*, nothing."

Fernandez used the term of endearment casually, easily. But his eyes were hard. "You know how these young girls are."

Women, she thought again, but let it go.

"Were you here the night of Tamara's death?" she asked. It hadn't occurred to her at the time, but now she wondered if police activity had extended to his office, if he had known right away. Even as she asked it, she realized it stood to reason—if the governor was there and a murder occurred in the statehouse, security would have moved immediately to protect him.

Fernandez stroked his mustache and smoothed his hair, though neither was out of place, then stood and walked slowly to the bookshelf. He lifted one of the heavy volumes, glanced at the cover, and moved it to another section before looking up at Maren.

"The smallest thing can seem so awful to them. A bill I wouldn't sign. Or a meeting I wouldn't take on one of her pet projects. It's all drama before thirty, isn't it?" He laughed—a rolling, teasing, full sound, then added, "I was in my office still at eight p.m. on a conference call when it happened. Delilah set it up for me; she stayed late to make sure it went smoothly. Technology is supposed to be our friend, but there can be so many glitches, satellites failing, who knows?"

Maren observed that the governor's mind seemed to have wandered away from Tamara's death to whether his phone system functioned correctly. She set her jaw firmly to force herself not to speak. She couldn't believe his insensitivity. They hadn't been talking about a hypothetical person who might feel this way or that, or even a "girl" who could appear through the library door any minute with a petty complaint. They were talking about Tamara Barnes, a young woman who until yesterday had worked for him. Until she was brutally stabbed and murdered.

A knock interrupted Maren's thoughts. Delilah stood at the threshold to the library.

"I'm sorry to bother you, Governor," she said. "Your next appointment is here."

Ray favored Delilah with the same head-to-toe appraisal he had given Maren, although he lingered longer at chest level, which Delilah accommodated by arching her back and bringing one hand to rest just above her considerable cleavage.

The governor reluctantly slid his eyes away and back to Maren. But then Delilah turned to leave and her rear view captured the governor's attention.

The small exchange put Maren's own history with Ray in the worst possible light for her. She shook her head, willing the memory and the discomfort away.

Maren's movement was slight, but Fernandez didn't miss it. He laughed out loud. Maren felt cruelty in the sound, although she knew it was probably only Ray's joy at the existence of willing women, of accessible power, or both.

She was relieved when he stood, adjusted his tie, and indicated that they were done.

* * *

Maren's visit with the governor had left her unsettled—there was, of course, his persistent one-dimensional view of women. (Well, two-dimensional if you counted front and back.) But there also was the act of his having summoned Maren for the first time since he took office. Although she supposed it made sense that as governor he wanted to know exactly what she'd said about him to the police.

The rest of the day hadn't gone much better. The legislative staff members that Maren pitched regarding the cell phone bill only wanted to talk about Tamara's murder. Well, that wasn't quite true—one was interested in Simone Booth's drowning.

Leaving the building, Maren passed by Senator Alec Joben's office suite—the exterior door, like most along the public corridor, was closed. She tried to picture herself dropping in to say hello. But memories of having failed Flirting 101 in high school and Subtle Seduction 202 in college came back to her. It wasn't that she hadn't been in intimate relationships. It was more that it was always so damn awkward to get something started, and then if it did, things had never ended well.

Once downstairs, Maren exited the building and sat on a wrought iron bench in the Rose Garden for a much-needed break.

Set on half an acre directly behind the capitol building, over 600 rosebushes in 150 varieties of color and scent lined winding pathways to a central seating area around a fountain. Officially named "The Women and Children's Peace Garden," the garden hosted Sacramento's youth who were invited to propose messages of peace, with forty-five chosen annually to be engraved on plaques dotting the small park.

"Peace is in the air, peace is everywhere…"

The breeze outside felt good after the stale capitol hallways, and the smell of roses was calming. The tension in her neck and back eased as Maren saw she had an incoming call.

"Are you quite all right?" Polly asked, her clipped, British tones breaking up over the line.

"I guess." Maren faced the other way to see if she could get better reception. "I don't remember Ray being like that. Not exactly. He knew what he wanted, but…"

"Oh, bollocks, you could always pick them." Polly interrupted. "If there were a rotten fruit in the basket, you'd have it out first. I've told you…"

Yes, you've told me, Maren thought, *many times*.

Maren loved Polly Grey dearly, but on the subject of Maren and romance her friend was relentless. Polly's zeal to "get Maren back in the game," as well as to reform Maren's taste in men, had only worsened since Polly's own recent engagement to Leonard Gilman, "a lovely bloke" and a medical resident six years Polly's junior. But even before that, Polly had hated Garrick Chauncey—Maren's most recent ex—from the beginning, despite Garrick's boatloads of money. Polly wasn't at all surprised when Garrick turned out to be a philanderer. And although Polly had never met Ray Fernandez, her opinion of him was equally low.

"What you need is a vacation," Polly said. "You're tethered to this place like an old mare at the stable. At least a weekend off. I've a colleague who has a condo in Palm Desert…"

Maren could picture Polly as she spoke. Barely five feet, with spiky, brown hair and several piercings in each ear, except for the generous sprinkle of laugh lines at her eyes and mouth she looked more the part of an art student than a high-level program administrator in the capitol. And Polly would never be taken for the single mom of a teen, although her son, Jake, would soon be fourteen.

"A trip away might be good," Maren conceded, before adding, "How well did you know Tamara Barnes?" She was unable to keep the governor's young staffer out of her thoughts.

Polly knew all the fellows—it was part of her job to screen applicants, ensure they were well matched to their placements, and help them with any problems they might encounter during their year of service.

"Not well. Tamara was a private little thing despite that sparkling smile and ginger locks."

Maren thought it funny to hear five-foot-tall Polly call someone little.

"I don't think the police believe it was a random killing," Maren said. "Maybe some link to her parents? I gather she was from a wealthy family—the car she drove, her clothes."

"Tamara?" Polly's British accent made the name almost unrecognizable. "No, not Tamara. She grew up a foster child— New York, I think. In a gifted program and then on scholarship to a college in New Mexico."

"Are you sure?"

"Yes, absolutely. It's the kind of thing that gets our attention here We see so few who transcend such a difficult background."

"So where did her money come from?" Maren asked. "It's not like the stipend you gave her could support a new BMW or designer suits."

"No idea."

"Anything else that made her stand out?"

"Other than her beauty?" Polly paused to think. "She did leave her plum fellows assignment with Governor Jack Caries midyear to do a special training. She was gone nearly six months. It caused a bit of a stir in the program. Fellows don't desert their posts."

"Training?"

"More of an internship," Polly said, correcting herself. "Near the Oregon border. Something about faith-based outreach to sign up the uninsured. Senator Rorie Rickman tapped Tamara for it—she and the senator attended the same church, the cathedral over on J Street."

Despite the obvious merit of the work, Maren wondered why Rickman would offer, and more importantly why Tamara would accept, a move from the governor's office to a gig so far away.

Maren bit her lip as she spun out theories, playing out the possibilities—church funds embezzled, corrupt local officials, somehow leading back through Tamara to the governor, to that "awful" thing he and Tamara did...

"Are you there? Love, can you hear me?"

Maren refocused, realizing Polly had taken her silence for a dropped connection. "I'm here, yes. Would you mind checking to see if you have anything else on Tamara's transfer? Perhaps there's something there. Something the police should know."

CHAPTER 8

Noel Kane lived in the epidemic of apartment complexes just off Highway 80 that had sprung up in the 1960s to cater to the growing population of students at the University of California at Davis, a lesser-known but highly respected sister school to UC Berkeley. Few Davis faculty members resided in the cookie-cutter apartments, preferring gracious homes on tree-lined neighborhoods closer to campus. But by nature cheap with himself and generous with others, Noel stretched his state salary where he could. Arms full, carting a briefcase and several books procured via interlibrary loan, he navigated the narrow hallways past giggling coeds with drinks, a young man carrying a bicycle, and another on a skateboard. The smell of pizza and a laughing "Dude, you didn't!" emanated from one open unit, the odor of pungent Indian takeout and a blaring reality show from another.

Noel hung his trench coat and fedora on an old-fashioned hat tree just inside his apartment, removing a dark brown cardigan with wooden buttons that hung there and slipping it on as he did every evening. The small living room housed a futon, bookcases from Ikea, and a poster of Albert Einstein with the quote "Truth is what stands the test of experience."

A short hall toward the back led to Noel's bedroom, which was next to a tiny bathroom tiled in an unfortunate shade of green. A swinging door to the right of the living room opened onto a functional kitchen dominated by a '50s dinette table and two swivel chairs where Noel worked and ate.

He extracted his laptop from his briefcase and placed it on the kitchen counter, his home screen set to CNN. He wondered whether the news had tired of the Tamara Barnes story yet. So far none had mentioned his sister's role in finding the body, although Maren's picture had featured prominently in earlier reporting on Simone Booth's death and the grandchildren's rescue.

He thought of his mother's body on the floor in their kitchen, the image soft and blurred like a faded photograph. He buttoned his cardigan top to bottom and checked the wall thermostat.

Gathering salad ingredients, Noel tore and rinsed fresh romaine lettuce in a plain white bowl, adding olives and sliced tomatoes. As he turned up the volume on the streaming news he dotted two chicken breasts with butter and rosemary and wrapped them in foil to bake.

Voice-over accompanied the picture on the laptop screen. "California's governor Raymond Fernandez left this evening for Hong Kong. Citing the fact that California boasts the world's ninth-largest economy, this governor makes it a cornerstone of his administration to develop strong relationships with our state's significant trading partners."

The video feed showed Governor Fernandez waving as he approached the Jetway, one arm around an attractive, trim-figured Latina woman in her late fifties, her black hair with a bold streak of white swept up off her forehead. The governor smiled broadly at well-wishers. His wife ignored the crowd. Her eyes never left her husband, intent with what could have been pride but might have been concern.

Noel was interested in that look—what it meant, what passed between the couple when they were not on camera. Romantic relationships fascinated him since he had spent much of his life alone, anticipating it would always be that way. Until he met Sally Castro.

Tall, thin, and strong, Sal had a softly lined and deeply tanned face, as though she spent every daylight hour outside to make up for working nights as chief custodian on the evening shift at the university science complex that housed Noel's office. Noel wasn't one for chatting, but Sal came through often when he was working late, and something about her put him at ease. Perhaps it was that Sal seemed genuinely interested in his work and in the science that made possible her employment.

Slowly their talks became personal. He learned about her past, and she about his. Both lost parents at a young age. Soon they were going out with Sal's friends, as Noel didn't have many. The one date Noel had arranged was to see a *Star Trek* themed band that covered popular sci-fi television and movie theme songs. Even that went well. And they spent time with Sal's four-year-old daughter, Bethany, although that came later.

Noel hadn't told Maren yet about the relationship. He wasn't sure why. He knew his sister wouldn't judge Sally Castro for her profession as a custodial supervisor or for having a child on her own after her divorce. But Maren's attempt to incorporate romantic partners into activities with Noel had failed miserably, no matter that it had been well intended. And he wasn't willing to do anything to risk what he and Sal had.

* * *

It was dark when Maren finally made it home. Although she usually found the walk through midtown Sacramento energizing, she was depleted. A feeling caused, to her mind, by *Death 1* and *Death 2*, a mental shorthand she'd taken to using for Simone and Tamara's premature passings. In some macabre fashion the nicknames lightened her burden. But as she reheated minestrone, Maren realized it wasn't Thing 1 and Thing 2 who made the mess in her favorite childhood story, but rather the Cat in the Hat himself. In fact, Thing 1 and Thing 2 had emerged from a box and magically cleaned it all up. And Maren knew there was no way either Simone Booth or Tamara Barnes could emerge from their respective boxes. So she tried to put the two tragedies out of her mind. She moved to the sofa with a cup of soup, looking forward to her evening routine of getting lost in a vintage mystery, one of her few non-work pleasures. Luckily, her current choice, *He Didn't Mind Danger*, was a 1940s tome about jewel thieves—no murders. She usually did her reading soaking in the spa in her backyard, but the cold air tonight made that less appealing.

Then she noticed the light blinking rapidly twice on her home answering machine—unusual since most everyone used her cell these days.

The first message was the cultured baritone of Garrick Chauncey insisting they have the dinner he had been requesting for the last two months.

Landlines and outdated answering machines must be the final recourse of former lovers, she sighed, thinking of Ray Fernandez reappearing via her phone at work and now Garrick at home.

Maren had dated Garrick Chauncey, a business professor at Sacramento State, for nearly two years. She was essentially living with him in his plush estate in East Sacramento when she was the inadvertent recipient of an anonymous fax sent to his home office that she found when trying to use the machine. "I'm glad we didn't sleep together yet, there is so much to look forward to..." signed with little x's and o's. Garrick said the fax was not for him, that it was for his buddy. But for Maren it was one lame excuse too many combined with a lot of suspect behavior. Plus the bastard was cheap to the core. Despite having made millions on clever business investments, Garrick insisted that Maren reimburse him for postage stamps when she lived with him and required that she split their "shared" food costs, which included top-grade beef and the expensive vodka he drank.

She missed things about Garrick, not the least of which were his arms around her at night. Still, the only closure Maren thought he deserved was the door in his face. And that had already happened.

She clicked delete. The next message played.

"Carlos Sifuentes here, Sacramento Homicide Division. We have not been able to locate Sean Verston. It looks like your home is his prior address. Call me, and if you speak to Mr. Verston, give him my cell." Sifuentes followed with his number.

Maren rubbed her eyes, then the back of her neck with both hands. She could tell from Sifuentes's tone that he felt she had intentionally kept something from him—check that, not just something, but the fact that she and Sean had "lived together."

Maren's back studio didn't have a separate street address, despite having its own kitchenette and laundry and no overlap with her living space. But this wouldn't be the first time someone had assumed the shared address meant more than an exchange of rent. She thought with frustration that if the police (and neighborhood busybodies) had done their homework they would know boy toys weren't her thing. Maren's weakness was older, powerful men—it didn't take a psychologist to find the roots for that attraction in her long-absent dad.

Well, no matter what Detective Sifuentes thought, she decided he would have to wait until tomorrow. No doubt it was important to the police since Sean would be able to explain whatever it was Tamara had shown him, the source of her distress that last day of her life. But Maren hadn't seen or talked to Sean since the night before, or more accurately since two o'clock that morning. Her calls to him had gone unanswered. Still, she was certain Sean wouldn't miss the Senate Health Committee hearing on their cell phone bill at ten a.m. tomorrow. Hailstorm, hurricane, or even homicide, Senator Rickman would expect him to be there.

The machine was silent, no other messages. Maren felt the familiar loneliness she had experienced nearly every night since her breakup with Garrick. She inhaled and exhaled once deeply, pushing the emptiness away, then turned her attention to Camper, splashing the last of the minestrone over the dog's kibble.

Camper could wag his whole body at the mere thought of food and was doing so now with such intensity that Maren thought he might levitate. Her spirits lifted a bit and she smiled to herself recalling Noel's assertion that attributing human feelings to animal behavior was inappropriate—"anthropomorphizing," as he put it. *Call it what you like*, Maren thought, *I wish a little minestrone could make me feel that good! Now cheesecake, on the other hand…*

But the soup was thick and warm and she found her place in the worn pages of the secondhand novel without trouble, giving her cause to reflect that sometimes it was the simple things that carried her through.

CHAPTER 9

Daniel Horatio Gold, chair of the California Senate Health Committee, opened Thursday's hearing promptly at ten a.m. His face appeared to be held together by a complex network of lines and wrinkles amassed over fifty years in politics. Drooping, thick, white eyebrows threatened to obstruct his vision.

Gold had been a local council member in a small town across the bay from San Francisco for decades before running for a seat in the California legislature. The only big fish in a tiny pond for so long, he had never forgiven the state senate for having thirty-nine other members, each one believing himself or herself to be Gold's equal.

With twenty-five bills on the docket including Senator Rickman's controversial cell phone bill, audience chairs in the large hearing room were filled. Since Maren was there to testify in support of Rickman's bill, she had arrived early to secure a prime seat.

"File Item 1, SB 104, Senator Camillo." Chairman Gold's scratchy voice boomed through the microphone as his small dark eyes scanned the room. "Is the senator here?" When he saw Camillo approach the lectern he nodded at her, but the line of his mouth remained grim.

Senator Trixie Camillo, a tall, heavy redhead in a dark pantsuit and pearls, smiled up at the seven present committee members before reading from prepared comments. "Thank you, Chairman Gold. This important measure would ensure that fire exits in California nursing homes are not locked from the inside at any time. A tragic death in my district last year was attributable to just such ill-conceived actions."

The kind of bill introduction that Sean prepares for Rickman, Maren thought, glancing around and noting he hadn't yet arrived. Not unusual, since staff often stayed in their offices working while keeping an eye on the hearings on streaming cable, coming down only in time for their own bills to be called. Even committee members were often late as they juggled jammed schedules. So it didn't surprise Maren when she saw Republican leader Joe Mathis make his way to a seat next to Gold after the proceedings had started, ignoring the chairman's pointed glare.

Camillo finished and Gold asked testily if there was anyone to speak in support of the bill, as though daring someone to bother him.

Eight witnesses filed up to the microphone to wait their turn.

How many people does it take to persuade the committee that fire doors trapping old people in a building must remained unlocked? Maren thought, glancing at the time. But she knew the answer.

With rare exceptions, legislators made up their minds on votes in advance of public testimony. They took direction from their party caucus, relied on staff analyses, were persuaded by lobbyists like Maren, or more often than not came to a decision based on their own preconceived notions. Even so, most recognized open committee hearings as an important part of the democratic process, perhaps because they permitted exceptions to occur based on public testimony in a political world that was increasingly hard for outsiders to penetrate with anything other than money.

After support for SB 104, the opposition had its turn. Nursing home operators argued that there was a compelling need to prevent addled elderly from leaving facilities. They produced charts to show that in the absence of locks the increase in the number of staff it would take to monitor patients would add significantly to the cost of care and thus to the burden on taxpayers who provided much of nursing home funding. They noted that last year's fire and resulting death of an occupant in a small nursing home in Senator Camillo's district was the only such incident in the capitol region in over fifty years—deeply regrettable, of course, but not a cause for a wholesale shift in policy.

Maren was reminded that there were nearly always two sides to lawmaking. It was rare that any bill was a slam dunk, start to finish. She reviewed her testimony on the cell phone measure and checked unsuccessfully again for Sean. He could be there, but if he was, she couldn't see him from where she was seated.

Maren's thoughts were interrupted by the next bill call.

"File 2, Senate Bill 246, Senator Joben," announced Chairman Gold.

"Thank you, Senator Gold," Joben said. "My bill has a simple and important purpose: to prohibit the use of the chemical bisphenol A, known as BPA, in the manufacture and sale of pacifiers in California." He quickly reviewed the impressive science. Exposure to BPA was linked to decreased intellectual capability, fertility problems, cancer, and more. As he spoke, Alec looked at each committee member in turn, his ramrod straight posture and unflinching gaze—undoubtedly habits from his days as a Marine—contributing to the urgency of his message.

Maren had thought of Alec more often than she liked to admit to herself, but she hadn't seen him since they parted the morning before.

"BPA has been banned in eight other states and many European countries. California needs to do the same. Far better to harm profits than to harm babies," Joben concluded.

A researcher and a public health professor spoke next, providing detail on the evidence that Joben had highlighted. Although the part of the pacifier that goes in a baby's mouth is BPA free, the plastic shield attached to it often contained the chemical. And babies weren't known for exercising caution in what they chewed or sucked on.

The witnesses in support were followed by a line of opposition rallied by Saniplaz, a plastics manufacturer located in San Jose, two hours south of Sacramento.

Saniplaz, with over 1,800 employees, utilized BPA in the production of a number of products, mostly food storage containers, but also pacifiers. The company saw Alec Joben's bill as the first step down a slippery slope that could end in a prohibition on BPA altogether.

Maren had experienced it countless times—a tense debate in the capitol that seemed out of line with the apparent stakes. But to participants the escalation was rational since the real fight was about something else altogether. Act II, behind the curtain.

Saniplaz witnesses argued there was no compelling proof that BPA was toxic, that instead the data the supporters had presented were merely the product of a spurious correlation, a "loose connection" masking the real cause of any illness and disability. Much more research was needed, they said, before a ban on such a useful and cost-effective material should be considered.

"Questions from committee members?" Gold asked, looking down at his bill list as he spoke and sliding his weathered index finger to the next item, indicating he was ready to go on.

"What about the free market?" Senator Joe Mathis asked. "Parents who are persuaded by the data can already purchase BPA-free products. There are many. Unless there's a clear and proven danger, why should we interfere in people's choices?" There was loud applause from the Saniplaz group.

"Order, order!" Senator Gold bellowed, slamming his gavel on the table. It looked like the first time the crotchety committee chair was having fun all day.

Alec Joben returned to the witness lectern. A Republican, he was respectful and brief in his response to Joe Mathis, his party's leader. "I agree that the government must limit its reach," he began, making eye contact with Mathis. "But in this case the evidence is more than sufficient to support a limited ban on the use of a clearly toxic chemical in baby products. I urge your aye vote. Thank you."

Gold called for a motion, and a roll call vote was taken. Senator Mathis and the other Republicans on the committee voted "No," but the bill was passed by the Democrats, who held a majority. It was an unusual outcome for a Republican-authored bill.

While collecting his papers Alec saw Maren in the front row and smiled at her.

She wanted to smile back. She wanted to engage him in normal, everyday conversation, to tell him that Ecobabe might be able to help with his bill. *It doesn't have to be personal*, she reminded herself. *It doesn't need to result in my being vulnerable.* But she couldn't quiet the throng of butterflies in her stomach. So she barely nodded. Joben seemed unperturbed. He smiled at her again and walked away.

Damn, Lois Lane would have done better, she thought as she watched him leave.

The next fifteen minutes passed at a glacial pace. With twelve more bills scheduled before hers, Maren resigned herself to being stuck in the hearing room for several hours in limbo. But then Chairman Gold announced with apparent disgust that SB 770, the cell phone driving ban, wouldn't be heard at all that day. It was being put over to a future committee hearing at Senator Rickman's request.

Maren's first thought was to be thrilled. Like getting out of school before the bell rang with an extra day to study for the test. But then she worried about what the postponement might mean.

Sean must have known; it explained his no-show status. But it didn't make sense to Maren—why on earth would Rickman postpone a vote on the bill without alerting her? Now that one murder had happened involving people Maren knew, her sense of the possible had altered considerably, and not for the better.

There was an exodus at the announcement of the cancellation of the cell phone bill as witnesses pro and con left. Maren spoke with several cell phone witnesses there to speak in support, letting them know she would notify them when the bill was reset for hearing. When the crowd thinned, Maren saw Rickman standing near the front door.

Maren picked up her satchel and made it to Rickman easily, carried along by the outward flow.

"My office," the senator said without preamble. "Now."

People were waiting three deep for the elevators nearest the hearing room, jockeying for position to board. So Maren and Rorie Rickman took the stairs the five floors up. There was no privacy, limiting conversation. It was quiet except for the echoing footsteps of lobbyists and legislators tramping up and down the bare stairwell.

Senator Rickman closed the door to her office and walked to the window. When she spoke it was so softly that Maren had to step closer to hear. "Sean was arrested this morning," she said. "For the murder of Tamara Barnes."

CHAPTER 10

"I received a courtesy call from the district attorney," the senator said. "The police were here within an hour of DA Sharpton's call to me, searching Sean's office. They took his computer." Rickman's voice rose, her color reddened, she paced a few steps in each direction. She stopped and looked pointedly at Maren, as if expecting her to make sense of this—that's what lobbyists do, make sense of things for legislators. But while Maren tried to ground herself in the here and now, to contribute something, she couldn't get past how surreal it felt standing in Rickman's office discussing Sean's arrest. She found herself unable to think of a single thing to say.

"He's my chief of staff, for God's sake! There's analysis in there that we need to get our bills passed." The senator walked purposefully to her desk and slid open the lower file drawer. Leaving it that way, she picked up her briefcase and retrieved a white physician's coat from a small cupboard. "I'm late for clinic," she said, crossing the office and walking out.

Maren stared at the door. Even given the circumstances, including Maren's unexpected vow of silence, Rickman's abrupt exit seemed odd. Then Maren took in the still-open file drawer. She had never known the senator to leave a paper out of place, let alone the relative unbridled chaos of an open drawer.

She moved behind the desk and knelt to see the drawer's contents. There were nearly twenty files marked *SB 770* filled with papers and notes. Many printed from the computer, some in Sean's hand.

"Can I help you?"

Hannah Smart's petite frame was stiff, her chin held high as she frowned at what appeared to be Maren rifling through the senator's papers.

Maren walked from the senator's office back to Ecobabe in a daze, carrying the large stack of files ten blocks without noticing their weight. (Hannah had backed off when Maren channeled her brother Noel's best don't-you-question-me look.)

Once inside her office Maren stacked the files in a corner on the floor. She didn't want to think about whether what the senator seemed to have done was legal—removing items from Sean's office in advance of a police visit. True, Rickman might routinely keep all work on current bills, including her staff's, in her office. But Maren thought it unlikely—it would make it difficult for Sean and others to get what they needed without interrupting the senator. And Maren knew if there was one thing valued by all legislators, it was the brief moments of privacy they had in their offices.

She decided to check her e-mails before tackling the files' contents—something routine to calm her. But it was no use. Maren got through only three messages in twice the time it would usually take her. The last was another "Invest Now!" missive from senrabyllit@talk.com. She wondered briefly why her spam filter had failed her before losing all interest in the screen. She shifted her focus to her cell phone, which sat silent on her desk. Willing it to ring.

It did—Maren picked up immediately.

"Maren, it's Rorie Rickman. The clinic operator said it was urgent."

Maren thought how best to frame her request. "Senator, I'm sorry to disturb you. Do you know where they're keeping Sean? I've been unable to get answers from the police." *Or from the district attorney's office or the newspaper that broke the story,* she thought. But she didn't see any reason to walk Rorie Rickman through each frustrating dead end, particularly since she would have at most a few minutes before Rickman had to return to her clinic patients.

"Sean's in county jail." The senator sounded weary. "I doubt he's permitted visitors."

"Do you know if he's hired a lawyer? I thought it might help if I spoke to him. Or her. I have years of history with Sean—as my intern, a tenant, now a colleague."

Rickman was silent.

Maren's stomach tightened. She eyed the orchids on her desk, wondering if she would feel better if she methodically tore off the blooms.

"Let me see what I can do," the senator finally offered.

Maren expected Rickman to hang up and was surprised when the senator spoke again.

"You know Sean's parents died a few years back, both of cancer, one after the other?"

"No, he never said." He'd mentioned only something about his mother being ill. She realized then how private Sean was with her, just banter and politics when they talked. And how alone he must have felt underneath it all. No parents. She could relate.

"This is Sean's first year with any real salary, and he has significant educational debts. With no family to turn to he will qualify to have a state-funded public defender." As if to quell any protests, Rickman added, "The Sacramento PDs are good."

Maren had interned briefly with the public defender's office in San Francisco during her last year of law school. So by "good" Maren knew the senator meant they were smart and dedicated attorneys but underfunded with a caseload of at least seventy-five defendants each.

Maren pictured Sean with the same confused look he had when Tamara Barnes came into Rickman's office, although now he was wearing an orange, prison-issued jumpsuit. That unsettling image was replaced by one of Tamara lying on the restroom sofa, arms crossed, feet together, still wearing her elegant grey pumps. Her eyes were peacefully closed, but her chest was covered in blood.

Maren spent the next hour scouring the web for detailed reporting on Tamara's death and Sean's arrest, but other than the fact that Tamara died from a single stab wound to the heart, there was little she didn't already know. The headlines were consistent in their enthusiasm: "Staff on Staff Murder!";

"Capitol Homicide"; "26-Year-Old Brutally Slain!"; "Legislator's Chief Aide Arrested in Grisly Crime!"

Fortunately, it didn't take Senator Rickman long to work her magic. By two p.m. Maren had escaped the media's collective joy in the tragedy and was standing outside the office of the Sacramento public defender at 700 H Street, only a few blocks from the capitol.

The tall, bland grey building was easy to find. If you could count and knew the alphabet, you could locate anything in downtown Sacramento. Moving from A to Z Street in one direction and 1st to 84th Street in the other, the rational layout made Maren wish the government processes housed within the city were as simple to navigate. Once inside, having shown her ID and acquired a guest badge, she was directed through a series of narrow hallways to a small office in the back. The door was ajar. The attorney inside was sorting through stacks of manila files on top of a scratched, cheap-looking credenza— more government-issued furniture.

Maren took in the woman's deeply burnished, luminous skin, high cheekbones, large coffee-colored eyes, and full red lips. Thick black hair fell gracefully to her collarbone, while the considerable curves of her body seemed hard-pressed to stay contained in a dark tailored jacket. A matching narrow, straight skirt ended modestly below her knees but served only to accent her shapely calves and long legs. In fact, Deputy Public Defender Lana Decateau was a dead ringer for Olivia Shell, the new-millennium starlet of Hispanic and African American descent, a 1940s bombshell glamour girl reborn in the modern era. Maren thought involuntarily of Jessica Rabbit of *Roger Rabbit* fame. *I'm not bad, I'm just drawn that way.*

"Ms. Kane, welcome. Please sit down," the attorney offered, revealing a lilting southern accent that, without intention, heightened her aura of femininity. "I apologize for the mess. We lost twelve lawyers in state budget cuts—those of us still here have double caseloads. We're suing the government to prevent staff reductions of another six." She gestured to Maren to sit in a folding chair before seating herself behind the desk. "The Verston case, isn't it?"

Maren wondered how Ms. Decateau could function daily in indigent criminal defense. Most of her clients must be lacking in basic social skills, and many, already incarcerated, were deprived of female companionship. For that matter, how did Lana (Maren was having a hard time thinking of her as anyone other than Olivia Shell) walk down the street without causing major traffic pileups?

But when the young woman spoke, Maren could see intelligence in her eyes and composure in her manner that would impede the otherwise instant erotic response she surely generated in most males aged fifteen to ninety-five. Because while being female, smart, and attractive was a turn-on for what Maren considered to be gold-standard men, she'd learned firsthand that other guys seemed to find the combination of the two threatening or at least off-putting.

Ms. Decateau's desktop wasn't faring much better than her credenza in the paperwork onslaught. She opened a new-looking file, pushing aside several others to make room. From where she sat, Maren had an upside-down view of Sean's booking photo, an intake form, and a number of loose papers.

"I understand you have information pertinent to the case?" Lana asked. Her southern twang made "case" sound more like "cay-yes."

Maren wondered if the attorney was thirty yet. Sacramento served as a training ground for young professionals before they moved on to "the big city"—San Francisco or L.A. Still, regardless of the woman's youthful appearance, Maren assumed Sean's case hadn't been given to a trainee. If the Sacramento public defender's office worked like San Francisco's, novice attorneys would be assigned only misdemeanors. A felony case like this would surely go to someone who could handle it.

"I was hoping you could tell me why Sean was arrested," Maren said. "What exactly happened—the news reports aren't saying much."

"Senator Rickman told me you're a friend of Mr. Verston. She suggested you might be able to help me better understand the circumstances that led him here." A fleeting smile offered a glimpse of the heights the young lawyer's beauty might reach if she weren't burdened by the seriousness of her profession. But Maren could still feel Lana Decateau putting her on notice—unless Maren could convincingly justify her presence there, her visit with the lawyer would be a short one.

"I've known Sean since his college days. He applied to intern at my company the summer he graduated. He later rented an apartment attached to my home. I feel some responsibility for him since I've helped guide his career." She thought of what Rorie Rickman had told her. "Sean's parents are no longer alive."

"I see," Lana said. "Certainly the senator's interest in this case is transparent, since Mr. Verston is her chief of staff."

Maren got the message, that she was only getting the public defender's cooperation because Rickman had insisted.

Ms. Decateau continued. "The information I can share with you will be public knowledge this afternoon. The mayor's office, working with DA Sharpton, plan a press release. The community is always interested in the details of a murder, of course. But in this case, they also want to know enough to have confidence in the arrest—to believe in it, with the murder happening as it did in an unrestricted area of a government building. There are questions of public safety."

Maren nodded. The multitude of crime procedurals on TV was evidence enough of the endless fascination people had these days with murder, imaginary and real.

"The police have a security video of Mr. Verston leaving the capitol building at eight twenty-five p.m. Shortly after footage of you and Senator Mathis arriving."

That's nothing, Maren thought. Sean told her he worked late that night. But before she could explain, Decateau said, "Mr. Verston used the exit closest to the bathroom where Ms. Barnes was found rather than the exit convenient to his office." The attorney turned to the next page in the file. "Although any surface in a busy public bathroom presents a challenge in terms of isolating fingerprints, one promising place to check was on Ms. Barnes's person. Not on the victim's skin—DNA tests might show something there later. But on her effects. In this case, her shoes." Lana's thick, black hair fell forward as she bent to read. She brushed it back with one hand in a single graceful motion. "There were two clear prints on Ms. Barnes's shoes that match Mr. Verston's. The police believe he arranged her body in the peaceful repose in which you found it, including lining up her feet so they were not askew."

Maren swallowed hard. She felt warm and unwound her scarf from her neck before managing a response. "That doesn't seem like much," she said finally, more firmly than she felt. "Tamara saw Sean earlier in the day. I was there. Couldn't there be other reasons he would have touched her shoes?"

Lana gave a small sigh. It was quiet, almost dainty. Maren saw it more than heard it, the woman's chest rise and fall.

"Can you think of any?" Lana asked. While her tone was soft, it was a challenge, not a question.

Think of other reasons he would touch her shoes? Maren knew there must be, but before she could come up with something, Ms. Decateau spoke again. "At any rate, other theories for the cause of the prints—even if far-fetched..." She paused and looked directly at Maren as though to caution her not to go there. "Such theories would be more likely to be entertained if it were not for Mr. Verston's clear motive."

This time Decateau skimmed through several papers before finding the one she wanted. "Based on the department's interviews, Sean and Ms. Barnes dated her first year of the fellows program. She rejected him. There are stories that after she broke up with Sean and got involved with someone else, Sean assaulted her new boyfriend, although no formal charges were filed. Sean has dated since, but apparently never found someone to replace Tamara. Photos in his apartment show he was carrying a torch, and according to the police, when Ms. Barnes recently made plans to marry it triggered the old if-I-can't-have-her-no-one-can response."

Sean and Tamara involved?

Sean assaulting someone?

Tamara engaged?

Sean Verston obsessed?

It was too much for Maren to process. She slid her chair closer to the desk to see for herself, but Lana Decateau had closed the file.

"What photos, what kind?" Maren asked, grasping for something concrete.

"Several candid shots. One taped to the corner of his computer screen. He would have seen it daily. It's a beach photo on a cold day, Ms. Barnes is wrapped in layers, a hat..." Lana pursed her lips and looked down. Maren thought she could see Decateau thinking of Tamara Barnes as a person, alive, rather than only as a victim, and the difficulty that caused the young attorney.

"There are also fourteen phone calls over the last few months from his cell to hers, lasting only a few seconds each. No return calls from her to him."

Maren had to admit it didn't sound good. Then she realized key information was missing. "Engaged to whom?"

Decateau found the name in the paperwork before looking up. "Caleb Waterston."

Maren's eyes widened, her mouth opened, then closed tightly. Now she knew she had fallen down the rabbit hole.

"Do you know him?" Decateau asked.

When Maren found her voice, it appeared to have gained several decibels.

"CALEB WATERSTON?"

She tried again, this time achieving a conversational volume but still unable to offer anything other than surprise and disbelief as she pictured the pale, emaciated, unattractive (at least to any nonreptilian being) lobbyist.

"He's…he's…Well, that's ridiculous." Maren stopped, realizing she was sputtering.

Lana kept her voice even. "I'm not able to comment on the appropriateness, or lack thereof, of their union. Evidence indicates it was recent, maybe a month or two. It appears they were trying to keep it secret, not unusual for staff-lobbyist liaisons, as you may know. But Mr. Waterston revealed the romance to a few friends and colleagues, sharing photos of them together. They looked like a happy couple. Homicide believes Sean found out about the engagement, and that was what pushed him over the edge."

On the walk back to her office, Maren realized Sean's attorney hadn't mentioned Tamara's comment that the governor and she had done something "awful." Maren worried the information that she provided in her interview with the police might be buried in the tsunami of papers in Decateau's office. She was sure that given Tamara's mention of the governor, something in the young aide's work for him had to be key to finding the real murderer.

And there was something else in the exchange in Senator Rickman's office the day of Tamara's death that Maren thought Decateau should be made aware of, something Maren had only reflected on after the fact.

Tamara went to Sean when she was truly upset—perhaps she had even feared for her life. That had to mean their post-romantic friendship was a mutual one, not a one-sided obsession on Sean's part. And to Maren's mind, the trusting looks that passed between Tamara and Sean that day gave clear evidence that Sean was not her killer. Maren had known Sean too long and too well to believe that his sincere expression of concern could have been masking a homicidal rage.

At the crossing at Eighteenth and L Streets Maren stopped at the light, pulled out her cell phone, and called the private line the lawyer had given her.

Lana picked up on the first ring and listened politely before responding summarily to Maren's concerns.

"Ms. Kane, your statement was not overlooked. Governor Fernandez has an alibi for the time in question. He was on a conference call from his office; phone records confirm it. He will be interviewed further as soon as he returns from an urgent trip to Asia. But don't expect too much," she cautioned. "And as for your belief that Mr. Verston and Ms. Barnes were on good terms, terms that would rule out the violence that followed, it's not uncommon for people to convey one thing and feel another; you must know that."

When the call ended, Maren felt flushed. She walked faster, almost stomping in her boots. Of course she knew people said one thing and did another. But murder? Besides, Lana Decateau didn't know Sean and hadn't been there that day to see what passed between him and Tamara.

Ten minutes later as she opened the door to Ecobabe's offices, Maren realized that with everything else that was said, she had neglected to pursue the primary purpose of contacting Sean's lawyer—assistance in getting into the jail to see Sean. As soon as she was settled at her desk, door closed, Maren made the call to Lana and the request. Lana's response wasn't what she expected.

"Is it true you have a law degree?" Decateau's tone was blunt.

Maybe an in-person visit and two calls to the attorney in one day were too much.

She fell back on what she'd learned in law school, advice for facing another lawyer's questioning. "Yes" or "No" answers, minimal elaboration—just the facts.

"Yes," Maren said.

"Have you taken and passed the California bar exam?"

"Yes."

"Any experience in criminal law?"

"Yes, an internship with the San Francisco public defender's office."

"How long?"

Maren had hoped Decateau wouldn't ask that follow-up. "Six weeks."

"Is there any reason Sean Verston wouldn't want to see you?"

What?

"No. None I can think of. He might be embarrassed. But I can't imagine, locked up like that, that he wouldn't want to see me. He and I..." Maren had gone off script, thinking aloud.

No matter. Lana cut her off.

"All right. Although you could visit Mr. Verston solely as a friend—if he were to agree to see you—in a high-profile homicide case like this it could be a lengthy clearance procedure for a brief conversation. I'll see whether I can bring you in as a legal colleague. Perhaps you will be able to encourage Mr. Verston to be more forthcoming with me."

Maren agreed, but when she hung up she was puzzled. She had assumed Sean would readily tell all he knew to his lawyer to speed his release. Although it could be he was in shock from the arrest.

As an Ecobabe intern Sean had been her apprentice, learning from her, following her lead on the best strategy to lobby high-stakes legislation. She hoped their experience in those roles might mean she would be able to help to guide him now.

CHAPTER 11

Sean pulled his knees to his chest and curled up on his side on the small bunk in the cell—clearly, the ancient metal frame and thin mattress were designed in an era when the average man's height was considerably less than his own.

Grey walls, a single dim light overhead, there was nothing to look at. He wanted his pills, a drink—anything. He didn't want to think about how he'd ended up here. He could feel Tamara's weight against him that one last time as he lifted her from the floor to the loveseat in the capitol bathroom, her blood soaking through his jacket to his shirt.

Sean rolled onto his back and rubbed his hands over his face, his forehead, his temples. Willing the image away. His hands were cold and it worked, a little, the feel of his own touch. He sat up, swinging his legs over the side of the cot. He didn't stand, there was nowhere to go. But the movement did something, tripped a switch in his brain. He realized that some good might come of his arrest, the speed of it. The finality. If he didn't fight it, if the police investigation stopped here, Tamara's secret could remain safe. Forever.

* * *

Sam Watson, chief of homicide at the Sacramento Police Department, leaned his considerable bulk back in his desk chair as though to distance himself from bad news. Beneath his bald dome Watson's sharp, green eyes focused on the two officers. "Let's have it, the update on the Tamara Barnes murder."

Detective Carlos Sifuentes had his tablet powered on, ready to retrieve the Barnes case notes—he was well ahead of the technology curve among local cops. He was also the only openly gay officer on the Sacramento force.

In his first six months post-hiring Carlos was closeted, harnessing the habitual swing in his hips and consciously lowering his soft, Latin voice half an octave from its natural tone. But past his probationary period Sifuentes came out strong. A gay officer in Los Angeles had been awarded over a million dollars for forced transfer to a position without advancement opportunities. Imagine the payout if Sacramento fired Carlos. The city would never risk it. So sure, the homicide division had a dress code, but Officer Carlos Sifuentes knew how to walk to the edge without falling off. Today it was a tailored grey suit with a brocade, vintage emerald vest and polished cocoa-colored boots.

"Sean Verston had motive and opportunity. History shows obsessive jealousy relative to the victim. He has been placed at the crime scene through his prints and also by his own admission, although he says Ms. Barnes had already been stabbed when he got there. He disappeared after the murder. We found him through an APB on his car, a 1982 gold and white Camaro. According to his roommates he hadn't been home overnight. He had his passport with him." Sifuentes scrolled further down the screen. "If Mr. Verston strangled the victim barehanded we'd be done. But death was caused by a single stab wound through her heart, with no recovery of the weapon. We've searched the capitol building, of course, and Verston's apartment and car. He may have dumped it leaving the scene; we're looking. Or maybe he flushed the weapon, in which case it's long gone through the Sacramento sewers."

Chief Martin circled his index finger in the air, indicating to Sifuentes to speed it up.

Sifuentes spoke faster. "Forensics estimates the blade was roughly half an inch wide, four inches in length—if the handle could be detached, perhaps...But I've seen a quarter sit at the bottom of a toilet for a long time through many flushes, so I don't see how..."

The chief's eyes simmered, turning a deeper green, which Alibi Morning Sun tracked as trouble. Morning Sun cut in. "That's it, Chief."

Watson leaned forward, grasping a pencil with both hands as though to snap it in two. It remained intact, but at risk.

"So if I get you right, the evidence all points to Verston, nothing's come up to contradict that. Still, it's circumstantial. He was there, he had reasons to kill the victim. He disappeared, he was a flight risk, so he was promptly taken into custody." Watson threw the pencil down on his desk. "With DA Sharpton's reelection coming up in June, he can't afford a screwup.

Especially not on a homicide that occurred steps from the governor's office in the capitol building."

Watson jabbed his finger in Sifuentes's direction, then glared at Alibi. "DA Mitchell Sharpton is the mayor's boy." Not that the detectives needed to be reminded of that. It was common knowledge. "I want a weapon or a witness. You're gonna give me an airtight road to a conviction of this Verston kid, nothing left in the wind. Understood?"

CHAPTER 12

Maren spent Saturday working. It was urgent. She had to craft a promotional piece about the cell phone bill, SB 770, before Monday. Rickman's office would circulate it to legislators and the press, and Ecobabe would feature it on their website as a marketing tool. Key content would be how many children's lives could be saved if the bill was enacted. Unfortunately, her writing wasn't going well. Sean in jail for murder was still beyond belief, and Maren was used to being able to help when things went wrong for those she cared about. But unless she could come up with Tamara's real murderer, she didn't see what she could do. And tracking down an unknown killer seemed a grandiose notion to entertain—where would she even start?

She checked her phone. There was a message from Noel canceling their weekly Sunday dinner—something about an urgent project. The next voice was Simone Booth's daughter's acknowledging how busy Maren must be but asking if an early dinner tonight might work.

Maren hated to keep putting her off—clearly, there was some measure of closure involved for Liza Booth-Henry in this act of thanking Maren in person. Maren didn't think she could face it alone, but with the right "date"...

Two hours later Maren and Polly stood just inside the entry of a small flat located on the second floor of a nondescript four-plex, not far from Maren's office in midtown. The eye of an artist was evident in Liza's choice of wall hangings and eclectic, colorful ceramic dishes on the glass-topped oval dining table. But an open door to a small study revealed the chaos that often follows a teacher home—John Booth-Henry's white laminate desk was covered with graded and ungraded exams. Books were jammed upright and sideways onto shelves, and some had made their way into piles on the floor.

"Can I get you a drink? Wine, sparkling water?"

In her late twenties, Liza Booth-Henry was lean the way some young mothers are from racing after their children rather than from dedicated workouts. Her shiny, brown, chin-length hair flipped up at the ends, framing an even-featured, attractive face. The sleek, black three-quarter-length pants, sleeveless black tur-tleneck, and black ballet flats she wore were '60s mod. Maren's hostess struck her as a cross between Barbie's best friend, Midge (minus the freckles), and an early Mary Tyler Moore. The only break in the unicolor look was a striking brooch of Liza's own design, a thin figure of indeterminate gender fashioned in flat silver, its outstretched arms supporting a quarter moon of bur-nished copper.

Polly chose red wine. Maren was about to ask for sparkling water when a streak of fur raced past, followed by a two-year-old girl in whirling, giggling Tasmanian devil-like pursuit. Seconds later, a boy with determined composure marched after the girl, gaining ground only because of his considerably longer legs.

"I'm so sorry...Maren, you'll remember..." Liza's mouth turned down. She faltered, not sure how to proceed given that Maren had met her children in a time of crisis. She tried again. "Maren, you'll remember Zoey and Zane. Mother's kitten, Nigel, has come to live with us. It's a bit of an adjustment for everyone."

"Mostly for Nigel, I'd say," Polly said, smiling when Zane came back into view carrying the cat wrapped in a bath towel, the feline's fuzzy black head peeking out, its ears back. Zoey followed closely, her cheeks puffed out and eyes narrowed, clearly poised to howl if Zane took the kitten completely out of reach.

Maren looked for recognition in the young boy's eyes as he walked by, but either her dry hair and clothes made her incognito relative to the awful day she had dragged him from the sunken car, or more likely he was choosing not to acknowledge her.

"Please, have a seat." John gestured to two modern-looking orange sling-back chairs arranged around the hearth. There was also a black leather love seat that looked more comfortable, but it was occupied by a variety of Lego and a teddy bear with one leg. (Pre-party cleanup had evidently been thwarted by the apartment's youngest occupants.) Tomato, onion, and garlic smells from the kitchen competed with jasmine-scented candles on the mantel.

92

"Your place is lovely," Maren said, watching her hosts for a cue as to whether she should perch on the edge of one of the unusual chairs or lean back in the slouch-like posture their shape encouraged. Liza perched, John leaned—no help there.

Liza looked around her. "It will be hard to leave. We've been here since before the children were born, but we've decided to move into Mother's place. There's a nice yard, a garden..." She paused, seeming to lose steam. "There really isn't any way we can express our gratitude to you," she said at last, looking directly at Maren. Tears were forming in her eyes.

John Booth-Henry, a large man with bushy black hair and black-rimmed glasses, took his wife's hand. Maren assumed he was intimidating to his high school students until they heard his gentle voice. "We had so little time," he said. "Simone only moved out here from New Jersey last spring." He looked at Liza, whose head was bowed.

Maren wondered if scheduling this get-together so soon had been a good idea. She pictured Simone Booth there with them, her white curls framing a grandmotherly smile as she cuddled Zoey on her lap or helped Zane with his latest Lego creation. Maren was suddenly tired. The emptiness Liza felt from her mother's passing was contagious.

"I understand she was a terribly talented journalist," Polly said brightly. "She must have left a wonderful legacy in her writings."

Thank goodness for Polly, Maren thought.

Liza gestured expansively. "Yes, there's so much of it. That's one of the challenges with the move. My mother wrote everything longhand and recorded her interviews on cassette tapes."

"Not even digital—real cassette tapes," added John.

"There must be thirty years' worth. Hundreds and hundreds of them. Some of them might be of interest to writing programs, or even museums—Mother did some important journalistic research. Especially on government activities and legislation, both when she was in D.C. and since she came here to Sacramento. But the labeling is unintelligible—random numbers, letters. No words or dates. It's like a code. She also left handwritten notes and backup documents that might hold the key, but I can't imagine having the time to go through them all, not with work and the kids..." Liza's shoulders slumped and her hands fell limply back into her lap as her burden of grief returned.

Maren focused on Liza's hands as they went from motion to stillness. She felt Tamara's hand in her own in those last moments, a young woman beyond her reach. Perhaps she could do something for this one.

"That could be a good project for my interns," Maren said. "They're all policy or political science students of one stripe or another. From what you say, there's likely a lot in your mother's research that they could learn from."

"Listening to the tapes might be educational." John adjusted his glasses with his free hand. "But it would take forever. I can't see you freeing your assistants for that many hours."

"They might be able to find a way to upload the tapes into the computer," Maren said. "Or perhaps a dictation program to translate them from voice to text. Then they wouldn't need to listen to each one. They could skim and highlight the transcriptions to pick and choose instead."

A crashing sound from the other room followed by an inhuman yowl and some very human crying brought both Liza and John to their feet.

John was out of sight first, returning with a kicking, scream-ing Zoey in his arms. Maren experienced déjà vu as she recalled Senator Alec Joben in the same posture with the toddler at the scene of Simone Booth's fatal accident.

John handed Zoey off to Liza, who spoke softly and stroked the girl's fine brown hair. The child ceased her resistance, laid her head on her mother's chest, and with thumb in mouth allowed herself to be taken back toward the bedrooms.

"The cat sought refuge at the top of the bookshelf," John reported. "Either that or there's a kamikaze kitten in our midst. Fortunately, the shelves were bolted to the wall as an earth-quake precaution. Still, most everything that was up there is now on the floor." He smiled, and in a somewhat theatrical ges-ture downed the remainder of his wine. "Although unclear how much of that was due to the cat, and how much Zoey caused in pursuit. Anyone else for a refill?"

Polly was game for another glass of red. Maren set her water down and asked if she might use the bathroom.

"Of course. There's only one, I'm afraid," John said. "Past the nursery. Sorry, it's a bit overrun with kid stuff."

Maren had noticed before that people with young children seemed to apologize often to the childless. She wondered if they worried whether she and others without offspring lacked the genes or the will to accept the discomforts that invariably accompany the joys of parenting.

* * *

John Booth-Henry's description of the small bathroom did not disappoint. Despite a clear attempt to organize, brightly colored children's plastic bath toys and child-safe body products claimed every surface, from the area around the sink to the sides of the tub. A blue toddler's potty competed with the adult version for the limited floor space.

After drying her hands on a My Little Pony hand towel, Maren adjusted her belt using the full-length mirror on the inside of the bathroom door.

On most days Maren's style tended toward artistic, avant-garde, or '60s hippie, depending on who was describing it— loose, flowing skirts, scarves, and jackets in peaceful, deep hues. Once, leaving a luncheon her oversized silk jacket—in a print reminiscent of a Monet watercolor—caught on a chair, which proceeded to drag behind her as she tried to leave. A colleague commented, "Maren, only you could make the furniture part of your fashion statement." But recently, with Polly's urging, Maren had purchased a white, above-the-knee, bell-shaped skirt with black embroidery along the hem. Tonight she paired it with a sleeveless white top, a broad black belt, and shiny, black strappy heels. *Not bad*, she thought, as she appraised her new look and noticed that even her dark curly hair seemed to be trying to behave itself

Before leaving the bathroom Maren dug into her satchel, retrieved her phone, and checked for messages. There were only a couple of routine work calls. It was odd not to see Sean's name among them. The two of them should be busy pulling together the cell phone bill strategy, talking daily about how to get the votes they needed to beat the opposition.

Getting it done without Sean wasn't optional; Maren didn't know if she would still have her job if she didn't at least demonstrate that she'd pulled out all the stops to secure passage of the cell phone bill. But what would once have been the only thing on her mind—seeing Ecobabe's legislation signed—had fallen so far that at times she had to remind herself to care.

She took a last look in the mirror—her face suddenly appeared older to her, greyer. She applied lip gloss and pinched her cheeks.

As she made her way back past the closed door of the nursery, Maren could hear new voices from the main room.

Both male.

Both familiar.

She turned the corner and stopped just inside the room.

Senator Alec Joben was accepting a beer from his host, John Booth-Henry. A younger man stood next to him, his prematurely receding hairline ending in a short, stubby ponytail. *Never a good look*, Maren thought. But his clothes were thrift-store chic—a '50s mustard-colored suit and a thin blue tie, which together almost made the hair thing work for him. Maren felt she knew him from somewhere, she wasn't sure where. But that was Sacramento—a small town despite its big-city aspirations.

Not that it mattered to Maren; the younger man wasn't relevant. She was mapping her escape strategy.

It was one thing to have hoped and imagined that Senator Alec Joben might appear at this thank-you dinner since he'd also participated in saving Zane and Zoey from the sinking car. In fact, it had occurred to her he might be on the invitation list when she chose her new outfit. But to have Alec actually show up unannounced was, well, unacceptable. She had wanted her next encounter with Alec Joben to be well thought out. Pro and con lists made and diagrams drawn, perhaps a role-playing session where Camper could be Joben. Because Maren felt she had two modes in life: carefully planned versus "what the hell just happened?" with the latter rarely ending well.

She looked more carefully at the two new guests, wondering if they could have come together. *If Alec Joben were gay, if they were a couple my problems would be solved.*. True, the thoughts Maren had been cautiously entertaining and then pushing away of a potential romance with Alec would be crushed. But at least the pain that actually reaching for love might cause her would never arrive.

"You know the senator," John Booth-Henry began. "And this is Ed Howard, our neighbor in the next flat."

"We've met," Howard said, stepping awkwardly toward Maren, nearly knocking over one of the chairs in the process, recovering, and extending his hand. "Spoken, actually. You prevented me from removing my belt." He stammered, then blushed, realizing that didn't sound right. "In the security line. At the capitol. Artists' Lobby Day," he clarified.

"Maren often has that effect on men," Polly said. Her British accent made the quip come across as droll, rather than crass. There was laughter, except for Howard, who blushed again before retreating to the chair Maren had vacated. Polly and Liza, chatting amiably, sat down. John was clearing the love seat while making more apologies for having children. Alec moved toward it, then slowed, waiting for Maren to seat herself first.

Musical chairs, she thought. She never was good at games. Still, she was sure there had to be a way out. Until Polly caught her eye with a stern *don't you dare* expression. Since Polly was her potential getaway driver, that narrowed her options.

Maren smiled at Alec. She hoped it was a smile and not a grimace, and tucked herself into one corner of the love seat. But while the senator did his best to observe the boundary she was setting, he wasn't a small man. They might as well have been in economy class in a commuter plane on Southwest Air.

Maren's breathing increased. She felt unnaturally warm. Her response to his proximity made her picture Garrick Chauncey—the last man she'd been intimate with—and she felt oddly guilty. She pulled her arms in tightly against her sides.

"Come here often?" Alec asked, smiling softly.

Is that flirting? Did he just flirt with me?

"No. Yes. I..." she began, marveling at how a simple conversation became a landmine when hormones were involved.

"I thought maybe you didn't venture out after dark," Alec said, his eyes not leaving hers. "I've looked for you at post-work events."

Okay, that was flirting—even I know that was flirting, she thought. *Unless he's worried I'm a vampire.* Fortunately, before Maren moved on to the possibility that Alec Joben suspected she was a shape shifter, Ed Howard cut in, leaning forward in his chair until it almost tipped over and he had to lean back again. "Senator Joben, I was starting to say, I mean, when we were standing..." He stopped and took an audible breath. "I have an appointment with you. Next week. I booked it with Shelly. No. Sharon, I think. I'm an artist, really, but my day job, I'm in hotel management, in training actually. I'm coming to see you about the bedsheet bill."

Bedsheet bill? Maren hadn't heard of that one—but then there were thousands of legislative proposals in California each session.

Alec Joben loved policy discussions; it was one of the reasons he had run for office. He shifted gears. "Ed, isn't it?"

The young man nodded.

"I understand management concerns about the cost to the hotels. But I'm worried about the health of the housekeeping staff that's why I'm carrying the bill. The time required in a bended position to tuck in the corners of bottom and top flat sheets hour after hour, day after day, as compared to sheet, changes using fitted bottom sheets, contributes significantly to workers' back injuries."

Ed Howard's blotchy complexion reddened. He licked his lips, and when he took a drink of wine to clear his throat, his hand was unsteady. But he was prepared on this topic and his content was clear. "New policies at forty-two percent of larger hotels permit guests to choose the option to skip sheet changes for days at a time to lessen the impact on the environment. But it also really reduces housekeeping staff's workload. The back injury data you cite is old. Really, hotels can have both—flat sheets which are less expensive in bulk, and injury rates still less than half what they used to be."

The two men parried, exchanging statistics back and forth, but it was not unfriendly. Maren tuned out their words, hearing only "*Blah, blah, blah bedsheets.*" She found herself observing Alec's strong mouth, his teeth and tongue moving as he talked, and imagining what else they might be good for.

* * *

The next morning when she got out of the shower Maren had a message from Alec asking if she would like to have a drink Wednesday night. Lana Decateau had also finally called—the attorney said she had cleared Maren to visit Sean as a"consulting attorney of record."

Maren left Alec a warm message accepting the invitation. She was happy to find it easier over the phone to act like a grown-up in romantic matters. Although she knew doubts would crowd in when she had to get ready for what was clearly "a date." If her past experience was any guide, fundamental questions would jam her most basic operating systems. *Was she good enough for him? Was he good enough for her?*

But for now, it was nice to be asked.

She turned her attention to Lana's message, jotting down the logistics to see Sean. Her work could wait—she grabbed her satchel and headed out the door.

The county jail at 711 G Street loomed large on the flat Sacramento landscape. Ninety percent of its 2,400 inmates were in for felonies. Three massive towers were crisscrossed with scores of narrow, tinted windows.

A short, older guard with white hair escorted Maren to an empty interview room with putty-colored walls, grey flooring, scuffed chairs, and a metal table. He left without comment. Within minutes Sean arrived accompanied by a second guard.

Rather than the orange jumpsuit Maren had expected, Sean wore prison-issue grey slacks and a grey button-front shirt. Several days' growth of beard darkened his face. His bangs, usually a fashion statement, hung dull and lanky in his eyes. The guard leaned against the wall, apparently planning to stay.

"I have a right to privacy with my client," Maren asserted, although in truth she had no idea what the rules were. Maren's legal experience was limited to drafting and reading proposed legislation and reviewing company contracts for Ecobabe. But she figured the same basic principle applied in all legal matters—ask for anything, you might get it. She added, "Uncuff him. I'll take responsibility."

"I'll be outside," the guard said, ignoring her request to remove Sean's handcuffs. But he did leave. *One for two*, she thought. Until she noticed a small window in the top half of the door enabling the guard to watch them inside.

Sean backed his legs against the chair before folding his six-foot-plus frame into it, by feel, like a blind man. He kept his head down.

"I don't believe for a minute that you..." Maren stumbled over the right choice of words. "That you harmed Tamara Barnes."

Sean looked up. He appeared to be taking in each aspect of Maren's expression—her eyes, the slant of her mouth—as though he didn't recognize her. Or maybe, she thought, he was measuring her, checking to see if she really believed in him. When he finally spoke his tone was hard, his hands balled into fists at his side, although the rest of his posture remained passive.

"I told Tilly—Tamara, I told her I would come to the governor's office when I was done. That she should wait for me. She was probably only there alone because I was late..." He broke off, swallowed. "I was almost to Tamara's office, the governor's suite. I heard something as I passed the bathroom." His face twitched; he grimaced. Maren pursed her lips and pulled her jacket closed tightly around her, also remembering that night, the body, the blood.

"She was on the floor," he said. "By the sinks. She tried to speak." Sean stared at the wall—Maren might as well not have been present in the interview room.

"I knelt to hear her. To hold her...She tried, but...she...there wasn't anything." His tears came hard. He made no effort to wipe them away.

Maren wanted to comfort him, but was conscious of the time, of the guard just outside the door. "You said she was on the floor? When I came in, that's not how..."

"The tiles were cold," he said quietly. "She was pale." His eyes were anguished. "I lifted her onto the couch." He looked down again. When he raised his head the vivid pain was gone, replaced by exhaustion, his lids heavy. "I don't know the rest, I don't remember."

"What do you mean?"

He spoke as if by rote, as if it was something he had repeated many times. "The next thing I knew I was outside. I heard sirens. I went home. In the morning I wasn't sure what was real and what wasn't."

CHAPTER 13

The key stuck. Maren had to wiggle it a few times, left, then right. Camper whined. It was a poor copy, but she felt lucky to have it since Sean hadn't returned the one she gave him before he lost the chance—to do that or anything else outside of jail.

It was cold in the small studio attached to her home. The wall-mounted heating and air conditioning unit she'd installed so that tenants would be comfortable was shut off.

Maren's interview with Sean had disturbed her. Not only because it was impossibly sad to see him locked up, but also because she was sure there were things he wasn't telling her. Some of what he said seemed heartfelt, as though he were trapped in the last minutes of Tamara's life. He had called Tamara by a pet name, Tilly—it felt real. But upon reflection, some of his other statements seemed rehearsed, and, she had to admit to herself, untrue. Not that she had good radar for that.

Maren tended to feel first and question later where emotions were involved. But she had noticed that in his summation of what occurred the night of the murder, he had omitted coming to see her.

She surveyed the small space. He had returned the black sofa bed to its original state, and the blankets and sheets were folded in a large open basket that she used for storage, as neatly as he had found them. In fact, it was unclear whether he had used them at all.

Maren's rental began as a master bedroom and bath. When she decided to convert it to income property, she provided a stacked washer-dryer in the large bathroom and turned the walk-in closet into a kitchenette. The twelve-by-fifteen foot main room was dominated by entries and exits— a front door, a back door to the courtyard that was shared with the main house, a door to the kitchenette, and another off that to the bath-room. Plus a good-size window on the wall between the built-in shelves and the closet, with a small flower box attached that the tenant could plant as they saw fit.

Camper did a cursory but enthusiastic smell check, nose to the floor, of all the rooms. Twice. Apparently satisfied with the results, he lay down in the one sunny spot under the window.

Maren pulled a bucket of cleaning supplies out of the single kitchen cabinet and dragged a folded step stool from behind the range. She started with the main room shelving first, spray-ing and wiping with a nontoxic vinegar solution top to bottom. Then she turned her attention to the baseboards, circumnavigat-ing the apartment on her knees, checking a corner that seemed loose, washing the edges carefully. Then the refrigerator. Next, inside the closet, where she found Sean's black suit jacket, neatly hung up.

Every inch of every surface. Not because she was looking for anything. Not because the missing weapon, the knife, could be hidden there. *Just a thorough and necessary cleaning,* she told herself.

Sweatshirt off, her jeans and T-shirt were dusty and damp, decorated with cobwebs and splashes of poorly aimed spray. She opened the window to let in fresh air and to help the freshly mopped floor dry.

That was when she saw it.

Not something left behind.

Something missing.

The key to the main house, to her house, kept on top in the second flowerpot from the left in the window box, was gone. She looked in and under all six pots, dug her hands into the dirt.

And came up empty.

She returned to Sean's jacket hanging in the closet and checked the pockets, feeling intrusive as she did so. There was a small, flat plastic container, unlabeled, with four pills in it, a receipt from a drive-through taco place, another from the California Department of Motor Vehicles. And some loose change. No key.

She returned to the main house. It was not yet four p.m., but she knew Polly would likely be home. She had worked out a schedule with the fellows program that permitted her to leave daily by three to pick up her son, Jake, from school, and then get in her compulsive exercise afterward.

Maren grabbed her phone and dialed.

"Slow down, love. Did Sean know about the key?"

"Yes." Maren kept her answer short, but in fact the key was originally kept there not only in case Maren locked herself out but also for Sean. When he lived in the studio, if Maren was traveling or working late, he took care of Camper, letting himself into the main house to feed the always-hungry dog or take him for a run.

"Anyone else know about it?" Polly asked. "When was the last time you used it?"

"No, no one. I don't know, maybe a year ago."

"Are you sure it didn't fall out of the flower box?"

Maren had thought of that and had searched the area thoroughly.

"I'm headed to the track." It sounded to Maren like her friend was already jogging down the hill, a little out of breath, using some runner's gadget to talk hands-free while she ran. "Why don't you join me? You can schedule a locksmith to come when we get back. You'll feel better for both, the run and the new keys."

Maren sighed. Polly thought a good run would remedy anything, but it wasn't high on Maren's exercise wish list. She far preferred the pool or walking city streets. She gave in once in a while to spend time with Polly. But not today. "I've been putting it off, but I have to get through the files for Rickman's cell phone bill. It's been reset for hearing. I suppose you're right about the locksmith. Although, if you think about it, if Sean took the key it doesn't matter now." *Since he's locked up,* Maren couldn't bring herself to add. "And I just don't see anyone else braving Camper's wrath to steal it." The dog door from the back of the main house gave Camper free access to the shared courtyard. And the big dog could "bring it"—true pit bull ferocity, despite looking deceptively like a friendly lab.

That's not to say Maren didn't take Polly's advice about calling a locksmith seriously. But it seemed foolish to her to incur the expense or trouble until she knew whether Sean had removed the key. Maybe he'd forgotten he'd picked it up, perhaps meaning to walk Camper in the morning, and then he was arrested and the key was inventoried with his belongings at the jail. So when she hung up with Polly she dialed again, this time calling Sean. But after being put on hold for an interminable time, she was told by the unidentified person who had answered only that "Verston is unavailable." *The trouble with jails,* she thought, *is you can't tell if someone's avoiding you or they're in lockdown.*

An hour later, after a halfhearted session with the cell phone files, Maren stood watering what was left of her front lawn, her thick hair pulled back in a clip as tendrils escaped on either side. She'd been so busy with everything else that brown was the new green, at least as far as her yard was concerned. She vowed to put in drought-resistant plants as soon as she had the time.

It was starting to get dark, and having done what little she could for the plants, Maren went inside and tackled her e-mails. Her laptop was glitching again. It took several reboots to get more than a blank screen. Hardly worth it—another senrabyllit@talk.com request to invest and a promotion for a dating club. She wished she had one of those programs that permitted her to create a custom filter to preselect and trash junk mail by characteristics—a specific e-mail address or keywords. Now that she thought of it, maybe she did, but it wasn't turned on. She decided to ask Noel to take a look since the problem seemed to be getting worse. Those investment e-mails were coming daily.

There was also a message from Garrick.

From: Garrick Chauncey <gchauncey@econ.sacstate.edu>
To: Maren Kane <mkane@ecobabe.org>
Re: Never say never...
Maren,
One lunch. You live with a man and then can't break bread
with him? Compassion, forgiveness, I know you believe in
these things. One lunch, I promise.
G.

Maren was having an increasingly difficult time holding on
to what had been wrong with her relationship with Garrick as
she passed days and, even worse, nights alone. She also found,
to her surprise, that her pending date with Alec made it seem
like a reasonable idea to see Garrick, too. Because that would
mean she was a woman who "went out with men"—plural, on
dates, plural. True, she'd never been able to do anything but
be monogamous and map things out. But she reasoned that in
the absence of having tried, she couldn't know what was possible. Not settling on one guy right away might take the pressure off and lead to a better choice in the end. And here was
her opportunity. Tuesday lunch with Garrick. Wednesday drinks
with Alec.

She started typing.

From: Maren Kane <mkane@ecobabe.org>
To: Garrick Chauncey <gchauncey@econ.sacstate.edu>
Re: Re: Never say never...
Garrick,
Tomorrow, Santa Fe Bar & Grill at noon.
M.

Maren closed the laptop. She was camped out on her living room floor digging through the large box of files collected from Rickman's office when there was a knock at her front door. Polly Grey walked in before Maren could get up to answer. The two friends had long ago abandoned the formality of waiting for an invitation before entering one another's homes.

Polly wore a fitted green tank top, black Lycra shorts, and a gold wristband. With her spiky hair and a warm sheen glistening on her skin from her run, she had an elfin look that contradicted her no-nonsense nature.

"What's all this, then?" Polly asked, stepping handily over stacks of papers on her way to Maren's kitchen to put a kettle on for afternoon tea. Despite having lived in the United States for over ten years, Polly's British-born habits endured.

"The cell phone legislation."

"Did you find a locksmith?"

"I'm working on it." Maren surveyed the mess.

"Is this new law of yours going to make it impossible for me to call Jake from my car?" Jake was Polly's only child, a thirteen-year-old whose existence defied teen stereotypes. Polite, happy, and respectful toward his mom, he played jazz saxophone and read classic literature. Although that's not to say he was above a marathon video game battle with his buddies.

"That's the plan," Maren said.

"Can I help?" Polly was well versed in bill analysis. Her annual preparation for new members in the Young Fellows program included teaching them those skills. It wouldn't do to have her charges placed in busy legislative offices without that knowledge.

"Last year a hands-free phone requirement for drivers became law. It was introduced by Senator Connor Smith of Fresno. Some new files have come to light; I'm taking a look." Maren didn't think it would be right to share with Polly exactly how those new files had turned up. She didn't wish to involve Polly in Rickman's decision to remove the items from Sean's office when he was arrested.

"I remember, I had to get one of those TalkFree headsets. Not cheap." Polly joined Maren cross-legged on the floor, passing her a mug of still-steeping mint tea and setting a plate of banana bread between them. Maren was rarely without healthy baked goods from the small bakery just up the street.

"There have been persistent rumors that Senator Smith's bill was originally drafted like mine, that it wouldn't permit any phone use while driving, hands-free or not. I'm trying to determine if that's true, and if so, why Smith softened the restrictions to allow talking hands-free. I haven't been able to reach the senator. He hit his term limits and retired out of state. I'm looking for notes or records on the original bill language."

"Okay," Polly said, picking up the nearest file and opening it. "This one is titled 'Vote Total'—looks like only Democrats voted for Smith's bill. There are notes here that Republicans worked to, and I quote, 'kill it.'" She opened a second file. "This might be interesting, refers to Mr. Caries, our dishy young governor at the time. Did you know he started a statewide jazz music program in the public schools? Jake idolizes him. But is he still around? Didn't I read somewhere that he popped off to Asia?"

"Africa—to start nonprofit schools for the poor." Maren gestured toward the folder. "Can I see that?"

Polly passed it to her, then took a bite of the banana bread. "This is good."

"It says here there was no signing ceremony for the hands-free phone requirement." Maren raised her eyebrows as she checked through the file again.

"They don't have those on every bill."

"No, but it's common when a governor signs a law affecting the public to gather sponsors and supporters for a photo opportunity. And Jack Caries, just out of Hollywood and photogenic as he is, made the most of those. I would have thought..."

Another knock at Maren's door. Polly hopped up to find her son, Jake, on the front porch. With flawless pale skin and dark hair and eyes, Jake was built on a small scale much like his mom. Although adults commented on his good looks, to Jake's dismay he was invisible to girls his own age, who seemed drawn to height and hulking evidence of hormone development even if it came with bad skin and scraggly facial hair.

When Camper heard Jake's voice he barreled through the living room, scattering several of the carefully arranged stacks of files on the floor.

"Whoa, Camper. Down!" Jake ordered, holding his palm flat in front of Camper's face in a signal the dog knew well. Camper complied and lay down, but his head remained upright and his entire body wiggled as his tail thumped on the floor.

"Can I take Camper for a walk?"

At the word "walk" Camper vibrated and, though well trained, barely managed to hold the down position. Maren smiled, the dog's joy cutting through her own layers of stress. After boy and dog happily departed she went back to work, homing in on a paper from the bottom of the box.

"What is it?" Polly asked.

"Senator Smith's chief of staff writes he was concerned about research that showed hands-free phones are not any safer than handheld phones in preventing accidents while driving. It's nearly two years ago. To my knowledge there was no such research until this year. If similar studies were available back then, a hands-free requirement would have been laughable, protecting no one." Maren waved the note in the air, clearly agitated. "Smith's bill would have been dropped—yet instead it was signed into law. How could research appear and disappear? If the reason it was ignored is that the earlier research was discredited, it will be a huge problem for my bill." She could picture her Board's disappointment. Her stomach sank at the prospect of two failed Ecobabe legislative campaigns in a row.

"There's writing on the back." Polly offered.

Maren flipped the paper over. The words "study canceled, Marjorie Hopkins dead" were scribbled in blue ink. Maren reread the note then moved to her laptop on the table by the hearth, opening the browser to Google the reference. Five years old, the core processor took its time. Finally, a window opened to the image of a pretty young woman, dark hair pulled back, black framed glasses, smiling. She was holding a toddler whose round face resembled her own, the smiles the same. The accompanying text was brief.

Marjorie Hopkins, PhD, age 33, junior researcher at the Department of Health Services completing a postdoctoral fellowship in communications and injury prevention, was found murdered Friday in an empty lot behind the Broads and Bards Café in Sacramento. There was no evidence of sexual assault. Police suspect a robbery gone awry. Dr. Hopkins is survived by her husband and two-year-old daughter.

Maren felt a chill. She realized reading of another death, one murder more, was different for her now, given what she had just been through. *At least Tamara Barnes didn't leave behind a child,* she thought, then caught herself. Maren didn't have kids. Did that mean her own death would be any less tragic? She turned to Polly. "The research stopped because the researcher died." Maren showed her friend the screen, noticing for the first time that Hopkins was killed on Polly's birthday, March 13. But if Polly made that connection, she didn't say anything, picking up instead on something Maren hadn't seen.

"Look at the byline at the bottom—it's that journalist, isn't it? The one who died in the accident."

Maren found the small print. *Simone Booth.*

There was another knock at the door. "It's bloody Union Station in here," Polly said, bouncing up to answer it.

Maren scrolled down the screen, finding a "read more" hyperlink in blue. She clicked it and was given access to the full article.

Still not much. A description of Marjorie Hopkins' happy childhood with two brothers and two sisters in Grinnell, a small college town in Iowa. Comments from two of the siblings. Highlights of volunteer work Marjorie had done, and lastly statements from a colleague about how wonderful Marjorie was to work with and from her boss at the Department of Public Health lauding Hopkins' initiative and dedication to innovative research. Nothing specific about cell phone use safety and no mention of Senator Smith's proposed legislation. But clearly, in preparing this brief obituary journalist Simone Booth had spoken to several people who might know more. Maren resolved to start her interns on the transcription of Simone's interviews sooner rather than later. And to ask them to begin by looking for tapes related to Booth's piece on Marjorie Hopkins.

Perhaps it was as simple as Senator Smith's staff having gotten wind of Marjorie Hopkins' proposed research that *might* show hands-free cell phones were no safer than holding the phone while driving. Then the study was scrapped when Hopkins died, and the hands-free bill went forward as planned. Over a year later someone learned of Hopkins' hypothesis and pursued the research that formed the basis for Rickman's bill. But still, Maren figured if she could uncover the beginnings of early research by Hopkins, it was almost certain that the well-funded hands-free phone industry would have unearthed it, too. And if anything Hopkins had written could be spun the other way—to say hands-free really was better—the profit motive would ensure that those companies would find a way to do that. Which, in turn, could jeopardize SB 770, Rickman's bill. Maren needed to be ready to respond if that was the case.

"Hullo, Doctor—raining, is it?" Polly always called Noel "Doctor" out of respect for his PhD, but she couldn't resist ribbing him about his ubiquitous trench coat, perhaps necessary in England but not, to Polly's view, in sunny California.

Noel either didn't get the humor or didn't take the bait. "Good evening, Polly." He surveyed the darkening sky. "No, it's clear, only a few cumulus clouds."

Now that Noel was here to make up for the dinner he'd missed Sunday, Maren set aside her work and pulled together an informal feast. Using grilled vegetables left over from a take-out deli salad and thick slices of whole-wheat bread, she made hearty, if meatless, sandwiches served with bagged sweet potato chips and apple slices. Unconventional, but Polly and Noel each cleaned their plates.

After dinner, the trio went out to the backyard, Maren detouring first down the stairs to the driveway to turn on the spa heater. Maren planned a hot soak outside later; maybe Polly would stay and join her. When installing the outdoor hot tub at the very back of the property, the company wanted to charge her an extra thousand dollars to run the needed electrical across the yard to have the controls wired at the spa. So a trip to her garage to set the spa thermostat and turn the bubbles on was part of her evening routine.

Friends and family.

A great marketing campaign for a cell phone plan, but in Maren's case the list would be too short to justify any group savings.

Noel and Polly.

If Jake hadn't left after returning Camper—and if Sean could have gotten a Get Out of Jail Free card—all would be present and accounted for.

The thick branches of a majestic, one-hundred-year-old oak shielded half the yard, creating a tree-house effect under its span. It was cooler outside than Maren had expected. Polly pulled the wool jacket Maren had loaned her tightly around her but complained that she could still feel the cold vinyl webbing of the chaise against her back. Maren sat on the edge of the spa while it heated, idly kicking her feet in the tepid water. Her mind kept returning to the two young women's murders. Tamara's, and before that Marjorie Hopkins'. Both stabbed, Both here and gone so quickly.

Camper was stretched out a few feet away, head on paws and eyes shut. Noel was halfway up a steep, unplanted hill that rose to her back fence, trying to get an unobstructed view of the night sky.

"Are you sure you don't want to join me?" he called. "With any luck Jupiter, Venus, Mars, and Saturn will be visible simultaneously." Struggling to get a foothold in the loose dirt, he paused to extract a five-inch-long collapsible telescope from his coat pocket. Maren wondered what else her brother kept in that coat—*he probably belongs to some nerd's portable-gadget-of-the-month club,* she thought fondly.

"Locksmith coming tomorrow to set you right, love?" Polly asked, shivering. She had no built-in insulation—the price for nearly zero body fat. She abandoned the chaise and joined Maren on the narrow deck that circled the old-style wooden spa, bending to test the water with one hand. Satisfied, Polly removed her running shoes and socks and sat shoulder to shoulder with Maren, apparently hoping for warmth.

"Yes." A white lie. Maren would get to it after she talked to Sean. Then she realized what was bothering her, why her mind kept circling what little she knew about Marjorie Hopkins' death. "Polly, the report said the police never found out who was responsible for the researcher's murder. Maybe it was the same person who killed Tamara."

Polly watched the bubbles swirling in the spa, frowning. "That's a stretch, love. That researcher's death was nearly a year ago. There must be hundreds of murders in that time span in our charming town. No reason for the bloke to be the same one." She looked up at Maren. "What makes you think they're linked?"

"Both young, professional women, government employees. No evidence of rape or sexual assault. Both stabbed. Neither woman involved in gangs or prostitution."

"That we know of," Polly offered.

Maren shook her head. "The Sacramento press lives and breathes scandal. If there were anything like that going on with an aide to the governor or with a researcher in the health department, a reporter would have dug it up."

"Got it!" Noel cried. "Jupiter, Venus, Mars, Saturn," he reeled off happily, as though the planets were on his friends-and-family list. "If only Spica were visible with this level of magnification," he added. "But that won't be until mid-April." At Noel's enthusiastic tone, Camper charged up the hill to join him. "Spica is a massive star—twenty-three hundred times more luminous than our sun," Noel continued, now in teaching mode. "It's a binary system. The second star, half Spica's size, rotates it at fifty-six miles per second." Camper, his large head cocked to one side, listened attentively, which was fortunate for Noel since Maren and Polly were preoccupied.

"Didn't the report say Hopkins' death was a robbery gone wrong?" Polly asked. "What about Tamara? Anything nicked?"

"I don't know," Maren said, realizing that hadn't come up. She wanted to call Lana Decateau right then to find out but figured the attorney would appreciate it if she waited until business hours to ask. Instead, Maren pulled her phone from her pocket and sent a text to Evie requesting that work begin on Simone Booth's tapes immediately. Because in addition to determining what Simone might have learned about the cell phone study as it related to Rickman's bill, Maren now also wanted to know as much as she could about the circumstances of Marjorie Hopkins' death.

CHAPTER 14

Once Maren had concluded that the missing key to her home had to be with Sean, her thoughts turned to the items she'd found in the jacket he'd left behind in her studio the night of Tamara's murder. Perhaps there was something there that might be useful to his case. So after Polly and Noel left, Maren reviewed the inventory laid out on the round pine table in front of her fireplace.

The receipt from the Department of Motor Vehicles appeared to be a printed record of an online transaction. It was torn at the bottom. Sean seemed only to have been interested in keeping the part that had his name and a confirmation number. She set that aside. She dismissed the loose change and the taco receipt as unimportant.

That left the pills. She dumped them out of the small travel case. Four flat, orange tablets with tiny printing on them. She could just make out the writing.

Wellbutrin 75.

The name was familiar. Maren powered up her laptop and looked it up. "A typical antidepressant, without the side effect of suppressing sexual performance common in many antidepressants."

She closed the computer and sat back in her chair. Maren had known many people that took mood stabilizers of one kind or another—antianxiety, antidepressant, or both. Sometimes integrated with counseling, sometimes not. So it wasn't surprising to find that Sean had them in his possession. Except for the fact that he was, in her experience, congenitally, or at least irrevocably, cheerful. Other than the night Tamara died, she'd never seen him truly down. Maren wondered if he might carry a "take in case of emergency" supply, although she thought she remembered hearing that for most people it took a while for the treatment to have an effect.

While mulling over the pills and what they might mean, something else occurred to Maren. She reopened her laptop and found the California Department of Motor Vehicles site. She tried a few links on the site and then found one where, by entering Sean's name and the confirmation number from the receipt, she could view the full transaction.

An order for a replacement driver's license. Maren smiled. *That would explain Sean keeping his passport on him. He would have needed it as identification until his new license came!*

Despite the hour, she couldn't stick with her earlier resolution to wait for the next business day. She immediately left a message for Lana with her findings, and asked that the attorney call her in the morning.

The next day Maren was ostensibly at work in her office, but too distracted to get anything accomplished, her mind on the call that finally came in at eleven a.m.

"I spoke with JPS," Lana said. "They did the usual intake on Sean. He didn't say anything about depression or being on medication. I've requested that they do a more thorough mental health assessment of him."

Maren knew from her internship at the public defender's office in San Francisco that JPS stood for Jail Psychiatric Services. Possibly the most understaffed unit in the jail.

"When will that be?" Maren asked. "If Sean is depressed with no support, going through this..."

"I've requested it urgently," Lana said. "But given the caseload in the jail for mental health, including inmates' immediate crises like psychotic breaks, that could mean weeks. I'll keep checking."

Maren heard Lana speak to someone in the background, then return to the call.

"The DMV record is helpful. I spoke with Sean and he says he told the police he had his passport with him because his driver's license was lost. That statement is not in the records that I received." Lana hesitated. "Even so, the fact that he only applied for the replacement online that night—after the time of the murder—could be problematic. There is the possibility that Sean intentionally dumped his license so that if he was caught later with a passport on his person it would make some sense, other than as preparation to flee..."

"Do the police really think Sean would have been that calculating?"

"Maren, the police think Sean is a murderer," Lana said. "So, yes, I do believe they think he's that calculating."

Maren could barely manage a civil good-bye to Lana as she hung up. She felt resentment and anger welling up inside her, like bad heartburn, only worse. Each discovery she made that she thought would help clear Sean seemed to her to be twisted by the police and the DA to prove his guilt. Picking up a loose paper, she crumpled it into a hard ball, and then spying the waste can in the far corner, hurled the ball toward it, missing by a long shot. She crumpled another paper, throwing it in the same general direction and hitting the bookshelf. Her third shot narrowly missed the photo of Noel on her desk. She made five more tries in mad succession—since she was taking no time to aim, it was not surprising that none went in.

"Maren? Shall I come back?"

Clay Zimbardo spoke softly as he pushed her office door open a few inches. She realized she must have left it ajar.

At twenty-six, Clay had been at Ecobabe only six months, a financial whiz kid with a degree in design thinking from Stanford—a relatively new field geared toward infusing innovation into a company's daily culture. Maren had hired Clay to take her organization's sales to the next level using the most modern strategies.

"No, it's fine," Maren said, adjusting her belt, which had slipped a notch during her poor imitation of San Francisco Giants ace pitcher Madison Bumgarner. "I was just thinking."

Clay nodded. Of average height with washed-out brown hair and pale brown eyes, he always seemed to Maren on the verge of fading away. She suspected that was one of the reasons he was so good at getting others to speak up with their new ideas. Completely nonthreatening, Clay seemed to take up little of the world's space, leaving room for his colleagues to feel empowered.

She noticed his gaze take in the graveyard of paper balls around her office. Clay cleared his throat. "I believe we've come to a good place in the iterative process with our sales field representatives. The rapid prototyping we undertook permitted them to consider new prospects. They'd like to expand beyond our primary network of independent toy and game stores to add product placement in big-box stores and major retailers." He smiled tentatively. "Utilizing only those outlets with ethical hiring practices and green, sustainable energy policies, of course."

As Clay spoke, Maren took a deep breath and the burning sensation in her chest left her. "I've got a meeting with Evie in a few minutes. Please e-mail me your recommendation on sales expansion and we can meet tomorrow."

She asked Clay to close the door behind him as he left. She picked up the mess she had made.

An hour later Maren and Evie were more than halfway through putting together the quarterly lobbying report to file with the state. Evie rose and went to the lone filing cabinet next to her desk to retrieve the needed numbers. Nearly everything in the Ecobabe office was paperless, stored on computers, but they still kept important financial and legal documents in hard copy.

Evie's office wear, a bright yellow sweater dress, was not typical for a woman of her ample proportions. But paired with shiny black boots and tasteful makeup it produced an end result many females would have been happy to emulate, and at least as many males pleased to embrace.

Maren was in the chic black and white outfit that she had worn to dinner at Simone's daughter's home. Evie noticed her boss's departure from her usual style. "You look nice—meeting downtown?"

"Thanks." Maren glanced at the time. "I'll be late if I don't get going." *Lunch with my ex isn't exactly a meeting,* Maren thought, *but close enough.* Just then, the door to the office suite opened and Liza Booth-Henry entered, Zane and Zoey trailing behind. Zane had a firm grip on his sister's hand.

"I hope this time is okay," Liza said, taking in the table covered in work. "I'm sorry to bring the kids with me."

There's the first apology. Maren thought she might be on to a successful drinking game for young professionals—take a shot of liquor each time someone with kids says they're sorry to the world at large for their offspring's existence.

"It's no problem," Maren said, standing to welcome Liza, demonstrating through her action that the work on the table wasn't urgent.

"It's just that I couldn't manage Zane and Zoey and the boxes at the same time..."

The tapes, Maren realized. *Evie must have called her after my text last night, and now Liza's here to drop off Simone's tapes and files.* "Come, I'll help you bring them up. The kids will be fine with Evie."

Evie retrieved a large box of colored pencils from her desk and was in the process of clearing papers for coloring space when Zoey, on tiptoe, managed to knock the box over.

"Are you sure?" Liza asked, moving to pick up the scattered pencils.

"Go on," Evie urged, a genuine smile on her face. She lifted Zoey onto her broad lap and pulled a chair closer so that Zane could sit next to them. "I have three little brothers."

* * *

"You probably noticed coming up that the elevators in these older buildings in midtown seem to have only one speed—slow," Maren commented as she and Liza exited the suite and headed down the hall. The single elevator in the Ecobabe building took the same time in transit as walking the three floors but was more conveniently located than the back stairs.

Liza smiled weakly. Maren noticed she was pale and thinner than when they met. She realized that the young woman's grieving over the loss of her mother must be starting in earnest, replacing the initial shock. It would be different, of course, than when Maren's own mother passed when Maren was only eleven. But Liza and Simone appeared to have been close the deep nature of the pain would be the same.

The bronze-colored door of the small elevator slid open with an unsettling creak, and the two women got in.

"How are you?" Maren asked.

"I'm okay. Work is a distraction. Although it's harder to coordinate my jewelry shows now. Mother took care of the kids when I had business to attend to. There are childcare services, babysitters, I'm sure—I should put up a notice. But Zane and Zoey miss their grandma. Especially Zane. I don't know that they're ready..." Liza's deep brown eyes matched her young son's, except that hers were so very tired.

Maren nodded. "If something urgent comes up, Evie works a flexible schedule. She can usually get away, or you could bring the kids here."

Liza laughed—it was unexpected, a sparkling, light sound. "In your office? Zoey would have it looking like Katrina hit. I call her my personal hurricane."

"Two-year-olds do have a special way with the world," Maren agreed, smiling. "But we're toymakers, one step removed from Santa's elves." The elevator door opened and she followed Liza out into the small foyer. "We've had interns bring their kids to the office—it reminds us of why we do what we do. You can get Evie's number before you leave today." The two women exited the building into the bright sunshine, the cold spring days finally warming up. "You mentioned moving. How's that going?"

Liza reached into a pocket of her coat and pulled out the key to a maroon mini-SUV parked in a loading zone in front of the building. "Mother's house is pretty full. She wasn't a hoarder, but she collected favorite furnishings, pottery, and art over a long life. John and I don't have much, but the kids sure do."

Liza lifted the hatchback as she spoke, revealing two clear plastic bins filled to the brim with cassette tapes and a third that contained brightly colored file folders.

"Let's take two now," Maren said. "I'll ask an intern to come down and get the last one."

"John loaded these up before he left for school. I guess I didn't realize how many there were." They each hoisted a bin. As they did, Maren saw Liza's gaze go to the multitude of colorful toys on the vehicle's backseat, wedged in around the two car seats. "Sometimes I wonder how Zoey would have fared in the days of the pioneers when her only possessions would have been a corn husk doll and a chalk tablet for learning the alphabet."

Maren thought the real question was not how Zoey would have managed but how Liza would have survived without an armory of distractions for her busy daughter.

The bins weren't heavy, just awkward to hold. Both women set them down as they waited for the elevator again.

Maren looked at the two bins, assessing the size, realizing there must be hundreds of tapes in there. "Do you know whether your mother left an index of any kind?" Maren asked.

Liza's brow wrinkled slightly as she shook her head. "I don't think so. I'm not sure what you mean."

"To the tapes. Having reviewed some of your mom's work, there are a few interviews I'm particularly interested in." Maren didn't see any reason to upset Liza by going into detail that the interview she was referring to related to the researcher's murder.

"I'm not sure. Mother wasn't much for electronics. She seemed to use her old computer only as a typewriter. We donated it to Zane's school. But John printed out what she saved on it—that's the box still in the car. You could check in there."

The elevator arrived, but it remained motionless on the ground floor even after the doors closed behind them and Maren had pushed the third floor button.

"Is this thing okay?" Liza asked, eyeing the elevator's control panel.

"Yes, it's fine. I think it's girding itself for the return journey." Maren hit the third floor button again, hoping they weren't actually stuck. "Do you have a firm move-out date?"

"We gave notice on our flat; we have to be out by April fifteenth," Liza said. "We'll have professional movers, so that's set. But I've had trouble getting an alarm service scheduled for installation. Mother's place is in a transitional neighborhood. Not bad, really, but not what we're used to. Our current flat is on the second floor. I like that. Mother's house is one story, everything street level."

A lumbering sound and a slight jerk signaled the elevator's intention to take them to the third floor.

"Where is it?" Maren asked.

"Eighteenth and Q."

"It's nice there. It might look a little rough around the edges in spots, but there are lots of families in the homes and young professionals in the apartments. You'll be fine."

"I guess," Liza said, leaning against the back wall to steady herself as the elevator shuddered. Evidently, going up was more difficult for the ancient conveyance than going down. "But since the murder of that young woman in the capitol building, I haven't felt safe. Thank goodness they caught the guy so fast. Still, it's a reminder there are crazy, violent people out there."

Maren felt cold. *So this is what's said about Sean now.* She didn't want to upset the young woman who was grieving, and it had been a casual comment. But she couldn't let it go entirely. As they stepped out on the third floor, Maren gripped tightly the handles of the bin she held and concentrated on keeping her voice even. "The person in custody in that case, Sean Verston. I know him."

Liza's face blanched. "I'm sorry, I..."

"No, it's okay," Maren said.

Liza reddened. "I shouldn't have assumed..."

"It's complicated. I recognize the police wouldn't have arrested Sean without what they believe are good reasons." She set the bin down as they reached the outer door to her office suite. "But an arrest doesn't mean a conviction."

At least Maren prayed that in this case it wouldn't.

CHAPTER 15

Sean's cellmate, Big Mike, was in the exercise yard. Sean took the rare opportunity to stand and stretch his arms over his head and then out to the sides, almost able to touch both walls of his seven-by-fifteen-foot cell.

At first glance it might have been a dorm room. On one side were two built-in bunks, above which a narrow window spanned the length of the wall with a vista-like view of downtown Sacramento. The tiny space also housed a steel toilet, matching sink, and two shelves. The clue that it wasn't typical housing was the single heavy metal door to the hallway and the world beyond locked from the outside.

Pre-arrest Sean Verston had shared the image of prison life that most of the public had from TV and movies. Inmates hanging out in "the yard," lifting weights daily, eating together at long metal tables, trading favors for cigarettes. A social life, albeit a tilted one. But once inside, Sean discovered a different reality. Like so many California jails and prisons, Sacramento County Jail was severely overcrowded. Too many men meant less rather than more time in group settings. Food was delivered to their cells and outside privileges were rotated, each man getting at most a few hours three days a week. So Sean did push-ups and sit-ups and ran in place in the cell when he could. If Big Mike was around (which was nearly always) they took turns—one of them on the bunk, feet off the floor, while the other exercised.

Not that Big Mike took up a lot of space. Five foot three, compact, with shoulder-length hair and a wispy mustache. But since they lived together, clothed and unclothed, Sean knew exactly where Big Mike was big, and that it was clearly a source of pride to Mike. Still, it hadn't kept Big Mike out of jail. Sean thought his cellmate might have been better off focusing on something else and coming up with a new nickname.

But then Sean realized, who was he to talk? Mike was in for robbing a convenience store brandishing a toy gun. He would be out in three to five years. While Sean was in for Murder One and faced life inside. "Maybe a few more inches below the belt and a cooler nickname and I'd only be in for robbery," Sean quipped aloud, needing to hear the sound of his own voice. It sounded hollow to him, and the lack of response from anyone tapped a feeling he hadn't had in years. Not since freshman year in college, when he'd lost interest in everything.

He tried to remember what he'd done to keep from sinking under the weight of too much course work, his mom getting sick with cancer, and Janie, his girlfriend, leaving him. Well, first there was the overdose on alcohol and pills—the only way he could figure then to stop the pain. Sean was hospitalized as soon as his roommates discovered him. After his discharge, antidepressants helped while he worked things through. He still went on and off the meds, only using them when things got bad, and fortunately they seemed to work quickly for him. Or maybe there was a placebo effect. Either way, they offered a safety net. But mostly he'd learned if he kept how he felt to himself, exercised strenuously, and had things he believed were meaningful in his life, he was okay.

Sean paced the small length of the cell as he considered how he might implement his "sanity strategies" while locked-down. He knew the odds of getting mood stabilizers inside were slim to none, having seen firsthand in the senator's office that money for mental health services for prisoners during an era of state budget cuts didn't make the top of any policymaker's funding list. He wasn't sure he wanted the pills anyway. They made him foggy and he needed a clear head for whatever questions might come his way.

Exercise was still good—he was finding a way. As far as not sharing his feelings went, that was easy. No one asked.

It had been only a little more than a week, but routine inside the jail made time elastic. Sean was better off than most since his days of being an isolated nerd in college were behind him. In the capitol he'd found a look that worked for him—dark suits and basic ties. He never veered from the formula. Plus, using his intelligence for humor rather than just for work made him popular among the other legislative staff and lobbyists. Even now, he had frequent visitors at the jail. Still, it was tough for friends and colleagues to know what to say. Sean suspected many thought he had killed Tamara in a fit of jealousy and rage. But they came anyway, awkward in their unstated forgiveness.

Sean had taken to asking visitors to bring him books. That way he could talk about the books they had read and the ones he was reading and stay away from real-life Sacramento stuff. Sean didn't want to know which bills had passed committee. Because in jail he couldn't help to pass a law that saved lives. He couldn't balance the scales. Worst of all, he was unable to block the hardest memories. Holding Tamara one last time as he lifted her onto the couch. Even when he was able to shut the desperate images and feelings out, he found himself lost in the emptiness that was left.

Sean felt around his waist for a belt, intent on gauging whether he could form a makeshift noose. He looked around to see how he might anchor it.

Not for now. Just in case.

But of course, the guards had taken his belt.

He swallowed hard and did twenty more push-ups.

* * *

The valet happily traded places with Maren, hopping into her vintage black Beetle convertible in exchange for a small white ticket that she tucked into a pocket of her purse. A sigh escaped her. She wasn't used to others driving her beloved car, not even for a minute. She'd owned it since high school. Plus, she felt out of her element. She generally avoided Old Sacramento, but she'd chosen the Santa Fe Bar and Grill so she and Garrick would be away from the capitol crowd. Not that there weren't nice things about it. The views along the riverfront were beautiful. The original cobblestone streets and restored covered wooden sidewalks offered a glimpse of Sacramento in the mid-1800s, when finding gold trumped politics as the city's obsession. Interesting art and clothing shops were mixed in with the purveyors of cheap souvenirs. But the area was often overrun with tourists—resembling Main Street in Disneyland minus the chance for a photo op with Pluto or Goofy.

A small, tasteful sign and a menu in a glass case distinguished the Santa Fe from the many casual restaurants on the block. Specializing in pizzas grilled in oversized clay ovens and featuring limited-press wines, their destination was distinctive and pricey. Maren guessed that by suggesting they meet there she was unconsciously testing Garrick's resolve, wallet first.

She saw him as soon she cleared the outer doors. Not a conventionally handsome man, Garrick Chauncey had coarse brown hair fuller on top than on the sides. With round hazel eyes and a larger nose, Garrick was rescued from homeliness by his critical intelligence, humor, and attentiveness to those around him. That and the fact that he worked out daily while watching global investment markets on the big-screen TV in his home gym. He was in better shape than men half his age and had the money to buy quality, understated clothes to show it off. Today he wore tailored grey slacks and an immaculately fitted sage-green dress shirt.

When Garrick saw her, he gave Maren a look so loving that she had to remind herself, "*Adulterer, cheapskate! Adulterer, cheapskate!*" Unfortunately, her mantra was having trouble getting traction in light of the memories that being close to Garrick evoked. Long passionate nights in bed, warm cuddly mornings in bed, and sweet stolen afternoons in bed. (She acknowledged that the memories were limited in scope, but still...)

"Maren," he said simply, kissing her gently on the cheek and stepping back. "You look lovely."

She had trouble finding her voice. Problems with basic speech with Senator Alec Joben and now Garrick Chauncey. She wondered if she was going to have to learn sign language now that she had resumed dating. She was rescued by a young blonde hostess in a buckskin minidress, bangled jewelry, and platform moccasins—Santa Fe hip, translated for the upscale end of the tourist trade in Old Sacramento.

Seated by an indoor cactus garden and waterfall away from the crowded riverfront tables, Maren and Garrick had some measure of privacy in the busy restaurant. She was regaining her composure and could not for the life of her understand why she had been fool enough to show up.

"I'm sorry about Simone Booth. But what you did, rescuing those children..." He looked at her intently. "It was extraordinary. Wait, I take that back—not for you. It's what I would expect."

Maren studied his eyes. Deep brown under heavy brows. "It seems a long time ago," she said.

"But finding that young woman murdered. Followed by Sean Verston's arrest." He shifted the small vase centerpiece to one side and placed his hand over hers on the table. "How are you doing?"

"I visited Sean. You've probably seen the press reports."

Garrick nodded.

Sean's internship and residency in Maren's studio had taken place before she and Garrick became involved. But Garrick was there for the frequent calls between Maren and Sean after Sean had moved out.

She eased her hand out from under Garrick's, reached for her water, and took a sip, afterward placing both hands safely in her lap.

"I know it looks bad," she said. "But Sean would have had every reason to be in the capitol building at that time, and once he found Tamara...found her dying...it makes sense to me that he was frightened, that he closed up and didn't share that with anyone. He's young and I'm learning he's a very private person, despite his glib exterior." She leaned forward to make her point. "And with Tamara working for the governor, the motive for the murder has to be political." As Maren gestured for emphasis, she hit the nearly full water glass to her right, knocking it off the table. It shattered noisily on the Mexican tile floor. Patrons on either side stole a glance at her before going back to their meals. It was the kind of place where people knew it was rude to stare at someone else's clumsiness.

A smiling busboy was there within seconds with a rag, which proved insufficient. He returned with a mop. When the mess was cleared and replacement water served, Maren found she'd lost the energy to discuss Sean, at least with Garrick. It felt suddenly futile. She leaned back in her seat.

Garrick seemed to get the message, moving to safer ground. "So how are things at Ecobabe? Still fighting the good fight?"

Maren was relieved to talk about work; she could do it on autopilot. "Ecobabe is sponsoring a driver's cell phone ban to expand on the hands-free restriction of last year. We're also supporting a bill to ban the chemical BPA from use in the manufacture of pacifiers."

"Who are the authors?" Garrick knew from his time with Maren that which legislator carried a bill could determine whether a lobbyist's life was heaven or hell.

"Senator Rorie Rickman, a pediatrician from Bakersfield, has the cell phone bill. She's good, although meticulous about detail. She reacts to any small error as though someone could die as a result, like being off by a decimal place on the dose on a prescription she's written. You know the old saying, what's the difference between God and a doctor? God doesn't think he's a doctor."

Garrick smiled, his eyes focused only on her, his forearm resting on the table. His hand close enough to hers to touch it again, but this time he didn't. Still, against her better judgment she was re-experiencing how Garrick's voice could make her feel. *An octave lower than anyone else's,* she noted, *able to make a simple rounded vowel into foreplay.*

She sipped her new water to buy time, then set her glass down carefully.

"Alec Joben has the BPA bill. Good guy," she added, before remembering that Garrick would know from the media that Alec was with her at the site of Simone Booth's accident. And if Garrick's jealous streak surfaced—it was never far away—he would expect that her work now with Alec Joben was a sign of something more. Despite Maren's intense loyalty to Garrick when they had been in a relationship. *Adulterers project their sins upon the innocent,* she had concluded at the time. But Garrick let her mention of Alec Joben go without comment. A good thing too, she thought, because this once he would be right about something more than work happening there. Or at least there was potential for a spark, even if she had lost the technique (assuming she had ever had it) to fan it into flames.

Maren was surprised when their meals came, since they hadn't ordered. "I called ahead," Garrick explained. "They can get jammed in here at noon, and I knew you had to get back to work." There was an organic green salad with goat cheese for each of them and one of the Santa Fe's famous flat crust pizzas to share, this one with blended cheeses, artichokes, and pineapple. Garrick had indulged Maren by ordering the pineapple topping, which he didn't prefer, knowing it was the way she liked her pizza. Despite herself, she found the gesture touching. It had been too long since she had shared a meal with someone who really knew what she liked. Then she noticed that Garrick hadn't ordered wine. While he didn't let alcohol interfere with his work, he never passed up a chance to have a drink (or two or three) to accompany a meal or social hour.

He saw her looking at the tableau and guessed her thoughts. "Would you like a glass of wine? Just because I'm passing doesn't mean you need to."

"Busy afternoon?" *Not that it stopped you in the past.*

"I gave up drinking. Taking Grey Goose vodka and wines off my shopping list saves me hundreds of dollars a month."

Maren set down her fork and appraised him more carefully. Garrick without high-priced alcohol was like the Hollywood Hills without the Hollywood sign, an iconic representation of his success. But Garrick's reference to dollars saved, no matter how many millions he had, was grounding for her. *He has a genuine Renoir in his living room and he's still counting pennies?* That was the Garrick she knew.

"If I could get an iced herbal tea..."

Garrick gestured to the waitress, who quickly returned with the tea.

"How are things at Sacramento State?" Maren asked.

"Classes hum along, dedicated and bright students." Garrick was not one to begrudge others their talents and successes. "My real challenge has come from a business deal. Getting the investors to agree on terms." Garrick spoke about interest rates and stock prices. Maren asked a few questions. They fell into an old, familiar routine: Maren the lifelong student, Garrick the experienced teacher.

When their plates near empty, the buckskin waitress came by to check on them. Garrick gave her his platinum credit card but made no move to go. Maren breathed in deeply, steeling herself for the purpose of their lunch together.

"Maren, I appreciate your seeing me..."

Here it comes.

"I know things ended on a bad note..."

A bad note? You call faxes from your paramours while living with me and the fact that I had to drain my bank account to keep up with our "shared" expenses a bad note? How about a bad symphony? Maren was getting ready to let Garrick have it when he interrupted her windup before the pitch.

"I miss you, Maren...I love you. I have changed. And I will change in any way that you want if you will come back.

Whoa!

In Maren's experience, Garrick was a liar when it came to affairs and cheap when it came to anything that he wasn't wearing or imbibing. But he'd never done anything but defend who he was and what he did. The word "change" was simply not in his lexicon, not applied to himself.

"Before you say anything," he said, assessing the look of shock on her face, "we're both strategists—you in the world of politics, me in the world of finance. We envision a goal and plan steps to get there. My goal is to be with you. I suggest a phase-in approach. We agree to three months of friendship—lunches, socializing, talking, nothing more. If that works for both of us, we then engage in three months of dating and whatever intimacy that brings."

Maren felt herself redden slightly, as intimacy with Garrick was an enticement and he knew it.

"If that goes well, we live together for six months, at the end of which we get married."

Maren could feel herself making a round cartoon "O" shape with her mouth, but she couldn't help it. This was beyond belief.

MARRIAGE?

Garrick had once said there was a reason women wear white at weddings and men wear black—the bride believes she is ascending to heaven, while the man knows it's his funeral.

Maren did the only thing she could do. She got up from the table and began walking, increasing her pace through the foyer and out the restaurant's front door.

CHAPTER 16

"Why not follow through and see Alec tonight? Before you decide about Garrick's offer." As she spoke, Polly sidestepped a soccer ball that had bounced directly in her path. A group of kids were kicking it around before school, some poorly. "Didn't you say you wanted to try out the horse before you ride it this time? What's the harm?"

Maren and Polly were midway through an early morning walk on the newly renovated track that circled the Sacramento High football field. It was a beautiful setting, tall eucalyptus trees framing the stadium under cover of a light morning fog.

"Maybe. But I've given it more thought. Dating Alec Joben would be complicated," Maren replied.

Despite their relatively slow pace, Polly was in full workout regalia. Form-fitting Lycra leggings and jacket, matching wristbands. She smelled like peaches from a new body wash and hand lotion marketed as age defying, which, according to Polly, all the celebrities were "going on about." The scent was awfully strong, and in any case, Maren never could understand why a woman would want to smell like a fruit. Maren was in sweats and the T-shirt she'd slept in, nursing a cooling herbal tea.

"And marrying Garrick Chauncey wouldn't be?"

"Garrick's not asking for marriage yet, it's..."

Another soccer ball—Maren kicked this one back, pleased with herself when it landed in the vicinity of the kids.

"I know. Friendship, then living together, then marriage," Polly said, repeating what Maren had told her. "But it all involves Garrick, a fatal flaw."

Maren was conscious that she worked Alec's name into conversations, found excuses to talk about him. So she really couldn't blame Polly for thinking he was Maren's path out of spinsterhood—a distant future Maren didn't ponder one way or the other but that seemed to weigh heavily on Polly on her behalf.

"Mom, I took four dollars from your purse for lunch."

Maren looked up to see Jake, Polly's son, calling through the mesh fencing that separated the path to school from the track. He was weighed down by a huge backpack, a gym bag, and his saxophone case, straps overlapping. He looked like a sherpa about to scale Mt. Everest.

Danny Paxton, Jake's best friend since preschool, caught up with him. Danny was carrying a similar load, although he got off easier with a clarinet rather than a sax.

"No problem," Polly called back. "See you tonight."

"Isn't it early for them?" Maren asked.

"Jazz band before school. So why not give this new bloke Alex a chance?"

Knowing there was no avoiding Polly's heartfelt desire to jump-start her stalled love life, Maren replied, "Alec. It's Alec, not Alex. Alec Joben. He's a new state senator from Yolo County, just south of here. There was a special election after the former Yolo senator died."

"Alec, then. Alec from Yolo. What would be the harm? Don't you have three months or some such nonsense while you and Garrick are just friends?" Polly had increased the pace. Maren tried to keep up without spilling her tea.

"Just for fun, tell me Mr. Joben's best qualities."

Maren had given considerable thought to Alec's attributes. "Intelligent, compassionate." She paused. "And honest—not manipulative. Which in the capitol is really saying something," she added.

"Ok, so he's a Boy Scout," Polly said. "How about his vitals? Obviously the man can look himself in the mirror in the morning without flinching, but do you find him attractive?"

Maren laughed. "Yes. He's tall, with that build, the dark hair..."

"So we have an upstart challenger, Alec Joben, a smashing personality, gorgeous, who can leap tall buildings in a single bound. Versus the defeated champ, Garrick Chauncey, who in the last bout for your heart was disqualified for dirty, low-down cheating."

Polly was smiling as she pumped her arms with each step, but Maren knew her friend was serious.

"It's not that simple," Maren said. "For one thing, Alec Joben is a senator, an elected official, and I'm a lobbyist. There are ethics. Rules. A legislator must declare any gift over ten dollars in value a lobbyist gives them, which has been interpreted to include non monetary gifts."

"You mean there's a form he would need to fill out if you had sex?"

Now they were both smiling.

"It depends."

"On whether shaggin' you is worth more than ten dollars?"

"No, on whether my 'shagging' him, as you put it, is intended to influence his voting record."

"What if he stays clear of any bills you're working on?"

"He could. But if a bill of mine is good for his district and he stays off it or votes no, he won't be serving his voters. And if he votes yes on it, as he would have done if it weren't my bill, it will look as though I bought his vote with my...my...behavior."

Polly conceded the point. But she wasn't giving up. "Still, there must be couples who meet that way."

"I suppose," Maren said. Although silently she was backtracking from both Alec and Garrick, wondering why she had ever thought agreeing to see two men would be simpler than the trouble she usually got into with one.

* * *

An hour later Maren was dressed for work and halfway to the capitol on foot. Her head was down and her eyes were intent on the screen on her smartphone, so much so that she narrowly missed colliding with a stocky woman in a black suit and too much gold jewelry exiting from a curbside Lexus. Maren thought she recognized Liza Booth-Henry's handiwork in the small burnished metal figures hanging from the woman's bracelet.

In forward motion again, Maren returned to scrolling down the phone's screen. She knew she should be focused on how to get the cell phone bill passed, but she figured other things she managed to do while walking to work didn't count. And she remained convinced that a person or persons unknown had killed Tamara Barnes, and that it was politically or financially motivated rather than love gone wrong. But even if it was a passion play, Maren would bet her house and her car that it had to do with her ex, Governor Ray Fernandez, not Sean.

She reflected on the image of Sean in Rickman's office kneeling before Tamara, listening attentively, not an ounce of jealous stalker in his posture. She contrasted that with Ray's wandering eyes (and hands)—Tamara's beauty and youth would have been a daily temptation as she worked alongside him in the governor's suite. Plus, Maren had experience with Sean when he was under stress and disappointment—employment in California's capitol was not for the faint of heart. True, she hadn't picked up on his depression—in fact, she was coming to realize she knew little concrete about his personal life. But unless he had multiple personalities, she didn't see how Sean's downtime behavior could be radically different from his calm and happy work repertoire—at least not to the point where it could include the capacity for murder.

So it didn't fit with what she knew—more than that, it infuriated her—that the DA and the police were locked in on Sean as their man. She felt she needed a hook, something to point them in a new direction. Tamara's mention of Ray Fernandez the day of her murder, that they had together done something awful, hadn't done it. So Maren returned again to consider the death of the young researcher Marjorie Hopkins. It still bothered Maren that like Tamara Barnes, Hopkins was a young professional woman, stabbed, with no sign of sexual assault, also involved in legislative work, albeit a step removed through her research.

Why couldn't there be a link, and it be one killer for both women?

Clay Zimbardo in marketing at Ecobabe had put the interns to work on his big-box store marketing project. The Ecobabe Board considered that a priority, so transcribing Simone Booth's tapes was on hold. But Maren figured she could do some research on the Hopkins homicide on her own.

There are so many murders in our charming town...

That was what Polly had said the night they hung out with Noel in Maren's backyard.

Maren decided to start by checking whether Polly was right, whether the sheer numbers worked against Maren's theory of a serial killer who, admittedly, worked slowly or simply had modest goals—two murders a year.

Plugging "Sacramento homicides" into her browser's search function, Maren found that there were thirty murders in the city in the past year. Horrible for each and every victim and their loved ones, but with a population of five hundred thousand, that didn't strike her as *so* many. One article reported that number was down from over a hundred killings five years prior. Credit was given to Chief Sam Watson, who shared it with his officers.

In an attempt to determine how many of those thirty deaths were from knife attacks—to find out if Tamara and Marjorie's deaths were part of a smaller subset in that respect, making a connection more likely—Maren tapped and scrolled, moving rapidly from one link to the next, reviewing reports on everything from armed robberies to gang-related drive-by shootings.

But she found only lurid case-by-case descriptions, no statistics that might help. So she expanded her search words and phrases—"Marjorie Hopkins," then "Broads and Bards," where the Hopkins murder occurred. Searching for a new angle felt familiar—Maren was adept at on-the-fly research. When a question was raised by a legislator, a quick answer could translate into the vote needed for success.

In the end, it was a brief local news piece on a cable station targeting suburbs north of Sacramento that had what Maren was looking for.

Cherrie Glazier, a former waitress at Broads and Bards, was being featured in a human interest piece. The camera zoomed in on Mrs. Glazier and her husband, Mark, as they stood in front of a modest storefront where workers were hanging an awning and putting finishing touches on the paint.

"What made you choose Roseville to locate your new restaurant?" asked a petite brunette reporter, her demeanor serious, leaning in with the microphone so as not to miss a word.

Cherrie turned to her husband, then back to the camera. The Glaziers were both in their forties, with short curly brown hair and broad smiles. In fact, she and Mark Glazier looked like they could have been twins, except that Cherrie's curves were in decidedly womanly places and his might have resulted from too much of her cooking.

"I couldn't consider downtown Sacramento anymore," Cherrie said. "I mean, not after that awful murder right where I worked."

The cameraman cut to the reporter. Maren thought her eyes seemed artificially wide, emphasizing—in case the audience might have missed it—that they were now talking *murder*.

Mark Glazier added, "A young woman was killed right in the parking lot of Cherrie's old place. Of course, it scared Cherrie. Well, me too. We didn't want to overreact, so we read everything we could about it. And we found out the police never caught the scum who did it. Stabbed that poor girl right through the heart, he did. Tragic."

Another shot of the reporter, nodding sympathetically, encouraging Mark Glazier to continue—as if to say to the viewers, pay attention, this is good stuff, not your run-of-the-mill human interest piece.

"After that, the big bar and restaurant in downtown just didn't feel safe to us anymore," Mark said, putting his arm around his wife and puffing out his chest. "I'm sure many patrons felt the same. I knew with Cherrie's cooking and my management skills, we could make a successful, local spot on our own, something away from crime and the big city. So here we are."

* * *

Deputy Public Defender Lana Decateau's daily grind consisted largely of battling obstacles and discrimination so that her guilty, impoverished clients might receive no harsher punishment than guilty, rich defendants who could afford private lawyers. Still, there were times when her task was vindicating the innocent. And she believed that Maren Kane's discovery of similarities in the Hopkins and Barnes murders—both women killed by a single stab wound to the heart—might be enough to shift Sean to the "presumed innocent" category from his current berth in the "he did it, the trial is a formality" class.

"Sifuentes here."

"Carlos, it's Lana. I'm calling about the Verston case."

"Lana, how are you? Verston, yes, Sean. How is he doing?"

"Not well. The food is bad." Their inside joke—Carlos asked how her clients were faring in jail and Lana referenced only the prison food. Even though both knew the nightmares of incarceration were so much worse.

"I should bring him my mama's special pupusas."

"I'm sure he would like that," she said. But Lana wanted to get down to business. "Mr. Verston doesn't belong in prison. I've filed to force his release based on the wholly circumstantial nature of the evidence—no weapon, no witnesses, no confession. His explanation of why he was at the scene is strongly consistent with the facts. But you know Judge Campbell—it's going to be up to DA Sharpton to acknowledge he has the wrong man and drop the charges."

Carlos lowered his voice. "I'm not sure I agree with your characterization of the evidence—the accused's fingerprints on the shoes of the deceased and a video placing him at the scene matter. Regardless, El Jefe, Mitchell Sharpton, will never say he has the wrong man. Only, perhaps, that he arrested the right man at the time and new information came to light so that man must now go free."

"Yes," Lana said, accepting the spin. "But my message, did you get it? Tamara Barnes died from a single, fatal strike with a knife through the heart. So did Marjorie Hopkins, eight months earlier. One murder might occur like that by luck—bad luck for the victim. But two separate incidents, surgically placed strikes killing young women in Sacramento? That's a modus operandi signaling one person responsible for the two crimes. And Sean was in DC that week with Senator Rorie Rickman, so he couldn't have killed Hopkins."

"It could be," Carlos said, "but it's speculation only, Miss Lana, you know that. And the Hopkins case is closed. Dead, mortado. It is in the cold case file, an unsolved murder chalked up to a robbery gone bad. If DA Sharpton brings the Hopkins case back up, he reminds the voters that he could not solve that crime then. And if Mr. Verston is released, it shows the public that DA Sharpton also has not solved this crime now. He is not going to do that unless you have something much more than an idea. Something conclusive." Lana could hear another man's voice in the background. Carlos paused, covered the phone, then returned. "I have to go. Please let me know when you are ready to go dancing. There is a new club by the river, the Water Wall. You need to get your gorgeous self out of that office."

When he hung up, Sifuentes lifted his jacket from the back of his desk chair and slipped it on, heading to the file room to see if Winston Chen, the clerk responsible for archived files, was around.

The Hopkins murder was less than a year old so the summary and index, if not sitting in backlogs due to state budget cuts in data entry, should be accessible to Carlos online. But given Lana Decauteau's concerns, the young detective wanted to see the original handwritten notes—everything that was there—to determine for himself if anything had been overlooked. He knew Decateau to be a solid attorney, one with ethics. When she was brokering a deal with the DA's office her client's guilt might not matter, but when sending a police officer out to substantiate a theory of innocence—for that he knew she must believe.

"Officer Sifuentes, what brings you down here?"

The old man, grey stubble as present on his chin and jowls as on the crown of his head, sat on a stool behind the counter in the basement office that bordered the evidence bays and file rooms. He had removed the pipe he kept, unlit, clenched in his teeth, and tucked it into a drawer. There was a strict no smoking policy in government buildings, but Winston didn't smoke anymore. He just liked to remember it.

Carlos pushed a paper across the counter, on which he had jotted down the essentials on the Marjorie Hopkins case. Winston reviewed it without a word before disappearing through a back door. Carlos regretted not having brought his computer tablet with him as he waited for close to ten minutes. But at least Winston eventually emerged with the file—it wasn't lost or checked out.

Back in his office, Carlos removed his jacket and returned it to the back of his chair. He seated himself and took a sip of now-cold coffee—there wasn't much that tasted worse in this life that he could think of. Opening the folder and sorting its contents, he was careful to note the order so he could put things back properly.

There were notes from the scene, including a statement that the victim's purse was missing. A few interviews with employees at the restaurant Broads and Bards. Nobody had seen anything. Although there was mention of a bartender who was on duty that night but had gone home for a family funeral, taking a red-eye to Milwaukee. It didn't look like anyone had ever gotten back around to talking with him. Finally, the coroner's report, documenting a single knife strike to the heart as the cause of death. No signs of a struggle, no other wounds or bruises.

Carlos read that the investigating officer had concluded Marjorie Hopkins was a woman in the wrong place at the wrong time. Victim of a random parking lot robbery that for some reason turned into murder—perhaps someone was coming or the perp was strung out on drugs so that the line between sparing a life and causing a death was inconsequential to him.

No arrest was ever made.

Then Sifuentes compared the Hopkins information with what he had in the Tamara Barnes case.

As Lana had indicated, both women were killed by one upward knife thrust through the heart. Lana had suggested that the single strike, where accuracy mattered, meant a hit by someone trained in lethal combat—an ex-Marine or Navy SEAL, special ops of some kind. But he thought that was most likely just Lana's way of looking at it. The way she should look it as a defense lawyer. But that didn't mean it was so—why couldn't the similarity be by chance? An attack in close quarters on a helpless woman where you didn't want her to scream. Why not aim for the heart? It could make sense to two different murderers—it would make sense to a smart kid like Verston.

Sifuentes kept reading.

Neither weapon was recovered. Based on entry wounds, the weapon used in the Hopkins attack was thick and serrated. Likely a kitchen knife of sorts. In contrast, the blade that killed Tamara Barnes was small, flat, and thin. It was surprising, he thought, that the smaller one did the job.

Sifuentes read both files twice before concluding there wasn't enough to reopen the Hopkins case, especially not with the way the DA was feeling these days. Three months out from his election, everything had to be clean, crisp, and packaged for the press.

CHAPTER 17

The next morning Maren spoke briefly with Lana. The attorney informed her that the police had been unimpressed by what they called "perceived similarities" in the Marjorie Hopkins and Tamara Barnes murders. Not that they could absolutely rule out a single killer, but with the evidence against Sean Verston and his absence from the state when the Marjorie Hopkins hit occurred, they didn't see it.

It had been an hour since that call and Maren was seated in the large public hearing room on the second floor of the capitol building. She felt more determined than ever to uncover whatever facts it would take to free Sean. She took a calming breath. *Don't let the bastards get you down.* She wasn't sure where she'd first heard it—she thought it might have been Kris Kristofferson or maybe U2. No matter, it seemed appropriate.

She turned her attention to the lecturn, where Senator Rorie Rickman appeared to be close to finishing her opening comments on SB 770.

Ecobabe's driver cell phone bill was finally being heard in the Senate Health Committee. If the bill died here, it would be over. Maren tried not to think of the consequences for her tenure at Ecobabe, although at the very least there would be no year-end bonus. She knew she had to focus instead on getting right the few things she had control over these days.

Last year's cell phone bill to enact a hands-free rule passed on a party line vote. All Democrats voting "Aye," all Republicans "No." That was typical—with party affiliation based primarily on ideological leanings, there was logical consistency in banding together in support of ideas with those who shared one's worldview. And while politics as a team sport might not be a thoughtful process, it simplified governing enough to make the massive workload California legislators faced possible.

There were, of course, rare bills that easily garnered votes from both Democrats and Republicans. But in most cases, they were uncontroversial. Like declaration of the third Tuesday in March as official "I Love My Dog Day." In contrast, a substantive bill like Ecobabe's cell phone driving ban—which would irk a significant subset of the public that wanted to do what they wanted to do when they wanted to do it—would require scaling the summit to get to "bipartisanland." A climb worth making since the governor would want cover from both parties before adding his signature, the final act that would turn the bill into law.

In practical terms, this meant Maren (and Senator Rickman) wanted not only the five returning Health Committee

Democrats who supported Senator Connor Smith's hands-free bill the year before to vote aye on SB 770, but also at least a few newly persuaded Republicans.

When Senator Rickman finished speaking, Maren approached the microphone without notes. Despite what was at stake, her arms were relaxed at her sides and her voice calm as she drew on years of experience speaking before committees just like this one.

"Last year this legislature took the courageous action of restricting cell phone use while driving to only hands-free technology. This year we seek your leadership to extend that to a full cell phone driving ban, to protect not only the lives of drivers, but also infants, children, and teens who might be harmed inside or outside the vehicle. Without this law, they will continue to be the unnecessary and tragic collateral damage in the communication revolution."

She cited statistics demonstrating that many of those injured or killed in cell-phone-related accidents were children and youth—inexperienced teen drivers or child pedestrians. With that as her close, Maren stepped aside so that Carolyn Garrisey could recount the story of her daughter's untimely death. Getting the call from an officer at the scene to inform her that Hilary was being airlifted to a hospital. Keeping vigil at Hilary's bedside, praying for a miracle, and finally removing her daughter from life support when hope was gone. All because Hilary's boyfriend was distracted while talking on his hands-free phone and tried to cut across three lanes without checking first.

The Senate Health Committee members were visibly moved. But emotion alone wouldn't be enough to pass the bill. When Maren and her fellow support witnesses stepped down, witnesses in opposition took their place. The first was a professor of statistics who in this hearing—unlike in a court of law—would not be required to reveal consulting contracts he had with cell phone companies. He criticized what he saw as weaknesses in the research. Sample size "too small," control groups "inadequate," and study funding "biased." Next, a representative of Citizens Against Big Government, a frequent player in the capitol, railing against the nanny state. Predicting that if an outright driver cell phone ban passed, lawmakers would soon require California citizens to wear crash helmets to walk down stairs and seat belts in their dinner chairs at home.

This hyperbole from witnesses was expected. But Maren was surprised to see lobbyist Caleb Waterston rise to fall in line with the opposition.

Maren looked for signs of grief in Caleb over the sudden death of his fiancée. But he appeared none the worse for wear. His color was never good, but he flashed an ingratiating smile at the committee as he took his place in the queue. He appeared nothing like Liza Booth-Henry, who acted like she'd had the wind knocked out of her in one blow with the news of her mother's death.

Waterston was joined by Lew Quintana, founder of Talk-Free Inc., a company that went from negligible net worth to hundreds of millions of dollars in value when the hands-free law was enacted. Quintana's political power lay in the fact that those millions enabled him to make huge campaign donations to prominent senators, including several on this committee.

When his turn came, Caleb presented an argument prettily packaged with words like "consumer choice" and "entrepreneurial creativity." But at its core Waterston's message was about the significant hit to jobs and the economy—and implicitly the senators' campaign coffers—if SB 770 were to pass. Waterston's voice was strained as he spoke, but to Maren's memory it always had been. She assumed his windpipe wasn't large enough in diameter to permit sufficient air to support a robust sound.

The contrast between Lew Quintana and Waterston was remarkable. Although physically compact and small in stature, Quintana had a booming, big man's voice. And unlike Waterston's carefully coordinated Savile Row lawyer's look, Quintana's shoulder-length, graying, beach bum hair clashed with a tan herringbone business suit and surprising two-toned tan and black shoes.

"Ladies and gentlemen, this bill would be a travesty to justice, to California, to our hardworking citizens," Quintana began, as though addressing a jury. "You've now heard the weaknesses in the bill sponsor's so-called evidence that a stronger ban is needed than the already powerful hands free restriction. Obviously, other states have not been persuaded. California is among ten states that protect our citizens through a hands-free law, but not a single state in these United States has found it appropriate or necessary to ban all cell phone use for all drivers."

Quintana pushed further, getting in a plug for his products. "Last year, motivated by the goal of greater driving safety under the new hands-free law, TalkFree Inc. expanded our offering of hands-free cell phone technology from Bluetooth wireless headsets to special in-car units, and from the most basic to those that operate through a car's speakers in stereo and incorporate full GPS systems. Presently, a full thirty-seven percent of California drivers own a TalkFree Inc. cell phone product to enable them to drive safely hands-free."

Maren was reminded again of how quickly TalkFree Inc. had introduced their products and dominated the market, while other companies were slow off the mark and forced to play catch-up.

"TalkFree's large market share is the consumer using the market to tell us what they want," Quintana bellowed. "Our systems make them feel safe and let them continue important communication while they drive, and that should be their choice!"

Caleb Waterston looked on approvingly throughout. Maren was sure he was barely suppressing his heh-heh-hehs.

"Thank you," Committee Chairman Gold said gruffly when Quintana, the last witness, was done. Gold then glanced around the dais, frowning, noting several still-empty committee chairs. "Lacking a quorum, we will defer the vote on this bill until additional members arrive."

Despite Chairman Gold's grimace, it wasn't unusual for testimony and votes to occur separately since legislators, possessing more human characteristics than they are generally credited with, can't be two places at once, despite the fact that they are frequently double-booked.

Maren pulled a draft of the Ecobabe finance report out of her satchel to review while she was waiting. Holding words on paper, in her hands she felt a bit like a nineteenth-century time traveler, surrounded as she was by individuals absorbed in their smartphones and computer tablets.

A movement from the hearing room door caught her eye. Maren looked up to see the temporary employee from the first lady's office. She recalled how the governor's receptionist, Delilah, lambasted the woman the day Maren was there to meet with Ray Fernandez. She still had a beaten look about her, shoulders stooped, even without Delilah there to administer the blows. She was dressed in a version of the Sacramento uniform—a dark blue pantsuit and red blouse. But it was baggy at the waist and hips. Her short brown hair lay flat and lifeless against her head. And while oversized glasses were the trend, the pair she had on looked like they'd been pulled from Salvation Army discards. She was waving one arm tentatively over her head, as though not really wanting to be called on by her teacher in class but figuring she should make some effort.

Maren checked over her shoulder to see if the woman might be signaling someone else, but there were no signs of recognition from the electronic army still buried in their smartphones and tablets. She tried to remember the woman's name. *Walter? Wexel? No, Wallis. That's it.* Maren made her way out of the room to where Wallis had retreated against the far wall in the hallway.

"The governor wants to see you," Wallis said. Her inflection made it sound like a question rather than a statement. She looked down as she spoke, twisting a small paper she held with both hands.

Maren was confused by the request. She couldn't leave her own bill hearing, and Governor Ray Fernandez would know better than to send someone to the committee room to ask.

"Wallis!"

A man's voice echoed from up the empty hall. As Wallis turned to see who it was, Maren noticed the ends of the woman's hair at the back, just above her collar, reflecting light. There were thin blond streaks—carefully placed highlights — apparently leftover from where the rest of her hair had grown out and been cut off. Maren thought it would certainly have improved the woman's appearance if she kept it up, but it must have been too expensive.

"I'm sorry, I have to go," Wallis said. The man who had called to her, a nondescript Sacramento type in a black suit and red tie, appeared to be waiting impatiently. "Please text the governor when you're ready," she told Maren. "The number's on here. He'll be at Westminster Church." She handed Maren the pink message slip she was holding, trying to smooth it out first.

Everyone in the capitol was familiar with Westminster— it sat directly across from Capitol Park at Thirteenth and N Streets. Built in the 1920s, its architects prepared first by traveling to Turkey to witness in situ the Mediterranean style. Their research paid off as Westminster Church faithfully reflected that exotic esthetic, rife with towers and archways and black iron latticework.

In addition to religious services, the church offered meeting space, free of charge, if the purpose was deemed worthy by its board. Coalitions to help runaway kids, that kind of thing. But for the governor to use Westminster to see her made little sense to Maren unless he was there for some other meeting. After all, he had an entire suite of offices at his disposal.

Hell, he has an entire state, Maren thought.

She tucked the note Wallis had given her into her satchel and returned to the hearing room, standing to one side since her prize front-row seat had been taken.

In the end, SB 770 lived to see another day, albeit with the same heavy weight strung around its neck that burdened Alec Joben's BPA pacifier ban—Republicans in solid opposition. Senator Rickman and Maren had their work cut out for them before the bill's next stop, a vote on the senate floor. Maren thought again how much harder it was without Sean there to help. He was connected with staffers on both sides of the partisan divide, and everybody liked Sean. *Or used to,* Maren thought, pulling her satchel close to her side to slip past a tour group blocking the hallway.

"Slow that train before the whistle blows!"

Caleb Waterston caught up with Maren as she exited the west side of the capitol building, halfway down the marble steps. A biting cold wind greeted her. The Sacramento weather could not seem to resolve to put both feet firmly into spring. As Waterston approached, Maren pictured his rickety figure being blown away, sucked up into the clear blue sky.

"I'm sorry for punting the ball upstream. It couldn't be helped," he said, out of breath. She supposed he was referring to the fact that he was on contract with TalkFree to oppose her cell phone bill, but, as usual, his peculiar turn of phrase made him difficult to follow. "If we can accept that as fresh snowfall, I want to talk with you about another matter."

Maren nodded acknowledgment and kept walking.

"I understand you and Ecobabe have hopped on the BPA bill as co-sponsors, jelly and jam, as it were. Sorry to say I'm on the other side of that one too, working with Saniplaz."

Maren could have guessed. Saniplaz had money to burn and Waterston was a willing furnace.

"I can't negotiate with you on that bill," she said. "You'll have to talk to Senator Alec Joben, he's the lead."

Waterston buttoned his heavy camel hair overcoat. "Understood. But I thought it would be helpful for you to come visit the new plant Saniplaz has opened dedicated completely to the green production of plastics. It's in San Jose, adjacent to the main facility. I could arrange a tour, and you can see for your-self that BPA is not a problem."

Maren hesitated. Noel had said something about a scientific interest he had in plastics made of vegetables. *Or had he said vegetables infused with edible plastics?* Plus, the BPA bill was Alec Joben's. Although she had succeeded in thinking about Joben less, when an opportunity did come up to spend time with him "by chance," it was hard to resist. And Maren thought there was a better-than-even-money possibility that Waterston was extend-ing the same invitation to visit the Saniplaz plant to Joben.

Waterston stuck firmly by her side as she continued toward her destination—she could see Westminster's central ivory-and-black church steeple across the street, its functioning bell tower and proud byzantine arches. She was getting close and had to do something—in addition to unwritten rules about tardiness, it was poor form to bring someone along to a gubernatorial meet-ing without prior clearance. That said, she wouldn't put it past Waterston to go for it.

"When?" Maren asked.

"Friday, four p.m. In and out before the herds of traffic, heh-heh-heh."

She did a quick mental calendar check. "Would it be all right if my brother, Dr. Noel Kane, joined us? He's a scientist at UC Davis." She paused, then added, "Have you invited Senator Joben? It is, after all, his bill."

Her suggestion to include Alec was either courageous or fool-hardy, she thought to herself.

Sensing a bargain in the making, Waterston closed the deal.

"Excellent! I'll check with the senator's docketeer. On Friday please check in at the front desk at Saniplaz. Four p.m. sharp.

Bring an ID—they have strict security—defense contracts and all. Sayonara! Tides before triumph, as they say!" he called as he left.

Docketeer? He really does need an interpreter, Maren thought. But as she stepped into the crosswalk she realized she hadn't expressed to Caleb her condolences regarding the tragic death of Tamara Barnes, his fiancée. She cut herself some slack for her poor manners. The pairing of the undernourished fifty-year-old contract lobbyist who would take any client for money with the idealistic, beautiful young staffer was simply unbelievable to her. She concluded that was likely why she didn't think to raise it. Or, she thought uncomfortably, maybe it was because Caleb Waterston hadn't seemed to need consoling.

CHAPTER 18

Two men, both in dark glasses, their muscular builds evident beneath brown utilitarian suits, stood chatting at the front entrance to the church. The shorter of the two strode purposefully toward Maren.

"This way, please."

He rounded the edge of the building to a large parking lot in back. Maren ran her fingers through her hair, resulting in what she hoped was a more attractive arrangement. Not wanting to please Ray Fernandez, but also not wanting to fall short of how he once thought of her.

There were two cars in the lot: an impressive black stretch limo and a small silver Mercedes with a convertible top that was closed.

The latter she recognized as the governor's private vehicle, but the limo was unfamiliar. She concluded there had been a prior meeting, perhaps with a large donor to talk money, necessarily accomplished away from the governor's office.

Orange cones had been placed at both entrances, blocking other cars from coming in. One of the security team moved them aside to let the limo leave, reestablishing the modest barrier afterward.

As she got closer, Maren could hear music from Fernandez's sports car.

Insoportablamente bella—unbearably beautiful. Brass and woodwinds punctuated Hector Zuniga's sultry voice. She found herself thinking back, hard-pressed to put a label on her past with Ray Fernandez. Not an affair, but certainly more than a flirtation. Whatever it was, the rich melody now filling the church parking lot had been the featured soundtrack.

The governor emerged from the driver's seat, the music louder through the open door. He took Maren by the elbow to steer her toward the passenger side.

"Let's take a ride."

"Where?" she asked.

He didn't respond. It was an assertion, not an offer.

She could refuse. *Governor or no governor.* But most likely the destination, if there was one, wasn't the purpose of their meeting. She assumed he wanted her in the car to talk because it was completely private. *About Tamara?* There wasn't time for her to think it through, but Maren figured that unlike the fate of unwitting cats, curiosity wouldn't kill her. At least not with a witness. As the security guard moved the cones aside to let them pass, she gave him a hearty wave.

Governor Fernandez turned the music down. "How did your cell phone bill fare?"

"Fine."

"The vote count?"

"Seven to four."

"Ah, our Republican friends are not happy with you, then."

Maren unwound her scarf and willed herself to be patient. At lunch with Garrick Chauncey the physical proximity had renewed her feelings for him, but she felt no latent attraction in Ray Fernandez's presence. Far from it. In fact, she wanted out of the confined space. But Ray was the sitting governor. She would need his signature on her cell phone bill and likely many others. So being with him was, at least from a work perspective, a good thing.

"I think Republicans will see the merits when I have more time to present the evidence. Hands-free mobile use while driving is simply not safe. And Senator Joe Mathis, head of their caucus, is a reasonable man." She looked out the window as she spoke. Nicknamed "The Emerald City," Sacramento was reputed to have more trees per capita than any other city in the world, except perhaps Paris. The California capital had over one million trees by the latest count, and wasn't stingy with variety—within a few blocks Maren saw maples, oaks, pine, and palm trees. She checked the side mirror to see whether a security detail followed. If so, she couldn't make it out.

As the governor neared the end of I Street, the Tower Bridge with its two thick, H-shaped arches came into view. *Only in Sacramento would a city allow its residents to vote on the bridge color,* Maren reflected. Gilded gold had won, in keeping with the capital city's status as the birthplace of the California gold rush. But once painted, the double-arch span was more of a yellowish brown. The color of something a puppy might leave behind in the living room before he was housebroken.

Fernandez looked relaxed, tapping out the beat to the music on the steering wheel, occasionally smiling at Maren as he changed lanes or came to a stop. The Mercedes revved impatiently as he downshifted and took the last exit before the bridge onto a side street leading down to the river. He pulled into a parking lot next to a small deli and removed his seat belt but made no move to get out, instead reaching for a briefcase in the small area behind his seat. He said nothing as he set it on his lap. The music continued to play, shifting from Zuniga to Luis Miguel singing No Sé Tú.

That's it? Maren thought. *A trip from one parking lot to another?*

She unfastened her seat belt and tried the controls to lower her window, then to open her door, but neither moved. Fernandez looked up and, seeing her futile attempt, pushed a button on his side. "Now," he said. "It will open now." He smiled broadly, as though he had given her a tremendous gift.

The fresh air coming off the river felt good. Although it lacked the salty smell of an ocean breeze, it had a pleasant, earthy quality. A couple sat at a round table on the patio of the deli, tossing pieces of bread from their sandwiches to a group of small grey songbirds with yellow markings. The birds chirped excitedly. Noel had once tried to teach Maren the difference between the Lesser Goldfinch, the Western Kingbird, and the Yellow-Rumped Warbler, all native to the Sacramento River region. She decided on Lesser Goldfinch for this crowd, although not with any certainty.

Meanwhile, Ray Fernandez had opened the case and extracted a document. It appeared to be an article or report three to five pages long. He closed and returned the briefcase to behind his seat.

"I want to speak with you about something," he said, watching her closely, his dark eyes serious. "It's time for you to make your mark. To show the world what you can do." He handed Maren the papers. She read the heading: *Children's Medical Services: Assistant Director, Environmental Safety and Injury Prevention. Responsible for liaison activities between Congress and the White House. Direct report staff of 11. Start Date...*

The next few pages provided a detailed job description for a high-level position in Washington, D.C. An immediate vacancy, to be filled within ninety days.

Maren looked up, trying to read from Raymond Fernandez's face what this was about. His eyes were lit up, his broad, mustached mouth barely containing a smile. She could see only a man whom she didn't know. Maybe never knew, despite what had happened between them. Perhaps the last music he played, No Se Tu—"I don't know about you"—should be their new theme song.

"*Es su destino,*" he said at last. "A position worthy of you. I have secured your interview. They..."

He stopped, frowning, as his BlackBerry, seated in a hands-free stand on the console, vibrated violently. He eyed the Caller ID—a number, no name—then lifted the phone with one hand as he opened his door with the other. He didn't bother to explain, closed the door behind him, and walked several feet from the car, leaving Maren with her unexplained destiny.

For a moment she was insulted, set aside as she had been so many times by him long ago. Still, he was now governor of the most populous state in the union, and Maren figured there

were at least a hundred, maybe a thousand things more important to the highest elected official of the state than a conversation with her.

She looked again at the position announcement.

*I don't want a new job…not even a big, important new job…not even a
high-paying, big important new job.* She tried out those statements,
and wondered if they were true. Or if they would be true if
anyone other than Raymond Fernandez had approached her
with this opportunity. And then there was the unanswerable
question of whether she would still have her current job if Ecobabe's cell phone bill followed the household hazardous waste
bill into legislative oblivion.

One thing she did know: she was hungry. The clock on the
dashboard, analog with silver hands and imitative of days gone
by, showed 2:35. She'd missed lunch. Fernandez was still on
the phone, gesturing emphatically. He had walked farther away
from the car so she couldn't hear, but she was sure from his
wide-open mouth that he was yelling. Maren's stomach growled
uncomfortably. She remembered Ray used to keep mints in the
glove compartment of his car, reliably there whenever they met.
She looked again through the window. He seemed no closer to
finishing his call. She pushed the button on the glove box. The
small, hatch-like door fell open. There was a manual for the
Mercedes and what looked like a spare phone charger, as well
as a soft leather pouch, probably registration and insurance.

Maybe in the back? She lifted out the pouch and the manual,
revealing the sought-after tin of mints. Next to it was a small
white hairbrush, travel size, trailing several broken strands of
beautiful, silky red-orange hair. Maren acted without thinking,

picking up her satchel from the car floor, opening it, and reaching for the brush.

She didn't hear him return.

"Sometimes I wish we could travel back those fifteen years," Fernandez said, his hand on the driver's door, his face inscrutable, the ever-present smile gone.

Maren shifted her hand to the right, passing over the brush and picking up the mints instead, and then closed the compartment quickly. She fiddled with the mint container to open it, not trusting herself to look at him, what her face might reveal.

"You found them. May I?"

He reached for a mint, his large hand brushing against hers. His knuckles were cold.

CHAPTER 19

Maren begged off from drinks scheduled for that night with Alec. He graciously said they should try another time. She asked if he'd received Caleb's invitation to tour Saniplaz that Friday. He said not that he was aware of, but that he would check with his scheduler. "Your scheduler, not your docketeer?" Maren had asked. They laughed together at Caleb's odd turn of phrase.

Afterward, she felt the conversation had gone okay, although she couldn't tell whether he had perceived her last-minute cancellation as a rejection or not. The truth was she needed something easier—someone easier—this evening. So she asked Noel to come over instead. Still, it turned out "easy" just wasn't on the agenda.

"I don't see why that matters," Maren protested.

Noel sighed. He was preoccupied. Bethany had fallen from the climbing structure at school that morning. A trip to the emergency room revealed she'd broken the scaphoid bone, one of eight bones in her tiny wrist. Noel was still processing the event.

Bethany had been pleased that the pediatric orthopedist's office had eleven cast colors available. She'd told Noel her friend Melanie would have picked neon pink, but she chose white because it was best to write on. Noel liked Bethany's way of thinking.

He had thought today might be a good day to tell Maren about Sal and Bethany, but Maren was already worked up and Noel needed a calm baseline for that conversation.

He tried again to reason with her.

"Two to six percent of the U.S. population equals six to eighteen million people. And that's only those who come by it naturally, through a mutation of the MC1R gene on their chromosome sixteen. That number doesn't account for the many who dye their hair."

"This wasn't dyed."

Maren set down a teak salad bowl brimming with fresh salad greens tossed with avocado slices, cherry tomatoes, and chopped walnuts.

"And it was a particular color of red, a deep red-orange," she said. "That has to change the math."

Noel tore off a piece of French bread and served himself some salad. "Assuming you're right and we could define the subset of people who have exactly that color of red, yes, it increases the odds the hair belongs to Tamara. But didn't she work for the governor? Aren't there other explanations for the brush being in his car?"

The timer rang for the quinoa and black bean casserole. Maren went to the kitchen, followed by Camper, who recognized the tinny-sounding bell as an indication that something edible was forthcoming.

"No," Maren said as she looked for an oven mitt. She slammed a few drawers in the process, finally opting to use a thick, plum-colored distowel to pull the hot dish from the oven.

Noel knew something of Maren and Ray's history. "So your assumption is Tamara Barnes and the governor were having an affair, which led to them both being in his car coming to or from their assignations. In the process you believe Tamara forgot her brush, which Ray Fernandez then stowed in the glove compartment to return to her at a later date?"

Maren set the steaming glass casserole on a hot pad next to the salad. Strong onion and garlic smells were offset by the sweet odor of chopped mango sprinkled on top. Camper took up his station under the table in case someone got sloppy.

"Sort of," Maren said as she spooned each of them an ample portion into individual blue ceramic bowls. "But the details aren't important. Tamara said she and the governor had done something awful. So that's the affair. Suppose Tamara was going to tell his wife, Martha, so Ray killed Tamara to keep her quiet? Or Martha found out, so she killed Tamara...Or..."

"Maren, stop. Details are always important. Without them, you may be engaging in false causality. It's like the single knife strike in the Hopkins and Barnes cases—with inadequate data..."

Maren cut him off. "I still think there's something to that. The police just aren't looking because they have Sean." She overfilled Noel's bowl as she spoke; beans and quinoa scattered on the table.

"There might be," Noel said. "But what you do know isn't enough. It's the same here. Even if the hair on the brush belongs to Tamara, and even if she and Raymond Fernandez were having an affair, you need to be sure all variables have been examined before coming to a conclusion. Didn't you say the governor has an alibi?"

"Yes. But I've been thinking about that, too." Maren set down her fork and pushed her plate aside. "Ray's alibi is that he was on a conference call at the time of the murder. People can do all kinds of things while participating on a conference call if there's not a video feed. Text, check their e-mails, eat dinner, for all I know they have sex while they're supposedly paying attention to a group of unseen people on the other end of the line." Maren picked up her fork, but rather than returning to the meal pointed it at Noel for emphasis. "I definitely could have killed someone on a conference call while other people were happy listening to themselves talk."

* * *

Maren left Lana a detailed message about the hairbrush in Ray Fernandez's glove box. She also asked whether Sean had gotten his mental health evaluation yet. As she hung up, her thoughts returned to her conversation with Noel.

Noel and Maren had lived with their father's mother for much of their childhood. She was a drinker and a worrier whose adult son had just disappeared, leaving her with his two children. She meant well and wasn't mean, but was ill equipped to look after them as they grieved the death of their mother and loss of their father. Maren became the head of the family by default, and for years now had been the only parent figure in Noel's life. She knew how difficult it was for her brother to trust anyone and how much he needed evidence, something solid, in order to believe in anything. The subtext of Noel's statements seemed to her to be an assertion that she was having trouble objectively assessing any information regarding Tamara's murder because she had such a strong preconceived belief that Sean was innocent.

Her stomach felt tense. The meal didn't sit well. *Not true*, she thought, *I'm checking everything*, remembering how thoroughly she had searched the studio for the missing knife, allowing for the terrible possibility that Sean might be the killer. She felt guilty even having entertained the idea, picturing how distressed Sean was that night when he came over, when he couldn't stand still, couldn't sit down, wouldn't even eat one of her shortbread cookies.

Then it came to her. A sick, cold feeling, a foreboding that she might find out in the worst possible way that Noel was right, that she had been blind to the obvious if it meant Sean was guilty. She jumped up and went to the small bathroom off the hall. Camper growled, alarmed.

I have to go to the bathroom.

She could hear Sean saying it the night of Tamara's death.

It was the only time, other than in the studio, that he was out of her sight.

And the missing key to her house? What if Sean had taken the key from the flowerpot because he planned to—strike that, he needed to—come back into her house when she wasn't there?

Maren started with the shelves above the toilet, pulling everything down, the basket of soaps, the stacks of towels. She combed through the drawers of the vanity. She breathed easier when each conquered space had nothing to hide. No knife. No weapon. Until she lifted up the small trash can, the kind with a foot pedal and closed top to keep Camper out. Underneath was a small, neatly folded plastic bag—lumpy, there was definitely something inside. Maren's face flushed, she felt tears welling up in her eyes.

It can't be.

She sat cross-legged and said a silent prayer before lifting the bag and spilling its contents. A heart-shaped locket on a gold chain clanked as it fell on the tiled floor, followed by the thud of a small white photo album. The necklace looked like the one Tamara Barnes was wearing the last day of her life, when she came into Senator Rickman's office. But Maren wasn't sure. She'd only noticed it then because Tamara kept gripping the locket.

The delicate chain was tangled. Maren picked it up gingerly. She felt odd, as though Tamara were next to her, watching. As she worked carefully to undo the knots she noticed the initials BC engraved on the back of the heart.

BC? Perhaps it isn't Tamara's after all?

Maren felt for the tiny clasp on the heart and opened it. The place for a miniature photo was empty, but the locket contained a lock of Tamara's hair, Maren was sure of it. It also made her more certain than ever that the brush in Raymond's car also belonged to Tamara. The tint and texture were identical.

Maren laid the necklace on top of the emptied plastic bag and turned her attention to the photo album. Inside were nearly twenty black and white photos of Tamara Barnes as a young child. They started with what looked like birth photos and stopped when she was no more than three or four years years old. The translucent, freckled skin, deep green eyes, pert nose— she was unmistakable, even then. The photos were candid. Of birthdays, on Santa's lap, toddling at the beach. In the last one she looked older, a preschooler, wearing a zip-front sweater with a kitten in a basket on the pocket and holding a matching kitten-themed purse.

There was never anyone else in the frame. Some of the pictures appeared to have been cropped to keep it that way.

Faced with photos of Tamara as a laughing, growing child, Maren thought again of finding the young woman's lifeless body that night in the capitol building. It made the loss that much bigger, and that much harder to put to rest in her mind.

CHAPTER 20

Friday dawned with a broad blue cloudless sky and unimpeded sunlight.

Maren took a sip of herbal tea and wished Polly hadn't already left for an early fellows meeting downtown. She had so much to share with her best friend, and one of their frequent morning walks would have been a good place to do that. But at least Polly's son, Jake, had taken Camper out last night. They didn't allow dogs on the community track, and Maren didn't have time to get to the dog park.

Resigned to walking solo, Maren stepped off her front porch to head down the hill when she saw them.

A tall blond boy had Jake's arms pinned behind his back, while a redheaded youth unzipped Jake's backpack, dumping the contents into the narrow street. He reached for Jake's saxophone case and tried to throw it, but it must have been

heavier than he expected. He dropped it. There was an alarm-
ing clanking sound when it hit the concrete. At the assault on
his beloved horn, Jake yelled and broke free, but the blond boy
reacted quickly, shoving Jake back to the ground and kicking
him once for good measure. Apparently satisfied, the two junior
thugs jogged off, grinning at one another.

Maren generally avoided running. But she was in a full-out
sprint when she passed Jake, kneeling, opening his saxophone
case to check for damage. When he saw her, his mouth fell
open.

The blond youth turned the corner of the gym before Maren
could get to him. But the red-haired boy stumbled on the football field and slowed to hold his side. Evidently, he wasn't much
more of a runner than Maren. He bent over, hands on his knees,
forcing his lungs to take in air. Maren had slowed to a walk but
was closing the gap. He looked up and started to move away.

"Hold it," she yelled.

He walked faster, still clutching his side.

Maren's anger doubled at being ignored. *What happened to
respecting your elders?* She charged blindly, finally calling up the
speed she needed and tackling him hard onto the grass.

He rolled over, face red, eyes wide. Incredulous.

"Don't you ever lay a hand on Jake Grey again," she warned.
She was on her knees now, leaning over him, her hands on
his shoulders, pinning him on his back. "If I hear of anything
happening to Jake I'll have you arrested, but not until my dog
takes a chunk out of you first."

The boy trembled. He didn't struggle against her, his body
limp. Tears seeped from his eyes. The expression on his
face reminded Maren she had just tackled and terrified a

fourteen-year-old youth. Not much more than a child, even if he was a tall and highly unpleasant one. She sat back to give him space, worried that the fall might have hurt him, then extended a hand. He pulled away.

"The thing about my dog? Not really," she said, in a softer tone. "Can you get up? Please. I'm sorry. I shouldn't have done that. I was upset about Jake. We both should do better."

The boy turned to look at her, then scrambled up and backed away, not responding.

Maren's sweats and T-shirt were covered with grass stains, her right elbow was scraped, and her hair looked like a cocker spaniel's on a bad day.

She stopped at home to get Camper, leashing him quickly, planning to tell Jake the dog could stay with him. She thought being with Camper would give Jake comfort and make him feel safe until Polly finished work. But by the time she had crossed the street to Polly's duplex Jake was already on the doorstep in a fresh T-shirt.

"The saxophone looks okay. I think it will play," he told her, bending to pet Camper as he spoke.

"How about you?"

He nodded, not looking up.

"What were you doing out so early?"

"Before-school jazz band rehearsal," he reminded her, taking a step toward the street. Camper tugged at the leash to follow him.

"Camper and I will walk with you," she said.

"No. Don't." Jake's young voice was firm. He started down the hill without them. He was favoring his right ankle, but his head was up and his back straight—all five foot two inches of him stretched to its limit.

* * *

At two p.m. the temperature was in the high sixties, the sky clear and cloudless. Maren stowed her overnight bag in the black Beetle's tiny trunk, slid into the driver's seat, and put the top down. She was looking forward to the two-hour drive south to San Jose. True, an insider tour of the Saniplaz plant wasn't a luxury weekend at a spa, but Maren was happy to be taking an extended drive. She was a road trip girl from way back. She tied a colorful scarf around her hair, slipped on her sunglasses, and backed down the driveway.

Camper stood on his hind legs in the living room, front legs propped on the windowsill so he could peer out and watch Maren's traitorous departure. But Maren knew all would be forgiven when Jake showed up to pet-sit and spoil the always-hungry dog with Camper's favorite peanut butter treats. She wondered if Jake had recovered from the morning, and whether he would tell his mom about the bullies. Or if she should.

Although the Dionne Warwick song suggested otherwise, there were several routes to San Jose, at least from Sacramento. It was hard to go wrong as long as Maren pointed her car south. Veering west toward the coast would take her through Richmond past Berkeley, but the weekend getaway traffic would likely be bad on a Friday afternoon, even this early. She could take Interstate 680, which her computer's GPS program tagged as the quickest. But 680 passed through numerous populous towns en route—Pleasant Hill, Walnut Creek—again raising the Friday traffic question. In the end Maren settled on Interstate 5, an uninteresting strip of concrete that traversed most of the state north to south but which had the distinct advantage of avoiding basically everything—human or man-made—that might slow it down.

She tried but couldn't get anything clear on the radio; too many dead zones. She found herself thinking again about the heart-shaped necklace and photo album Sean had left in her bathroom and hoped she had done the right thing.

Neither item seemed to offer new information. There was already ample evidence that Sean had been in a relationship with Tamara, which would explain his possession of her childhood photo album. Although doubtful that he would have his former girlfriend's consent, Tamara likely left it at his place and he failed to return it. Part of the unintended custody agreements of records, CDs, and photos that always occurred in sudden breakups.

It's not like it was a weapon, she reflected, reliving her relief when she first discovered that the bag under the waste can in her bathroom did not contain a knife.

Plus, Maren really did expect Sean to be exonerated, and if she turned over the album to police storage it might be damaged or hard to get back. She believed that in his grief Sean deserved to have some memories intact.

The necklace, however, was another matter. If it was the one Tamara had on the day of her death, how and when did Sean get it? Did he remove it at the scene, or did he see Tamara before that, despite his denials? And the small lock of hair inside might be important. On a hopeful note for Sean's defense, the "BC" engraved on the back of the small gold heart might be the killer's initials, or at least a clue to who he was. Maren felt there were too many unknowns to keep it to herself. So she had called Lana Decateau and left a message about the necklace, omitting any mention of the photo album.

When she reached the Saniplaz address Maren followed signs to parking and navigated the narrow, circular ramp up two floors, only to find both full. Circling back down to the basement floor, she maneuvered her Beetle between two SUVs that had no business parking in spots marked "Compact Only." Taking off her scarf, she checked her hair in the mirror. Rather than being flattened into compliance, her dark curls rebelliously popped up in all directions. She settled for putting on lip gloss, grabbed her satchel, and squeezed out between one of the behemoth vehicles and her car. Her legs needed stretching after the two-hour drive, but otherwise she felt good.

Looking around to determine how to get access from parking to the Saniplaz plant, she saw four exit doors, one in each corner of the garage. They were each a different color—muddy brown, muddy blue, muddy green, and muddy purple—with no labels. She felt like a *Let's Make a Deal* contestant. The brown door to her left was the most worn. Assuming that meant it was also the most used, she chose that. Bingo. Inside was an elevator and a small brass-colored sign indicating "Saniplaz, Inc. 2 nd Floor."

The modern lobby, high ceilinged and constructed primarily of gleaming metal and glass, stood in stark contrast to the dismal featureless garage. The lobby walls were punctuated by videos on big screens heralding the joys of plastic. It looked like Walt Disney had designed the space, a possibility reinforced by a smiling Snow White look-alike receptionist at the front desk.

Maren was signing the log in exchange for a visitor's badge and a bright green carryall bearing the Saniplaz logo when Caleb Waterston came hurrying toward her.

"Maren, so glad you made it." He extended his bony hand to shake hers. She was struck again by how much the man needed an infusion of at least ten thousand calories.

"Caleb, hello. I didn't realize you would be here."

"I didn't want to have a VIP like you negotiating the complexities of a corporate carrot without me, heh-heh-heh."

A corporate carrot? She was trying to figure out what that could possibly mean when Waterston continued.

"Unfortunately, Senator Joben had other canyons to climb so he won't be with us today."

Maren hoped her expression remained appropriate—she was going for minimally let down. She wondered if Alec not showing up was a message to her, that just when she'd decided to roll the dice and see what might happen he'd gone sour on the idea of dating a lobbyist. Especially only a few months into his first term, deciding against it—against her—would be the politically smart thing to do.

"We could start," Caleb said, "but I thought your brother was joining you."

Maren couldn't believe she'd forgotten about Noel. She'd turned her phone off on the drive since sound through the TalkFree hands-free speaker system was hopeless when the convertible top was down. She checked her voice mail. Sure enough, there was a message saying he was stuck in traffic. She figured he must have chosen to take one of the more interesting but less favorable routes. He told her to start the tour without him, that he would call when he got there. There was also a message from Garrick Chauncey. They hadn't spoken since their lunch together and she still didn't know what to say to him. She hit save without listening and turned back to Waterston.

"Noel's delayed. While we have a minute, I wanted to ask you about Senator Rickman's cell phone legislation. I understand why TalkFree opposes, but can we…"

A monster of a man molded into a white coat and holding a clipboard interrupted them.

"Ms. Kane, Mr. Waterston, good afternoon. The plant closes in an hour. If we want to see any of the action we need to move. I'm Dr. Samuel Jones, vice president of the Go-Green Initiative here at Saniplaz."

At least six feet four inches tall, three hundred pounds, bald, with thick sideburns and a goatee, other than his clothes he looked like a bouncer at a hip club, not a plastics executive. Given the difference between Snow White's puffed-sleeve dress and hair bow at the desk and this guy, Maren had to give Saniplaz points for letting employees express their individuality. She tabled her thoughts about the cell phone bill and determined she would get back to Waterston about that later.

Dr. Jones began the tour's narrative as they walked. "What you will see today is the cornerstone of the Saniplaz Go-Green Initiative. As you no doubt know, most plastics are produced using petroleum. That is accomplished in increasingly eco-friendly ways in our main facility. But Saniplaz is always looking for alternatives that can be eco-effective and provide our customers with the quality and durability they need."

Eco-effective? He may look different, but he sounds the same, Maren thought as she listened to what appeared to be a standard corporate spiel. *He should try telling the people in the gulf at ground zero for the BP spill that oil is increasingly eco-friendly.*

The trio passed through several hallways that fed into offices before reaching a large set of double doors emblazoned with a life-size image of a stick figure with a line through it and the words "Danger, Industrial Production Area." Maren thought privately that the stick figure was a pretty good rendering of Caleb Waterston. Dr. Jones reached into a side locker and pulled out a hard hat and safety goggles for himself and handed similar gear to Maren and Caleb. He reminded them to check that their phones were off for the tour. Then he swiped a card through a keyless entry. There was a click as the doors unlocked and he pushed one open, gesturing for them to go in.

The space was cavernous, filled with pulsing machinery dominated by three huge steel cylinders. There were only three workers in sight, all in white coats and safety gear, checking various dials and panels. Jones shepherded Maren and Caleb to one side.

"As I noted, most plastics are made of nonrenewable petroleum. However, in this new Go-Green facility our plastics are all corn-based. We purchase the raw materials—resin pellets distilled from corn—from a plant in Iowa, ship them here, and then use that as the basis for polyminecine plastic. Not only is the source renewable, the end product is biodegradable."

Caleb was smiling smugly, proud of his client's achievements. Maren had to admit she found the idea of corn-based plastics pretty cool. Jones walked them through the various stations of production and introduced them to staff along the way. Maren was sorry Noel was missing this. Not only would he have enjoyed it, he could have asked the hard questions about by-products from corn processing, including how much energy it took and why the chemical BPA was still needed. She had tried but was unable to decipher the technical responses.

Back in the entryway Maren thanked Dr. Jones and Caleb Waterston, promising to follow up with any questions Senator Joben, author of the BPA bill, might have. She also asked Caleb to give her a call about TalkFree and the cell phone legislation as soon as he could. When they had left she turned her phone back on and checked for messages. Only one—Noel again. She felt a moment of disappointment, realizing she was hoping for the call from Lana Decateau that would tell her there was a break in the case, that the police knew they'd made a mistake and Sean was being processed for freedom.

Maren hit play.

"I'm sorry I'm late. Four hours for what should have been a two-hour drive. Please call me." Noel was clearly frustrated.

She tapped the callback icon on her phone screen. He picked up on the first ring.

"Noel Kemp here."

"It's me, where are you?"

"Saniplaz. There was a four-car pileup, injuries, ambulances." He paused. "But I'm here now, parked on a side street a few blocks from the plant. I couldn't figure out the maze of one-way streets to get to the entrance. I'm walking...wait, that looks like the parking garage."

"That means you're at the main building. The parking garage occupies the three bottom floors. Meet me at the lowest level— my car's near the brown door. I can drive you to your car and we can have dinner. I'll tell you about the tour. I have lots of questions for you."

Noel hung up and walked around the block until he saw external stairs down to the garage. The complex was nearly empty. Clearly, most of the Saniplaz employees had gone home for the day. Maren's VW was parked against the opposite wall. He took out his phone to let Maren know he had located it. But mid-dial he sensed something and looked up to see an ominous figure dressed head to toe in black, including a black ski mask, crouching behind Maren's car.

At that moment Maren entered the garage, head down. She was rummaging to get her ringing phone from her bag as she walked, oblivious to the imminent threat less than ten feet away.

Noel shouted at her to stop as he dropped his phone, ignoring the cracking sound as it hit the concrete. He took off at a sprint towards her, his long legs covering the space quickly, his trench coat billowing behind him.

The dark figure rounded the car toward Maren and rose to standing, a knife held high in one black-gloved hand. Noel threw himself the last few feet into the narrow gap between his sister and her attacker. He knocked Maren backward, then felt the cold steel drive deeply into his side. Maren's landing was cushioned bottom-first on her soft satchel, but Noel hit hard, free-falling, arms outstretched onto the unforgiving cement floor.

The assailant shifted Noel's limp body, quickly patting the trench coat pockets, pulling Noel's wallet from one.

"What's going on?" Caleb called, seeing the tangle of bodies as he entered from the opposite end of the lot near a shiny white Volvo, his car key in hand.

The figure in black dropped Noel's wallet at the sound, backed away, then turned and ran. Maren managed to sit up and crawl toward her brother. He lay facedown on the ground, his head turned toward her. She saw the protruding knife and felt his warm blood as it stained his coat and flowed onto the concrete, fast. Too fast. His eyes were closed, his breathing rapid and shallow.

Caleb reached them.

"What the hell is happening?" he said, his voice shaky.

"Shut up Caleb. For once, shut up! Call 911! And give me your jacket."

Caleb pulled his suit coat off and dropped it next to Maren as he fumbled to get to his phone.

"No reception." He waved his phone helplessly.

"Go outside. Now!" Maren ordered, pressing the jacket to Noel's side in an effort to stop the bleeding.

CHAPTER 21

Maren's eyes ached, her throat was dry, and she felt stiff from her fall. She had been at Santa Clara Valley Medical Center for three hours, watched over by a police officer, a small pudgy man with a body odor problem who, despite his uniform and badge, looked like he would have a hard time subduing any assailant. San Jose police had said the attack in the garage appeared to be a random robbery attempt—parking structures were a popular target. Perhaps that was why they didn't send their top man. Still, any attack with a knife sent gears whirring in Maren's head these days. She would think about that later. For now, her head only had room for Noel.

She tucked her feet underneath her on the hard vinyl chair and pulled the blanket the hospital staff had given her up to her neck. She couldn't stop shivering. There was that awful hospital odor. Not a clean smell, although a mixture of pine and chemical disinfectant was dominant. Beneath it Maren felt she was breathing in something primal, the desperation of sickness and death. She thought of her mother's last days in intensive care, then willed herself back to the present.

The ambulance had come to the Saniplaz lot quickly, para- medics barking at each other in code, taking action to stabilize Noel. She rode in the back, crowded alongside Noel's stretcher with an attendant who fiddled with dials and an IV while they traveled at what felt like mach speed through the San Jose city streets, sirens blaring.

"Noel, I'm here. It's okay."

Maren held Noel's hand in hers and continued speaking to him throughout the transport, although she had no sign he could hear. His fingers felt icy cold and he never opened his eyes. The feeling inside her was like an acid wash, the pain beyond anything she'd ever experienced. The what-ifs were sim- ply too terrible to consider.

At the hospital the paramedics maintained their pace, wheel- ing Noel away on a gurney through two double doors. Maren was told to wait at the entry. After fifteen minutes she got in line at the intake desk behind a short, thick-waisted man in a T-shirt and plaid shorts, a business type who looked like he'd been golfing, although Friday night didn't seem the time for it. He leaned against the counter and drawled lazily giving a long, detailed description of the barriers he had encountered when he tried to pick up his wife's medications at the hospital pharmacy. He seemed neither angry nor frustrated, just intent on a full, calm hearing of his grievance. It appeared to have nothing to do with emergency care and the staff tried to tell him so, but he persisted, never checking over his shoulder to see what kind of line might be forming behind him as the minutes ticked by. When he was finally done to his satisfaction the man turned and walked out, failing to make eye contact with those he had kept waiting, including Maren.

What, you think if you don't look at us, we don't exist? Maren fumed. She wanted to smack him, but she couldn't remember ever having punched anyone. Except Noel, when they were kids. The memory of her brother made her need for information more urgent. All she could get out of the harried desk staff was that Noel had been taken for a CT scan and evaluation. She returned to her seat, occasionally moving around to stretch or pace. The magazines on the table beside her were out of date, and she had no ability to focus anyway. She checked twice more at the counter; no news of Noel. Nearly an hour passed.

"Ms. Kane?"

The doctor who called her name as he entered the waiting area was young and tall with caramel-colored skin. He wore the requisite physician's white coat over mint-green surgical scrubs.

"Yes, over here," Maren said, standing as she spoke. She felt she would be better able to take any news the doctor had if she was eye-level with him, or at least close to it.

He walked toward her and gestured that they both should sit back down. But it had taken all Maren's energy to stand up and she couldn't reverse the process. So they stayed standing as he extended his hand, speaking in a softly accented voice, "I am Doctor Wihabe."

"Hello."

"Please, would you not be more comfortable sitting down?"

She wondered if this small talk was a test to see how long she could tolerate the doctor not telling her anything about Noel's status before they had a new attempted homicide on their hands and she was the guilty party.

"Where is Noel? May I see him?"

"I have good news and bad news about your brother."

Seriously, good news and bad news? Can't you come up with a more reassuring opener than that?

She didn't trust herself to say anything, so she waited.

"The good news is that the knife nicked only a small branch artery, rather than a major line. So the blood loss seemed a lot, but it was not enough to be life-threatening. Also, the blow to the head as he fell does not seem to have done any significant damage. His brain function is normal."

She didn't think she would ever hear anyone describe Noel's brain function as normal. But yes, that was good. And the bad news?

"The intake report said he was running and leapt up to block the assailant from striking you."

"Yes."

"When he landed, his head was up, and his chest hit first. It is the reason his head injury was minor. Like what do you call it when diving, a belly flat?"

"Belly flop," Maren offered. *Noel's lack of athletic prowess finally did him some good?*

"Because of the trauma when his chest took the impact of the fall, your brother sustained a small tear in his aortic artery. This is not from the knife at all—from the fall, yes?"

She nodded.

"This, then, is the bad news. The result is a very serious injury. The aorta might tear further and the wound could become life threatening. We will try to fix it to prevent that, but we need first to be sure everything else is as it should be. His ribs are bruised, not broken; that is good. We need to also be certain that no other organs, for example, his liver, kidney, or spleen, have been compromised. Then we will see if surgery can be done to repair the tear in the aorta."

Maren felt herself go numb, then hugged herself tightly. *Noel has a torn aorta?* She asked the doctor in a childlike tone, "My brother...has injured his heart?"

Dr. Wihabe responded gently. "Yes. I guess that is a right way to say it. You can see him if you like. He is heavily sedated, as we must keep his blood pressure low so that the aortic tear is not exacerbated. After you see him, you should go home. Rest. Come back tomorrow. We will not do anything until he is stable for at least twenty-four hours." Maren said nothing, so he tried again: "I will ask a nurse to take you to him now."

She heard Dr. Wihabe say he would *try* to fix it and that it could be *life threatening*. But those words were unacceptable, so she filed them accordingly, out of conscious reach.

When Maren got to Noel's room he was asleep. The nurse advised her he was on heavy painkillers and blood pressure drugs. Deep purple bruises spread from the right side of his face down his chest, and both his palms were torn and discolored. But the biggest shock was seeing him without his fedora and trench coat—in his white hospital gown Noel looked so vulnerable. Unprotected, unarmored. At least the knife had been removed and his wound was wrapped in gauze.

Maren picked up Noel's cell phone from the bedside table for safekeeping and instructed the nurse to call if anything changed. It wasn't until she had checked into a Marriott three miles north of the hospital, changed into her flannel pajama bottoms and T-shirt, and climbed into bed that she realized she hadn't called anyone about what had happened to Noel.

Their mom was gone, dead sixteen years now, and their dad might as well be since neither Noel nor Maren had a number or address for him. No other siblings. Was there anyone to call?

Lana needs to be told.

Maren knew what the San Jose cops were saying, a robbery gone wrong. With a knife as the weapon. But what was the saying—once burned, twice shy? No, that wasn't it. Because for Maren this made three times. Marjorie Hopkins, Tamara, and now her.

Maren couldn't believe this attempt on her life was random, even if it was in a city two hours south of the capital. There was at least a chance it was related to the others. Terrifying for her, yes, but Maren would think about that later. Right now, a similar attack, with Sean in jail, had to work in Sean's favor.

She started to dial Lana Decateau's number when she saw "6 missed calls—Sal" scrolling across the front of the mobile, and realized she was holding Noel's phone, not hers. She turned it over and saw the crack in the case in the back from when Noel had dropped it, but the phone itself looked okay.

Sal? It must be urgent, six times on a Friday evening.

Maren debated whether she should return the calls at ten p.m., and with such bad news. She checked Noel's recent phone log first and found calls to and from Sal nearly every day for as far back as she could see.

She wondered who could possibly be that significant in his life. She gave in to her curiosity and hit call return for Sal. A woman answered on the first ring. "Noel! Where are you? I thought you were coming back tonight, it's so late."

Maren didn't know how to begin. "This is Maren, Noel's sister. I'm sorry to bother you, but I saw the missed calls and..."

"Maren? Where's Noel?"

"I'm sorry to ask, but who are you? I mean, I know you're Sal, I called you, but who are you?"

"Oh. I'm Noel's, ah, his friend. We're together, dating. But what happened? Why do you have his phone?"

Dating?

Maren stopped herself from asking all the questions she suddenly had. She realized it wasn't the right time to catch up on relationship news, even if in Noel's case that merited thorough investigation.

"There's been an accident," Maren said. "Noel's hurt. It's okay. He's in Santa Clara Valley Medical Center in San Jose. I just left there. They may operate tomorrow but he's resting tonight."

"Operate?" It sounded like Sal would jump through the line if she could. "What? Why?"

"It's not the knife wound—" *That was a mistake*, Maren realized, too late.

"KNIFE WOUND? What do you mean? Let me talk to him, now!"

"I'm sorry, I'm exhausted, I'm not doing this right. Someone tried to attack me, Noel saved my life, he jumped between us. The knife wound is small, but he fell hard and has a tear in his heart and they have to fix it. I'm..."

"We'll be there in...let's see...three hours tops. We'll go straight to the hospital."

"Okay, I'm at the Marriott, room two eight-four. I..." Maren was interrupted by a dial tone.

Whatever else Sal is, she's a doer, Maren thought. For all the terrible news of this evening, the fact that her brother, Noel, had a girlfriend, one who could communicate like a normal human being and who clearly cared deeply for him, was some consolation.

But as Maren snuggled down under the covers, calmer than she had been since this whole mess started and determined to get some rest, she stiffened and opened her eyes wide.

We? She said we? Who the hell is she bringing with her?

CHAPTER 22

Fortunately, the wisdom of the body can outrank the panic of the mind. Maren was physically and mentally exhausted and soon fell fast asleep. But her respite had only lasted a few hours when she was awakened by a loud knocking. She sat up, her breath coming fast, throwing off the covers. The police may have thought the attack on her was a robbery, but she was far from convinced.

She opened the drawer of the nightstand and pulled out the Gideon Bible provided with each room, raising it over her head, ready to land a righteous blow if need be.

"It's Sal," a woman said. "Sal Castro."

Noel's phone, the messages.

Maren opened the door. Standing before her was a tall woman in her late thirties dressed in a navy work shirt and matching pants, the only feminine touch a tiny gold cross on a chain around her neck. She had chin-length dirty blond curly hair. Her face was tanned and lined, her deep-set, blue eyes worried. She held a sleeping child, three or four years old, wrapped in a blanket, face hidden from view.

"Is it okay if I put Bethany down?" Sal asked as she struggled to pull back the covers with one hand and deposit her sleeping charge on the bed. "The hospital wouldn't let me bring her into intensive care." She added once the child was settled, "I have to see Noel."

Maren would have said that she understood, would have offered a supportive comment, had she not been transfixed by the now-exposed features of the sleeping girl. A cast on one arm, her free hand was tangled in silky, red-orange curls framing her pale face, sprinkled with translucent freckles. She wore a zip-front sweater with a kitten in a basket hand-embroidered on the pocket.

The sweater was identical to the one worn by the child in the last photo in the album that Sean had hidden. More than that, it was clear to Maren that the child she'd seen in that photo and in all the photos wasn't Tamara. There was a powerful resemblance to Tamara, yes, but the photos were of this child.

"Are you all right?" Sal asked, taking in Maren's glazed expression.

Maren turned away, picking up her room key off the nightstand. She willed her face to remain blank. "No, fine. I'm fine, really." She handed the key to Sal. "What's her name?" And she couldn't help herself from saying, "Your daughter—I mean, she is your daughter?"

Sal accepted the key and crossed the room quickly, her hand on the door, the need to see Noel pulling her as she spoke.

"Bethany." She turned back and gave a weak smile. "Is it okay if she stays with you? Noel said you're good with kids."

"Yes, of course," Maren managed, realizing Sal might be having second thoughts about leaving the child in her care.

"Call me if she wakes up. You have my number in Noel's phone."

Maren eased herself into a chair and stared at the peaceful child before her. This was the child in the photo album, it had to be—the kitten sweater, her features. Maren's mind raced. *But how? Why would Sean have those pictures unless this child is somehow related to Tamara? Sal's daughter, but adopted? Or Tamara's niece? There has to be a blood connection to Tamara.*

Maren had so many questions. But she took a deep breath and consciously let go, for the moment, of the need to understand. She had to do that to survive, as it was the end of a day that couldn't possibly be understood. Not, at least, until Noel was out of harm's way. She lay down carefully on the other side of the large bed, hoping not to wake the girl. But Bethany Castro opened her eyes, rolled over, and wrapped her hand around Maren's dark curls before tucking her knees up to her chest and falling back into a deep sleep.

Maren lay like that, she wasn't sure for how long, when she heard a key in the lock. When the door opened she was startled to see Sal, back so soon, fury in her eyes.

"They wouldn't let me see him, only family is allowed! Damn it, I don't know what to do!" Sal paced the room, running both hands through her hair, grabbing at its roots in frustration—she looked ready to break a lamp or chair.

"Who did you speak with?" Maren eased off the bed.

"Some guy at the front desk. He wouldn't let me past the entry. Family only, he kept saying." Sal walked over and adjusted Bethany's blanket as if by habit but didn't stop talking. The child didn't stir. "I got mad and he finally said he didn't need this grief, that he was going off shift in fifteen minutes and if I didn't leave he would call the police. On me!" She looked at Maren. "I guess I did get a little assertive."

Maren had to smile. She knew how hard it was to be a strong woman in the world. *Our lack of subtlety is not often appreciated.*

"What did you tell the guy, about who you are?"

"Noel's girlfriend," Sal answered, as though that would be obvious.

"Okay. You said he was going off shift? Maybe you can get a fresh start." As she spoke, Maren reached behind her neck to unclasp the thin chain that passed through the simple gold band, its patina worn, hidden from sight under her shirt. Her mother's wedding ring. She had not taken it off since her mother's sudden death. But it was time, she figured, if not for this fierce woman, then for whom? She slipped the ring off the chain and handed it to Sal.

"Put this on, tell them you're Noel's wife. He'll have a bit of a shock when he wakes up," she said, smiling, "but he'll understand."

Sal didn't blink, didn't pause. Maren thought Sal might get teary, but this was a woman on a mission. With a little effort Sal wiggled the ring onto her finger. A tight fit, but she managed, then gave a quick thanks and was gone.

Maren felt calmer, seeing the intense connection Sal clearly had to Noel. It made her more confident there would be time for questions later. She lay back down and was not surprised when Bethany rolled toward her once more and reached out her hand for Maren's hair.

CHAPTER 23

Sal returned at two a.m. to collect Bethany. She told Maren she'd booked a room in the same hotel and that she would be using vacation time to stay until Noel could return home.

Maren was unused to having anyone else look out for Noel, and she wasn't sure yet how she felt about it. Plus, interacting with Sal—for any reason—was complicated. Maren tensed inside each time she thought about Bethany and the photo album Sean had hidden in her home. Because that mattered too, she realized—not just that Sean had the album with photos of Bethany, but that he thought it worth concealing. She thought it supported the possibility that Bethany was Tamara's daughter and Sal had adopted her. But the path to get from here to there remained unclear unless she flat-out asked Sal. And that seemed way out of bounds. So Maren started the morning with the beginnings of a headache. And when she listened to her voice mail messages it only got worse.

Lana Decauteau reported that the hairbrush in Ray Fernandez's car hadn't gained any more traction with the police as potential evidence than Maren's Hopkins-Barnes single-killer theory. The governor's alibi had checked out. Participants on the two-hour conference call at the time of Tamara's death testified to the fact that Ray was actively involved in the virtual meeting, speaking frequently. And his receptionist, Delilah Wade, corroborated his story, stating she had been in the inner office with him, taking notes. (Maren had to wonder if that was all the busty blonde had been doing.) Also, security cameras were located such that the governor could not have exited his inner office and made it to the bathroom where Tamara was killed without detection. Yes, the cops acknowledged, that could be Tamara's brush in Ray Fernandez's car. She worked for him and could have left it there on the way to a public event or other function. They sounded just like Noel in that respect.

In short, the police had no intention of harassing a popular sitting governor and inflaming the press unless they had more than an aide's hairbrush to go on.

Maren guessed that by this time she should have this seen coming. She was beginning to believe that Detective Morning Sun and his crew wouldn't believe Sean was innocent unless Maren brought them the actual killer gift-wrapped with a bow.

As she waited for the elevator, Maren turned her mind to Ecobabe and her work. The cell phone bill was scheduled for a hearing in two weeks in Senate Appropriations, the fiscal, or "money," committee. California legislative fiscal committees don't evaluate the right or wrong of a proposal in terms of content or even ethics. Their only charge is to consider the financial stress the bill might mean to the state. Maren's task for Senate Bill 770 was to convince committee members that the net costs of enforcing the cell phone driving ban—police time, paper processing, court dates—would be zero, fully paid for by fines levied on drivers that chose to flout the new law.

Maren pulled her phone from her satchel and sent a text to Evie about the need for a cost analysis on SB 770, asking her to put Ecobabe's two interns on it. As she did so, she remembered that Elliot, a senior intern in his second year at Ecobabe, was busy helping Ecobabe's junior intern, Nadira, with Clay Zimbardo's marketing proposal. Figuring out a way to transcribe Simone Booth's tapes had been next in the queue, but she would have to push that back one more time.

* * *

Noel was sitting up, the hospital bed adjusted lounge-chair fashion. His eyes were lightly closed. Maren noticed how long his sandy lashes were against his pale skin. The doctor had warned Maren that her brother would be resting most of the time since the blood pressure drugs were paired with sedatives to make the long hours of immobility needed for his heart to heal bearable. Still, Noel had his hat back on. Silly as it looked, Maren found that to be the best sign of all.

"Noel?"

He opened his eyes. "How are Sal and Bethany?" His voice was weak but clear.

Although it was on her mind at the mention of the child, Maren wasn't comfortable asking Noel about Bethany's adoption, not in his condition. "At the zoo," she said. "Busy exploring San Jose, at least when Sal isn't here giving wifely support." At least she could enjoy teasing her brother about his faux spouse. Noel didn't seem to mind. He never questioned Maren's decision to give Sal their mother's wedding ring.

"How is Ecobabe managing?"

"Since Sal's here I'm planning to get back to the office today."

He nodded. "I don't imagine the capitol can go on for long without you."

It was hard to tell with Noel whether he was kidding, and it was generally safest to assume he was serious. "The government will be fine. It only shuts down when Democrats and Republicans have more than their usual catfights. Not when they're short a lobbyist." She smiled, although as usual Noel didn't seem to register her attempt at humor. "I can come back if you need me. Sacramento's gone mostly virtual anyway, communication via e-mail, text. Although my laptop finally crashed for good yesterday. No hard drive."

"I'm so sorry," he said, genuine pathos in his voice. To Noel, the death of a computer was a notable passing.

"It's okay. Ecobabe sprang for this." Maren pulled an iPad mini from her satchel. "There's an Apple store a few miles from here." She flipped the small tablet over in her hands, then back again. "It's much lighter and easier to carry around than my laptop. But I haven't been able to figure out how to get to my Ecobabe e-mails—it keeps redirecting me to the main server."

A light came into Noel's eyes that she hadn't seen since his injury. "Are you able to leave it with me? I can play around with it and give you a tutorial when you come back. The university has me on medical leave, and it's not like I have a full schedule here." He glanced around the small spare hospital room, an open curtain revealing an empty bed the twin of his own.

"That would be terrific," she said, handing it over, then hesitantly leaning in to give him a kiss on the cheek.

Noel looked directly at Maren. "I love you."

She tried to remember having heard him say those words since their mom had died, to anyone.

CHAPTER 24

There couldn't be any worse news on Sean's case—at least none that Maren could think of. And it was all her fault.

When Lana explained that if Sean obtained the necklace in the course of Tamara's murder it could add robbery during a homicide to the charges and make Sean eligible for the death penalty, Maren argued.

Loudly.

"It wasn't robbery. When Sean found Tamara he wasn't thinking. I'm sure he just wanted something tangible to remember her by. Maybe he's the one who gave her the necklace. And it wasn't removed during the commission of a murder because Sean didn't kill anyone."

If Lana was bothered by Maren's outburst, she didn't let on. "There was already concern that whoever killed Ms. Barnes robbed her of her laptop and phone, since neither has been recovered from her office or home. But no witnesses came forward to indicate that she had them with her at the time of her death, so until now a murder-for-profit special circumstance under California law would have been hard to prove. But now, with the necklace clearly traceable back to Sean from his visit to your home the night Tamara died, it will be up to the DA to decide how to treat the new evidence."

Maren knew the attorney was leaving unspoken the DA's tough-on-crime platform for his reelection campaign and how that might play into the charges he would bring against a defendant in the murder of a young and beautiful public servant.

She closed her eyes, her jaw clenched. She felt a desperation foreign to her, the need to do something, anything to stop the train wreck that seemed to be Sean's case. She had only one card left—she didn't know how it might fit into the case, and she certainly wasn't looking forward to sharing it since all her ideas seemed to be shot down with the phrase "given that we have the prime suspect in custody..." But she couldn't give up just because people refused to listen. Maybe the information would lead to a motive and then to the real murderer. So Maren dropped what she expected to be a bombshell. That it was likely that Tamara Barnes was survived by her daughter, a three-and-a-half-year-old girl.

"There must be hundreds of red-haired, freckled little girls," Lana said upon hearing Maren's latest theory. "There's no reason to believe this one is Tamara Barnes's child."

Maren was thankful Lana didn't have Noel's scientific training or she might have to hear statistics on the worldwide incidence of redheads and something about mutated genes all over again. She spoke evenly, trying not to let her frustration show.

"It's not only that she looks like Tamara. But she does. Exactly like her."

"I understand there's a resemblance."

"This child was adopted at birth."

Maren had learned that much from Noel without having to disclose her suspicions about Tamara being Bethany's birth mother.

"And on the back of Tamara's locket are inscribed the initials BC. This child's name is Bethany Castro. I bet a test would show the lock of hair inside the locket belongs to Bethany, not to Tamara." Maren paused. "When I met Bethany last night she was wearing a zip-front sweater with a hand-embroidered kitten in a basket on the pocket. It's the same one in a photo album with pictures of Bethany Castro since birth. It was in Sean's possession and..."

"What? When did Sean give it to you?"

Maren felt cold. She took a deep breath. "It was with the necklace. He left it in my house."

"You withheld evidence?" Lana's voice was steely, no trace of southern belle any more.

"No. I mean, yes, I kept it. But I didn't see any way it could be relevant to the crime. I thought the photos were of Tamara as a child, and I assumed Sean had it from when they were dating, that it had nothing to do with that day, with her death. I thought..."

"Yes, well whatever you thought, your actions were wrong. Thankfully, it's only been a few days since you found the album, during which time you were attacked and your brother was seriously injured—there are reasons you would not have been thinking clearly. As long as we turn it over now, I don't believe DA Sharpton will prosecute you for obstruction of justice."

Not thinking clearly? Maren bristled. That wasn't what had happened. She wanted to protest, but Lana wasn't finished.

"In the future, you are not to assume or interpret anything that remotely relates to suspects or victims in this case. You are to share that information with me and only me, and you are to do so immediately, is that understood?"

Maren agreed. But she also asked that she be able to explain personally to Sean why the police had the necklace and the photo album, and in turn, that he be given a chance to answer the questions this new evidence raised—she had many.

They met that afternoon in the parking lot next to the jail. Lana Decateau wore a dark grey fitted pantsuit with a turquoise silk shirt. Her glossy black hair was held back by a single charcoal stone clip. The simplicity of her outfit did nothing to mute her glamour.

Remembering her last visit to the facility, Maren wondered if Lana had selected her clothing to match the grey-on-grey color scheme inside. But they were shown to a different interview room this time, one with hideous, salmon-gone-bad-colored walls—grey would have been a relief.

Sean appeared thinner, more angular and muscular than when Maren last saw him. He had deep circles under his eyes made more pronounced by the shadow of his bangs, which, lacking the styling gel he had at home, fell heavily across his forehead. Maren reflected that ironically his new look—harder, disheveled, and wanton—would make him more attractive to many women than the clean-cut Sean of old.

Lana had been able to get Sean a mental health evaluation. The technician's notes, shared with Lana as required by law, stated that although Sean showed signs of depression, it was more likely he had an antisocial personality disorder. Maren was sure that opinion was biased by the fact that Sean was charged with a brutal homicide and imprisoned as a result.

"Sean, we're here because Maren found the things you left in her home, the necklace and the photo book." Lana's normally soft southern tones were clear and assertive.

Sean registered no surprise. His eyes were on Lana, but they seemed vacant, disinterested. His cuffed wrists lay heavy in his lap.

"The prosecution has the option to seek the death penalty, as your possession of the necklace adds robbery to the charges and murder for profit as a special circumstance. I need you to help me understand what happened."

Still Sean didn't react. He looked past the two women and stared at the wall.

Maren opened the topic gently. "I know Tamara has a child."

Sean leapt so suddenly from his chair that it fell backward against the wall with a thud. He spun in a circle, then crashed both cuffed fists down on the metal table. "You're crazy!" he bellowed.

A guard was in the room within seconds, followed by another. It was difficult for the two to restrain Sean as he thrashed in all directions, but they finally managed by getting on either side, each grabbing one arm tightly so that he was pinned between them. A third guard ushered Maren and Lana out.

CHAPTER 25

Not what Maren had expected. Although she had to ask herself what was the range of reactions Sean might have had to hearing Maren knew Tamara had a child. Or hearing Tamara had a child, period. Maybe even that was news to Sean. Maybe it was Sean's child. Or that other guy's child, the one Sean beat up.

Maren wondered whether it would have helped if she had asked those questions of herself first, before blurting out to Sean what she knew. Or what she thought she knew.

She decided her new mantra would be "I might be wrong, I might be wrong." Like the Little Engine That Could from the childhood story saying "I think I can, I think I can." Only she would say it backward—sort of. Maybe it would help her get to the truth if she could remain open to the possibility that some of her hunches might be dead ends.

Maren tried to think all this through as she rushed to drop off papers on the cell phone bill at Senator Rickman's capitol office, arriving just as Hannah Smart, Rickman's receptionist, was leaving. It occurred then to Maren that maybe Hannah could fill in some gaps about Sean's history, since the young woman worked with Sean and, more than that, seemed about as keyed into capitol gossip as anyone around. So Maren asked if Hannah wanted to sit down over a drink at the end of a long day, get to know each other a bit better.

Hannah responded that she had a lot of work that evening— no time to go out for a drink—but agreed to go downstairs on site to the cafeteria for something quick.

"Does he seem okay? I mean, it has to be so hard." Hannah's high-pitched voice carried in the senate basement cafeteria—the large, hollow space had brick walls and a high, beamed ceiling. "How does he look?"

The salad bar, grill, and refrigerated drink case in the cafeteria were modern—stainless steel and glass. But the seating area was populated by what looked like multiple cast-off dining-room sets. Mismatched wooden chairs with curved backs huddled around scratched, worn tables. If there was fraud and abuse in California's government, the misappropriated funds weren't being spent on a luxurious furniture budget.

The two women had their pick of seats. It was a little after six and the cafeteria was nearly empty. Not surprising, since legislators were en route to their home districts to see family and constituents over the weekend, and most staff were already at one of the many capitol happy hours, decompressing.

They chose a table near the wall. Hannah sipped a bottled water, then began rearranging the items on her fruit plate by color. "Sean couldn't have done it." Red grapes and strawberries on one side, cantaloupe and orange slices on the other. "You don't think so, do you?"

Maren generally felt young people didn't get the respect they deserved. In another era teens and twenty-somethings full of energy and drive would be the rulers, while she and her peers would be dead at forty from illness or childbirth. But Hannah, with soft features that were almost a blur, gave off nothing to suggest she might be capable of building a civilization or sustaining it.

"Of course not," Maren said. "I'm certain Sean will be exonerated." She took a bite of her chocolate-chip muffin, then kept her tone casual. "I heard there was a fight a few years ago, a young man Tamara dated after Sean?"

"Oh, it was awful!" Hannah said, although she appeared to relish the memory. "Sean and Tamara had been talking at least six months."

Maren had learned from Polly's fourteen-year-old son, Jake, that "talking" was a modern-day euphemism for "seeing one another." Meaning the two people were romantically involved.

"It was sad when Tamara dropped Sean. They were so cute together," Hannah said, tightening the band on her thin ponytail. "But there was this other guy. He worked in the capitol gardens, on the landscaping crew. He definitely had that bad boy thing going. Shaggy dark hair, buff, always in a blue work shirt rolled up to show tattoos, jeans, heavy boots." Hannah's eyes got a little dreamy as she recalled the man's description.

"Do you know his name?"

"Bobby. No, Billy. His last name was Italian. Machiavelli, I think." Hannah finished her water but her fruit was untouched. She eyed Maren's muffin.

Machiavelli?

"Would you like a bite?" Maren said, breaking off a piece.

Hannah accepted the offering but didn't eat it, placing it instead on her fruit plate. It didn't work with either color scheme, so she set it in the middle. "Sean called in sick and word got around that he had punched that guy. Someone had seen Billy in the rose garden pruning, with a black eye. But my girlfriend Jill knew Sean's roommate Sarah, and Sarah said Sean was really the worse off of the two. He had bruised ribs, his arm was in a sling, and his face was swollen. He didn't come back to the office for ten days."

"How long were Billy and Tamara together?"

Hannah moved the muffin piece over with the grapes and strawberries, then back to the middle of the plate. She seemed to have only a designer's visual and spatial relationship with her food. "That was the weird part." Hannah's small eyes widened. "First Billy disappeared. Then Tamara and Sean started talking again. Well, it seemed like it. She was up in our office a lot."

"What do you mean disappeared?"

"Disappeared—you know, not there anymore."

Maren nodded, although she had been hoping for more detail, not the textbook definition of the word.

"About a month later, maybe less, Sean and Tamara both went into Senator Rickman's office. They closed the door, and no one came in or out for over an hour." She lifted the muffin piece—it almost made it to her mouth—then put it back down. "When

Tamara came out I could tell she'd been crying. Sean looked angry. I'd never seen him like that."

Maren's phone buzzed; it was set on vibrate. Caller ID showed it was Alec Joben. Virtual bells rang in Maren's head—*so he's not done with me!*—although she couldn't tell whether her brain was trying to signal alarm or celebration. But she hit ignore and tucked it back in her satchel.

"Oh my gosh, it's late," Hannah said, checking her own phone. "I've got to catch the bus."

"When was that, the meeting in Rickman's office?"

"What? Oh, spring. We had policy hearings. Maybe March?"

Maren wished she had her car so she could offer Hannah a ride and continue talking. "Did you ever find out what the conversation in Senator Rickman's office was about?"

The two women carried their dishes to the drop-off station, Hannah's still full. "A few weeks later Tamara left the governor's office to do a six-month internship up in Flax, something at the church up there. I guess it was that. It must have been a great career opportunity for Tamara to leave her fellows assignment with Governor Caries just like that. It all happened so fast."

* * *

Maren tilted the rearview mirror of the Beetle, rearranging her dark curls before getting out. Three women in business suits emerged from a nearby green Camry. Maren was glad she'd changed into jeans, a plain black sweatshirt, and her tennis shoes in a capitol restroom before making the drive.

Dos Arboles, an unimpressive small town of strip malls and inexpensive housing fifteen miles north of Sacramento, was home to a newly built indoor shooting range. "Shoot the Lights Out!" was freshly painted in red script above the doors on the front of the large warehouse-style building.

When Alec Joben called to suggest that instead of a drink, Maren meet him here so he could give her a few pointers on how to handle a gun, her unspoken response was that he'd made a one-way trip to crazy town. In fact, if anyone had asked her New Year's Eve what she absolutely was not going to do in the coming year, shooting a gun would have been high on that list. Maren had never held a gun, had no interest in guns, and her gut told her she was safer without one. Beyond that, her employer, Ecobabe, had carried bills to restrict and regulate gun ownership in California, arguing they were a public health threat to children and teens based on both intentional and accidental injury and death statistics. Even before the federal government considered reinstating a national ban on assault weapons in the wake of several tragic, high-profile mass shootings, Ecobabe had joined other nonprofit advocates in persuading California to pass the strictest gun statutes in the country.

Maren didn't want to admit to herself that a chance to be alone with Alec Joben might outweigh all that. She'd managed to limit communication with Garrick to e-mails and a phone call, and he hadn't raised his marriage proposal. But she knew it was likely his offer had an expiration date. She'd put him off for any in-person meetings, even if they were supposed to be in "the friend phase." Meanwhile, her contact with Alec had been so limited, truly in the angst-without-benefits category, that she had decided it was time to figure it out, to put up or shut up. Or maybe to put out or shut up; she would have to see how things developed, and possibly check with the ethics commission about this whole lobbyist-dating-legislator thing.

Maren also had to acknowledge that the attack at the Saniplaz facility had left her open to considering options for self-defense. Anyway, trying out a weapon at a recreational target range, she reasoned, was still a far cry from owning a gun or keeping one in her home.

Maren heard the low, even hum of Alec's blue Ranger before she saw the truck round the turn on the frontage road. He left a few spaces between it and her Beetle as he pulled in.

Joben stepped down from the large cab easily, although Maren recalled from the day they pulled Liza Booth-Henry's children out of the water that the distance from the raised truck seat to the ground was considerable, requiring her to jump.

The senator was dressed in his daily Sacramento attire—a dark suit, white shirt, and red tie. In contrast he carried a small, khaki duffle, clean, but worn and frayed. It looked like it might have seen combat. She wondered if that was where he kept his Glock and bowie knife.

"Any trouble finding it?" he asked as he set the bag down to take off his jacket and expertly loosen and pull off his tie, folding both neatly on the front seat of the truck before locking up.

Maren had no natural sense of direction and considered GPS one of the great inventions of the modern era. "I used my phone," she said, tugging at her sweatshirt and holding on to the hem, unsure what to do with her hands. She felt the familiar warmth that flushed her cheeks whenever she stood near Alec, and took a step back.

"Ready?" he asked, smiling. When she said nothing he turned toward the building, waiting for her to take the first step. She reminded herself that this didn't have to be difficult. Maybe it could even be fun if she could get out of her own way.

Two heavy glass doors opened into a bland entry space painted white and peppered with signs. A poster proclaiming *First-time Shooters Welcome* featured an image of a woman similar in age and appearance to Maren—evidently, she was one of the new range's target demographics. The one next to that heralded the venue as *Family Friendly!* with an image of a smiling couple and their teenage son and daughter, each holding a gun against a background of orange and gold foliage. There were also schedules of classes in gun safety and self-defense, each boasting a curriculum approved by the National Rifle Association.

Alec gestured toward the men's room down a short hall to the left. "I'm going to change. Why don't you have them start setting you up with a rental and I'll be right there?"

Inside a second set of doors was a seating area with a new-looking green-and-brown plaid sofa, several large chairs, and a coffee table. It was similar to what might be found in a modest hotel lobby, except for the *Gun Digest* and *Gun and Garden* reading options. And a faint smell of gunpowder that persisted despite a heavy-duty ventilation system, made evident by a loud whirring sound and measurable indoor breeze. Maren knew from her environmental studies that breathing lead residue over time could be deadly, so she assumed the cooling system was a legal requirement. Only one of many rules a place like this would need to comply with before opening.

Counters and racks crowded with guns, ammunition, and shooting paraphernalia lined both sidewalls. But Maren's attention was locked straight ahead, where behind a large, bulletproof glass pane were twelve shooting bays separated by khaki-colored, numbered metal partitions. Each bay appeared able to hold two or at most three shooters. She could see individual targets set at varying distances between fifteen to thirty feet from where the shooter would stand. Only a few were occupied. Either the range was too new to have built up much clientele, or more likely four p.m. on a weekday wasn't their rush hour.

A fit young man wearing a red polo shirt with *Shoot the Lights Out* embroidered above the pocket came out from behind the counter. He had neatly combed, short brown hair and wire-rimmed glasses, and looked like he would be more at home working in a library than a gun store. An older man wearing the same model shirt with the name *Hank* embroidered over his pocket stood near the register jotting numbers down on a notepad. There was a strong resemblance between the two and Maren wondered if it was a family business.

"I'm Kirk," the younger employee said in an upbeat, professional manner, offering his hand to her to shake. "Welcome to Shoot the Lights Out. What can I help you with?"

Maren remembered her assignment, even though she felt strange saying it. "I'd like to rent a handgun."

Kirk frowned, not the reaction she expected.

"I'm sorry." He gestured to one of the many signs on the wall behind the older man. The range seemed to communicate primarily in writing, undoubtedly another legal requirement.

No Rentals to Solo Shooters. No Exceptions.

Upon seeing it, Maren recalled news coverage of an incident in which a depressed man in his sixties, experiencing financial trouble, decided to rent a gun at a shooting range and used it to commit suicide. In contrast to someone who needed a rental, gun owners could shoot themselves in the privacy of their own homes, using their own weapons. That perceived distinction led regulators to ban renting a firearm to someone on their own, despite permitting a lone gunman to shoot without a chaperone, so long as they brought their own weapon.

"I'm not alone," Maren said. "My friend is just changing; he should be out in a minute."

"No problem; if you'd like to take a seat over there, I can help you when he comes out."

Maren took a seat in the waiting area and idly leafed through a few magazines. It was astonishing and sobering to glimpse into the gun culture, to see the variety of guns a person could legally buy.

When Alec reappeared he was in jeans and a grey T-shirt. Maren was reminded of his image in soaking wet clothes after the rescue—the size and tone of his arms and chest made obvious then and now that he'd not given up weight training when he left the Marines. She wondered how many hours a day he must spend in the gym.

Kirk was busy with another couple that had just come in. He waved to Maren when he saw Alec, then held up one finger in a "be with you in a minute" gesture.

"So. A lobbyist," Alec said, smiling as he sat down next to her on the couch. "What made you choose that?"

"It's a part of what I do. It's a small company. I wear quite a few professional hats, and lobbying is one of them."

Joben's phone buzzed. He extracted it from a pocket of his jeans and began reading a text. Completely absorbed, he seemed to have forgotten Maren was there until he had exchanged several texts and then put the phone away.

"Sorry," he said. "Where were we? Oh yes, lots of hats." He smiled again.

Behind the counter Kirk seemed to be having trouble finding the couple what they wanted. He called Hank over. This might take some time.

"How about you?" Maren asked Alec. "What drew you to public service?"

His phone buzzed again. "Sorry," he said, before taking it out and checking the message. "Excuse me." He got up and walked a few steps away, speaking in quiet tones before returning.

"My ex-wife," Joben said. "She always did have the worst timing. My boys are with me this weekend, although she may find some way to screw that up." He frowned, shaking his head.

"Boys. How old?" She tried to process him as a father.

"Eighteen months. Each. They're twins."

Eighteen months? How long could he have been divorced?

But now at least it made sense to Maren that Alec, nonplussed, had known how to hold the wriggling, crying two-year-old Zoey at the scene of the accident. "Do they live nearby?"

"Yes, Auburn. My wife—ex-wife—has family there. She never could cut the cord and grow up. A daddy's girl, you know. Daddy this, Daddy that." He mimicked a woman's high-pitched tone.

Before Maren could think of what to say to that, since *No, I don't know, my father abandoned me* seemed a little harsh, Kirk approached.

"I apologize that you had to wait. Please, come with me." Kirk led them back toward the counter, taking up his post behind it. "Do you know what you would like to shoot today?"

Maren raised her eyebrows. "I assumed we would be shooting targets."

Kirk laughed. "Sure, I get it! No, I mean what caliber, what make of firearm?"

"Can we see the .38 special and the magnum .357?" Alec said.

Kirk unlocked the case and removed the chosen guns.

Alec picked each one up in turn and examined it with what appeared to be an expert's eye.

CHAPTER 26

The two women sat comfortably, sipping their tea. Maren put her cup down and lifted her hair off the back of her neck so she could get to the clasp. It took her a few tries before she was able to unhook the necklace and set it on the table in front of her. Next to it were two small keys, each with a hole in the top, enabling her to slide them easily onto the chain where her mother's wedding ring used to sit. Sal, still with Noel in San Jose, hadn't returned it yet.

Polly leaned back in the wooden chair and eyed the two metal boxes sitting on the pine table in front of Maren's fireplace. One was coated black steel, rectangular and flat, only a few inches in height. The other was shiny aluminum, shaped like an old-fashioned lunchbox with a handle. Each had a lock on top matching the keys Maren now wore on her neck.

"So if I have this right, love," Polly began as she reached for a whole-wheat scone and broke it in half, "You're asleep. An intruder breaks in. All you have to do is unclasp your necklace, take it off, remove the two keys from the chain, go to the top shelf of your closet, take down the two boxes, fit the right key into the gun box, take out the gun, fit the other key into the ammo box, take out the ammo, load the gun, and you're ready to go." She pursed her lips together to keep from laughing.

"Well, yes." Maren said, frowning. "But there's Camper. He would bark; that would give me a warning and some time. Besides, I don't think I would ever actually load the gun. I would just use it to scare someone away."

"Hmmm," Polly said, now more concerned than amused. "I thought this Alec bloke taught you how to shoot—wasn't that the purpose, the last resort if the bad guy had a gun? It doesn't seem to me an unloaded gun is anything but a distraction. When you could be locking the bedroom door and calling 911 you'll be fiddling with all these bloody boxes and keys."

Maren looked down; her cheeks began to color slightly and she toyed with her tea bag, swirling it in circles in the mug.

"How did the lesson go? You never said," Polly asked. "You can't shoot the blasted thing, can you?"

Maren looked up, eyes wide in protest, but quickly gave up the charade. She smiled, then started laughing and couldn't stop. "No," she said when she could finally catch her breath. "Not at all! I never even came close to the target. The gun jumps back when you shoot, it doesn't hold still."

Polly laughed, too. "All these years in cowgirl boots and you can't handle a six-shooter?" She picked up the teacups and headed for the kitchen. "Well, that's for the best, then. Why have one at all?"

"It's rented. I hate to fail so miserably at something. Even something I don't really value. Alec still thinks I can learn. I can only legally keep the gun for three days before I have to go back to the range and take a Handgun Safety Certificate test." She reached into her satchel hanging over the back of her chair and pulled out a thirty-page booklet, dropping it heavily on the table. "This is the study guide—I'll take the written test and show I can load and unload a firearm safely; then I can purchase or rent my own long term or borrow Alec's for up to a month."

Polly knew better than to argue with her friend when studying and a test were involved. A lifelong student, Maren could no more walk away from that challenge than she could stop breathing—it was part of who she was.

"We better get going," Maren said as she stuffed the manual back in her bag and picked up the two gun boxes to store them. "It will take us three or four hours at least, and that's if we don't run into traffic."

Polly had made clear to Maren that one night midweek in the tiny town of Flax near the Oregon border was not at all what she had in mind when she had suggested a getaway to Maren. But Maren hadn't been able to find anything online about the church project Tamara was involved in up there or why it had caused Tamara to leave the capitol for six months. Maren thought understanding that gap in time might lead to the murderer—and going in person seemed to her to be the only way to find out. Plus, Rickman's cell phone bill was in some trouble—not enough Republican votes—and a key legislator was from Flax. The councilman who had sponsored Tamara's internship might be able to help with that. Polly chided her about work before play, but in the end acquiesced when Maren pointed out that getting out of Sacramento had to be good, wherever they went.

* * *

The contrast between man-made contributions to the landscape—mostly gas stations and dated motels—and the majestic beauty of snowcapped Mt. Shasta, reaching ten thousand feet toward the heavens, couldn't have been greater. Polly and Maren breathed in the brisk mountain air. Maren wished her jacket were long enough to warm her legs or that she'd worn pants instead of her usual calf-length cotton skirt. At least her red boots and thick socks kept her feet warm.

Once a thriving lumber mill town, Flax was now a modest vacation spot for those who wished to hike, fish for trout in the nearby creeks, or take a final break en route to Oregon. The northernmost state line of California was less than an hour away.

Maren rechecked the address. "Councilman Breed's office is up the hill a block."

Polly's office records indicated Vance Breed was the councilman who supervised Tamara while she was in Flax. Young Fellows had to be placed with an elected official to receive their stipend, so Tamara did her church outreach work based in Breed's office, tagged as community service for which he got some credit.

Polly was well prepared for the mountain weather in heavy, fitted black leggings, a bright blue turtleneck with a black ski jacket over it, and matching blue-and-black striped gloves. Only her many ear piercings and spiky hair kept her from looking like a typical Flax tourist. They left Maren's Beetle behind and headed up the sidewalk along the wide street, the mountain still in view.

"You know this is close to where the Lemurians live," Polly said, increasing her pace. "Under the mountain, in a series of tunnels."

Maren pictured some variant of fuzzy animal. A mole or meerkat.

"They're said to appear in white robes at midnight," Polly added.

White robes?

Before Maren could ask (and she wasn't sure she wanted to know) she saw number 840 on the right, a plain two-story office building with a sloping, shingled roof. A real estate agent's office occupied the bottom floor. Three small suites above were accessible only by a weathered exterior staircase.

Maren started up the stairs. Polly followed, still eyeing the majestic peak that dominated the skyline, weighing the odds of subterrestrial beings. "The continent of Lemuria sank under the Pacific Ocean, but some of the citizens—the Lemurians—escaped and made it to Mt. Shasta."

"All I know about Mt. Shasta is that it's a volcano," Maren said. "It erupts every six hundred years. It's been two hundred years since the last time, so I think we're safe."

Maren was grateful for the metal banister guarding the drop along the walkway outside the second-floor offices. A small engraved sign by the door of Suite B indicated she and Polly were in the right place: *Office of Councilman Vance L. Breed.*

Inside, a young woman sat at a faux wood desk in front of a circa 1990 computer. Her face was blotchy and tired. She wore a red headband and a green-and-red plaid sweater that accentuated her uneven complexion and made her look like she'd missed the calendar's steady march from the Christmas holidays into spring. Easy to do in a village hamlet surrounded by pine trees.

One wall of the small space was host to three beige metal cabinets and a folding table that held a coffeepot, some magazines, and brochures. There were two deep, faded armchairs across from it. Together, they apparently constituted Breed's version of a welcome wagon.

Behind the receptionist's desk was a solid interior door bearing the nameplate *Councilman Vance L. Breed*. Maren felt there could be no doubt about who occupied the internal office, but she also knew that most politicians rarely tired of seeing their name and title in print.

"We have a one o'clock appointment with Councilman Breed," Maren said, approaching the desk. It was 12:55 p.m.

"He's at lunch." The young woman blew her nose before continuing. "I'm sorry, I can't seem to beat this cold." She tossed the tissue in the wastebasket under her desk and pulled out another one. "You can have a seat and…"

Just then the exterior door from the walkway opened and a small man entered carrying a backpack, one beige pant leg hooked up with a strap (a look favored only by bike riders), revealing a surprisingly purple sock. What was left of the sparse hair on his head was nearly hidden under a cap that said "Flax Underwriters." A wrinkled beige suit coat did little to dignify the cheap-looking blue dress shirt he had underneath.

When he saw his guests Councilman Vance smiled broadly and extended his hand. "Ms. Kane? I was expecting you. Pleased to meet you." Evidently, Maren's slightly more formal wear made her distinguishable as the leader of her delegation of two. "And this is...?" He turned to Polly, looking down at her, apparently happy to see someone shorter than he was for a change.

"Polly Grey," she said.

"English, are you? I love the English." Breed turned to his assistant, his voice louder than necessary: "Did you get coffee? Grace, did you offer them coffee? Let's head inside, I keep the heater in there—Grace doesn't like it too warm." He crossed the few feet to his office and opened the door. An executive-size desk covered in Flax-themed mugs, pencil holders, and knick-knacks nearly consumed the floor space. He could have opened a wing of the local gift shop. Plaques and framed certificates congratulating the councilman on everything from presiding as the grand marshal at the Flax Independence Day festivities to coaching a local Little League team filled the walls.

"Sit, sit!" he said with the joviality of Santa Claus, in keeping with the winter wonderland theme the receptionist had set, despite the fact that he was sized more appropriately for an elf. He gestured to two chairs pressed into a corner. "Now, how can I help you? You're up from Sacramento—I gather there's legislation you wanted to speak to me about?" He took Maren's offered business card. "Ecobabe, eh? That's a good one!" He chuckled heartily.

Maren wasn't sure what the joke was, but she smiled. "Yes, SB 770. It would prohibit drivers from using cell phones of any kind, including hands-free. I understand you had an unfortunate accident here last year where a tourist was on their hands-free phone and hit a young man on a bicycle."

"Little Jimmy MacVale. He was okay, but gave us all quite a scare. Bad concussion. Missed a few weeks of school. His mama was beside herself." Breed had a concerned expression, mouth down, brows furrowed. Maren thought it looked camera ready for the press.

"I'm very happy to hear he's okay," Maren said. "But others have not been so fortunate. I know you have a lot of visitor traffic here, unfamiliar with the roads. Senator Rorie Rickman is the author of the bill, and she thought you might be able to help with your district's senate and assembly votes." While she spoke, Maren extracted a briefing packet on SB 770 from her satchel and handed it to Breed. "In particular, I understand you might be close to Senator Schmoley. It would be wonderful if you could help him to understand the need for this bill."

"Well, I don't know." He was scanning the papers. "Seems to me talking to my wife on a phone hands-free in the car while I'm driving wouldn't be any different than talking to my wife in the passenger seat. Are you Democrats planning to outlaw that, too?" He grinned—"gotcha, didn't I?" look on his face.

Maren was glad he'd asked. Despite the way he did it, it was a reasonable question many people had. "When your wife's in the car with you, she can see, at the same time you do, a truck veering out of its lane about to hit you. She'll stop speaking while you quickly make a critical decision as to what to do, decide whether to brake or accelerate out of the way. But if she's on the phone, she'll have no idea what's happening on the roadway and may distract you by continuing to speak, even demanding your attention if you don't answer."

"Hmm, well, if you say so." The councilman seemed to be thinking it over.

"There's also research that shows that the incidence of accidents driving hands-free and holding the phone is the same—no benefit from setting the phone down if you're still talking on it. But no phone conversations at all while driving, then we see an improvement." Maren didn't want to push the point further than that. "I believe you know Senator Rickman?" she said.

He looked up, smiled, and gave a booming response twice as loud as Maren's question. "Oh yes, the senator, lovely woman!"

Maren knew nothing warmed a small-town politician's heart more than connection to a higher-up elected official, especially one who was rumored to be running for governor the next year. Even if Senator Rickman was, from Breed's viewpoint, in the wrong party.

"The senator speaks highly of you."

The councilman positively beamed.

"She mentioned you took on one of her young colleagues, a legislative aide, to do an internship here. Something about outreach for health care services to the uninsured through one of the local churches. It was a few years back."

Councilman Breed's smile disappeared. His mouth closed up, suddenly tight. He took off his cap and smoothed his thinning hair, his eyes scanning his desk, no longer looking at Maren. No more spirit of Santa, not even an elf. Breed picked up a mug, set it down, then lifted a jar of paper clips, examining it.

"Tamara Barnes." Maren added.

Breed dropped the paper clip jar with a clatter. He focused on retrieving them one at a time, head down as he spoke. "Hmm. No. I don't think so."

"Tammy, you say?" Now he shook his head vigorously. "No."

Maren glanced at Polly questioningly. Could her friend have gotten the wrong file? True, it was a while ago, but it wasn't like Breed had twenty employees and Tamara would be hard to pick out of the crowd.

"That's odd," Polly said. She was giving Breed one of her patented, laser-like stares. "I completed the paperwork personally to place Tamara here."

Breed continued to shake his head "no" and avoid eye contact with both women.

There was something decidedly not right, Maren thought. Why the sudden intense discomfort? What would it matter to Breed if they had the name or the intern's placement wrong?

Maren concluded he must be lying—she saw no other explanation for his body language and his inability to speak. She thought for a moment, then decided to give Breed a way out, even if it was through enough rope to hang himself.

"There must so many people in and out of your office," Maren said. "Perhaps a description would help?"

Breed still didn't look up.

"She's short, heavyset, with black hair," Maren said

"Thick glasses," Polly added, clearly understanding Maren's tactic and joining in. "A little homely, to be sure, pity that. But a hard worker..."

Maren thought Polly might have overdone it.

Councilman Vance L. Breed swallowed hard. He looked at the two expectant women across from him. He saw no malice in their expressions, just friendly curiosity.

"Yes. Of course," he finally agreed. "That was a busy time for me, I wasn't in the office much. Out helping constituents. But, of course. I remember her now." A bit of his bluster returned. "Tamara Barnes. Yes, of course!"

Polly smiled at Maren.

Maren smiled at Polly.

The councilman smiled at them both.

"Now, back to this bill," he said. "I'm not sure our folks up here will go for that kind of government interference. And since Jimmy MacVale is okay..."

Polly and Maren walked back to Maren's car in silence. It wasn't until they were inside Maren's car and underway that they agreed Vance Breed's willingness to embrace the existence of a short, heavy, black-haired Tamara Barnes could only mean one thing. Clearly, the esteemed councilman had never met the real Tamara at all.

CHAPTER 27

Maren's GPS failed to take into account preparations on the main street of Flax for the evening's farmers' market, which blocked access to several side streets, one of which was the direct route to the Ridgeway Bed and Breakfast where Polly and Maren had reserved a room for the night.

Polly suggested they take the nearest right turn open to them, then try right again to get around the outdoor market's street closures.

"Ridgeway Lane—there it is." Polly pointed just as Maren passed it. There was no traffic on the narrow tree-lined residential street, so Maren opted for slowly backing up instead of trying an illegal U-turn. Looking over her shoulder for clearance she suddenly hit the brake, stopped reversing, and pulled up to park along the curb.

"Come on," Maren said, grabbing her satchel from the back-seat. She looked both ways, saw no approaching cars, and crossed the street.

"This isn't our..." Polly started to protest, but Maren was already standing in front of a large, pale blue Victorian-style home that dominated the block, set back from the street. A winding walkway of paving stones led from the road to the front door. On either side were expanses of deep green lawn—no need for sprinklers in this part of the state. Two tall pine trees bordered the home.

But what had caught Maren's attention was not the architecture or the landscaping. It was the three young pregnant women in their teens, or at most early twenties, bundled up at a table on the front lawn with warming mugs in front of them and two others nearby, also pregnant, entertaining a toddler. Five pregnant young—very young—women.

There it was, in front of her. The reason Tamara Barnes might have needed six months away from prying eyes at the capitol. Maren smiled at the young women as she passed them on a beeline to the entrance to the house, Polly hurrying to catch up.

"Yes? May I help you ladies?"

The woman who answered the door was eighty if she was a day, and Maren wouldn't have been surprised to find she was in her nineties. Her dress was appropriate for the Victorian-era home—deep blue satin with a black lace collar and heavy black belt. Its only nod to modernity was the length, ending just below her knees rather than reaching the floor. The woman's silver-grey hair was neatly coiffed, swept back from her forehead above whisper-pale blue eyes.

"We're here to inquire about a former resident. We have a friend, a colleague who stayed at..." Maren glanced at the inconspicuous brass nameplate to the right of the door. "Here, at the Farmer Home for Catholic Women. About four years ago. We were hoping we could speak with you about her."

The sound of the toddler's giggles could be heard across the lawn as one of the women showed the child how to play patty-cake with his small mittened hands.

"I can't share information about our residents." The woman looked from Maren to Polly, her eyes narrowing, her paper-thin brow creasing in thought. Her mouth remained soft, sympathetic. "It's our policy."

"We understand," Polly said, "but these are special circumstances."

"They always are, dear." The woman smiled slightly as she moved to close the open door.

"Our friend, Tamara Barnes, has died," Maren said. "She was murdered."

The woman pressed one palm flat on her chest, her knees wavered, and her mouth dropped open. Confirmation that she had known Tamara, yes, but Maren was afraid she might also have given her a heart attack. Maren moved quickly, putting her arm around the woman's tiny waist to support her as she helped her to a faded loveseat inside the entry hall, coats and umbrellas hanging on hooks beside it.

The woman took several long, deep breaths, waving Maren and Polly off with her hands. "I'm all right. Please, find Gena."

Polly headed down the hall, glancing into doorways as she called for Gena. She returned with a young woman in jeans and a clean blue T-shirt wiping her hands on a dish towel. When

Gena saw the older woman she rushed to her side, took both her hands in hers, and started to speak, but was interrupted.

"I'm quite all right, Gena. Please, bring us tea in the parlor."

"Yes, Mrs. Farmer."

Of course, there's a parlor, Maren thought, the crisis apparently over.

Polly, Maren, and Mrs. Farmer walked slowly to a side room with elegant red-striped wallpaper, several high-backed chairs, and a piano with a padded bench. Gena stayed with them, a step behind, until she had settled Mrs. Farmer comfortably in an armchair and covered her legs with a soft afghan throw. She glared at Maren and Polly as she left, likely accurately attributing blame for the incident to them.

Mrs. Farmer's eyes filled with tears. "Tamara. Such a lovely girl. And her baby, so beautiful. A gift from God, even if it was in the most awful of circumstances." She sat up straighter. "Tamara was with us six months, you know. We all loved her."

Maren didn't like the characterization of a baby born out of wedlock as awful circumstances, but she acknowledged that Mrs. Farmer had a right to that opinion. In any case, the woman seemed intent on doing good rather than judging people for it.

"She'd gone through so much already." Mrs. Farmer hugged herself. "Violence must have followed her like a dark cloud." She shook her head. "I thought it was behind her. I thought she said he had left." Mrs. Farmer wrung her hands, turning a small diamond wedding ring on her finger around and around as she spoke. Her voice was tremulous, barely audible. "When a man does that to a girl...when he takes her like that. Without her consent, leaving her with child. Who knows what else he might do to her?" She shivered. "What he might do to anyone?"

* * *

Maren was quiet as she and Polly drove the short distance to the Ridgeway Bed and Breakfast, this time with no unscheduled stops. There were still missing pieces, to be sure, but some things had become clear. Tamara left Sacramento because she was pregnant—she came to Mrs. Farmer's to have the baby. *To have Bethany.* The resemblance, the hair color, Tamara's locket with the initials BC. It seemed altogether too much to be a coincidence now.

But why did Tamara choose Flax? That appeared to have been engineered by Senator Rickman. And how on earth did Bethany end up with Sal Castro as her adoptive mother? She refused to believe Noel could have known about the connection since she was certain if he did, he wouldn't have hidden it from her, at least not after Tamara had been murdered.

That night, while Polly slept in the four-poster bed, Maren sat at the small writing desk in a corner of her room, laptop open. Very little on the Farmer Home. Notice of a few fund-raisers. Registered publicly as a nonprofit. Then Maren realized there was one place she might be able to get more information—one person she could ask.

* * *

"The senator will stop back here before she leaves for the day. You sure you wouldn't like coffee?" Hannah's high-pitched voice filled the small waiting area of Rorie Rickman's office suite. Now that Hannah and Maren had eaten together (or more accurately, Maren had eaten and Hannah had looked at the food), Hannah treated Maren with something approximating warmth, although the young woman couldn't quite get all the way there.

"No thanks, Hannah."

Just then Senator Rickman arrived wearing a white doctor's coat, a stethoscope around her neck and a briefcase in one hand, returning from her afternoon volunteering in a low-income children's clinic in West Sacramento.

Rickman's eyebrows rose when she saw Maren. They didn't have an appointment. But she inclined her head toward her inner office as she kept walking, which Maren took as an invitation.

Removing her medical coat and reaching for a tailored red blazer on the back of her chair, Rickman slipped her arms into it as she spoke. "What is it? Not problems on the bill, I hope?"

"No." Maren shifted uneasily from one foot to the other. "I was wondering if you might help me understand something about Tamara. Tamara Barnes."

The senator frowned. "I can try." She gestured to Maren to sit in one of the plush chairs across from the desk as she came around to sit in the other.

"I went to Flax yesterday. To meet with Councilman Vance Breed. I thought he might be able to help us get Senator Schmoley's vote."

Rickman leaned back in her chair and folded her hands on her lap.

"My friend Polly Grey went with me. We decided to make a brief getaway of the drive, to stay overnight." Maren felt herself sweating under her silk jacket, her shoulders tensing. "Polly runs the fellows program. She asked the councilman for feed-back regarding Tamara's internship in his office."

"I see," Rickman said. She stood and walked to the large window in her office. The early evening Sacramento sky was cloudless, the blue deepening as the sun set.

In a posture Maren did not remember seeing her in before, the senator wrapped her arms tightly around herself. She continued to look out the window away from Maren as she spoke. "And you found that Tamara never actually worked there." Rickman's tone was even.

"Yes."

Maren knew there was no point now in being anything other than transparent about what she knew. "After that I went to Mrs. Farmer's place. Her home for Catholic girls. I know about the baby. About Tamara's stay there."

Rickman sighed. She relaxed her arms and turned back toward Maren. "So you didn't really go up to Flax to get Schmoley's vote on the cell phone bill?"

"No."

"Good." When she turned back to face Maren, Rickman had the smallest of smiles on her face. "I was wondering what kind of crazy fool lobbyist I was working with who wouldn't know to pick up the phone instead of driving across the state for one vote." She returned to the chair next to Maren and sat down. "It sounds to me like you know everything there is to know."

Maren had trouble getting the question out.

"The father?"

"I don't believe that's for me to disclose." Rickman paused. "I'm not saying I know, but if I did I wouldn't tell you."

She heard the senator's refusal to answer, but couldn't stop herself. "Is it Sean?"

Rickman's features became hard, cold, her mouth set. She appeared to be appraising Maren carefully before she spoke again. "Tamara's...situation...there is nothing more personal. To carry a child, to give it away at birth. This may be the hardest decision a young woman can make."

Maren nodded.

Rickman stood and picked up her briefcase. "I know because I was in that situation myself."

Maren felt her jaw drop, then closed it quickly.

"I was very young and involved with an older man, a prominent politician." Rickman moved toward the door. "I didn't tell him about the baby." She took a deep breath. "I stayed at Wilma's—Mrs. Farmer's home. Later, many years ago, one of her largest donors moved from Flax to Sacramento and joined the board of my church. Tamara attends services there, too. I mean, she attended services." Rickman shifted her briefcase to her other hand. "Our church sponsored an annual fund-raiser for the Farmer Home. Tamara worked at the fund-raiser as a volunteer, heard the speeches, knew all about the Farmer Home and its services in Flax. When she found out she was pregnant and contacted Mrs. Farmer, the first call Wilma Farmer made was to me. Everyone who stays at her home must have a character reference. Wilma is very careful about the environment for the girls—the young women—and their children."

Maren had so many questions. She tried to choose carefully among them.

"Do all of the women who stay at Mrs. Farmer's give their babies up for adoption? Some looked like they had older children."

"Every baby that is born at Mrs. Farmer's is welcomed with love. Where they live after that, who will be their family—that varies."

"How do they place the babies? The ones who don't stay with their mothers?" Maren pictured Bethany and Sal Castro, desperate to find the connection.

"There are different avenues, but most often through a network of churches affiliated with the home. A couple in one of the congregations might want a child, they attend a fund-raiser, an informal application is made."

A couple, Maren thought. *Or a single woman.* She remembered noticing the tiny gold cross that Sal wore with her work uniform the night Sal came to see Noel. *It shouldn't be hard to find from Noel whether Sal attends church,* Maren thought. *And whether that church is in the network that supports Mrs. Farmer's home.*

Rickman's voice was strained as she eyed the door. "You know that I'm considering a run for governor next year. If I do, my history will come out. You uncovered Tamara's secret. Someone will uncover mine. I told people I trusted at the time." She turned back and her eyes locked on Maren's. "Just as I'm telling you now."

Maren nodded.

"I don't know who else you may have spoken to about what happened to Tamara—the choice she made—or who you might plan to. But please think carefully before you share the secret of a woman who can no longer protect herself or her child. A child that she cared enough about to bring safely into this world."

CHAPTER 28

Marilyn heard the siren before she saw the black-and-white in her rearview mirror. She pulled over to the shoulder.

"License and registration." Officer Ernesto Landry watched the driver as she reached for her purse, which was perched in the backseat on an empty child safety seat. *Twenty, maybe twenty-two*, he figured. *Pretty.* Although the shellacked platinum hair and heavy eyeliner didn't help. *Marilyn Monroe with an edge.* The male passenger was closer to thirty, with curly dark hair and tan skin—ethnicity hard to figure. *We're all mutts*, thought Landry, who was a quarter English, a quarter Scottish, and half Portuguese.

The passenger opened the glove box slowly, like he knew not to spook a cop. Landry registered it. *Might be something to that.* But he dismissed the suspicious feeling, chiding himself. Ever since his buddy got shot on a routine traffic stop a month back,

Landry didn't view anything as innocent. Ernesto knew he'd have to move past that or he'd have another ulcer.

"Your left taillight is out. Texas plates—you here visiting?"

"We're moving here," she answered politely.

Seems sober enough. The male passenger smiled, a little too broadly.

Landry handed the driver a citation for the broken light. "Be sure to take care of this or the fine will run into some money." He looked at her Texas driver's license a second time before returning it. It matched the vehicle registration—Marilyn Lewis. But he'd put a fiver on Marilyn not being her given name.

As Officer Landry drove away, Billy stuffed the ticket in the glove box.

"Jerk!"

"Doing his job, babe," Marilyn said, smiling before pulling off the shoulder and easing back into traffic. "I can't wait to see her. Do you think she looks like you?"

Billy had only seen the kid once, when he had shown up to get money from Sal that first year. He had no idea before that visit that there was a baby and hadn't cared when he found out.

"You said she had red hair, but she could have your eyes. I don't care what she looks like. I just can't wait to hold her."

So happy, Billy thought, *and we don't even have the kid yet.*

Marilyn told Billy shortly after they met that she couldn't get pregnant. Fine with him, made it easier when they were having sex, everywhere, all the time. They hadn't slowed down, either. Marilyn seemed to like it as much as he did as long as he didn't do the rough stuff. She liked be treated like a lady. Fair enough, she'd been raised that way—ritzy Houston royalty. So

Billy went elsewhere. A few bucks did it down in the barrio. No need for her to know.

Really, the only problem with Marilyn that Billy could see was that she didn't just want sex, she wanted a baby.

Man, did she want a baby.

When Marilyn found out Billy had a kid being raised by his sister, there was no stopping her. She had gotten a second job, saved money for this move, even bought the damn car seat. And she was counting on Billy to make her dreams of motherhood happen.

It was a pain. He still wasn't sure what the big deal was with a kid, but Billy knew he had gotten lucky with Marilyn, and he wasn't going to screw it up. Much better than when he was with that uptight Catholic girl back in Sacramento.

That one had wanted it too, Billy recalled. *The prim and proper ones always do. No matter what they say, before or after.*

So he was willing to do what he needed to keep Marilyn happy. He told her his sister would be more than ready to stop single-parenting and give the kid to a proper set of parents, a dad and a mom. But he wasn't as sure about that as he made himself out to be.

Billy was high when he showed up that last time at Sal's, and she had been anxious for him to leave. Not that it was anything new. Sal hadn't wanted Billy around for a long time. Ever since he started wanting fun in his life and was willing to take some risks—and use weed and blow—to get it. Meanwhile, Sal seemed stuck in "Ms. Responsible" mode. He figured that was why Sal accepted the kid from Tilly in the first place. Out of a sense of duty. His older sis was such a straight-arrow goody-goody. If she saw now that he had changed, that he had a good woman, that he stayed sober most of the time (Marilyn didn't like him using), Sal would hand the kid over.

He remembered the tiny baby sleeping in the crib. True, Sal had made him sign some paper she wrote on the spot saying he gave up rights, something like that, he couldn't remember exactly. Then she had given him money, more than she usually did.

But she can't buy a baby, he reassured himself. Or at least he didn't think she could. *Anyway, things are different now, Sal will see that*, he told himself, still more conclusively than he felt.

It was after ten p.m. when they pulled into the lot in front of a Motel 6 in downtown Davis. The next day they planned to check out apartments and Billy would apply for temporary landscape help or construction jobs. Marilyn wouldn't work so she could get the mom thing going. She insisted on that. She had even endured a visit with her old man to rangle some extra dough. They would visit Sal, make nice, show how stable they were. Not ask for anything. He hoped Sal wouldn't take long to see what was best. As soon as they had the kid he wanted to get back to Houston. Sacramento was too law-and-order for him.

As he carted their bags from the car to the motel room Billy had a pleasant thought. *It will fall in love with Marilyn. Everyone does.* Then he corrected himself. *She. She will fall in love with Marilyn.* At least, he was pretty sure he had it right when he told Marilyn his kid was a girl.

CHAPTER 29

The squeaky wheels of gurneys rolling past, call bells ringing, and unintelligible announcements in hospital code over the loudspeaker all faded into the background as Noel concentrated on Maren's iPad.

He scrolled though icons at the bottom of the home screen until he came to an image of a globe and clicked on it to access the Internet. Once in, he could see Maren's problem. The tablet had been set up by the retailer with a drop-down list of major platforms: Google, Yahoo, AOL. He tried each one before determining that www.ecobabe.org was established through a Gmail account in Google. He figured Maren had gotten stuck because she missed that step. After that it was simple—he used her e-mail address and password to get to the administrator functions, which included a link to mail. He could view her list of sixty-two unopened messages. Maren definitely had some catching up to do. Noel would have stopped there, but something caught his eye.

Maren was terrible at visual challenges; she always had been. Even as a kid she would throw partially completed jigsaw puzzles up in the air in frustration, dodging the pieces as they fell, then moving on to something free-form—painting or clay. Noel was the opposite. He took comfort in the patterns he encountered in life, like how their mother methodically set knives, forks, plates, and spoons on the table always in the same order. So when he saw that an e-mail from the same address with the same subject line had arrived in Maren's e-mail each day at 12:01 for the past two weeks, his interest was piqued.

To: mkane@ecobabe.org
From: senrabyllit@talk.com
Re: Urgent--Investments!

It was not only a clear pattern but also an unusual one since marketing spam on autosend was typically randomly generated to avoid detection by ad blockers. Groggy from his medication, Noel fought the wave of sleep that pulled at him, the desire to set the tablet aside and look at it later. He was concerned that the messages were malicious, perhaps carrying a virus. Given the recent demise of Maren's laptop, he felt he better take a look rather than leave it to her. He might need to delete the message since opening it could activate the virus. But then again, he didn't want Maren to miss something important, in the off-chance this wasn't spam. The gears in his overactive brain whirred.

Then he saw it.

Didn't Maren say Sean called Tamara by a pet name, Tilly?
Senrabyllit@talk.com
Senrabyllit is Tilly Barnes written backward.

There were two attachments.

Noel's heart was racing.

Suddenly, a shrieking alarm went off in the hospital—it appeared to be coming from the monitor by his bed. He heard running footsteps, then shouting. Someone wrenched the tablet from his hands. Noel felt a stinging prick as the needle went in. He struggled to speak but fell silent as the powerful sedative began to do its work. He could barely make out the voices.

"Were we in time?" asked the nurse.

"His heart rate was dangerously high," Dr. Wihabe replied. "We will not be able to image the heart to view the aortic tear to see whether there is any new damage until he is stable."

"But will he be okay?"

In a gesture uncharacteristic of a busy doctor, Wihabe removed Noel's hat and gently adjusted his head on the pillow. "I do not know," Noel heard him say, the last words he could make out before he lost consciousness. "It is now between Mr. Kane and his God."

CHAPTER 30

Noel had given everyone a real scare when his heart rate escalated and his blood pressure suddenly shot up. The episode could have been fatal. Maren felt terribly guilty that tinkering with her iPad had evidently been too much for him.

Doctor Wihabe explained that they had gotten there in time and were keeping Noel heavily sedated in an induced coma-like state. The goal was to slow Noel's heartbeat for as long as it took to ease pressure on the aortic tear so it would heal. It was frightening, but the doctor assured Maren and Sal that it was a necessary step for this type of injury and would not cause Noel any permanent harm.

Sal still had vacation time that she could use to be with Noel, but it was impossible for three-and-a-half-year-old Bethany to stay day and night at the hospital. So Sal and Maren worked out a weekend visit for Bethany at Maren's.

Maren was sure now that Bethany was Tamara's daughter—
all that was missing was placing Sal at a church connected
with the Farmer Home. But Maren had taken Rorie Rickman's
warning to heart—unless Maren could find a compelling link
between Bethany and Tamara's murder to help Sean with his
case, she would be wrong to delve into a secret that Tamara
was not there to explain or defend.

Maren purchased foods Sal recommended for the visit—gold-
fish crackers, baby carrots, chicken noodle soup, peanut butter
and jelly, and whole -wheat bread. Not much different from
when Maren was little, except for whole wheat replacing the
squishy, white Wonder bread she remembered.

She heard the car door slam out front. Maren shut Camper
in the backyard for the initial greeting—she didn't know how
Bethany might feel about such a big dog, and Camper had a
tendency to go for an unaccompanied run if he got out the
front door or up the driveway on his own.

Sal unlatched Bethany from her booster seat and the little
girl climbed down. She navigated her descent particularly well,
given that she had one arm in a cast and the other clutching a
small red corduroy elephant. Meanwhile, Sal began to unload
what looked like luggage for three weeks at sea. Maren came
down the stairs in time to carry the car seat inside.

"Who is this?" Maren asked, looking at the elephant.

"Daniel," Bethany replied solemnly, hugging the battered toy
closer as she dragged a small rolling suitcase behind her using
her good arm.

"Well, hello Daniel," Maren offered, "We are happy to have
such a distinguished guest."

Bethany rewarded Maren with a smile. She showed Bethany and Sal to the tiny guest room, a converted breakfast nook off the kitchen. The room had two windows, one overlooking the drive and the other the garden out front. There was a single bed, a desk with a computer, and a small stuffed armchair. Sal started to unpack Bethany's things, but Maren offered to handle that. "It's a long drive back for you, and there will be traffic."

Sal acquiesced and knelt for the serious business of saying good-bye to her daughter. She had told Maren that Bethany was used to being left with sitters and friends since Sal worked most nights. Still, this weekend would be the longest they had been away from one another.

Bethany wrapped her arms around her mom, cast and all, kissed her, and then pushed Daniel toward Sal with the command "Kiss Daniel!"

Sal did so with appropriate reverence and then rose, turning to Maren. "Thanks again." Maren noticed Sal was still wearing the wedding ring, even away from the hospital.

"We'll be fine. We'll have a great time. Daniel will take good care of us."

Bethany frowned. "No, we will take care of Daniel. He's the baby!"

After several more hugs Maren and Bethany stood on the porch and watched Sal drive off.

Not a tear. Courageous kid, Maren thought to herself.

Maren gave Bethany a tour of the rest of the house and the backyard. Not surprisingly, Bethany was most taken by the hot tub. "Let's go in, let's go in, I want to swim!"

"It's not really for swimming," Maren told her, although she could see how to an almost-four-year-old it might look that way.

"It's a big bathtub, more for soaking. Besides, I'm betting that cast of yours isn't supposed to get wet."

Bethany looked very serious. She carefully set Daniel by her feet so that she could use her good hand to support her injured arm, holding it straight up away from her body where Maren could clearly see it.

"That is pretty true," Bethany said, "but this is not a plaster cast. This is a fiberglass cast." She said fiberglass very slowly, to be sure Maren got it, raising her eyebrows as though it were a great discovery. "And fiberglass should not get wet. But it will not fall apart like plaster if it gets a little wet." Bethany eyed the cast and turned it slightly to show top and bottom. "A little wet," she emphasized, "would be fine."

Maren nodded, suppressing a smile.

"I have special plastic bags that go over my cast for baths." She carefully guided her arm back to her side and picked up Daniel again. "And this is like a big bathtub, for soaking. It's not for swimming." Having fed Maren's own words back to her to make the case, Bethany giggled at her own cleverness making her curly red-orange hair bob and ivory skin flush.

"I see," Maren said, now smiling, too. "Let's get dinner and let our food settle a bit. I'll call your mom and make sure I understand how the bags work and that this is okay with her, and if it is, then we'll go in the water."

Bethany was hopping in place. "Mom will say yes! She'll say yes, I know it! She knows how very careful I will be!"

Maren and Bethany returned to the kitchen and set about making peanut butter and jelly sandwiches and noodle soup. Bethany explained that Daniel wanted his sandwich with the crusts cut off, so she would like hers that way, too. Maren smiled. *Some things don't change, whole-wheat bread or not.*

* * *

The lone figure was pleased to find Maren Kane's street quiet—no traffic or walkers. Getting down the driveway to the chosen spot between the garage and the neighbor's fence was easy, concealed by overgrown bougainvillea vines. But the waiting was unpleasant.

Seven thirty. Nothing. Eight p.m. Still no Maren Kane. Then there were voices.

"You dressed quickly. Are you warm enough? It's good to have our swimsuits underneath to be ready, but it will take the spa a while to heat up. While it does we can sit on the edge and count the stars."

The figure in black recognized Kane's voice.

"Isn't the bathtub that way? Where are we going? Daniel doesn't want to go down those stairs."

"The stairs lead to the garage. We have to go there to heat the water."

The target wasn't visible at the top of the stairs from around the corner of the garage, but the assailant could hear the conversation clearly and didn't like the sound of things.

A second speaker, a child. First, the trench-coat guy appears out of nowhere in the parking structure and now she's got a kid with her?

There was more talking as Kane and the child entered the garage.

"What's this for?" the girl said.

"That one turns on the bubbles. And this dial heats the water."

Pulling on a black ski mask, the hidden intruder quickly tried to weigh the ethical score generated by murdering an adult if the accompanying child was spared. And suppose the kid got in the way. Collateral damage?

There were mechanical, whooshing sounds as the gas heater engaged.

They would be out and headed back to the house any minute now.

No more time.

* * *

Upstairs Camper pushed his nose under the back door and breathed deeply. There was a bad smell—the smell of adrenaline, the raw smell of a hunter. The dog door was latched tight. He scratched at it and started barking.

Bethany grabbed on to Maren's hand at Camper's outburst and pulled Daniel closer. "Don't worry." Maren stroked the child's soft red curls. "Camper really wants to get out tonight since you're here."

Camper abandoned the immovable door and pawed the side window, finding only the mild resistance of a screen.

"Okay, honey, that's it," Maren said. "Let's go get Camper." She led Bethany out of the garage onto the driveway, the short flight of concrete stairs in sight.

Every muscle tense and coiled, the weapon firmly gripped in both hands, the attacker rounded the corner and raised the gun...

Camper leapt into the screen, forcing it out and clearing the steps in a single movement. Snarling, roaring, he hit the stranger with the full force of his weight just as the gun came up.

A quick loud pop, then another.

Maren screamed, buckling to her knees. One of her legs felt nothing, then everything at once, the pain searing. Bethany wrapped her arms around Maren's waist, still clutching Daniel.

Camper crouched low, ears back, and growled a deep warning, but the assailant chose to ignore it, pushing swiftly upright off the ground and firing again. Camper took a bullet as he lunged and bit hard on the shooter's upper arm, sending a third bullet off target and into the air.

Maren managed to stand, Bethany's arms still wrapped around her, the child's face now buried in Maren's side. Dragging her bleeding leg, Maren willed herself and her small charge up the stairs, each step like another bullet piercing the wound. They made it into the guest room. No lock on the door. But Maren's cell phone was on the desk charging. She dialed 911.

"Help us, help, someone is here. My dog needs help."

"Calm down, ma'am. Slowly, please. What is this about a dog?"

Maren heard another shot, the breaking of glass. She hung up.

"Get behind me," she told Bethany firmly as she sank to the floor on her knees, facing the door. She shielded the girl with her body, despite signals from her leg ordering her to lie down. To give up.

CHAPTER 31

The evening had passed in a blur. A medley of sirens wailing from an ambulance, a fire engine, and police cars—it seemed every emergency vehicle in Sacramento had been called up. Maren woke the next morning across the street in Polly's home in a cocoon of drugs, the dull, muted pain in her injured leg like a far away, unasked-for visitor. A vision of Alibi Morning Sun floated before her eyes, but she couldn't be sure if the detective had actually been there the night before. If he was, she had no idea what he might have said.

"You're up, love, that's good."

Polly's skin was drawn. There were deep lines Maren had never noticed before around her eyes. She set a tea tray on the desk next to the bed before engulfing Maren in a tight hug. Maren saw that her friend's face was wet with tears, although that didn't stop Polly from berating Maren for having the audacity to get herself shot.

"You had me right worried! I was downtown when it happened, and I came back to a bloody circus on your lawn."

Maren found it hard to move her lips, like she'd been to the dentist and was maxed out on Novocain. She could only manage one word.

"Bethany?"

Polly smiled. "Don't worry, that little one's rosy. Her mum's here, arrived in the wee hours last night."

Maren's sense of relief was immeasurable but brief as she felt her shoulders sink, her head drop to her chest, and a drug-induced sleep overtake her. It was hours before she awoke again. She could hear Polly in the next room calling to Jake that there were cookies and milk on the table—normal sounds and actions as though it were a normal day. Maren was beginning to wonder if she would ever have one of those again. She winced as she reached for her cell phone, then adjusted herself on the bed, propping a second pillow behind her, although there was no comfortable angle for her injured leg.

Shortly after Sean's arrest, Maren had programmed Lana Decateau into her speed dial. She was glad for it now, as it meant she didn't have to go through her phone contacts alphabetically for the lawyer's number. Even small moves were difficult. Her leg was throbbing. She wondered for a moment how brave souls with chronic pain did anything—it must take courage just to live. Then she realized her mind was drifting from one thought to the next without edits due to the pain drugs the doctor had prescribed. She tried to rein in the randomness of her thinking, worried if she wasn't careful she might say things to Lana like, "Wow, totally." She was pretty sure that wouldn't be appropriate as a near-murder victim when speaking with the attorney of her friend, Sean, who was a near-murderer. *Near-murderer? Is that even a word?* She realized this whole "communicating while on drugs" thing was going to be a challenge.

Fortunately, when Maren reached Lana, the lawyer did most of the talking. And it was clear from Decateau's first words that she was fully in the loop with the police on what had happened.

"I told Morning Sun I would update you this morning—he's leading the investigation," Lana said. "He didn't like the look of you last night."

So the detective was there. Maren was relieved to know she hadn't been hallucinating, at least about that.

"The lab analysis is back. Your attacker's name is Wallis Jane Lisborne. No priors, no record. Last known address is Hollywood. She listed her profession as actress on the lease application, and her reference was an acting instructor who does local workshops. But looks like Lisborne has made the bulk of her living in stunt work. She's had decent-size parts in B movies. Out of that apartment over a year, no address we can find since. A black Volvo sedan registered to her was parked a few blocks from your house, packed suitcases in the front. Probably preparing to flee after the attack, but it could be she was living out of it. I'm not sure what other leads the police are working to locate her, but they must be starting with hospitals and urgent care centers. The blood Ms. Lisborne left on your driveway from the wound your dog inflicted was considerable."

"I don't understand," Maren said. "Wallis? Wallis who works in the first lady's office, for Mrs. Fernandez?" She wondered if she had heard Lana correctly.

"What? No." Lana thought for a moment. "Maybe. Tell me what you know."

Maren described her brief encounters with Wallis. She shared that she only had heard the one name—she didn't know if it was Wallis's first or last.

"In your opinion, could that be the person who shot you?"

"I guess." Maren paused to picture Wallis. "Although she seems the opposite of a stuntwoman. Afraid of her own shadow, mousy. Not athletic at all. I suppose that could be her acting ability."

Suddenly, Maren had an idea. She thought it was a good one.

"Maren, are you there?"

Maren realized she would need to speak for Lana to know her thoughts.

That's damn inconvenient, she mused. *Someone should work on that.* "I had this idea," she said. "Would Wallis have used her real name working in the capitol? And wouldn't her employment with the first lady have come up when the police ran her prints?"

"Maybe not," Lana said. "It depends how long Wallis worked there—with state budget cuts there could be a backlog of employees not yet entered into the computer. Or it could be she used a different last name. I'll let the police know. I'll call you later."

"But this clears Sean, right?" Maren asked. "Now that they have a real murderer to go after?"

Lana paused.

Maren hated phone pauses. In her experience they were never followed by anything good.

"The police are seeking Wallis Lisborne in connection with two attempts on your life, and the related assault on Noel. There is nothing to link her to the death of Tamara Barnes." She added in a gentler tone, "I'm sorry."

Maren had scarcely hung up when the phone rang again. She checked, Caller ID: Garrick.

"Maren, I just heard. Are you okay?"

"Fine," Maren said, noticing for the first time that the pattern of Jake's quilt was a montage of tiny musical instruments in almost abstract form.

Wild.

"You were shot," Garrick said. "Does fine really capture it?"

Maren closed her eyes before speaking in an effort to stop the symphony of instruments on the blanket from intruding into her thoughts. "I had a near miss, a flesh wound." In fact, it was more than that. The bullet had missed the bone and no surgery was needed, but it tore a chunk of muscle and took some flesh with it as it exited. Although the wound would leave a gnarly scar, the doctors expected a full recovery. "But Camper had the worst of it; he..." This time it was Maren's emotions, not the drugs, that made it difficult for her to go on. "The vet had to amputate. Camper lost a leg."

"Can I come see you?"

She took a deep breath. She felt confused as thoughts about her options for romance pinballed around in her head.

Could Garrick have changed? Would he not cheat on me this time? And what if Alec Joben weren't a senator? Is he the one, is that anything real? Did I dream he has twin toddlers?

Ultimately, she found herself concluding that her priority needed to be to stop getting herself attacked at knifepoint and shot at long enough to figure these things out! At least for the moment she loved the simplification of planning that was evidently generated by prescription opiates.

Her call waiting beeped.

"Garrick, it's the other line, I'll call you back."

She was starting to feel dizzy from the handoffs.

"Ms. Kane?"

"Yes?"

"Dr. Wihabe here. We were able to reduce your brother's sedation. It had to be done gradually. He is conscious now, but very groggy. Still, he asks repeatedly for you, something about an e-mail. It seems important, he wants you to look at your e-mails."

"Can I talk to him?"

"He is too weak and easily agitated. If I let him know you have gotten this message, perhaps it will calm him."

She asked the doctor to update her on Noel's condition if there was any change. He agreed to do so and hung up.

Maren laid back on the bed and fell asleep again. Twenty minutes passed and she woke to her pain increasing, up to six on a scale of one to ten. But she also felt the drug haze lifting. She wondered how often she was supposed to take the meds, at the same time resolving she would tolerate a higher level of pain if it meant she could think more clearly.

Pulling aside the covers, she eased herself off the bed, good leg first, letting out a small cry as she put weight on the bad one. Polly appeared almost instantly from the other room. She held a cane. "The doctor said you can try this when you feel ready. But don't be barmy and start prancing around yet. I can get you all you need."

"Thanks. I'd like to go to the bathroom." She remembered there was a half bath to the right of Jake's room. "When I'm through, would it be possible for me to use your computer? I left my iPad with Noel."

"Of course, love." Polly helped Maren up, gave her the cane, and supported her the painful few steps to the bath. When Maren emerged, she told Polly she'd like to try sitting on the sofa. She didn't relish the idea of getting back up onto the bed. The couch was lower, easier in that respect, although she still made involuntary sounds of pain as she tried to settle in. Polly bit her lip, witnessing it, then left the room, returning with an older laptop similar to the one Maren used to have.

Having found a position as close to comfortable as she was likely to get, Maren put the computer on her lap, booted it up, then opened her Ecobabe inbox easily on the familiar platform. She scanned for the e-mail the doctor said Noel wanted her to see.

No e-mails from Noel. Nothing.

Then Maren noticed a recent message marked with a star. She decided that must have been Noel, since she never used the star function. It was from senrabyllit@talk.com, the spammer that had been contacting her to "Invest Now!" for weeks. Maren clicked on it.

Maren,
I think they're watching me. Sean will know what to do.
Tell him to protect what is mine, always.
I know he will.
TB

Maren lost all color, her face nearly white. Just then Sal arrived through the front door with Chinese takeout. Seeing that Maren was in distress, she crossed to her side and reached to take the laptop from her. "You shouldn't be working yet."

Maren snapped at her, "No! No, it's here! It's this! This e-mail!" Her eyes were wide as she stared at the screen, her hands shaking where they remained on the keyboard.

Polly was literally running as she came back into the room, having heard the commotion. She stopped herself, apparently taking in the absence of blood or an assailant. She sat at the end of the sofa, gingerly, but the shift that her weight caused in the plush surface of the cushions elicited another groan of pain from Maren.

"Sorry, love." Polly got up and knelt on the floor beside Maren instead. "You've had quite a go of it. I know you don't want to get behind at work, but any e-mail can wait. Why don't you look at that later? I'm sure Ecobabe will understand."

Maren, head down and brow furrowed, ignored Polly as she clicked on the first attachment to the e-mail. It contained boxes of numbers and graphs, one after the other, all in the same format, labels of *Yield. Close. Volume.* There was something familiar in it to Maren, but she wasn't sure what it was.

Then Maren opened the second attachment, and all else faded away. A scanned copy of a credit card receipt: $17.16 at Broads and Bards Café, Sacramento, 7:18 p.m., March 13 of the prior year. Easy for Maren to remember since it was Polly's birthday. And the day Marjorie Hopkins was murdered. The charge receipt was signed by Wallis Jane Lisborne.

A crashing sound from Polly's room, where Jake was teaching Bethany to play checkers, caused Sal to exit, leaving Polly to negotiate with Maren to put the computer away. But once she understood that it wasn't routine work, but rather a possible link between last night's attack on Maren and Marjorie Hopkins' murder, she appeared as keen as Maren to sort it out. Within minutes she'd made tea and found a yellow notepad and a pen. She sat cross-legged on the floor near Maren on the sofa, and the two women spent the next fifteen minutes going over what they knew about the crimes, and what it all might mean.

"It's not obvious," Polly concluded after reviewing for a second time the notes she'd made on the yellow pad. Polly had insisted on acting as scribe, despite Maren pointing out that her head was now clear, and the bullet had hit her leg, not her hand.

"This charge receipt puts Wallis Lisborne at the scene of Marjorie Hopkins' murder," Polly said. "But we're lacking a motive."

"And a weapon. And a witness," Maren added, reaching for tea on the small folding table Polly had set up for her, which also now held her cell phone and Polly's laptop. Everything a wounded woman might need. "We also don't know how Wallis found out that Tamara had the charge receipt, or how Wallis discovered Tamara sent it to me."

"Yep, we're right screwed. Unless we learn more."

Maren hoped Lana would think differently. Ever since she had failed to mention finding Tamara's necklace to Lana— resulting in a possible death penalty charge for Sean, too horrible for words—Maren had strictly adhered to the first rule of working with the public defender. As laid out by Ms. Decateau herself. That all new information on Sean's case was to go to Lana first. Period. No questions or delays. But it had been three p.m. when Maren dutifully forwarded to Lana Tamara's e-mail and the attachments. The sun would soon be setting through Polly's living room picture window, and still no response.

Maren took a sip of tea, ignoring the two Oreos Polly had set next to it, and tried another angle. "But Wallis must have known Tamara sent the receipt to me. Why else would she try to kill me? Twice." Maren was certain the assailant at the Saniplaz parking lot had also been Wallis. "That gives Wallis the same motive to kill Tamara that she had to kill me. Knowledge of evidence against Wallis in the Hopkins murder."

"Okay, love, right. But that still brings us back to square one." She circled two items on the notepad. "What was Wallis's motive to kill Marjorie Hopkins? And how did Tamara get hold of the receipt to begin with?"

"Maybe there's something I missed in the other attachment," Maren said. She leaned to reach for the laptop and a fresh wave of pain shot through her thigh, causing her to emit another involuntary groan. She wondered if at some point she would be able to control when she made sounds and when she didn't. Polly jumped up and got the laptop for her. "You sure you don't want more of those pills the doc left?"

But Maren wasn't listening, as she was back in research mode, reexamining the first attachment to Tamara's e-mail. "Yield...Close...Volume..." Maren remembered now where she had last heard those words. *Garrick.* Stock values! The attachment was some kind of investment record.

Maren knew the police could find someone to interpret the document if they thought it mattered. But they had ignored all the other leads Maren had given them. So Maren went back to the e-mail from Tamara, selected "Forward" from the drop-down menu, and began typing.

To: Garrick Chauncey
From: Maren Kane
Re: Financial Document

Garrick,

The attached documents were sent to me by Tamara Barnes on the day she died. In fact, every day since then, through autosend. At any rate, I just read them now. One is a charge receipt. The second looks like it has something to do with stock prices and trends. Any chance you can interpret it? I was

She stopped typing midsentence.

She realized she failed to call Garrick back after he phoned that morning to check on her. It wasn't an oversight—she was avoiding a substantive conversation with him, as she had been for days. And now, at a deep level, she knew she couldn't keep procrastinating when things got hard. Acting only on impulse. Not after almost being killed—twice. And finding corpses—twice. Life really was too short.

She looked up from the laptop and addressed Polly. "I'd like to make a call. Privately."

Polly eyed Maren but said nothing, apparently correctly interpreting Maren's expression as meaning this was not a negotiable request. She moved to collect her papers and headed to her bedroom to join the others.

Maren looked at the phone in her hand and punched in the numbers. Garrick had been booted off her speed dial, but that didn't mean she'd forgotten how to reach him.

CHAPTER 32

Garrick Chauncey tried to regain possession of his left arm—it was losing feeling, pinned under her neck. Worse yet, her tangle of long blonde hair was starting to itch. He gave up on delicacy and pulled free in one harsh movement. She didn't wake.

He stood under the strong jets in his marble shower, looking out at the private fern garden beyond the glass enclosure. He reflected, as he often did, on how nice it was to be rich.

Misty was lovely. Garrick had met her the way millionaires meet models and actresses in California. At somebody's party where a man's money, not his age, mattered. Garrick had made a habit of these young women for several decades—he got older, they didn't. But having turned the corner at forty-five, he wanted some measure of stability, maybe even children.

Garrick was surprised it was taking Maren Kane so long to see things his way. He was sincere that he loved her, and despite the fact that she was soft rather than firm in places, Maren did something for him and to him that that those girls did not.

Not that he would give up the Misty's of the world entirely. He would just have to be more careful.

As he stepped out of the shower, his phone rang.

"Garrick?" Maren's voice seemed far away.

"You sound like you're in Budapest." He didn't bother to towel off, donning a thick, beige terry robe hanging on the back of the bathroom door.

"I'm at Polly's. Maybe it's a bad connection. I can call you back on her landline; it will take me a minute to get to it."

"No, it's fine. How are you?"

"Okay."

He started toward the kitchen, down a long wide hall accented by a Picasso, strategically lit. As he passed the master bedroom Misty called to him. "Garrick, darling, come back to bed. Where are you?"

Damn. He covered the phone.

"Garrick, are you there?" Maren asked.

Misty called again, loudly, more insistently. "Garrick?"

He hung up on Maren in midsentence and returned to his bedroom. Kissing Misty lightly on the forehead, he told her he was late for a conference call meeting and moved to the large walk-in closet. Dropping the robe to the floor—the maid would take care of it—he dressed quickly in lightweight navy wool pants, a sky-blue silk shirt, navy cashmere socks, and Italian loafers.

He opened the sliding glass door and walked quickly to a broad slate patio under the trees. Once he was seated in a comfortable Adirondack chair, his feet up, Garrick hit redial.

"I'm sorry. That bad connection got the better of us."

At first he thought the line really had gone dead. After a moment Maren spoke.

"I can't agree to marry you."

Not what he had expected.

"Maren, you've been through a lot. Let's wait and talk about this later."

"I don't think I love you anymore."

His right eye twitched. His free hand involuntarily formed a fist. The intense jealousy that had been his shadow for as long as he could remember sparked.

"Who is he?" His voice came out as a growl.

"No one. But you and I...I can't. Not again. I need to move forward in my life. Not back."

He calmed slightly. There was another man, he could hear it in her voice. A crush, maybe an infatuation. But not someone else's arms around his woman. Because that was what Maren was, he realized.

His.

Garrick's fist opened. He flexed his broad fingers. He took a deep breath and wound down the trajectory of his emotions. He was accustomed to tough deals, to hesitant clients and competitive bids. *Rule number one, ask only questions that require a "yes."*

"I understand. But I'm here for you. As a friend. You know that?"

It might take time, but the way Garrick saw it, until Maren Kane walked down the aisle with someone else, the prize was his to win.

* * *

As much as she wanted to know what the documents Tamara had sent her meant, Maren decided to give Garrick a few hours before sending the e-mail asking for his help interpreting them. Still, he had said he was there for her and would be her friend. At nine p.m. she completed the e-mail to him and sent it. Then she took a pain pill as prescribed and slept for twelve hours. It might have gone on longer, but the next morning there was a soft knock on her door at seven a.m. It wasn't jarring, but it was enough to bring her to consciousness. Maren opened her eyes to an unexpected view of Jimi Hendrix cradling a guitar, gold satin scarf tied around his head, shoulders rolled, and hips thrust forward. Jimi communing with his music, which, as fate would have it, he would have limited time on earth to make. Next to Hendrix, Muhammad Ali's upper body glistened. His face was lit up by an infectious grin as his famous "speed of light" anchor punch—executed in four hundredths of a second, according to Ali—targeted an opponent's jaw. The photographer had caught the moment immediately before contact.

Maren rolled gingerly from her left side onto her back, carefully pulling herself into a sitting position against the headboard. The pain in her leg greeted her this morning, but either she was getting used to it, or it was less insistent. She resolved again to go for as long as she could during daylight hours without the pain meds. She hated how groggy they made her feel. In response to the gentle knock, she called out with an invitation to enter.

Jake opened the door but stopped there. He pulled at one sleeve of his black T-shirt, the image of a cartoon dog on his narrow chest wrinkling as he did so. Polly had insisted to

Maren that police protection or not, she stay with them a day or two, at least until the swelling in her leg was down and she was proficient with the cane. In truth, Maren knew Polly was determined that she not return home until Wallis was caught. But Maren wanted to be home, not in small part because she hated displacing Jake onto the sofa.

Jake remained in the doorway, surveying the scene.

Maren tried to look welcoming, but it was hard when she had taken over his room. Her overnight bag lay open, clothes spilling out on the limited floor space. The work Evie had dropped off yesterday at Maren's insistence filled Jake's small student desk.

"Thanks again for letting me borrow your room," Maren said, following his glance as it captured her appropriation of every inch of his space. "I know how inconvenient it must be."

"I need a new reed," Jake said. "For my sax. Sorry, before-school jazz band rehearsals." Maren cringed inwardly at her memory of having tackled the kid who bullied Jake on the way to one such rehearsal. "The last one I had in the case broke." He shifted in place, from one foot to the other, his black, high-top Converse making a squeaking noise on the wood floor.

Maren realized she might need to be overt in indicating that this was still his domain, that she hadn't taken over completely. She'd learned in her brief experience teaching art to high school students that adolescents could regress from mini-grown-ups to children needing adult direction in minutes. A bewildering age for those going through it and for those on the outside looking in.

"Please, come in," she said.

That seemed to do it. Jake crossed to his desk, stepping over her open suitcase, and rummaged through the top drawer before finding a small foil-wrapped Jazz #2 reed.

274

He was almost out the door when he stopped. He looked down at the reed in his hand, turning it over as he spoke. "Is Camper okay?"

At her mother's funeral while her father wept and Noel sobbed, Maren had bitten her lip until it bled rather than permit herself to cry. Since then her eyes might water, but she kept any real hurt locked deep inside. Not a matter of pride, but of privacy. But at Jake's question something strange took hold of her. It started with an uncontrollable shaking in her shoulders followed by a soft, low keening escaping from her mouth. Maren hunched over and wrapped her arms around herself in a futile effort at containment of the utter, bereft loss of control she was experiencing. Then the tears came, her nose running and her face soaked within minutes.

She didn't know how much time had passed, but when she looked up at the doorway, Jake was gone.

That must have terrified him.

She remembered what it was like to see an adult in her life completely lose it, and wondered if Jake would suffer nightmares as she had.

But in a moment he was back at her side. "I found this website," he said as he pulled the rolling desk chair, a worn cast-off from someone's office, close to the bed and opened the inexpensive laptop he held, covered with stickers of musicians. He didn't look at Maren, his eyes fixed on the keyboard as he clicked and typed. But his voice, though tentative, was hopeful.

"See? It's called tripawds.com." He turned the screen toward her. "It says here it's better to run on three legs than to limp on four." He pointed to a banner at the top of the site.

Maren could see images of a golden retriever leaping for a ball, then a corgi petted happily by two small children, both animals with three legs.

"There are cool things you can buy that help with balance so the dogs can get around more easily. Plus training videos..." Jake's voice was gaining strength. He hazarded a glance at Maren to see if she was getting it. "And look, people blog about their dogs, what happened to them, how they're doing. I bet Camper would be featured. Since he's a hero."

"He is that," Maren said, a few new tears escaping her. But this time she found it didn't hurt to cry. She realized having someone stronger, even if that someone was fourteen years old, made a difference.

She rubbed her eyes with both hands, then looked directly at him. "Camper will be home in a few days. If you make a list we can figure out what he might need. I don't know when I could do a blog, but if you..."

Jake was up again, headed out the door. "I'm on it. My friend Danny is a really good writer, he can help."

* * *

A few hours later, Polly was at work and Jake at school, but Maren wasn't entirely alone. A black-and-white patrol car was parked across the street in front of her house making sure Wallis Lisborne didn't make another appearance.

Maren was getting around pretty well, although leaning heavily on the cane and taking only a few steps at a time. A patch the doctor had given to her to put directly over the wound contained a numbing salve that helped a lot. She'd been able to cut the oral pain medication dose in half and intended to stop it altogether as soon as she could.

Polly's square dining table made a better work surface than Jake's small desk, so Maren sat in one of the four padded matching chairs, her left leg outstretched.

She opened Polly's laptop, on loan since Maren's iPad was still with Noel. The first two messages of the morning were from Noel. He expected to be discharged soon. Not that it meant he was ready to function at anything close to full speed. He would be on bed rest for at least two weeks. More likely the hospital needed the bed, or his insurance limit had kicked in. Still, convalescing at home had to be better than the sterile environment of an inpatient unit.

Maren rubbed both eyes, stretched her neck, and took a moment. She thought she and Noel, the Kane siblings, made quite a pair now. *Gimpy and gimpier.* But they were alive. Both of them. And she knew better than to take anything for granted anymore, especially not that.

She turned back to her inbox. A new note from Garrick.

To: Maren Kane
From: Garrick Chauncey
Re: Tamara Barnes Attachments

Maren,
The document is a history of three different stock prices over the past six years. It runs their value and other parameters up through two months ago. Company names aren't listed. Many stocks show similar patterns over time, but one

of my research assistants should be able to identify these with the programs I have.

More interesting is where the investments are located. The credit card receipt is charged to the main account, the investment partnership, held in a savings and loan in Albuquerque.

New Mexico has extremely permissive laws with regard to investor anonymity. All someone needs to park assets there via a limited liability corporation is to give a company name and provide an address for the principal office and a registered agent who lives in New Mexico. The owners don't show up on any public record.

Garrick

Maren moved too quickly, putting weight on her leg before she had the cane in place. She winced but kept going, realizing she would need to keep her phone at her side from now on. She found it in the kitchen on the counter where she had made tea.

"Polly Grey speaking."

"Polly, it's Maren. Did you say Tamara Barnes went to college in New Mexico?"

"Yes. Born in New York, college in Albuquerque." She thought for a moment. "University of New Mexico. She graduated with honors. Why?"

"The document I sent Garrick, the attachment from Tamara's e-mail. It's an investment account. Stocks, located in Albuquerque. The partners can be anonymous, all except the local agent." Maren was talking fast. "Wallis Lisborne had access to the money. If Tamara did too, it might explain her expensive car and clothes, and how she got the charge receipt, the evidence placing Wallis at the Hopkins murder."

"Hold on, love." Maren could hear Polly talking to someone else, the sound of a door closing. Then Polly was back. "How does this help Sean?"

"If we can find who was on that account, if there is someone else, that might be the person Wallis worked with to kill Tamara. Clearly, there's money behind this somehow, and we're getting closer." A pain shot through her leg. Maren leaned against the counter for support but didn't stop talking. "Tamara said she and the governor had done something awful. That must be it—Ray Fernandez must be a partner on that account."

"Maybe." Polly hesitated. "I still don't see how being part of this investment account links to any of the murders—Hopkins, Barnes, or the attempts on your life."

"It is, it must. It's just that everything's so complicated. But I'll figure it out. Or the police will." Maren moved back to the sofa and gratefully took the weight off her leg as she sank down into the large cushions.

Once the call had ended Maren took a sip of her tea, cold now, and suffered a moment's doubt. She thought about the hunches she'd had so far on Sean's case and how they had played out.

The similarity in the methods of killing in the Hopkins and Barnes cases, a single knife strike through the heart, had suggested to her one killer. The police hadn't agreed, at least not without something more. The hairbrush with strands of orange-red hair in Ray Fernandez's car also hadn't meant anything to anyone but her. And Bethany Castro being Tamara's child wasn't linked to Sean's case in any way she could see yet, not enough to expose Tamara's secret.

She thought back to Rorie Rickman's warning. To be thoughtful. To be careful. Generally good advice—Maren knew that. She just wished it weren't so hard for her to follow.

* * *

Sal insisted on carrying Noel's bag and his briefcase in from the car while he waited on the pullout sofa bed in her living room. Noel was on strict orders of bed rest for at least several weeks, and Sal wouldn't hear of him going home alone to his apartment to fend for himself.

Noel lay on top of the covers, his hat and coat still on, while Sal started dinner and Bethany played upstairs.

He was taking time to adjust to the idea.

Not that it would be his first overnight at Sal's. They always started like this, with him on the sofa bed. They had agreed that Bethany shouldn't be exposed to the fact that he and Sal were sleeping together unmarried. It wasn't a strict religious code for either of them, although Sal went to church regularly. It stemmed from their shared concern that young children were highly impressionable. Neither of them wanted the future teen Bethany sleeping with someone just because she thought they had sanctioned it.

Sal's modest Davis townhome had two bedrooms and a bath upstairs, with the living room, eat-in kitchen, and half bath downstairs. In the past when Noel had stayed, he moved upstairs to Sal's room for the night after they were sure Bethany was asleep, setting an early alarm for the next day so he could be back downstairs making up the sofa bed when Bethany woke in the morning.

Their strategy only failed them once, when Bethany had a nightmare and knocked on Sal's locked bedroom door at two a.m. Before Sal could say anything Noel jumped out of bed and hid in Sal's walk-in closet. He stayed there for nearly an hour while Sal comforted Bethany, until the child fell asleep and Sal carried her back to her own room.

When Sal teased him about it later—an hour was a long time to wait in a closet—Noel only looked at her puzzled, failing to see the humor in what he felt was a logical and reasoned action on his part.

But this time would be different, more than a night or two. Several weeks, an extended stay. Noel hadn't lived with anyone since college. Then only a semester passed before he found he was ill-suited for roommates. They seemed uncomfortable with him, despite his trying to stay out of their way. As far as Noel could tell, the problem was simply who he was. Noel reasoned that if he moved in with Sal, the chill that followed him would become obvious to both Sal and Bethany. He might lose them, a risk he was unwilling to take. As he was preparing to get up and tell Sal that he would be fine in his own apartment and needed to go home, there was a knock at the door.

* * *

Sal wiped her hands on a dish towel and went to see who it was. Likely a door-to-door salesperson or petitioner; they always chose the dinner hour to find people at home. Annoyed, she turned the stir-fry to low so it wouldn't burn.

Billy Machelli stood on the stoop, hands jammed deep in the front pockets of his jeans, his curly dark hair longer than Sal remembered it. A heavily made-up, platinum blonde woman stood next to him, her eyes struggling to stay open under lashes thick with mascara. Her smile was more childlike than the rest of her, something sweet and genuine in it. It was hard to tell her age, but Sal guessed the woman was younger than Billy. That was his type.

"Hey, Sis, great to see you," he said.

"What are you doing here?"

"This is my fiancé, Marilyn Lewis. Seeing as how I'm getting married, I had to introduce you two."

Billy took Marilyn's hand and started to step inside, but Sal blocked him.

She acknowledged Marilyn with a nod, keeping her eyes on Billy. "If this is about money, call me and I'll..."

"No, I have a job. We just want to be with family to share our news."

"Mommy, Daniel is hungry."

Bethany took the stairs carefully, holding the banister with her free hand and cradling her stuffed elephant, Daniel, with her cast against her tiny chest.

Noel's medication made him dizzy, but he was up in time to intercept Bethany's path toward the entry. "Let's go in the kitchen and feed Daniel," Noel said, taking the little girl's free hand and turning her towardsthe back hall. "I'm hungry, too," he said.

Marilyn gazed at Bethany's retreating figure.

There was a longing, a depth of feeling in that look that gave Sal a chill. She remembered her own days when all she wanted was a child. And in that moment Sal knew. This visit wasn't about money. It wasn't about a marriage.

It was about Bethany.

Her daughter.

Billy's daughter.

CHAPTER 33

Evie dropped off all files and work on the cell phone bill at Polly's at Maren's request.

Included was a draft of the cost analysis for the upcoming Appropriations Committee hearing. As she read it Maren was feeling more confident about the bill's chances—Ecobabe interns Nadira and Elliot had done fast and good work. Their computations showed that fines paid by violators would cover the cost of enforcing the cell phone driving ban. The bill would, therefore, be "revenue neutral," the magic phrase legislators loved to hear, meaning a bill would neither add to nor deplete state resources.

Assuming the bill did clear Appropriations, Maren was confident it had enough votes from Democrats to pass both houses of the legislature. But she was concerned that unless she could build support from Republicans, the governor might not sign the measure since it had the potential to anger so many voters. There were many drivers who would not want to have their cell phone access taken away while enduring one of California's many notoriously long commutes.

Maren rifled through papers on Polly's dining room table until she found the files that Rorie Rickman had pulled from Sean's office and computer. While Maren had the vote count from Senator Smith's hands-free bill, she wanted to see if there were specific notes on Republicans still in office now who voted against Smith's bill back then—anything that might give her a handle on how to approach them. Nothing.

She turned to more recent documents. The agenda from the Health Committee hearing. Support and opposition letters and testimony. Nothing there either, at least not anything that seemed likely to serve as a magic bullet to remove Republican opposition.

The work was tedious and slow-going, but Maren was feeling better and able to stay focused. She'd been able to replace the heavier prescription pain medication with over-the-counter pills. Things were also finally looking up for Sean. Lana Decateau was busy on another case, so Maren hadn't heard much from her lately, but enough to know that the police were following up on the investment account. Maren was certain they would find that Tamara Barnes was the New Mexico link. That would explain how Tamara had access to Wallis's receipt. And Maren thought Ray Fernandez had to be their likely backer, getting the fund started. She guessed Ray had had an affair with one of the two women, Wallis or Tamara. Most likely Tamara. Noel and the police might have viewed the location of that hairbrush in the glove box of his car as innocent, but they didn't know Ray like Maren did.

She set her work on the bill aside and pulled up the investment document again. She and Garrick had spoken to walk through it. She'd been surprised how easy he was to talk to since their "just friends" discussion.

Garrick explained that two of the stocks showed typical returns. Four to 8 percent annually, with some years better, some years worse. But a third performed extraordinarily, jumping over 300 percent twice in the history. All told, from six years ago through two months prior to today—the period tracked in the document—an investment of $100 would have yielded a fifteen-fold return—$1,500. And a million would have become $15 million.

Maren looked again at the graph for that stock and the periods when it had peaked.

She also went back to the original cell phone documents. The dates the hands-free bill passed a major committee, then each house. And she recalled Lew Quintana, president of TalkFree Inc., testifying that 37 percent of Californians now owned a TalkFree hands-free instrument for their car. Since the passage of the law.

She hit speed dial for Polly.

"Slow down, slow down, love." Polly seemed to be having trouble following what Maren felt was so simple.

"Tamara, Wallis, and Ray were betting on the outcome of bills. I don't know what the other two stocks were, but I've compared the most successful investment from the document Tamara e-mailed with TalkFree's history—it's a perfect match."

"Hold on." She heard Polly talking to a young man, likely a fellow in her program. It never paid to call her at the office. Maren paced the length of Polly's small dining room. Not very effectively, using her cane, but she couldn't sit still.

Polly returned to the line. "So they invested in TalkFree?"

"Right," Maren said, giving in to the growing ache in her leg and sitting down. "The value of the stock was nearly stagnant, no real change, until it skyrocketed after the hands-free bill became law. That maps exactly to the value of the highest-performing stocks in the investment account in the documents Tamara sent to me."

"Let me get this straight. An insider like Wallis, working in the capitol, could follow which bills were introduced in Sacramento, assess the potential for a company's bottom line, and invest in those she thought would top off when the new law is enacted? Is that legal?"

"Yes. Garrick confirmed it—not only that it's legal but that it likely happens all the time. First, because it doesn't need to be an insider. Anyone can look up bill proposals online, read them, and consider their potential for making a company money. Of course, people on the inside would be better at it, have a better idea of whether a given bill is likely to pass, sort of like how knowing personally the players on a football team, their aches and pains that don't hit the media, improves your chances at betting on whether they'll win." Maren realized she was on a bit of a tangent about who could do this. "But the key word in terms of the legality of it is 'potential.' There's no guarantee the bill will pass, it's not rigged, it's not a sure thing."

"Okay." Polly paused. "So?"

"Suppose Connor Smith's hands-free bill hadn't become law. Which would likely have happened if Marjorie Hopkins' research had been completed back then showing that a driver's conversation on a hands-free phone is no safer than holding the phone. The bill would have become a worthless idea. It would have died. And anyone who had invested in TalkFree or other hands-free cellular companies based on their expected performance under the anticipated new law would have lost all their money." Maren swallowed hard. "The motive, Polly," she said. "That's Wallis's motive to kill Marjorie Hopkins. It was to stop the cell phone research, or at least delay it long enough for Smith's hands-free bill to be signed, TalkFree's stock value to soar, and the money cashed out."

CHAPTER 34

As she shifted the cold compress to better cover her aching eyes and block out the seedy motel room, Wallis Jane Lisborne reflected that Marjorie Hopkins was a woman who had deserved to die.

The two first met at a busy coffee bar up the street from Wallis's downtown Sacramento apartment. Wallis was post-morning-workout, and Marjorie had just dropped her two-year-old at preschool. Both needed caffeine to jump-start their day.

Marjorie, in her early thirties, had straight dark hair pulled back in a pink velvet bow. Her round grey eyes with dark lashes were magnified by chunky black glasses and stood out in an otherwise plain face. She was chubby, but in an "I'm a busy mom, I'll get to the baby fat later" kind of way. In contrast, Wallis, more than ten years Hopkins' senior, was hardbodied from years of sustained effort. Her well-tended form was her meal ticket in L.A.—no stunt or stand-in jobs without it. Her soft brown close-cropped locks, artfully highlighted with gold, were styled straight from a magazine, and she wore the latest, hippest clothes, even if she could only afford a few now that she was a desk jockey. Working for a temporary agency, currently placed in a law office as a file clerk, she was a far cry from her Hollywood stuntwoman days.

The third time they ran into each other Wallace stepped in line directly behind Marjorie. It was rush hour, eight people in front of them. Marjorie turned, pushing her glasses back up on her nose as they threatened to slide all the way down. She smiled at Wallis's now familiar face. "We seem to have the same schedule."

Wallis made a point of looking past Marjorie to the counter, avoiding further eye contact in the hope the chitchat would stop there.

"I just couldn't believe my little girl today. First it was a tantrum over breakfast. Suddenly she doesn't like bananas. I mean, who doesn't like bananas? What two-year-old doesn't, anyway?" Hopkins' face was animated, her bobbing head causing her to have to adjust her glasses again.

The line edged slowly forward. Too slowly for Wallis.

"Then she wants an apple, and we don't have any. She's screaming 'appies, appies, no nanas.' That's what she calls them, appies and nanas. So cute, but I couldn't be late to work."

"Uh-huh."

"Bryan took over for me, he's so sweet. He knows we're expanding at work, and Shauna wanted her pink fuzzy socks. They were in the laundry and..."

Seriously, socks? Wallis decided a good offense had to be better than her wilting defense. Any topic was preferable to nanas and fuzzy socks. And if this gabby woman's office was expanding—she thought that was what she'd heard her say somewhere in her endless narrative—maybe there was a job in it for her someplace that didn't take the temp agency's 25 percent off the top. Not likely, but you never knew unless you asked. "So your office is expanding? Are you hiring?"

"Oh, no. I'm a postdoctoral fellow at the Department of Public Health," Marjorie replied, switching topics without taking a breath. "We've been crammed into some temporary space and our physical office is expanding. My own work is at a good place, though. I'd been looking at hands-free cell phone and car accident data, and I realized there was a good project there..."

Too bad. Wallis had nearly tuned out completely when Marjorie began to describe with some excitement—clearly she was dying to talk about it with someone—the initial results of her rough analysis of the data, that hands-free phones were worthless as a safety measure in the car.

"I've been checking and cross-checking. I don't want to share it with my supervisor until I'm sure. The industry will attack it, so it has to be just right." Marjorie's mouth was still running—which tests she planned to do, the variables—but Wallis Lisborne didn't need to hear any more.

Wallis quickly and easily made what should have been an unthinkable decision.

"Marjorie," she began with her most sincere, take-pity-on-me expression, "I know so few people in town. I've only been here a few months. Do you think we might go for drinks or dinner? I know you have Shaina, but..."

"Shauna. It's okay, so many people make that mistake. I wanted to name her Tara, but Bryan just loves the name Shauna..."

Wallis tensed. *If I pull on her ears hard enough, maybe her tongue will fall out.* Instead she managed, "Shauna, such a beautiful name. How about Thursday after work?"

"Bryan has softball. Maybe, let's see...tonight? I mean, if it's not too last minute. I know Bryan will be home, I'll have to ask him, but I bet he'll want to, he's always telling me I should go out for a girls' night."

Their coffees were ready.

"Why don't we meet at Broads and Bards?" Wallis asked. "Sixteenth and Q. You know it? Seven p.m."

"Well, I'm not sure, it seems fine, but what if I can't make it, let me get your number and..."

"My mobile's on the fritz. I'll go, if you can't make it, no problem, I'll grab a drink on my own and we'll try another night. At least it will get me out of the house." Pulling from her acting workshops, Wallis gave a convincing pitiable expression and then looked conspicuously at her watch. "See you tonight."

* * *

In the end it was almost too easy. The rental car, the sharpened knife in her purse. A sandwich and a cold beer first at the busy bar alone, blending in.

"Marjorie, nice to see you. The most amazing thing, someone painted a mural on the back wall of this place. You have to see it, animals in the jungle, a spaceship..."

Leading Marjorie to the back of the restaurant. Marjorie, who started babbling the moment Wallis stopped speaking. Wallis put a hand over the woman's mouth and the torrent of words turned to muffled screams. A quick, hard stab up through the heart, pulling Marjorie's body along behind the dumpster and letting it fall in the dark by the field. Just like the scene Wallis had rehearsed over and over again as the stuntwoman for Gwyneth Paltrow in *Dead Wrong in Chicago*.

Except Sacramento wasn't Chicago, and this time the knife was real.

* * *

Wallis gingerly lifted the dressing on her arm, wincing at the pain. At least it didn't look any worse. She had slathered on two tubes of Neosporin and covered both of the deep gashes with gauze, hoping the over-the-counter antibiotic would have some effect. She knew she should see a doctor and get stitches to reduce the chance of infection and improve the appearance of the wound when it healed. But she couldn't risk it. Emergency rooms and urgent care centers would surely be alerted to watch for someone with her injuries by now. She hoped the Kane woman had her so-called pet up to date on rabies shots.

Lying down on the lumpy bed, Wallis wondered whether Maren Kane led a charmed life or if this hit had just been wrong from the start. First, there was the little girl. Kane lived alone. The kid was a surprise and it had shaken Wallis. She had never hurt a kid, not even a little bit, and didn't think she could. Then the damn dog got out and it all went to hell.

Knives were Wallis's first weapon of choice. Simple to obtain, no bullets to load, no trigger locks to disarm. She had trained with them for stunt work in several films, including her two favorites: *Knife Fight Before Dawn* and *Knife Fight Before Dawn II*. True, the films weren't high art or blockbusters—straight to video as it turned out—and had almost as many scenes of women having sex with one another in prison as they did of knife fighting. Still, Wallis felt it had been a good experience. Since then, she believed knives to be the most ethical way to go into combat of any kind. They required the courage to face the target up close. Wallis felt that when possible, a human life deserved that, not death from thirty feet at the pull of a trigger. But getting it done quickly and cleanly on Kane's property meant using a knife was too risky. That approach had already failed once in the parking garage at Saniplaz in San Jose.

So guns it is, Wallis had concluded unhappily. Still, she had some training there, too. In *Crack Shot* Wallis was the stand-in for Julia Roberts, who played a crack-addicted prostitute who stalked and shot her pimp and a whole lot of bad guys. Roberts was cast against type. Wallis recalled it hadn't done very well.

Wallis initially tried positioning herself at the top of the cul-de-sac where Maren lived, hoping to have a clean rifle shot at Maren getting in or out of her car. But the street curved just before Maren's home, so it was around the bend and not visible from the hilltop.

On the third day of scouting for options Wallis had finally found something promising. Stationing herself in the backyard of the unoccupied house next door—mail stacked up, owners on vacation—Wallis observed that every evening sometime between seven and eight p.m. Maren exited the back door of her house and descended the four concrete steps to the garage at the end of her short driveway. Kane disappeared into the garage for under five minutes, then passed back through the gate up the stairs and into the house, reappearing minutes later with a book and towel that she took to an outdoor spa in the corner of her yard by the trees. The dog followed her and would lie down next to the tub while Maren soaked and read.

The single most important part of this scenario from Wallis's perspective was that Kane shut the dog in the house while she went down the stairs to the garage. Maybe the beast would run loose down the driveway if Kane didn't.

Once, while filming an action flick geared toward the PG-13 crowd, Wallis was attacked by a rottweiler that was supposed to look vicious but be nice. It turned out to look vicious and be vicious. Twelve stitches and a staple later, she figured they would put the dog down. But the dog was a star (or at least more of a star than Wallis), so it stayed. Kane's dog had a similarly massive head and jaws, although it looked to be some other breed. Gun or no gun, Wallis preferred not to have it in the equation when she was taking her shot.

Yet that was exactly what had happened. She again cursed her luck. That was all it had been, *bad luck*.

Returning to the present, Wallis heard a door slam in the next room and the TV through the wall, canned laughter on a sitcom. She slipped under the bedspread and pulled it over her head to mute the tinny sound but thought better of it when the musty smell of the bedding enveloped her. She got up and headed to the bathroom to wash her face. The mirror had a crack through the bottom and the faucets were rusted. The place was a complete dump, but at least the guy at the front let her crash with no ID, just an extra fifty bucks in cash.

Still, there was a silver lining. She knew her man would find her here. This was the place they had agreed upon if they ever needed it, where he wouldn't be known. And while he hadn't come to the room—it was too risky—he'd left something for her at the front desk. She looked again at the small gold box no bigger than her palm. She had been saving the contents for as long as she could, for what it meant, for what it said about how he felt about her. But she was hungry and the hunt for her must be in full force by now. Getting food would be difficult; she was certain she'd been identified—she'd left enough DNA in blood at Maren Kane's house to flood a lab.

Wallis removed the top carefully, wanting to save the box as a keepsake. The three chocolates inside were lopsided. They looked handmade. It reminded Wallis of the fancy candy film that companies sometimes had on sets for the stars, where there might be some left over for the stunt doubles and crew.

She closed her eyes and took a bite, savoring it on her tongue. The first one tasted like hot chocolate. No, cinnamon, maybe mixed with coffee. She couldn't wait to try the rest.

CHAPTER 35

"Where? When? How?" Maren asked. She'd been taking a break from work, lying on Jake's bed on top of the covers when Lana called. She sat up.

"They found Wallis Lisborne's body in a low-end motel room. North Hollywood, ten a.m. this morning," Lana said, her voice crackling through a bad connection on the line. "The Do Not Disturb sign was on the door, locked from the inside, the maid couldn't get in. The room was only paid for one night. The manager didn't bother to go in to check, he just called the police. Given the likelihood of drug overdoses and fights in that neighborhood, he might have had the department on speed dial."

"She was murdered?" Even if the victim was Wallis, Maren didn't think she could take another murder.

"No. It looks like suicide. The investigation is ongoing, but initial blood work indicates an overdose of a mixture of strong prescription sedatives."

"Did Wallis take responsibility for Tamara's death? For Hopkins'? Was there a note?"

"No."

"Still, it's clear now, right? The cell phone bill was worth millions to anyone who bought into TalkFree. Wallis killed Hopkins to stop her research from going forward and protect that investment." Maren had e-mailed Lana the tracking that showed that the key stock in the investment partnership was the hands-free cell phone company. For once, Lana seemed impressed with Maren's theory and said she'd get it to the DA right away.

"It was Wallis, it was all her," Maren said. "The murders, the attacks: Marjorie Hopkins, Tamara Barnes, me. And Ray, the governor, he was part of it, backed her with money. It'll come out when they crack the investment partnership. When will that be?"

"Legal cases are complex, we don't have..."

Maren got off the bed and walked to the dining room, scarcely leaning on her cane, adrenaline pushing her ahead. She picked up the investment record. "Wallis and anybody else who was smart in this thing likely cashed out their TalkFree stocks sometime in the last few months, after the date the quarterly document I sent to you was issued. Because Rickman's total cell phone driver's ban is gaining steam, and if it passes there's no reason to purchase Talkfree's equipment for driving since under the new law, use of any phone while driving—including hands-free units—would be illegal."

"I know, but..." Lana tried to get a word in edgewise.

"So since Wallis almost certainly sold the stocks and had cash in hand when she killed Tamara and tried to kill me, it wasn't about money anymore. Instead, Wallis would have wanted me dead because she believed I had evidence against her for the murder of Marjorie Hopkins. Evidence that was sent to me by Tamara Barnes. That's also Wallis's motive for Tamara's murder." Maren finally took a breath. "Wallis Lisborne killing herself. That's terrible. I mean, not really since she wanted to kill me, but terrible because of whatever craziness was driving her. And terrible because now she won't ever be able to explain herself. We won't get a confession. But the important thing is Sean had nothing to do with any of this." Maren had asked if a new angle cleared Sean over and over so many times that she felt like a long-playing record with the needle stuck. *But this time...*

Lana spoke softly, her southern lilt reasserting itself. "The DA's office agrees that Wallis Jane Lisborne had a motive to kill Tamara. They appreciate what you have found, and they are moving to subpoena the stock records. But to get the documents from New Mexico, where the intent of the law is to shield investors, will take several steps. It's another jurisdiction. It will take a few days at least to prepare the request for the order and move through the channels of both states."

Okay, Maren thought. *A few days, a week. Sean will be able to hold on. He'll have hope.*

But Lana wasn't done. "Getting ahead of ourselves won't help. It's only an idea for now. And the suggestion that the governor is the silent partner in the investment—there's simply no evidence for that yet."

Maren considered bringing up Tamara's hairbrush in Ray's car again but was able to stop herself.

"And the police have a competing theory based on the investment information you sent." Lana paused.

One of those long phone pauses that Maren hated. She started pacing again.

"The police believe Wallis Lisborne, coming into money, paid Sean to kill Tamara Barnes. Sean was the one with access, he was seen leaving the building at the time, his fingerprints were on Tamara's shoes, and he was picked up in the probable act of fleeing the country." Then she added, apparently anticipating at least one of Maren's protests, "Lost driver's license or not, he had his passport."

Maren barely felt the cane slip from her hand, didn't hear the clatter as it hit the floor. She didn't bother to retrieve it, stepping back, leaning against the wall in Polly's dining room for support. It didn't seem possible to her that the web of violence and drama entrapping Sean hadn't yet fallen away. In fact, it seemed to stick to him more tightly with each new revelation in the case.

Maren took a deep breath, willing herself to speak slowly. "Sean found Tamara already stabbed, he told us that." Her anger rose, she couldn't help it. She stomped her good foot, putting weight on her bad leg, causing her to wince. "Anyway, that's ridiculous. Wallis pay Sean? Why on earth would he kill someone for money?"

Maren knew as soon as she said it that it must sound to Lana like a silly question. Why does anyone kill anyone for money?

"As the police see it, in addition to Sean's motive of obsessive jealousy toward Tamara, he is nearly one hundred thousand dollars in debt for college and graduate school. Wallis's new-found investment millions could solve that."

This was too much for Maren. "You've got to be kidding me," she sputtered. "If every lawyer, doctor, and other professional with significant student debt killed someone to pay off their loans, there would be none of us left!"

* * *

Standing outside Senator Rorie Rickman's door, Maren ran her free hand through her hair. She knew she was a mess. Her deep blue cotton skirt and silk jacket were wrinkled, pulled out of a suitcase at Polly's, and her thick curly hair was out of control. She figured she looked like she'd been through several hours of a crowded Black Friday sale at the mall.

But she was there. Despite wanting to drop everything to march down to DA Sharpton's office and explain how ridiculous the paid hit man idea was when applied to Sean, Maren had missed too much work already. She knew if she didn't get back to it she'd be without a paycheck and the cell phone bill would be dead. So she had pulled herself together, more or less, and made it to the capitol for the first time since the shooting. It had helped to remind herself that she was there to help Senator Rickman prevent cell-phone-related accidents and deaths.

After a brief wait in the reception area—Hannah was out ill; a young man was filling in—the senator appeared and walked Maren back to her office. Maren eased down into one of the plush armchairs in front of the senator's desk and composed herself.

"I appreciate your coming, especially under the circumstances," the senator said. "We can keep this brief. Can you give me an update?"

"Senator Joe Mathis still plans to ask the Republican Caucus to oppose your broad ban on cell phone use while driving," Maren said. "He sees it as an infringement of personal freedom."

"Where does that leave us?"

"Republican Caucus opposition, if Joe Mathis is able to get it, will generate negative press. Worst case, it could lead voters in Democratic districts to ask their representatives to turn against our bill. Even if we scrape through the legislature, a weak vote could generate a gubernatorial veto."

Rickman pushed her chair away from the desk and looked out the window at the tall trees bordering the capitol on the east side. "Can't we counter with data about the deaths the driving cell phone ban would prevent?"

"We can. We will. But TalkFree has a war chest in the millions to spend on ads against the bill. If Republicans give them ideological support, we could have a real problem." For a moment Maren was pulled back to Sean's case—the thought of TalkFree, all that money. But she didn't think it was appropriate to share that information yet with the senator. The police were still running everything down. Fortunately, the senator's BlackBerry rang, breaking Maren's runaway train of thought. The senator ignored the call and continued.

"Strategy?"

"I recommend we find a Republican senator to join you as coauthor on the bill as soon as possible," Maren said.

The senator frowned. Maren could see Rickman weighing the options. Reaching across the aisle from one party to the other inevitably meant giving something to get something. Still, sometimes it was the only way.

"All right. I'll ask Senator Joben. He's moderate and might find the evidence compelling on its merits."

Maren opened her mouth to protest, to suggest someone else, but Rickman was already dialing.

"Alec? Rorie Rickman here. I don't know if you're aware of my bill to ban all cell phone use by drivers. SB 770...I'd like you to coauthor...Maren Kane, it's an Ecobabe bill...Okay...And Alec, I have to let you know, Senator Mathis is planning to ask your caucus to oppose...Yes. All right."

Rickman hung up. "He says he'll consider it provided he is given equal control over the bill, both content and strategy." Rickman smiled wryly. "He doesn't want to pretend he cares if he doesn't. Althought I don't see why not—men do it all the time." She shuffled through some papers and handed one to Maren. "Share this with him. Maybe he can save the day, he looks enough like Superman."

Maren barely registered she wasn't the only one who saw Joben's resemblance to the Man of Steel. She was silently racing through arguments she could polish that night, when she was home and calm, to persuade Rickman to refuse Alec's conditions and choose someone else for the bill. She didn't know what she wanted from Alec yet, if anything, but his being a coauthor on Ecobabe's bill would rule out romance while the bill was in process. She doubted her bosses, the members of the Ecobabe board, would ignore the gossip and bad press that might follow, even if both she and Alec were willing.

"Alec can meet you now, downstairs in the cafeteria."

Now?

The senator stood, came around the desk, and picked up Maren's bag and cane for her. Maren accepted the senator's assistance and started the awkward process of standing. Cane first, avoiding any weight on her bad leg.

When Maren was almost to the door, Rickman spoke. "Any progress with Sean's case?" The senator's lips were tense, her eyes moist. She looked uncharacteristically old and vulnerable.

Maren couldn't bear to explain the latest developments, and besides, she didn't believe the murder-for-hire charge could possibly hold.

"I hope so," she said.

A few minutes later Maren pushed open the heavy bathroom door down the hall from Rickman's office on the fourth floor, having avoided the ground-floor facilities since Tamara's death. She paused before the full-length mirror.

Her hair and outfit hadn't started out well that morning and her eyes showed fatigue. She applied lip gloss and was about to call it a day when she glanced back to adjust her skirt. She had to admit that view looked okay. Polly once said the problem with "arses"—as she called them—was they follow women around throughout their lives but fail to keep up, sliding south or jutting out with extra weight. Maren was reminded that wasn't the case for her, then felt silly for being thankful for something so shallow.

Although slowed by her injury, Maren still made it to the senate basement cafeteria before Alec Joben. Legislators were almost guaranteed to be late given the demands on their time. She purchased a bottled water and sat in a colonial-style chair that looked like it had been discarded by someone's grandparents. Her phone rang.

"How's the leg, love?"

"It's good," Maren lied. Going without prescription pain pills to keep her head clear each day was a challenge.

"What time will you be home tonight?"

"I'm not sure," Maren said. "I think this will be the last night. You've been so kind, but..."

"Don't be daft, you're right entertaining. Always saying something barmy."

Maren thought there was a compliment in there, although when Polly's British slang kicked in, Maren could never be sure.

"How's Leonard?" she asked. Maren couldn't imagine trying to keep a relationship alive between Minnesota and California, but she supposed Skype and FaceTime (and who knew what else) combined with texting and e-mailing must help.

"Good. He'll be popping out in a few weeks for a conference. Speaking of which, how is the lovely senator from Yolo?"

"I'm waiting for him for a meeting right now. Not my idea," she added. "And he's late."

"His cape caught on something?"

Maren had to smile. "Probably. Anyway, looks like Alec will be joining the cell phone bill as a coauthor. Rules out exploring anything personal."

"I don't see why. It sounds like an opportunity to me. I see candlelit strategy sessions in your future." Polly paused, then became serious. "Combining work and pleasure wouldn't really jeopardize your job, would it?"

"It could. But it's not only that. This bill has to be my first priority. Getting involved with one of the key players on it could hurt my judgment."

Or hurt me, Maren thought privately. She flashed on Alec's rapid-fire criticism of his ex-wife and their short-lived marriage despite having twin toddler sons.

CHAPTER 36

Alec's work meeting with Maren Kane had been brief, but as was the case with all his encounters with her, she stayed on his mind.

He stood up from the large desk in his inner capitol office and went to the dorm-style refrigerator behind it, pulling out a bottled iced coffee. As he took a sip he thought about the deep blue-green of Maren's eyes. He'd never seen that shade before. And more than that, there was something in the way she came a little apart each time he saw her that was endearing to him, a signal she could do with a protector, a partner. A lover. Even though her outward behavior said otherwise.

There were the work issues, of course, but nothing insurmountable there. He'd seen the '90s movie with Michael Douglas as the president opposite some actress Alec couldn't name as the lobbyist Douglas fell in love with. It had a happy ending. That was all that mattered.

Alec's brief marriage had been a disaster. Freshly back from combat in Afghanistan, he'd only known his wife—whom he'd met through a friend—four months when he proposed. She hadn't been pregnant then, although many in attendance clearly thought so. But it likely happened on their wedding night, and things went downhill from there. Rose whined daily about her morning sickness. She let the house become a mess and burst into tears when he pointed out dust in the corner or a sticky spot on the counter. He knew he was a bit obsessive about cleanliness, but there were worse things to be. By the time his sons were born, he not only didn't love Rose. He didn't like her.

The screwup with Rose was the main reason he was happy to let things go slowly with Maren Kane. *When you're comfortable, that's when it's gonna happen*—that was what Michael Douglas, the president, told the lobbyist, what's-her-name, in that movie. Then they ended up in bed. Alec hoped he could make Maren that comfortable.

He turned back to the stack of bill proposals on his desk and drained the bottle, ready for the caffeine to kick in. When he first arrived in Sacramento, Alec was surprised by how many of his colleagues voted on bills they'd never read, relying exclusively on recommendations from their party caucus and information from lobbyists, interest groups, or staff. He was less judgmental about it now—he understood there weren't enough hours in the day to do all the work being a state legislator required and still have any kind of life.

At 5:01 his scheduler, Sharon, showed the two men in. He knew the skinny guy, Caleb Waterston. They had sparred over several bills in the short time Alec had been in office, the most important one being the BPA prohibition in the manufacture of pacifiers. But he couldn't place the other man. Graying, shoulder-length hair, weight-lifter shoulders and a broad chest in an expensive suit, and the silliest two-toned shoes Alec had ever seen.

"Senator Joben, this is Lew Quintana, CEO of TalkFree Inc." Caleb made the introduction.

Right, Alec realized, *the cell phone billionaire.*

Alec moved from behind his desk to a small conference table by the window and asked the two to join him.

"We understand you signed on as coauthor to Senator Rickman's SB 770 to ban cell phone usage while driving," Caleb said. "We hoped you might reconsider."

Word travels fast, Alec thought.

Lew Quintana broke in, unnecessarily loud in the small space.

"Senator Joe Mathis, chair of your caucus, was close to getting an opposition position on that bill from all Republicans in the senate when you joined the other team. What you've done is not smart politics, Joben, it's bucking the party line."

Alec ignored the disrespectful use of his last name by someone he had just met. He knew what Lew Quintana meant and why he was pulling the power play. If the new cell phone ban passed it would cripple TalkFree's business—no need for hands-free phone equipment for driving if it wasn't legal in California. But passing the bill would be no easy feat—Quintana and the cell phone lobby gave heavily to every new legislator's campaign fund, Democrat and Republican, including Alec's. It was not an unusual strategy for those who had resources, putting legislators of both parties in their debt.

"I think if you go back and reread the bill, you'll find there are things you don't like about it, reason enough to pull your endorsement and your vote. Happens all the time." Quintana said this as though it were a done deal. As though his asking would make it so.

Alec had changed his mind about bills before. Once he had signed on as a coauthor on a bill that would have required all California insurance companies to cover training children in specific eye movement exercises that some believed helped treat learning disabilities. But when Alec learned that studies were conflicting and major physician groups felt the practice was ineffective, he knew it was too early for a mandate and withdrew his name.

The cell phone bill, however, was different. As a U.S. Marine Alec had taken the corps motto to heart. *Semper Fi. Ever faithful to corps and country.*

And as an elected official Alec developed his own similar but personal motto for service in the capitol. *Faithful to the ideals of democracy and serving constituents.* To Alec Joben's mind, that pledge was nonnegotiable. He also relied upon advice his father had given him. *Never get in a pissing match with a skunk.*

Alec stood and extended his hand.

"Mr. Quintana, I want to thank you for taking the time to meet with me."

For one glorious moment Lew Quintana thought he had won, that it was that easy to get this tall ex-soldier to roll over for a dime.

But as he grasped Lew's hand Alec said without rancor, "My name stays on the bill."

Then he turned to Waterston. "Caleb, I believe you can show Mr. Quintana out."

Quintana turned bright red, leaned forward, and looked ready to let Alec have it, but Waterston firmly guided his client out, knowing it was better to find the votes they needed elsewhere.

As Alec started to collect his things Sharon reappeared, trailed by a young man finishing a text on his smartphone as he walked in.

"Senator, Mr. Howard wondered if you might have five minutes." Ed Howard looked up apologetically, his blotchy skin worse than Alec remembered it.

"The bedsheet bill," Sharon added.

Alec wanted nothing more than to leave and get in a few sets at the gym. Still, he concluded that by listening to this young man—who had no money or influence to offer—he might be able to clear his office of the stench of the influence brokers that had just left.

"Please, Mr. Howard, have a seat."

* * *

Maren crossed the street from the capitol and entered the double glass doors to the high-rise Hyatt on K Street. Dawson's dark wood-paneled restaurant and upscale saloon-style bar on the first floor of the stately hotel was quiet. The post-work capitol denizens had come and gone, and the late-night crowd wasn't there yet.

Her leg was throbbing like hell and her efforts to set Sean free were in tatters. And what stung most was that Lana, as Sean's attorney, seemed incapable of doing anything but parroting back to Maren the DA's theories, all of which implicated Sean. To be fair, she knew Decateau was bound by the process and the law. But *so what?* Maren was over it. And now Alec Joben was coauthoring the cell phone bill, a move rife with likely complications. Each of those things seemed to require thinking, making decisions about what she would and would not do. But what Maren wanted—what she needed—was to stop thinking for a while. And to stop hurting. This whole getting shot thing was becoming a drag. She made her way to one of the padded leather stools at the bar and lifted herself onto it with effort, adjusting her leg at an angle for minimum pain.

The bartender, who had been rinsing glasses at a sink at the other end of the bar, approached. He was a good-looking young man with wavy black hair, dressed in the Dawson's uniform. Black slacks, a crisp white shirt, and a green velvet vest. He looked scarcely old enough to drink, let alone to mix and serve alcohol.

"What can I get you?" he asked, smiling to reveal straight, white teeth that Maren was sure must have benefited from braces.

Maren smiled back, with effort. She was out of her element, couldn't remember the last time she'd been in a bar alone. Then she saw a green, bound folder an arm's length away leaning against a vase with a single rose. There were several similar settings strategically placed the length of the bar.

Appletini, B-52, Salty Dog, something called Sex on the Beach made with vodka, peach schnapps, cranberry juice, and orange.

None of them was appealing. Maren put the folder back.

Then it came to her.

"Whiskey, please."

She unwound her ivory knit scarf to stash in her bag, channeling her image of a crusty cowboy with a bullet in his leg choosing his drink based on the maximum anesthetic quality. *That would be whiskey.* At least she was pretty sure it would be.

The young bartender's smile wavered. Evidently not the order he'd been expecting. In fact, Maren realized he'd probably already mentally poured her a glass of fruity chardonnay.

But the young man rallied.

"Bourbon or scotch? We have Maker's Mark, Wild Turkey, Glenlivet..." He turned and gestured to a row of bottles of varying shades of amber liquid lined up on glass shelves behind the bar.

Maren was lost. "You choose," she said finally, forcing a smile again in what she hoped was a reassuring manner. A drink had seemed a good idea to her, but not if it took so much thinking. Not thinking had been the goal.

The barkeep reached for Old Potrero, an expensive rye whiskey bottled in San Francisco and known for its easy, smooth taste.

"Neat or on the rocks?" he asked. "A splash of water, a twist of lemon?"

Oh my God, Maren thought, *was I supposed to study before I came in?*

"You choose," she said again. It had kept things moving the first time.

The young man poured the drink neat in a shot glass, put it on a coaster, and set a highboy filled with water over ice next to it.

Maren sipped it. Harsh, but it wasn't as bad as she'd feared. She ordered bruschetta from the bar menu and asked for a second drink. She was tired of the pain in her leg, and she figured a few drinks couldn't be any worse than the opiates the doctors had ordered that she'd stopped taking. Those had really messed with her head.

She couldn't remember when she'd last had two shots of hard liquor. College? She began to experience a warm feeling. Looking down at her red boots, she pictured herself again as a cowboy from the Old West, the bullet from a shoot-out successfully removed, now relaxing after a long day dealing with cattle, cattle thieves, and other cattle-related things.

She was about to order a third shot of whiskey, really it wasn't bad, when it occurred to her that maybe she had been wrong. Maybe that wasn't what cowboys drank. She sat with that thought for a while until it wandered off, reappeared, and wandered off again.

"Tequila," she said when the bartender returned.

He appeared to be studying her face to see if he had missed something in the cues that had made him think she was going to be a one-drink, dignified customer. He made no move to fill her order but instead slid the still-full glass of water closer to her. Maren took a sip to make him happy, then repeated her request. "Tequila, please." She really did feel better, a measurable dulling in the pain.

He acquiesced and rattled off options. "Cabo Wabo Blanco, 1800 Silver, El Tesoro Anejo, Patrón Silver, Pepe Lopez Gold, Suaza Tradicional..."

Apparently ordering tequila is an advanced, graduate-level drinking challenge, she realized. *At least when compared to whiskey. And had he really said Cabo Wabo?*

He was still going.

314

"That one," she said, interrupting him.

The tequila definitely seemed smoother going down than the whiskey, although whether it was the type of spirits or the fact that she could no longer feel the burning in her throat was unclear. Either way, it wasn't what she expected because it wasn't enough. If anything, she could recall more vividly Sean sitting in jail facing a death sentence. It was too horrible to contemplate. Maybe one last drink would blot things out. She really needed a rest from her own brain.

But while she was deciding whether and what more to drink, she had a new thought. It was the fact that she hadn't slept with anyone since Garrick, although that thought, like all others at this point, had a tendency to wander. But she searched for it and it returned.

She thought of the happy ending in that '90s movie, the one where Annette Bening as the lobbyist and what's-his-name who played the president got together at last.

And so what if Alec didn't like his ex-wife and was a bit snarky about it. Not unusual, maybe warranted.

It took her some fumbling though her bag to find her phone and then another minute to get to Joben's private cell number in her contacts.

"Alec? It's Maren. It's not about work. I'm at the Hyatt. Can you meet drink me for now?" True, that didn't sound quite right, but she was pleased she had proffered the invitation.

"Where are you exactly?" he asked.

"Dawson's," Maren said.

She set the phone down on the bar, the line still connected, as she reached for a napkin to clean up some water she had just spilled. She couldn't hear Alec as he spoke.

"Maren? Maren? Can you hear me? Stay put, I'm coming now."

Maren was finding the bar stool to be increasingly unreliable. It appeared to have developed at least one, if not two, wobbly legs. She slid down, amazed at how fine her leg felt, and headed for a booth at the back, bringing her empty tequila glass with her. She left the bruschetta untouched along with her phone on the bar and crossed the room without incident, which she felt was an accomplishment since the lighting appeared to be insufficient.

It seemed it had only been minutes since her call when Alec stood at the threshold to the room. He looked for a moment at Maren, the empty shot glass in front of her, then went to the bar. He returned with two waters and her cell phone, which the bartender had picked up and offered to Alec to return to her.

She smiled, her face lit up.

"What's the occasion?" Alec asked, setting the waters and her phone down as he sat across from her in the booth. "Are we celebrating something or killing the pain?"

"We're celebrating." She knew it was true as she said it, her earlier worries now lost, or at least buried. "Being alive, we're celebrating being alive. Being happy. Being cowboys."

"Okay, cowgirl," he offered with a smile. "Let's move this rodeo along and get you something to eat."

As she returned his smile, Maren realized that somewhere deep, underneath the alcohol, she had definitely had enough of awkward moments and failed conversations with this man. She slid across the booth and leaned into him, kissing first gently, then deeply. Her head spun. A little. *That was nice.* But then her head spun a lot, and she felt herself slipping, sliding. Her vision swam...

When Maren woke the next morning she was in the Hyatt in a hotel room in bed. Alone. Fully dressed. Except for her boots, which she could see were lined up neatly on the floor beside the bed.

Then she noticed the handwritten note on the nightstand beside a small tin of aspirin and a bottled water.

Take two. No roping and riding today. Call me when you get up.
Alec

CHAPTER 37

Maren's head hurt. Her stomach churned. But she figured it wasn't that bad, considering. She would have expected a whiskey and tequila hangover to be worse. Maybe it was the healing effects of ginger ale and saltine crackers. Polly said it worked for morning sickness—why not hangovers? Still, when she thought of Alec Joben, Maren's stomach flipped badly. She had ignored the request in his note that she call him, so that morning he had called her and she let it go straight to voice mail. She knew where things would go from here. Clearly a gentleman, Alec Joben would check up on her. And then let her know he didn't date crazy people. And while she couldn't remember everything from the night before, she was pretty sure her behavior put her in that category.

She hoped the phone would ring again but that it would be Lana Decateau saying a subpoena on the investment account had been issued and Ray Fernandez's involvement was confirmed. She remembered vaguely having been angry with Lana last night, but this morning she couldn't remember why. The attorney seemed to be doing all she could for Sean. And on top of that she was putting up with Maren, which Maren knew couldn't be easy.

It would also be nice if a call came from staff to a Republican assemblyperson saying they had dropped their opposition on the cell phone bill. Only four days until the final vote in the assembly. *And she was five votes short.*

In fact, given all that was on Maren's mind, it was impossible for her to tell whether her current symptomatology—which was affecting her head, stomach, and more—was solely from too much alcohol, or whether it also signaled the beginnings of a nervous breakdown.

No matter. *Duty calls.* Maren dressed and headed for the capitol, a little shaky, but on her feet.

By two p.m. Maren and Carolyn Garrisey had been at it for hours, visiting every Republican legislator that Maren thought might swing their way on the bill if they personally heard from Carolyn, the mother of Hilary. Hilary Garrisey, the prom queen who had died. No success. They received sympathy but not pledges for votes.

"Ms. Kane?"

Maren turned to see Selmeyah Zaki, chief of staff to Joe Mathis, hurrying toward her in the narrow capitol hallway. Selmeyah wore a dark suit, matching pumps, and a hijab wrapped around her head. It was a simple, modern variant of the Muslim head covering in the Spanish style, a lightweight triangular scarf tied at the neck that revealed about five inches of Selmeyah's dark hair and a pair of dangling copper earrings.

"Ms. Kane, do you have a moment to speak? Inside?" Zaki asked, gesturing to Mathis's office.

"Yes." Maren turned first to speak to Carolyn. "I can meet you in the basement cafeteria when I'm finished here if that's okay. Do you know where it is?

"No, please, I would like Mrs. Garrisey to join us." Maren realized Selmeyah must have seen Carolyn testify at the hearing, if not in person, via streaming on the capitol channel.

The three women went into Senator Mathis's private office. The walls were adorned with pictures of the senator with Republican luminaries including President George W. Bush and Governor Pete Wilson. There was also one of Mathis with Rorie Rickman, despite their different political parties. He had his arm around her, and they were both smiling. He was at least ten years older than Rickman, but in the photo they both looked very young. She remembered something Rorie Rickman had said about when she found herself unexpectedly pregnant, that the baby's father had been an older, married politician. Maren wondered.

"Please, sit. Water?" Selmeyah asked. Both women nodded yes, and as Selmeyah poured from a pitcher on the table she began. "Senator Mathis is not here today. Last night his neighbor was hit by a car. She is elderly; her pelvis and jaw were broken. There may be other injuries, possibly more serious."

"I am so sorry," Carolyn said.

"She is a widow; the senator has known her and her family for thirty years. She has been in surgery all day." Selmeyah leaned forward, speaking more quietly. "The man who hit Mrs.

Canendi, he is a businessman. He was on the phone closing an important deal." She paused. "Hands-free." She looked from Maren to Carolyn. "He was using a speaker, but his phone lost signal, and in his agitation and desire to get the client back on the line, he did not see Mrs. Canendi in the crosswalk."

Maren felt horrible. She knew where this was going, but she still felt horrible.

"Senator Mathis has reconsidered his position on your bill. He will be holding a press conference later today and calling other legislators to ask for their aye votes. If you would, please advise Senator Rickman."

"Of course. I will." Maren said, the line of her mouth grim. "Please convey to Senator Mathis our prayers for his friend."

"That poor woman," Carolyn Garrisey said as she and Maren reached the elevator at the end of the narrow hall of legislative offices. "What happens now?"

"It's over. Joe Mathis is powerful. With this change and the press on his side, he will shift the votes easily. The bill should come up Monday on the assembly floor. You'll be able to watch the debate and see the final results online. I'll send you the link."

As they exited and walked across the capitol grounds, Maren was not in a celebratory mood. In addition to her sadness over the pain and uncertainty faced by Senator Mathis's neighbor, Maren was reminded that too often a single personal incident, rather than thoughtful policy, determined outcomes in Sacramento. The tendency of legislators to use laws to address the difficulties and tragedies in their own lives was both human and highly dysfunctional. She had seen that dynamic lead to good laws that she believed in, like this one, but also to bad laws inconsistent with irrefutable evidence about what was best for California.

* * *

"It's contagious."

Polly's voice sounded weak, like she was calling from her hometown of Louth, England, rather than from across the street in Sacramento. "Bloody hell..."

"What is it? What have you got?" Maren asked.

"Your hangover! You get off easy, and I've been chucking my insides out all night, eight hours of it. And all I had was a pint after work."

"I'm so sorry." Food poisoning or the flu more likely, but Polly had her own way of looking at things. Maren's own stomach, only recently settled, lurched at the thought. "Is there anything I can do?"

"Would you take Jake and Danny out to San Loomas this morning? They have auditions for the Governor's Award, the scholarship. If you can drop them, Marty will bring the boys home. He loves jazz, plus, he's hoping for a look at the guv."

"Ray Fernandez has a jazz program? And who's Marty?"

"Marty's the new IT guy at work, he volunteered when I called in sick. No, not that governor. The handsome one. Jack Caries. I told you about it. I gather it's supported now by some foundation, plus Caries' own funds. Not much chance Danny or Jake will qualify, but their hearts are set and I...oh no...I'll need to call you back...ugh..."

From the sound of it, Polly was starting round two of Maren's hangover.

Maren checked her calendar. Camper had a vet appointment at eleven a.m. An important one to recheck how his leg—well, the absence of his leg—was doing. Fortunately, the vet was midway between San Loomas and home and Camper was a good traveler. If Maren brought him along with the boys, she should be able to do both.

She freshened Camper's water and knelt down to give him a belly rub, his preferred expression of love, second only to food. As his tail thumped heavily on the floor in gratitude, she marveled at his recovery. From what Jake had said, Maren understood that the loss of a front leg is hardest for a dog since they carry 70 percent of their weight up front rather than on their rear legs. On top of that, many dogs who have a leg rendered useless through injury or illness are able to adjust over time as the limb weakens and then wears out. A bullet shattering the bone had given Camper no similar transition period. But other than giving up his spot on the couch for a dog bed on the floor and finding it easier to run than walk—which according to Jake was common—after the first really difficult days Camper's routine seemed largely unaffected.

Maren selected a soft red cotton calf-length skirt, a turquoise-blue sleeveless top, and a batik print blouse and headed to the bathroom to shower.

Dressed, waiting for a bagel to toast, she checked directions online and found that the boys' auditions were held only a few miles from Shoot the Lights Out. She walked back to the bedroom and retrieved the two locked metal storage cases from the top shelf of the closet. The outer cases were purchased, not rented, so no point in lugging them back. She removed the keys from the necklace around her neck and extracted the gun and bullets, which without their trappings fit easily in her satchel.

Drop the boys, return the gun, get Camper to the vet. A good morning to kill two—make that three—birds with one stone.

Figuratively speaking, since she'd never fired her weapon outside the indoor shooting range.

The police had dropped Maren's protection—with Wallis Lisborne dead, Maren was no longer considered at risk. The cops believed Wallis's co-conspirator was in custody in the person of Sean Verston. Maren disagreed on that central point—she was sure if Wallis had an accomplice he—or she—was still out there. And if not, there had to at least be someone who knew more than they were saying, someone who could link Wallis to Tamara's murder. Still, Maren didn't feel personally threatened anymore. Whoever it was had to believe they had gotten away clean. Why start a new mess?

Maren checked the time. She was due to meet the boys at Polly's place at 7:45 a.m. Still ten minutes to spare. She opened her iPad and tapped on the Capitol News link. It wouldn't do for her to work the capitol ignorant of major events.

The video feed showed an eager young blonde reporter in a tangerine dress interviewing a staff member of former governor Pete Wilson.

"Do you think the governor regrets his support of ballot measure Proposition 187?" she asked, her stern expression conveying that such regret might be appropriate.

Wilson's former aide, now in his sixties, had an even, pleasant voice. He wore a simple navy suit, no tie, and gestured easily as he responded. "In the 1990s there was great concern among the voters, as there is today, about the influx of illegal immigrants into California and the strain it puts on our state's budget. Governor Wilson supported Proposition 187 to prohibit undocumented immigrants from obtaining taxpayer-supported services and the voters agreed with him, passing it by a large margin."

The reporter's frown deepened. "But that law was found to be unconstitutional. In particular, banning immigrant children who came here through no fault of their own from attending public school or getting health care was later viewed by many as cold and even harsh. Has the governor changed his stance on this?"

Again, the aide responded calmly. "No, I've spoken with the governor on several occasions, he still believes..."

It was rare that Maren could feel a virtual lightbulb go on in her brain as an idea took hold, but there it was. First her conversation with Polly, now this...

She knocked over a stack of papers on the end table as she reached for her cell phone.

Lana, pick up. Pick up!

"You have reached the private and confidential phone line of Lana Decateau, Sacramento Deputy Public Defender. Please leave a message."

"Lana, it's Maren. Look, I realize something. I was wrong—we were wrong. When Tamara said she and the governor had done something awful, she wasn't referring to Ray, to our current governor. Once a governor, always a governor, they keep that title. Especially people who worked for them don't say 'former governor.' It's just governor, forever after." Maren paused for breath, but barely. "Fernandez has an alibi. True, he could still have engineered it without being involved in the actual murder. But when Tamara said 'we've done something awful,' I'm betting she was pointing to Jack Caries. It's worth a look, isn't it?"

CHAPTER 38

Jack removed the price sticker from the Balvenie forty-year-old single- malt scotch. $3,800 a bottle. Not a trivial amount, even for him, but it would be worth it. Next he fiddled with the cell phone. Larger than his own, but still not out of the norm. It looked like the latest in smartphones. He tested the hidden recording capability and found nothing so obvious as a beep or a microphone icon.

There was a soft chime from the entryway. Caries slid the phone and bottle into his briefcase, latched it shut, walked to the door, and opened it. When he found attorney Lana Decateau standing there, he said nothing. A moment passed, then another. She had made an appointment; he expected her. But he had not expected *her*.

"Governor, thank you for seeing me."

Jack took in her flawless skin, large, deeply lashed coffee-colored eyes, and full red lips. She was dressed in a caramel-brown suit that complemented her skin tone, a lavender silk blouse underneath highlighting her curves. Thick, black hair fell loose and heavy around her face. He couldn't help it, he just stared.

Fortunately, Ms. Decateau appeared used to the lag time most men and some women experienced in functioning when she arrived as she courteously waited for him to regain his powers of movement and speech and invite her in. When he did, Jack showed her into a small living room with high ceilings. It was filled with a riot of color—reds and pinks and bright greens and blues—from the sofa and chairs to the pillows, tapestries, and paintings on the walls. There were modern and period pieces side by side. A grand piano was clearly the centerpiece.

Caries gestured to a lime-green cushioned settee and Lana sat down, while he chose the piano bench across from her. He watched as she pulled her phone from her purse and checked to make sure it was off so they would not be interrupted.

"I appreciate your taking the time to see me," she said. "My investigator is out sick, and with budget cuts, I'm the only stand-in. I expect that having run the state, you can understand." She smiled. "I'm here to try to better understand the relationship between Ms. Barnes and my client, Mr. Verston, who I'm sure you're aware is in custody as a suspect in her murder. He was found at the scene, but there was no weapon and the DA is leaning heavily on a motive of jealousy. Did you know Mr. Verston?" Her southern accent, the ups and downs of it, carried well in the space designed for the acoustics of jazz.

"Sean worked with my office on legislation for Senator Rorie Rickman. I didn't know him, just in passing."

"Did you have occasion to see Sean with Ms. Barnes?"

"They dated when she first came to work with me." He paused. "I gather it didn't end well."

"When you say you gather, did you witness anything between them or did she speak of it with you?" She brushed a loose lock of hair back off her brow.

"I didn't ask. She didn't say. But there was talk around the capitol, and when Tamara took a leave for several months some thought it was to get away from Sean."

"Nothing concrete, nothing you saw or got directly from Ms. Barnes?"

"No." Jack laid his hands on the baby grand's keys, softly, without sound. "Tilly is...was...family to me, a sister, really, but we didn't talk about everything." Still looking at the keys, he tried again. "We knew we could count on each other, though." He looked up. "Maybe you have family like that?"

"I wasn't aware you and Ms. Barnes were acquainted before she came to Sacramento."

"We were both foster kids in New York City. It's a big population there, of course, but we were placed in a special program for gifted kids. I was several years ahead, but we took the same city bus to the internship. When I left I told Tilly—Tamara—I told her to look me up if she ever got to California. She did, and I meant to look out for her..." Caries' eyes unfocused, and he looked down, silent. Then glanced at his watch. "I'm sorry, I have to go. It's the annual jazz award auditions." As he stood he asked, "Do you like salsa?"

Lana tilted her head, her eyes on his. "The condiment or the music?"

"Either...Both."

He smiled as he grabbed his briefcase and jacket and escorted her to the door.

* * *

Fortunately, it was foggy and the air was crisp and cool. Although Camper didn't mind, Maren hated leaving him in the car and would never do so if it was warm out, windows cracked or not. From her advocacy work related to child health and injury prevention she knew that at eighty degrees outside the interior of a vehicle could reach one hundred twenty. And the weather was shifting in Sacramento; any day now it would be one hundred in the shade.

The football field at San Loomas High, home of the Fighting Panthers, was dotted with white-canopied booths. Gangly boys and a sprinkling of girls, most of whom outpaced the boys in height and maturity, were scattered across the expanse of artificial turf. Nearly all were toting instruments. Jake and Danny were in line for the woodwind table. Jake shifted uneasily in his oversized suit and unfamiliar tie.

"We're here. They're fine."

Maren had called to reassure Polly, who sounded weak and tired.

"Marty said he would ring when he arrives, I gave him your mobile," Polly said. "You can't miss him. Over six feet, Genghis Khan mustache. But you don't need to wait, you can leave now if you like. Jake can reach me."

"Get some sleep," Maren said. "I'll stay until Marty comes." *At least if he gets here before the sun burns through and Camper needs rescuing,* she thought. It was nine a.m. She figured she had until ten.

Jake and Danny returned, each holding a bright blue folder with the California seal in gold on the front. Among the papers inside was a sheet detailing the history of the award that featured a photo of its founder, Governor Jack Caries. Thick, wavy brown hair, large blue eyes. The man must have been born camera-ready. Except for teeth that just missed being perfect in a way that said, "I'm a man of the people, not a movie star."

Maren took a deep breath. She had seen Jack Caries many times and knew him slightly through her work, but it gave her a start to see his image now that she believed he might bear some responsibility for the deaths of Marjorie Hopkins and Tamara Barnes.

She reminded herself that she had also been sure that Ray Fernandez had a role in the murders. In fact, the list of her deferred or denied hunches was now bordering on embarrassing. Still, she reminded herself *no pain, no gain*. Or something like that.

"Can you help me with this?" Jake removed a badge from the folder, his name in large black letters on a white background with a blue and gold ribbon proclaiming "Governor's Jazz Awards, Invited Musician." She pinned Jake's badge on his jacket, did the same for Danny, and then, consulting the schedule, shepherded the boys toward the school's auditorium.

According to the agenda, an opening band would play, followed by "Remarks by the Governor." Then award hopefuls would head to their assigned classrooms for auditions. Thirty-three finalists—three from each of the eleven instruments—would be selected to return another day to play chosen pieces before an august panel of experts.

Maren found three seats together about ten rows back. She took the one on the aisle so she could exit easily when Marty showed. Twenty minutes past the program's official start time and the auditorium was still three-quarters empty. She heard late-arriving attendees grumbling about a shortage of parking and long lines to get packets and badges.

Jake and Danny kept busy on their smartphones, texting friends and playing games. Maren found it odd that two best friends seated next to one another weren't directly interacting, but she knew it had become the norm.

She figured she might as well join in and opened her iPad. The most recent e-mail was from Evie, an update on the interns' work on Simone Booth's tapes.

> Maren,
> I think you're going to want to take a look at this.
> Simone left 634 tapes. Tapes 629, 630 and 631 are interviews with Hopkins' sister, colleague, and boss. 632 is an interview with Caleb Waterston. 633 and 634 are two interviews that Booth evidently intended to do, but never happened. For each of those a tape is labeled, but it's blank. One was a scheduled interview with Tamara Barnes the day of Ms. Barnes's death. The second was intended for an interview with you, "date to be determined."
> Evie.

Maren was reeling. She reread the e-mail three times. In addition to the background interviews Simone Booth had done for Marjorie Hopkins' obituary last year, it looked like she'd recently undertaken research on Rickman's cell phone bill, with plans to speak to Maren and Waterston. That made some sense, since the new cell phone bill linked to the first cell phone bill, which, in turn, related to Hopkins' research. But why had Booth planned to interview Tamara?

Before she could gather her thoughts, the house lights dimmed and the audience broke into applause. Maren quickly powered down the tablet and looked up to see a young Asian American man with shoulder-length black hair in a shiny purple jacket and narrow print tie tuning a stand-up bass. A heavyset, pale, redheaded teen stood at the front of the stage fiddling with the mouthpiece on his sax. The two were soon joined by a guitarist and more horn players—trombone, trumpet, clarinet, as well as a short, dark-haired, acned young man carrying an oversized silver horn that Maren didn't recognize.

She would have to unravel the connections in Simone's work later; there was nothing she could do in the dark. She became aware again of her young companions, Jake and Danny.

Jake had put his phone away and seemed transfixed by the scene unfolding before him. "Look, a French horn," he whispered to her. "And there's an oboe," he said reverently, eyes wide, as though spotting a White-throated Needletail, which Maren understood from Noel to be one of the rarest birds in existence. "You almost never see them in jazz bands," he added wistfully.

Until then Maren hadn't known a fourteen-year-old could be wistful.

The musicians ceased their individual activities and launched into "Take the A Train," a Duke Ellington tune that Maren recognized. Despite the young age of its members, the band was really good. As the song hit its stride, Jack Caries, walked on stage staying off to the side, giving the musicians his full attention and nodding slightly to the music. When they finished

Caries approached an empty microphone center stage, just his height, evidently set in advance for him. His voice was clear but soft as he spoke into it. Not commanding—enveloping.

"Let's thank the musicians. These are last year's Governor's Award Winners. They sat where you sit now."

When the applause subsided he brushed his thick brown hair off his forehead and scanned the room slowly before speaking again, as though inviting each person into the conversation. "There are no wrong notes in jazz..." He waited a beat. "If I hit a G when the chord calls for an A, it won't matter. Not unless I stay stuck on the music as written." Again, a measured pause. "If instead I reach for a new sound, a new moment, if I break through to the unknown..." Caries' voice rose. "That's jazz...that's truly jazz."

He turned purposefully and crossed the stage to the baby grand, casually seating himself. He placed both hands palms down on the cover before opening it to display rows of perfect black and white keys.

Caries' left hand set the rhythm diligently, a repeating tone. His right joined in to craft the melody with a delicacy that begged the listener to hear nothing else.

It wasn't greatness. But it was beautiful.

Maren sat stock-still, absorbed. Wondering if a man who could feel so deeply and create such music would also willfully end a life.

CHAPTER 39

Camper was stretched out the length of the Beetle's backseat. He lifted his large head to sniff through the gap in the window. Maren opened the door and took the big dog's weight against hers to help him down, a now-familiar routine.

Camper wobbled several steps, then leaned into a loping stride, momentum aiding his balance. He circled a nearby tree and lifted his hind leg, remarkably poised on his two remaining limbs for the moment it took to complete the important task of marking the trunk.

The loud sound of crickets chirping caught Maren off guard until she remembered that Jake had changed her phone's ringtone to "sounds of nature" for her. She wasn't sure yet if she liked it.

"New Mexico turned over the investment agreement."

Maren took a breath and leaned against her car.

"Tamara Barnes opened the account when she was a senior at the University of New Mexico. You were right about that." Lana paused. "There are four partners in the fund. Governor Raymond Fernandez is not among them; Jack Caries is. It looks like you were also correct that Tamara was referring to him."

Camper had returned and lay at Maren's feet, head on his paws, his eyes following her.

"In addition to Tamara Barnes, Wallis Lisborne, Jack Caries, and Caleb Waterston owned shares."

Maren opened the car door and sat on the passenger seat. She didn't trust her legs to support her. "Caleb?" First he shows up on Simone's interview list, now here. "That doesn't make sense."

"Caleb did the legal work. Amendments to the partnership were drafted by him and kept in the files. Mr. Caries put his share in a blind trust once he was elected, so although he might have done the administrative work himself since he also has a law degree, under the circumstances it would have been unwise."

"So the investments were legal?" Garrick had said as much, but Maren wanted to hear from Lana what the police and district attorney's experts thought.

"Yes. Even the governor's role. When he put his investments in a blind trust it meant he no longer knew what was kept and what was sold. When he signed the hands-free cell phone bill, of course, he might have hoped the TalkFree stocks were still in the account, that he would make millions. But he had no way of knowing; it wasn't a sure thing."

Still, even long odds might be incentive enough to make sure the bill passed and to be complicit in Marjorie Hopkins' murder, Maren thought.

With her free hand she fiddled distractedly with the radio knob on the VW. It was loose and Maren had meant to get it fixed. She inhaled deeply. "So, Sean is not a recipient of the partnership."

"I'm getting to that," Lana said.

Maren shifted the phone to her other side. "What do you mean? You just gave four investors. They're the ones who need to be looked at."

Maren heard papers rustling.

"Sean is not a partner, that's true. But each investor in the partnership account that Tamara Barnes forwarded to you had the option of designating a beneficiary to inherit their funds from the trust in the event of their death." Lana cleared her throat. "And if both the investor and his or her beneficiary died, the agreement was structured such that the deceased investor's share would be split among the remaining living investors."

Lana paused. A long pause.

Maren's shoulders tensed again.

Lana finally resumed. "Each investor's individual share of the account across all stocks and cash currently stands at five point three million. Caleb Waterston's beneficiary is his mother, living in Florida. Wallis Lisborne didn't name a beneficiary. She might have been unaware of the clause. It was buried deep in the paperwork."

Another pause. Maren realized Lana was reading from notes.

"Jack Caries' beneficiary was Tamara Barnes. Neither the governor nor Ms. Barnes had family to speak of, and they seem to have forged a sibling bond when both were foster kids in New York. Similarly, Tamara Barnes's share was originally designated to go to Jack Caries if she died. Quid pro quo," Lana said.

"That gives Jack Caries a motive for wanting Tamara dead, for working with Wallis," Maren said, relieved, now understanding where this was going. She got back out of the car and leaned against it, feeling the warming sun. *So the police have a new suspect. A difficult one, to be sure. A former governor.* But she'd already figured that out, and this had to be good for Sean.

"Originally, yes, it would have," Lana said. "But the day before her death Tamara Barnes altered the terms of the agreement, designating a new beneficiary. She had a legal notary witness a statement removing Jack Caries and leaving her full share in the event of her death to Sean Verston."

Maren's stomach dropped. When she spoke, her voice was strained. "Five point three million?"

"Yes. Everyone but Caries had converted their TalkFree stocks into cash a month or more ago. Since his share is in a blind trust, his fund manager is making independent decisions. In any case, the amounts are still divided by the agreement equally. And unfortunately, this dovetails with the prosecution theory that while Sean may have been fueled by obsessive jealousy when he killed Tamara Barnes, he was also motivated by money," Lana said. "Lots of money."

Lana hung up. Maren was shaken by the call, but she managed to get Camper settled on the front seat and was navigating toward the exit of the lot when she saw Jack Caries pull out ahead of her. He must have left immediately following his welcome speech. It made sense since he wouldn't be needed again until the finalists returned in a week or so.

Caries' car was futuristic, low-slung and sexy, but snub-nosed in the front, the headlights resting far back from the grill. The body, gleaming silver with black accents, was lopped off in the back, square rather than rounded. Tesla, the manufacturer's name, was in tall, thin letters spaced the width of the rear bumper.

Maren recalled hoopla over Caries buying the vehicle for his personal use in his last days in office. It was electric and environmentally green, but anyone who ponied up the one-hundred-thousand-dollar price tag wasn't pinching pennies on gas.

Maren felt a chill as she saw Caries driving. He had to be the one who engineered all this. Neither Wallis nor Tamara could have done it on her own, she was certain. Waterston was just the legal hack. He made the money, but he didn't have what it took to pull this off. And it wasn't Sean. But there was nothing she could do to prove that. Not that she could think of yet, anyway.

She remembered again Sean that day in Rickman's office, his manner, kneeling to look into Tamara's eyes. *How Tamara had sought Sean out when she was afraid.* True, that was beginning to feel like a slim thread, but she couldn't let it go. She wouldn't.

Glancing at the time, Maren saw she could only make Camper's vet appointment if she headed there right away. She pulled out after Jack Caries, one car between them, turning right toward the entrance to Highway 5. As they approached the on-ramp Maren could see traffic at a standstill a mile in the distance. She was stuck once for hours near that spot when a big rig jackknifed and blocked all lanes. She knew there were back roads that would take her to the vet's office in midtown, but lacking any sense of direction, she would need GPS to figure out the way. She'd resigned herself to pulling over, looking up the address, and loading it into the phone when she saw Jack Caries' roadster inch out of the line and make a hard left at the next light. Odds were he was heading to the capitol area and knew another way. Maren eased the Beetle over, gunned the engine, and accelerated through a yellow signal at the intersection, following Caries' lead. Camper slid partway off the seat, but they made it.

There was sparse traffic so it was easy to keep Caries in sight. He was on the phone hands-free or talking to himself. Maren reflected that hands-free technology made that brand of crazy look normal. Either way, he was engrossed in conversation. Something serious, his matinee-idol smile in storage for the moment.

After fifteen minutes through barren country landscape, things began to look familiar to Maren. There was a gas station, then a succession of small shops. Well-kept, upscale, with a village-like feel—if villages catered to residents who bought Prada and Tiffany. At the crest of the hill Caries turned left again and Maren slowed, realizing she'd been there before. A fund-raiser for a state senate candidate, posh food and free-flowing money, held at Caleb Waterston's house, just a block up the road.

She made the turn and pulled over in front of a Georgian-style mansion with an expansive front lawn that must have cost a fortune to keep green. She could see Waterston's fab concrete-and-glass '70s split-level home four doors down, stark and ostentatious. Jack Caries' sleek, silver car in the driveway made the place look *Architectural Digest* ready.

Maren helped Camper out. He headed toward the lawn until she chided him and he came trotting back. They started down the broad, sloping street. *Nothing suspicious, just a woman on a walk with her dog on a fine day.* In any case, Maren felt her activities were innocent enough. She didn't have a plan, not even a hope of hearing what might be going on behind closed doors between the two men. But she knew the meeting had to mean something. She couldn't just drive away.

Having gone only a few feet, Maren realized she'd left her cell phone in the car, in her satchel. Since her injury she felt bare without it. She couldn't get to the phone quickly enough if she had to make a call. So she went back for it.

Maren had just unlocked the car door and taken hold of her bag when she heard a yowl, then a growl, and Camper was off, down the hill and across Waterston's driveway as an orange flash of fur disappeared under the Tesla and out the other side. Camper skidded, narrowly missing the car, then rounded the corner toward the back of the house after the cat, in full three-legged pursuit.

"No, Camper!' Maren stage-whispered before recognizing that was completely ineffective. "Camper, no!" she tried again, a little louder, slinging the satchel, unreasonably heavy, over her shoulder and walking as rapidly as she could toward the scene of the chase, not wanting to alert the occupants inside but needing to get Camper out of there before he ended up with a scratched eye or worse from his feline quarry.

That was when she heard it.

A gunshot.

Then another. From behind the house.

At the same moment it dawned on her why her bag was so heavy. She had a gun, too—her gun. She hadn't had time to even think of returning it once Lana had called.

Maren dropped the bag and pulled the weapon out, gripping it with both hands, holding the gun straight-armed out in front of her as she had seen cops rounding blind corners do on TV. She knew her gun wasn't loaded; she wasn't daft, as Polly would have put it. But that wasn't the point. She couldn't—and she hoped wouldn't—shoot anyone. But if Waterston thought breaking up an unwelcome cat-and-dog fight in his yard required a weapon, he had another think coming. And if something worse was happening, she figured better faux-armed than not armed at all.

She found the cat where the short driveway ended. A fat, orange, smug-looking creature, it was fifteen feet up a massive eucalyptus tree, giving Camper the stink-eye. Camper, for his part, was circling the trunk madly, pausing only to jump on one leg to get closer to his target, although not by much.

There was a four-foot-high wrought iron fence separating Caleb Waterston's yard from the wooded expanse where the cat and dog were failing at détente. Maren could see one end of a dark-bottomed Olympic-size swimming pool with a diving board, flanked by chromelattice chairs, matching tables, and lounges. The rest of her view was blocked by Japanese hollies, tall and thin, wedged together as a privacy screen. She could hear but not see a waterfall or fountain feature at the far end.

Maren set her gun down on the ground and quickly unbuckled her belt, slipping it off. She walked toward Camper, took hold of his collar to get his attention, and looped the belt through the collar like a leash. It was uncomfortable for Camper to keep his balance on three legs walking when tethered, she knew that. But there was no other way to secure obedience while he was in hunt mode, and she had to get him out of harm's way.

Toward the front of the house she was able to circle and secure the belt through a thin handle on a side gate, giving Camper the down and stay command with her hand before going back to retrieve her gun. She couldn't leave it, and she wanted out of there. She would call the police when she reached the street and relative safety. But as she bent and picked up the weapon she heard a moan—a deep, terrible, pain-filled sound. She edged closer to the fence and squeezed in front of the hedges to see. Her gasp was audible when she witnessed the scene.

Jack Caries lay sprawled on his back, arms flung open on both sides. Blood seeped from his right shoulder. Caleb Waterston stood a good six to eight feet away, a .38 revolver in his right hand hanging limp at his side. His large head seemed possessed by a tremor, rocking loosely on his neck, making his resemblance to a ballpark bobblehead toy more marked than ever. Eyes wide, he saw her.

"Maren," was all he managed. "Maren."

Waterston's brain seemed stuck on repeat.

He tried again. "So good of you to come."

What is this, a tea party? she thought.

Then Caleb seemed to remember Jack Caries a few feet away. "Terrible. He came to kill me. A black moon on the horizon." He looked down at the gun he was holding—each thing seemed new to him. He laid it on a small white resin table near the edge of the dark-bottomed pool, then eased into one of the scoop-shaped latticed chairs.

He looked back through the gaps in the hedges, seeing Maren again. "There was a struggle. I trumped the eagle, the thing went off, an accident."

Caries moaned, moving one hand to his shoulder, where it quickly turned red with the steady flow of blood. *If something isn't done right away...*Maren shifted her gun to her left hand and opened the gate.

"Call the police," Caleb said, his reedy voice weak. "There's a phone in my study." He gestured to a sliding glass door at the back of the house. "I can't believe it, an assassin in my own yard." He looked back at Jack. At Jack, who started to rise, to lean on one hand and pull himself to sitting but gave up the effort. His eyes rolled back in his head.

Caleb Waterston's face distorted at Jack's movement. He stood and reached for his gun.

"No," Maren said, "It's okay now."

She walked toward Caleb, placing her own gun on the table next to his, noticing a cell phone and two highball glasses there. It reminded her this was a setting for poolside drinks and conversation, not firearms.

She moved between Caleb and Jack, taking off her jacket, kneeling and wadding it up, pressing it against Caries' wound to stop the bleeding.

"He can't hurt you," she said to Caleb even as she focused on Jack, on trying to keep him with her. "You call the police, see the phone there? I'll do what I can."

Jack Caries spoke. His voice hoarse, urgent. "Liar..."

Liar?

He tried to speak again, but he was so weak there was no sound. She leaned in to hear. "Caleb...Wallis..."

"No!" Caleb's high-pitched voice cut in, almost a screech. She turned and saw he had his gun trained on her. His hands were shaking. "It's too bad, really. You should have gone in the house when I asked you to. Then Jack would be dead when you came out; he would have nothing to tell you. You should have!" As Waterston spoke—incensed, passionate—the shaking increased. His entire frame appeared in motion, rocking side to side, buffeted by winds that weren't there. "Now Jack will have to kill you. Because you got in the way when he came to kill me."

Maren moved slowly to one knee as Caleb's gun vibrated with his tremors. She understood now.

Caleb.

Caleb and Wallis, it was the two of them. Marjorie Hopkins' murder, then Tamara.

She figured she had only one play.

"Caleb, it's okay. I understand. This is Jack's fault. Jack's the bad guy."

Caleb's arm dropped slightly, weakened; the gun wavered.

"Let's call the police together; let's tell them." Maren's voice was gentle, reassuring. "They'll believe us, you and me. Like you said, Jack will be gone by then. It's better if there are two of us here to tell it." She stood as she spoke, arms out from her sides, empty-handed, her palms open toward him.

Caleb lowered the gun a little more, thinking. Watching. As he did, Maren charged, launching herself at him, knocking them both backward into the pool, Waterston dropping the gun on the concrete as he fell into the water.

He struggled to get back to the side, his shoes and heavy clothing making it difficult for him to move in the pool. But he made it, grabbed the weapon, and stood in the shallow end, his thinning red hair dripping water in his eyes. He aimed first in one direction, then another, the gun tilted down—no idea where Maren was. Only that she was under the shimmering blue surface somewhere, the dark grey bottom and sides of the pool deepening the color of the water, obscuring his view.

Maren had swum to the far end below the diving board. She was in her element, looping back and forth underwater, coming up for air only when she had to. She felt like a pop-up duck in a shooting gallery.

She tracked the sound—finally, her firearms training came in handy. Waterston's .38, like hers, should hold six bullets, although some .38s chambered up to twelve. She'd need to take that chance.

She heard two gunshots before she got to the yard. There had been four since, or was that three? It was quiet for a minute, so she surfaced for air. Caleb was waiting, ready, and took another shot.

Fortunately, it was wide of the mark. *Damn, NOW that's four*, Maren realized. She pushed off the far wall and took broad strokes under water, keeping her eyes open despite the burning chlorine. She locked in on Caleb's spindly legs, his pants billowing loosely around them. Caleb was turning, heading for the pool steps, probably to reload. But she got to him within seconds, pulling him under, then wrapping her arm around his chest firmly from behind. Surfacing, she cradled Waterston against her like she would to save a life, a drowning man. When she pulled him toward the side he kicked and writhed, but to no end.

CHAPTER 40

Maren numbly watched the newsreel of Jack Caries' body covered with a sheet as it was wheeled from Waterston's home. The next image was of her, wrapped in a deep blue blanket, her hair matted like a wet poodle's.

"Here." Alibi Morning Sun set the coffee cup in front of her. It was a nice gesture—he couldn't have known caffeine would make her ill.

Her dry change of clothes was a set of heavy, oversized grey sweats provided by the department with *Sacramento Homicide* printed on the front. But she still felt deeply cold. The paramedics had given her drugs, one by IV—she guessed for the shock. But while she felt bone tired, she could think clearly. They didn't seem to be the mind-altering type she'd been prescribed for her leg. In fact, that was the problem. She didn't want to think or to remember any of this.

"We appreciate your statement, your persistence on this case," Alibi Morning Sun said. He was wearing a wine-colored dress shirt, a black tie, and black pants, dressed more formally than she remembered him. He leaned his large frame against the wall of the interview room, arms crossed. "And your heroism," he added.

Yeah, right, she thought. She had managed only to save herself. Jack Caries was gone. She leaned over the steam coming from the coffee, breathing in the scent and the idea of warmth. There was a knock on the door. Morning Sun stepped outside. He returned trailed by Carlos Sifuentes carrying a computer tablet.

The junior detective's cologne was as Maren remembered it— sandalwood with a hint of lime.

"It will not be much longer," Sifuentes said, sitting down across from her. "You and your dog will be home soon." His soft Latin accent was pleasing.

"Where is he?" Maren couldn't believe she'd forgotten about Camper, tied in the down position while all the drama had occurred. With the waterfall in the background he could have been barking up a storm and she wouldn't have heard.

"Our canine unit officer, Terry Dolenz, is with him. They're outside the station walking. The big dog gets around well on three paws, yes? I have a shepherd mix, sweet."

He adjusted the brightness on his tablet's screen, then became all business.

"Governor Caries, he went to Caleb Waterston's with a purpose. He brought a specially designed digital recorder. It looks like a cell phone, but with greater audio capacity and without a telltale red light or icon when taping. We believe Mr.

Caries, the governor, suspected Mr. Waterston of wrongdoing. He wanted to get the evidence on tape. And we assume Mr. Waterston was forthcoming in conversation because he believed the information would die with Mr. Caries today."

Maren remembered the phone on the poolside table.

"The media, they are very busy with this. You will be asked questions," Sifuentes said. "Chief Watson asked us to share this information with you, for accuracy, to minimize confusion for the public." He fiddled with his tablet a minute, finding the program he wanted.

Maren sat up straight, running her hands over her face, rubbing her eyes. She reached for the cup, then remembered it was caffeinated coffee, not tea.

"Wallis Lisborne did not kill herself. Simone Booth did not die of a heart attack. Both were murdered by Mr. Waterston. Poison, inside chocolates. Mr. Waterston confessed this to Governor Caries prior to shooting him."

If there was any adrenaline left in Maren's body, it was firing now, as she thought out loud. "Because Simone knew about the link between the cell phone bill, the money, and Marjorie Hopkins' death. Or she was close to finding out." Her stomach was churning. She pushed the coffee cup farther away.

Sifuentes raised one eyebrow at Maren. The police had just now uncovered that information. But he glanced over at Alibi, who nodded at him to keep going. Sifuentes scrolled down his tablet. "Ms. Booth interviewed Caleb Waterston about Senator Smith's cell phone bill. The one that means we must now drive hands-free. She'd found a possible link between research undertaken by Marjorie Hopkins and jeopardy to the massive profits that Waterston's client, TalkFree, enjoyed after the bill's passage."

"I have a tape of that interview," Maren said. "I have all of Simone Booth's interviews that she recorded; it must be in there," Maren said. "She planned to interview Tamara; that's probably why she was murdered—Waterston and Wallis knew Tamara wouldn't lie about the investment account and that it was only one more step to link to Hopkins' murder." Maren bit her lip hard. She wanted to scream at not having gotten to the tapes sooner while she was chasing down dead ends in Sean's case instead.

Morning Sun stepped out of the room. Sifuentes continued. "Ms. Booth thought only that Mr. Waterston was a source from which to learn about the cell phone bill. She did not, it appears, know that Caleb Waterston stood to benefit personally from Hopkins' death—from the stock he owned—as did his girlfriend, Wallis Lisborne." He looked up to see if Maren was following.

"Wallis Lisborne and Caleb? In a relationship?" Maren experienced déjà vu from when Lana Decateau had told her Waterston was engaged to Tamara.

"Yes, they became involved back when Ms. Lisborne was in L.A., a stuntwoman on a film that Mr. Waterston invested in. They met at a party at the producer's. We gather from the conversation today that Governor Caries was living in Hollywood at the time too, and the three knew one another. It was the basis for the investment partnership." Sifuentes paused to tap the screen. "The day Simone Booth interviewed Mr. Waterston, she let him know she had an appointment the next day to interview Ms. Barnes." He looked up. "It is good that you have evidence of that, the tapes you speak of." He tapped on the keyboard again and waited for it to load. "Apparently Mr. Waterston, as you said, figured Tamara, part of the investment group but not involved in Hopkins' murder, might have an attack of conscience."

Morning Sun returned. "A friend of yours is here. Polly Grey. I've asked her to wait."

Polly. Maren realized her best friend—and everyone else— would have seen her on the news. Reports of a governor murdered by a lobbyist would have taken over all the Sacramento stations.

"Status?" Morning Sun asked Sifuentes, knowing that Carlos could turn a ten-minute report into an hour.

Sifuentes moved faster, ticking off points on his fingers. "One, Marjorie Hopkins was killed by Wallis Lisborne to prevent Hopkins from completing and sharing research that might stop the hands-free cell phone bill." He looked up at Maren, acknowledging her role in identifying that link. "Two, Ms. Booth was killed by Caleb Waterston so she would not continue to investigate Marjorie Hopkins' murder. But Tamara Barnes followed Simone Booth's lead and uncovered evidence on the Hopkins murder." He looked up again. "Which Tamara endeavored to share with you outside the state e-mail system since she felt she herself was in danger."

Maren's eyes were heavy. The events of the day were catching up with her. But she nodded.

"This led to Wallis Lisborne's attacks on you." Sifuentes raised a third and then fourth finger, picking up the tempo. "Three and, finally, four—Caleb Waterston decided Caries and Wallis must die. Waterston reasoned that when all of this was done, no one would be left to collect on the investment but him. He wanted to be a very, very rich man." Sifuentes shook his head.

Maren was tired. So tired. It was too much to take in.

"Four?" Alibi Morning Sun's deep brown eyes bore into Detective Sifuentes.

Sifuentes frowned, looked at the tablet. "Yes. Caleb Waterston and Wallis Lisborne were responsible for four murders. Wallis for Hopkins, Waterston for Booth, Caries, and Wallis. Four murders." He looked at Maren, then back at Morning Sun. "Four."

Morning Sun said nothing. He figured his young detective would get there best on his own. But Maren stood up suddenly, swaying a little. She gripped the edge of the table for support as she spoke.

"There is one murder more," Maren said. "The one Sean is charged with, the one he's still in jail for. Tamara Barnes. The similarity in the knife strikes, Tamara uncovering the charge receipt, the evidence against Wallis. Wallis Lisborne must have killed Tamara. What is it you look at—motive, opportunity, means? Didn't she have them all?" She took a deep breath. "Did Caleb Waterston say anything about Tamara Barnes's murder?"

Sifuentes reddened, then smiled.

He tapped the tablet again. "Yes. I skipped a screen. Technology is our friend until it is not, yes?" He lifted up a hand, palm spread, all five fingers showing. "Five, it is five murders. Ms. Barnes's murder should have been second on the list. In fact, it seemed the cause of Jack Caries' visit to Caleb Waterston. If you like, I can play that section of the audio." He looked to Morning Sun—with Maren Kane listed as a consulting attorney of record by Lana Decateau in Sean Verston's defense, she would have access to the tape soon enough.

Maren sat down, folding her hands on the table in front of her as she leaned forward to hear.

CHAPTER 41

"It's been too long." *Jack's voice.*

Then Waterston. "Rum, no ice?"

The sound of liquid pouring—the recorder disguised as a cell phone on the table next to the glasses.

"Which reminds me, I brought you a little something to celebrate." *Jack again.*

"Forty-year-old Balvenie? A celebration must be in order." *Waterston.*

The sound of clinking glasses. Laughter—Waterston's unmistakable heh-heh-heh.

"But what happened to make it so...complicated?" *Jack.*

Maren rose and stood behind Detective Sifuentes. Despite there being no images on the tablet other than a graphic of the sound level, up and down.

"Marjorie Hopkins' death was Wallis's idea." *Waterston.* "She found out Hopkins could sink our investment with her research, so Wallis took care of it. The journalist figured that out. A tower of blocks and cards in the end. Unfortunate. I know how you feel about Tamara."

"Kid stuff, times change." *Jack.*

Jack's bluffing, Maren thought, *keeping Waterston talking.*

"Tamara told me she wanted out of the New Mexico funds. Her behavior became unpredictable and jumpy. I came across her crying like a little girl. She had stumbled upon something linking the account to Hopkins' death."

No response from Jack.

Waterston again. "I made the decision."

"Did you..."

"Me? I have no stomach for violence."

"But wasn't it hard for Wallis to kill another woman? And someone she knew?"

"No. As Wallis told it, the knife cut through Tamara's heart easily, soft as butter."

A scuffling sound, a crash, maybe a chair tipping over.

"Okay, okay, calm down. You're right. I took care of Wallis, didn't I? Justice was done. A little poison in chocolate. She and that journalist both had a sweet tooth. In its own way, a kite across the harbor. I'll get us some food, let's start over. After all, chess satisfies, not checkers."

The graphic on the screen was flat, registering no sound.

It's over, Maren thought, but Sifuentes raised a hand.

The sound of one gunshot. Then another. The two that Maren had heard through the fence. Nearly a minute passed.

Then Waterston's voice.

"Maren." *A pause.* "Maren."

CHAPTER 42

Sal Castro pushed away her coffee and peanut butter cookie. She looked across the diner at Noel seated alone in a corner booth. Peering over an open newspaper in his fedora and trench coat, he looked like a 1940s government agent from central casting staking out the mob.

Noel had refused to let Sal meet her brother on her own. Sal thought he might as well be wearing a sign saying "Don't look at me, I'm inconspicuous."

Billy entered the café and slouched toward her, a walk he had perfected in his teens that said *you can't make me do anything*. He pulled a chair out from the small table where she sat and turned the chair around so he could sit astride it. His back was to Noel, whom he appeared not to have noticed.

"You going to eat that?" Billy asked as he lifted the cookie off Sal's plate and took a large bite.

Sal watched him, saying nothing.

Billy kept eating.

"I'm getting married," he finally said, mouth still full. Billy looked straight at her, no hesitation, no fumbling. He seemed to Sal to be working from a script in his head. "I've changed. I'm clean."

Sal had heard it before.

Billy smiled—that smile that had charmed so many women— one lopsided dimple in his even, tanned face. "I want to see my kid. I want her with me."

Sal's stomach tightened. Noel couldn't hear, but he could see Sal's expression. He set his paper down.

Sal laid both her palms flat on the table and leaned toward Billy. "You can't do that. Bethany is my daughter; I've raised her. I love her." Then added, "You have to think of what's best for her."

"I have rights."

"You don't."

Billy looked down. "I've seen a lawyer." He reached over as he said it, taking Sal's coffee now, too.

At Billy's movement toward Sal, Noel stood.

"Did you tell this lawyer that you fathered this child through rape?" Sal said, her voice even.

"Tamara's gone, rest her soul," he said, his jaw clenched. "We were a couple. That's our child, not yours." Then Billy went all in. "You will let me spend time with her or I will tell Bethany that I'm her father."

Sal paled. She leaned back, away from the threat.

Billy didn't see Noel coming, didn't feel Noel once he was standing behind him. "Where do you think Tamara Barnes went that last night after you left her?" Noel said. He spoke softly, almost intimately.

Billy turned his upper body, a hard maneuver while astride the chair. When he succeeded, it took him a minute, but he recognized Noel.

Billy turned back to Sal, sounding every bit the little brother. "What's he doing here? You said just us. You said Marilyn couldn't come."

Noel took another two steps, moving into Billy's line of sight. "Tamara Barnes went to the emergency room that night. What you did to her without consent left a physical record."

Billy stared hard at Noel, then pushed himself off the chair, standing so he could face Noel. They were both tall men, but Billy packed muscle on his frame from construction work and must have outweighed Noel by fifty pounds.

Noel spoke firmly. He was used to outsized college boy-men whose size gave them confidence even as their brains trailed behind. Reading the confused, even frightened look on Billy's face, Noel was secure his bluff would hold. "You have twenty-four hours to leave town or I will turn Tamara's medical records and her sworn statement that you are responsible for her rape over to the district attorney. As a tenured member of the scientific faculty I expect they will give my involvement in the case significant weight."

Billy's mouth turned down; his shoulders drooped. He looked back at Sal. "C'mon, sis. It's Marilyn. She'll be good to the kid."

Sal had been processing what Noel said. *Did that really happen? Did Tamara go to the hospital and were there records?* But at the mention of Marilyn, Sal realized what was at the heart of her brother's plea.

Billy would never have come back for Bethany if his girl-friend hadn't wanted to play mommy.

"You will tell that young woman that you were mistaken," Sal said as she stood, a head shorter than Billy and Noel. "You will tell her that Bethany is not your child, that you've seen a DNA test I produced from the real father. Tell her Tamara Barnes lied to you about your being her baby's father. In fact, I don't care how you do it or what new lies you spin, you will undo the damage you've done by leading Marilyn into thinking you had a ready-made family for her."

The sibling resemblance was increasingly clear. Both Billy and Sal looked ready to break something, preferably over the other one's head.

Noel put his hand on Billy's shoulder and started to speak a word of caution, but Billy had had enough of being lectured to by this fop. He pulled back his right arm, hand in a tight fist, target in sight.

It was over in seconds as Noel Kane swiftly ducked and kneed Billy in the groin before Billy's punch could connect. Billy collapsed, moaning, knees to his chest on the ground.

Sal smiled. The pain her little brother was now feeling would subside, and it was nothing compared to what she would have felt had he succeeded in tearing Bethany from her. In fact, Sal would have cheered, if she weren't conscious of the few other patrons in the restaurant watching them. Instead, she eyed Noel appraisingly. And couldn't resist teasing him. A little.

"I'm impressed. Although I would think Spock's death grip would have been your first choice to incapacitate him."

"A common misconception," Noel responded, calm but serious. "Humans don't have sufficient tensile hand strength to execute that—it only works if you're Vulcan."

CHAPTER 43

Standing next to Lana in the capitol restroom, Maren was finding it difficult to get ready. Lana's thick black hair shone as she brushed and twisted it into a knot at the nape of her neck. It was too hot to wear it loose. Meanwhile, Maren's curls were giving new meaning to the word "frizz." The mirror seemed to Maren to yield two options. Movie star siren on one end and frazzled working woman on the other. She wanted to trade sides.

Polly was oblivious to Maren's engagement in a silent beauty contest. Her short, spiky hair never needed combing. Besides, she was wrestling with understanding Caleb Waterston's involvement in the murders. "So the bloke poisoned the journalist Simone what's-her-name because she was on to the Hopkins murder, and then he poisoned Wallis Lisborne to keep her from talking and also for the investment money?"

Lana nodded, carefully blotting the dark red matte color on her full lips. Not, as Maren observed, that they needed any help.

Lana tightened the black belt on her deep green sleeveless sheath, accenting her hourglass figure. Maren adjusted her scarf. Brown to match her cane.

"Maren, you figured out it was one person who killed Hopkins and Tamara. But for Waterston to also be involved in Tamara's death—wasn't he engaged to her?"

"No." Both Maren and Lana answered at the same time.

Maren let Lana finish. "Caleb faked his engagement to Tamara after Tamara's death, cropping group photos at capitol events so it looked like just the two of them. He thought it was a good cover for the fact he and Wallis Lisborne had been involved since her Hollywood stuntwoman days. Caleb's the one who brought Wallis up here."

Polly finally faced the mirror as she spoke, appraising her black miniskirt and black-and-white geometric top. She seemed satisfied. "It's too bloody much to believe."

Maren shrugged. She had known Caleb Waterston for years and it wasn't as surprising to her. "I doubt Caleb started with murderous intentions. But with the clause in the partnership that living investors split dead ones' shares to the tune of millions of dollars, the temptation to eliminate partners must have been too great. Especially with Wallis starting things off with Tamara's murder."

"The background check showed Wallis Lisborne had an extremely abusive mother," Lana said. "Wallis seemed to find an outlet for those issues through feigned violence in the stuntwoman work she did, often killing women according to script.

But at some point the line between staged and real blurred for her."

The three women left the capitol building on foot despite the fact that Maren's leg was aching. She had been overdoing it, no question. Fortunately, Lana's car was in the lot right across the street. As they waited for the light to change to cross at Tenth and L, Maren saw Alec Joben approaching from a block away.

Maren hadn't seen him since that night at the Hyatt.

She tried to steer Polly and Lana behind one of the big oak trees on the edge of Capitol Park.

"What are you doing?" Lana protested.

Too late. Alec had seen her. He broke into an easy jog, heading toward them.

Jogging? Is he really jogging in his suit in ninety-degree heat? Maren looked for somewhere better to hide.

"It looks like someone is happy to see you," Polly remarked, watching the handsome senator gaining ground.

Lana noticed Maren turning in circles. "What are you doing?"

Alec was there before Maren could get her brain and body coordinated to choose and implement an escape route.

Then it happened. What always happened when men were first confronted with Lana Decateau, real-life screen goddess. Alec stopped functioning. He stared at Lana. Her perfect oval face, flawless skin, the slight scoop in the neck of her soft-green fitted dress, the curves, so many curves, then the long legs without stockings in black leather pumps.

Maren was lost. Despite coaching herself that he was flawed and that it was a bad move, given their work, to start a relationship, her heart hadn't listened, and the heartbreak she expected had arrived.

There is a biological imperative for a straight male when faced with a perfect physical female specimen to honor it, to react. Alec did just that. And in some men the physical response takes over.

But not Alec. Within a moment he could speak. He introduced himself to Lana. And then she might as well not have been there.

He turned to Maren and pulled her toward him, his arms around her waist, and kissed her.

She kissed him back, encircling his neck with her arms and stretching up as he leaned down and into her. When more than a moment had passed, Alec moved his mouth from hers to her ear and quietly spoke.

"I've missed you. It's hard to find a good cowgirl in the city."

* * *

Governor Raymond Fernandez sat down with his wife, Martha, for an early, private dinner at the window table in the bedroom overlooking their back garden. In their move to the capitol upon his election, Martha and Raymond had chosen to live in a modest home in midtown Sacramento in a diverse neighborhood reminiscent of their L.A. roots. The historic California governor's mansion had long since been retired as a residence, last used by Governor Ronald Reagan in the '70s. Each governor had found more comfortable and less expensive quarters, while the old mansion was opened to the public and used only for special events.

Tonight the server brought the meal to their bedroom and left so they could eat uninterrupted on one of their rare unscheduled evenings at home. The imperatives of gubernatorial security meant fences, alarms, and capitol security on the premises at all times. The best they could do for privacy was keep to their room.

As he moved to the table, Fernandez reflected how glad he was that "the episode" with the Barnes girl was resolved. Frightening. Maren Kane was also nearly killed—twice. He owed her a special thanks for figuring out that "the governor" Tamara Barnes referred to in the investment scandal was former governor Jack Caries and not him. He was disappointed that Maren hadn't decided to go for the Washington position—she would have been good at it, and it would have been a great connection for him to have on the inside there. But no matter, it was her choice.

Tragedy had struck the California capitol during his term. His predecessor in the governor's seat, Jack Caries, and Tamara Barnes both murdered. And a journalist. Evidently tapes she had made were going to provide evidence in the case against Caleb Waterston.

Caleb Waterston. The worst of what the lobbying profession had to offer. Money for votes, and now murder for money.

Fortunately, in all this mess the signing ceremony that afternoon for the driver cell phone ban had gone well. Both Republicans and Democrats voted for the bill in the end. It had taken a tragedy, a neighbor of Republican Senator Joe Mathis being seriously injured. Still, Fernandez was glad the two parties had gotten together, whatever the reason. Controversial bills were never easy, but possible for him to sign if there was bipartisan support.

Content, he lifted the silver warming cover off his plate and tried a forkful of the chicken mole. Fernandez hadn't wanted to replace the chef for the governor's mansion when he was elected, but he had heard Governor Caries was a pot roast man and was concerned whether he could go four years without the Mexican dishes of his childhood. He needn't have worried— Caries' chef could cook anything. But Caries wouldn't be enjoying any more meals of any kind.

Really a shame, he thought.

"Feeling better, dear?" his wife asked, watching him eat with gusto after days of picking at his food. "You seem more yourself."

"Yes, it was just exhaustion, I'm sure. We'll have to think hard about that second term. Maybe better to have time to ourselves instead of trying to solve the intractable problems of this state." He left unmentioned that he had decided to let Delilah go as his receptionist. Maybe then he would get a little more rest. "I hear Senator Rorie Rickman might be interested in the job. Perhaps I will endorse her..."

* * *

It was sticky hot, even at seven p.m. Summer weather was early, pushing its way into the Sacramento Valley. The fog was gone. Sean didn't seem to notice. He left his black suit coat on and didn't bother to loosen his red-striped blue tie.

*Or is that a blue-striped red tie...*Maren smiled to herself. Despite the sad occasion, she was so happy to see him free. There were days when she had doubted it would ever happen.

Alec Joben wasn't there. He had left to attend a caucus meeting. And she knew if this clicked for them, Alec would be on his phone, or late, then later, then absent, much of the time. It was okay with Maren, at least for now. She figured that could all be worked out later. *Or not.* There was too much for her to be happy about in this one moment to let the thought of future problems spoil it.

When she caught up to them, it made six adults and one child forming a small circle around Tamara Barnes's grave.

Sean, Maren, Polly, Lana, Sal, Noel, and Bethany.

Sean Verston kept his head down, ignoring the tombstone, unable to look at the engraving. The flowers he brought were wilted. Daisies were Tamara's favorite, but they didn't hold up. He laid the small bouquet on the grave, then took a crumpled paper from his pocket. He read quietly, still not looking up.

"Tamara Barnes. Beautiful. Smart. Very smart. Funny...Sparkling."

* * *

His voice cracked. He stopped. Maren closed her eyes and willed him strength.

Sean put the paper down, unable to finish what he had prepared. He looked around at the unexpected group there with him, into each of their eyes, before he spoke again.

"Tilly, heaven has welcomed you. But we love you still."

The informal service over, Bethany found an open area of grass unmarked by graves for now. She set Daniel, her stuffed elephant, down nearby and was whirling in circles, finally falling in a cascade of laughter, then stumbling dizzily toward Sean, begging him to come play. He walked over, spread his arms out under the open, cloud-free sky, and began to spin.

Maren stood, observing them. One hand on her cane, with the other she lifted her hair up off her neck and took a deep breath. Lana and Polly joined her, one on either side. Maren took in their presence, feeling fortunate, recalling the walk with death she and Noel had almost taken. And the close call Sean had with the wheels of justice, which had almost veered off track.

Bethany, her red-orange hair tangled and her clothes spotted with grass stains, squealed with delight as Sean staggered after his last spin, struggling to stay upright. He steadied himself, picked up Bethany, and held her in his arms as he walked toward the three women, grinning. At first Maren thought he was smiling at her, but then realized he was looking past them. She wondered what had lifted her friend's heart.

She didn't yet know that Sean's pain was eased, in part, by the knowledge that he would soon start the paperwork to put the millions Tamara had left in his name into trust for Bethany Castro, with Sal Castro as executor until Bethany turned twenty-one. Tamara had made the switch in beneficiaries from Jack to Sean the last day of her life, and Sean intended to make good on his promise to protect what was hers. Always.

Even if she had known about the money, Maren would have been the first to asserted that Tamara's inheritance couldn't be the cause of Sean's broad smile. There was too much tragedy associated with it.

Sean reached Maren.

"Feel like going to a wedding?" he asked.

Maren, Polly, and Lana turned back to see Noel on one knee holding Sal's hand in his.

Not in a cemetery—and your hat, take off that hat. Oh, Noel. But Maren could see from where she stood that Sal's eyes were brimming with tears, and Sal was nodding yes...

THE END

ACKNOWLEDGMENTS

If my experience is an indicator, bringing a book to publication requires an eclectic mix of brilliant and hard-working individuals. Tremendous thanks to Inkshares: Tess Klingenstein, Angela Melamud, Jeremy Thomas, Matt Kaye, Thad Woodman, Larry Levitsky, and most of all Adam Gomolin (who "discovered" me the day I discovered him).

Also grateful to talented consulting editor Harrison Demchick, skilled copy editor Shire-Baden Brown, and gifted independent developmental editor Kristen Weber, whose counsel through several initial drafts was invaluable.

Special thanks to Loran Calvin, Lillian Montalvo and Katherine O'Regan (you know why).

Finally—really first, last, and in the middle—love and gratitude to family, friends, and colleagues who made this possible through their support and encouragement. I can't name each of you here, but you know who you are.

Did I say finally? One last thanks: to the amazing Erin, Matt, and Nathan, the true shining stars in my small universe. I am forever grateful for you.

ABOUT THE AUTHOR

A former local elected official, author Kris Calvin knows politics from the inside out. Educated at Stanford and UC Berkeley in psychology and economics, Kris has been honored by the California State Assembly and the Governor's office for her leadership in advocacy on behalf of children. *One Murder More* is the first in Kris Calvin's new Maren Kane mystery series.

One Murder More was made possible in part by the grand patrons who preordered the book on inkshares.com. Thank you.

Abby Wills

Alice Kuo

Alisa M Kimble

Amy Whittle

Angela Melamud

Aparna Kota

Basil Fthenakis

Calvin Family

Christopher Tolcher

Council-Galper Family

Crawford-Jakubiak Family

Danielle Kilchenstein

David Nied

David Plenn & Shelly Stephens

Dean Blumberg

Debra Beadle

Ellen S Jaffe

Erin & Matt Haney
& Nathan Calvin

Errol R Alden

Gary J Shapiro

Geoffrey T. Fong

Harry Pellman

Heather Lamson

Ignatius Family

Jackie Diamond

Jerilyn Schmidt

Joan M Hall

John M Kikuchi

Joseph Atlas

Joseph Henry

Judith Darnell

Katherine O'Regan

Kenneth Nakamura

Ken Slaw

Kimberly A Kerr

Kristie Sells

Laura E Mabie

Letitia Clark

Lia Margolis

Lillian Montalvo & Ken Hardy

Lucy Crain

Lynn Hunt

Marcia F Mascorro

Margarethe Humbert

Marlene M Abraham

Mary Blodgett

Mary L Doyle

Mary Nicely

Meena Harris

Michael A Weiss

Myles & Ida Abbott

Milton Arnold

Nelson Branco

Nicole G. Blankenship

Noga Niv

Pamela Postrel & Mindy Blum

Patricia Winkel

Paula Whiteman

Paul Qaqundah

Peri S Gunay

Peter B Manzo

Phyllis Agran

Regine Verougstraete

Richard H Markuson

Richard Llewellyn

Richard Pan

Richard Vorisek

Robert Adler

Shannon L Udovic

Steven H Nakano

Steve Shore

Stuart, Dana, & Will Cohen

Taejoon Ahn

Tamar Shoval Kidron

Teresa Grimes & Charles Loveman

Thomas F Long

Tomás M Torices

Touraj Shafai

Tracy L Trotter

Vanora l Savig

Victor A Robinette

Victoria M Arriola

Walter M Fierson

Wendy Lazarus

Wilbert H Mason

William Froming

William H Webster

Yasuko Fukuda

INKSHARES

Inkshares is a crowdfunded publisher. We democratize publishing by letting readers select the books we publish—we edit, design, print, distribute and market any book that meets a pre-order threshold. Interested in making a book idea come to life? Visit inkshares.com to find new projects or start your own.